CW01432585

DEADLY
REMAINS

By Kate Ellis

KATE ELLIS
DEADLY REMAINS

C

CONSTABLE

CONSTABLE

First published in Great Britain in 2025 by Constable

1 3 5 7 9 10 8 6 4 2

Copyright © 2025 by Kate Ellis

The moral right of the author has been asserted.

A CIP catalogue record for this book
is available from the British Library.

ISBN 978-0-349-44293-8

Typeset in New Baskerville by M Rules
Printed and bound in Great Britain by
Clays Ltd, Elcograf S.p.A

Papers used by Constable are from well-managed forests
and other responsible sources.

FSC
www.fsc.org

MIX
Paper | Supporting
responsible forestry
FSC® C104740

Constable
An imprint of
Little, Brown Book Group
Carmelite House
50 Victoria Embankment
London EC4Y 0DZ

The authorised representative
in the EEA is
Hachette Ireland
8 Castlecourt Centre
Dublin 15, D15 XTP3, Ireland
(email: info@hbgi.ie)

An Hachette UK Company
www.hachette.co.uk

www.littlebrown.co.uk

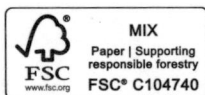

For Roger

1

The story had it all. Wartime spies. A beautiful young secret agent going missing in mysterious circumstances. A gallant young pilot. Tragedy and heroism. Drama and sacrifice.

Barry Brown tidied his files. He'd been working all day, even though it was Sunday, a day of rest for most. His research into the air crash in 1943 had been making good progress. Until he'd stumbled across a startling development; a story potentially so strange and unlikely that it might have come from the pages of a whodunnit. But first he needed to make absolutely sure of his facts.

He pushed the files to one side, hauled himself out of the armchair's warm embrace and went to the fridge to fetch himself a can of beer. He felt he deserved a drink, especially after the awkward encounter he'd just endured. But as he was about to open the fridge door, he heard the doorbell ring.

His heart sank. If it was who he feared it was, he wasn't sure whether to let him in again. He'd already said all he had to say and he didn't want to discuss it further. Barry wasn't a man who enjoyed conflict.

He hesitated for a few moments before opening the front door.

Half an hour later, Barry Brown lay dead amid a jumble of empty files. The debris of his work.

The royal family shot out of the jeweller's a few seconds after the alarm began to sound. The man in the King Charles mask took the lead, with the Queen and the Prince of Wales following close behind. Soon they reached the getaway car parked in the alleyway at the side of the shop; a top-of-the-range BMW SUV driven by the Princess Royal, who'd pinched it from its rightful owner the previous evening.

The jeweller and his assistant, Janice, cowered behind the counter with their hands on their heads as instructed. But as soon as they heard the roar of the car's engine receding into the distance, Janice rose from her hiding place to survey the damage. Mr Parker, the jeweller, more cautious by nature, hesitated; he was afraid the raiders would return and punish them for raising the alarm. He'd seen the gun. And the Prince of Wales had looked as though he was prepared to use it.

'We need to call the police,' said Janice firmly as she crunched across the carpet of broken glass. The raiders had smashed the display cases before loading the contents into holdalls.

'They told us not to.'

Janice had always suspected Mr Parker was a coward. She ignored him and picked her way noisily into the back room. It was time to call in the professionals.

2

'It was them. Honestly, Chief Inspector, it was the royal family.' The jeweller, Mr Parker, was in a state of agitation, but this was hardly surprising given what he'd just been through. They were sitting in the shop's back room, sipping the weak tea his assistant had provided before going off to supervise the glaziers, who'd just arrived to repair the damage.

DCI Gerry Heffernan scratched his head, trying his best to keep his face straight. 'Well, if it is them, they should be easy to find. You say the Prince of Wales threatened you with a revolver?'

'Yes. And he looked as though he was prepared to use it.'

'You mean the man wearing the Prince of Wales mask?' said DI Wesley Peterson. He wasn't normally a pedantic man, but he felt the need to establish the facts.

Parker managed a weak smile. 'Yes, yes, of course. I don't mean the actual royal gentleman himself. That would be ridiculous, wouldn't it? There were three of them, wearing rubber masks – the kind they sell in joke shops. The King, the Queen and the Prince of Wales. They all wore black – like some sort of uniform.'

'And according to a witness, someone wearing a Princess Royal mask was driving the getaway car,' said Gerry. 'The vehicle was caught on camera and we have evidence that it was nicked from a house outside Neston last night. Now think hard, Mr Parker, is there anything else you can remember about these people? Anything at all? Accents, or ...'

'The person in the Queen mask was definitely a woman. It was only the King who spoke. He ordered me and Janice to crouch down behind the counter and not to try any funny business.' Wesley saw the man shudder. 'As they were leaving, Janice triggered the alarm. I was frightened they'd come back and ...'

'But they didn't.'

'No. I heard the car starting up. That's when Janice called the police.' Mr Parker hesitated. 'You asked about accents. Well I could be wrong, but I think the King had an accent rather like your own, Chief Inspector. I think he was from Liverpool.'

'That should help to narrow it down,' said Wesley. 'This is the fourth similar raid on jewellers' shops in the south-west, and the robbers always wear royal family masks. Did anything unusual happen in the weeks leading up to the raid? Any new customers with Liverpool accents, for instance? Anyone who aroused your suspicions?'

Parker glanced nervously in Gerry's direction. 'Well, er ... *you* came in, didn't you, Chief Inspector. Purchased a silver necklace, as I recall.'

'That's right. Birthday present for my daughter.'

Wesley saw a fond look appear on the chief inspector's face, as it did each time he mentioned Alison. Gerry hadn't been aware of her existence until a couple of years ago. It wasn't until her mother was dying that she'd confessed that Alison's biological father was a young sailor she'd met

4

in Liverpool when she was eighteen. He had sailed off unaware of her pregnancy, and she'd kept her secret until the end. When Alison discovered her father's name and searched for him, she found that he'd left the Merchant Navy long ago and was now a senior detective down in Devon. Her appearance had come as a shock, one that Gerry's other daughter, Rosie, was still coming to terms with. His son, Sam, however, had welcomed his new half-sister with open arms.

Parker looked uncomfortable. 'I'm afraid you're the only person with a Liverpool accent who's come into my shop over the past few months, Chief Inspector.' He hesitated. 'And the man in the King mask had a similar build to yourself.'

Gerry didn't seem to have picked up on the man's implied accusation, and Wesley made a great effort to conceal his amusement. 'Is there anything else you can think of?' he asked.

Parker shook his head. 'Nothing I haven't put in my statement.'

Wesley caught Gerry's eye and stood up, satisfied they'd learned all they could for the moment. 'Thank you for your time, Mr Parker. And if you remember anything else, however trivial it may seem, please don't hesitate to contact us.'

Parker remained seated, and as they left the room, Wesley turned his head and saw that the man was staring in Gerry's direction.

'I'm sure Mr Parker thinks you've taken up a new career as an armed jewel robber,' he said once they were out of earshot.

Gerry snorted. 'The pay might be better, but I can't stand the taste of porridge.'

5

They returned to the police station, where a message was waiting for them. A man had been found dead in a rented holiday cottage a few miles from Morbay. And it looked as though the premises had been ransacked.

Little Rockington was the sort of English village that featured regularly on calendars and attracted camera-happy visitors from both sides of the Atlantic. Sweet thatched cottages lined a village green with resident ducks swimming on its pond. At one end of the green a pretty stone church stood surrounded by memorials to bygone generations, alongside a tiny thatched café that served Devon cream teas to the tourists. It was the last place you expected to find violent crime – unless it featured in the pages of the cosier kind of murder mystery.

A CSI in a white crime-scene suit greeted Wesley and Gerry at the front door of the pink cottage overlooking the green. 'The victim's through there,' he said with a jerk of his head.

'What happened?' Wesley asked. All they'd been told was that it appeared that the occupant of the cottage had been injured in the course of a burglary.

'He was found by the cleaner. She called an ambulance, but it was too late. The doc's been and said he's probably been dead since last night. It looks as though the place has been searched, but there's no sign of forced entry. He sustained a head injury, and that's probably what killed him.'

'Do we have a name for him?'

'Barry Brown. According to the cleaner, he's renting this place for a few weeks.'

'OK if we take a look inside?'

'You'll need the proper gear,' the CSI said, chucking a

couple of packages in their direction. Wesley caught his neatly, but Gerry fumbled with his and dropped it on the ground. Once Wesley had put on his crime-scene suit, he watched Gerry struggle to fasten his zip over his belly. The DCI kept promising to go on a diet, but so far this hadn't happened.

As soon as they were ready, the CSI led the way through a tiny hallway into a living room with a low beamed ceiling. The place was a mess. Drawers had been opened and the contents strewn over the floor. A laptop charger was still plugged in, but there was no sign of a computer. Several empty cardboard files lay near the inglenook fireplace, but the detectives' eyes were drawn to the dark-haired man lying face-down among the debris, a small patch of dried vomit beside his head. In the kitchen area at the back of the living room two clean glasses sat upside down on the draining board but there was no sign of a bottle.

'Has someone called the pathologist?' Gerry asked. At times like this he liked to have Dr Bowman's input.

'I think the doctor called him. He'll be on his way.'

'Any sign of a phone or laptop?' Wesley asked.

'Nah. The intruder must have taken them, probably to sell down the pub,' the CSI said with a roll of his eyes. 'All this for a few quid, eh.'

Wesley picked his way carefully up a steep, narrow staircase that would cause any modern-day building inspector sleepless nights. Once he reached the tiny landing, he made for the larger of two bedrooms. A double bed took up the lion's share of the space. Something on the small bedside table caught his eye.

'Isn't that a Rolex?' he said.

The CSI had followed them up and was lurking behind

7

Gerry in the doorway. 'I noticed that. Worth a flaming fortune, those watches. I'm surprised they missed it. Someone was careless.'

'They were only careless if theft was the motive,' said Wesley quietly. 'Maybe our killer wasn't interested in valuables. Perhaps he or she was after something else.'

Gerry looked puzzled. 'But what?'

Wesley turned to face him. 'We need to find out more about the victim. Maybe the attacker didn't pinch the laptop to sell on. Maybe he was more interested in what was on it.'

They made their way downstairs again, where a couple of constables were hovering around the front door.

'Anyone had a word with the neighbours yet?' Gerry called out, causing the two men to stand to attention.

'Just about to do it, sir.'

'Well get on with it. I want to know all about the victim. Name, occupation, home address, whether anyone else is staying here and if he had any visitors. If any of the neighbours saw anything, I want to know. Where's the cleaner who found him?'

'Being given tea and sympathy by a neighbour on the other side of the green.'

'In that case, that's where we'll start. We'll handle that one ourselves, but I want a team over here going door-to-door asking questions.'

3

It was a warm late-July morning. No mist. No rain. Only a pale blue sky dotted with light clouds and a slight breeze blowing over the vast expanse of Dartmoor. According to the email sent to all participants the previous evening, it was expected to be perfect digging weather.

Michael Peterson, at the age of thirteen, had feared that his classmates would scoff at his plans for the summer holidays, so he'd said nothing. It was bad enough being the only mixed-race boy in his class and having a father who was a police inspector, without spending his vacation engaged in something that might be associated with the old and untrendy. Michael desperately wanted to fit in, and he'd been worried that his mates would tease him if they knew that his honorary uncle, his dad's old university friend Neil Watson, had persuaded him to take part in an archaeological dig over the summer. Not that Michael had needed much persuading, because excavating the site of a crashed wartime aircraft sounded exciting. Besides, he'd always thought of Uncle Neil as a bit of a hero, an unconventional Indiana Jones figure. But he knew others might take a different view.

His mother, Pam, had given him a lift to Neston and

he'd caught the local train to Exeter, where Neil had picked him up in his battered car and driven him to the village of Moor Barton. When they reached the Gornay Arms, the old white pub where everyone was to meet, Neil gave a welcoming speech. According to records, the plane they planned to excavate was a Lysander. It had been en route from an airfield near Millicombe on the south coast to a base in north Devon when it had crashed in September 1943. The pilot had somehow managed to escape but later died of his injuries. There was no record of anyone else being aboard, and as no body was found in the wreckage, it was assumed that the pilot had been flying the short hop from one Devon airfield to another alone.

After Neil had said his piece and delivered a short briefing about health and safety, the group made their way to the crash site, Michael keeping close to Neil's side. The people nearest his own age were a group of archaeology students who chatted together as they walked. For a moment he began to wonder whether signing up for the dig had been a mistake. But he knew Uncle Neil and his father would be disappointed if he gave up on day one.

When they arrived at the site, a desolate patch of moor a quarter of a mile outside the village, Michael stood to one side and watched as members of the local metal-detecting society swept the ground with their machines while Neil marked out the location of the trenches he wanted to open. A small mechanical digger stood by, ready to delicately remove the top layer of earth as soon as he gave the signal.

While he waited, Michael studied his fellow diggers. As well as the students, there were the members of a local archaeology society, who were mostly in their post-retirement years. Then there was a group of well-built men who seemed to stick together. He guessed these were the former soldiers Neil had mentioned. They were participating as part of a project, but Neil hadn't told him much about it.

The soldiers stood slightly apart from the others and their conversation seemed terse and serious, as though they'd lost the habit of small talk. The volunteers from the archaeology society, in contrast, gossiped merrily and laughed at jokes Michael couldn't quite hear. He noticed that one member of this group was standing a little way from the rest, watching them warily. He was probably in his late sixties, although Michael found it hard to tell. He was lanky, with a long, pale face and a small grey beard, wearing an open-necked checked shirt and an old beige bucket hat. Michael did his best not to catch his eye, because he looked like the kind of man his parents used to warn him against talking to when he was younger.

The man turned his head to look at him as though he'd realised he was being scrutinised, so Michael shuffled closer to the group of students. One of the girls, petite and pretty, with auburn hair tied in two long plaits, gave him a wary smile, as though she'd sensed his embarrassment and taken pity on him.

'Hi,' she said. 'What's your name?'

'Michael,' he answered, aware that his cheeks were burning.

'I'm Harriet. Pleased to meet you.' She offered her hand and he shook it, surprised by the formal gesture.

'Come and join us. We don't bite.'

He gave her a grateful look and sidled towards the group of students. They were chatting about things he didn't quite

11

understand, but he stood there trying to look as though he belonged and wishing something would happen. He hadn't expected there to be so much hanging about.

Feeling a little bored, he couldn't resist glancing round to check whether the man in the bucket hat was still watching him. To his surprise, he saw him sneaking away towards a dip in the landscape as though he didn't want to be seen.

Neil was still in deep discussion with the metal detectorists, so Michael thought it would do no harm to find out what the man was up to, providing he kept his distance.

'Where are you going?' Harriet asked when he tried to slip away. It seemed she'd appointed herself to look after him.

'I thought I'd take a look round; get the lie of the land,' he said, trying to sound casual and wondering whether his father's work was a bit like this. Following suspects.

'You won't have time for that. Come on. We're starting.'

His guardian angel had spoken.

Landscapes shifted and changed over the years, but Pelham Jenks knew at once that this was the right place. He shielded his eyes from the sun and turned slowly until he saw a large rock shaped like a sleeping sheep half hidden behind a bank of yellow gorse.

The only sounds he could hear were the bleating of sheep and the mewing of a pair of buzzards circling the green and empty landscape like harbingers of death. He thought the tall granite tors in the distance looked like the brooding towers of satanic churches. But he told himself he was being overimaginative; a flaw in his character that had left him friendless during his distant teenage years – and made him wake screaming in the night, convinced he was being buried alive.

He'd brought a trowel with him, but he hesitated. What if the archaeologists ventured this way and noticed that the ground had been disturbed? But the dig was some distance away, so with any luck, nobody would spot what he was about to do.

As he made his way over to the rock, he carried out some swift calculations. He'd only been six years old at the time and memory could play tricks. But the dip in the ground a couple of yards in front of the boulder looked horribly familiar, and he could see that the spot was marked by a small heap of tumbled stones, as though someone had once built a little cairn, which had collapsed over the years.

He closed his eyes, and the scene flashed through his head: the sound of the spade hitting the ground and the scent of disturbed earth as he hid behind the rock watching the unceremonious burial of his own older brother.

Tears stung his eyes as he realised that the memories were real and not a product of his overactive childhood imagination.

And now he needed time to consider what to do next.

Little Rockington was normally filled with tourists taking selfies, and it occurred to Wesley that it would make an excellent setting for a cosy TV crime drama. Although the word 'cosy' hadn't sprung to mind when he'd seen the state of his latest crime scene.

The cleaner who'd found the dead man was called Kylie Mountjoy; a single mother of two who worked for an agency that, in her words, sent her all over. She was obviously shaken by her discovery but still alert enough to make a good witness. She sat in the neighbour's chintz armchair puffing on a vape as though she was in need of comfort. Every so often she picked up the mug on the table beside her and took a sip, pulling a face as she did so.

'Linda knows I don't take sugar, but she insisted. Said it was good for shock.' She spoke in a whisper to avoid offending their hostess, a slim middle-aged woman with expensively streaked blonde hair and the tanned, lined complexion of a habitual sun-worshipper, who was now busying herself noisily in the adjoining kitchen.

'Some people believe that,' said Wesley, who was sitting beside Gerry on the sofa opposite. It was a small room with low beams, similar to the dead man's cottage. He looked round and noticed a trio of photographs featuring a smiling little girl on the mantelpiece.

Kylie put down her mug and leaned forward anxiously. 'I saw blood on his head. Do you think the burglar hit him? Is that how he was killed?'

'We're not sure yet, I'm afraid. We need to ask you a few questions, if you're feeling up to it.'

She nodded. 'Of course. Fire away.'

'What can you tell us about the victim?'

'Only that his name was Barry Brown and he said he was here to do some work. He'd booked the cottage for three weeks and I was sent in by the rental company to clean once a week. I only saw him the once before today. That time he was busy on his computer. And before you ask, I've no idea what he was doing. I just got on with my cleaning. I haven't got time to be nosy about what my clients get up to.'

'Of course not,' said Wesley. It would have been good

14

if she'd snatched the opportunity to look over the man's shoulder to see what was on the screen, but he knew from long experience that life was rarely so obliging. 'He didn't say anything to you about his work?'

'No. He wasn't the chatty type.'

'Can you tell us any more about him?'

Kylie considered the question for a moment. 'He wasn't that old – mid thirties, maybe. And he was pleasant enough. Polite but distant, if you know what I mean. I got the impression he was here to do a job and didn't want any distractions. He had a nice car – a red BMW. It's still in the residents' parking spaces down the street; I noticed it earlier while I was parking on the road,' she added, looking at her watch. 'Look, I'm already late for my next client. They're only in the next village, but . . . '

'Just one more thing? This cottage is on the other side of the green. Why didn't you go to one of the neighbouring cottages?'

Kylie smiled. 'That's easy. I headed straight here because the other places are holiday lets and I don't know the people who are staying in them. I know Linda because she's one of my clients.'

'That makes sense. Well, I don't see any reason to keep you any longer. We have your contact details if we need to speak to you again.' He hesitated. 'Are you sure you feel up to carrying on after the shock you've just had? We can always get someone to notify your agency.'

She sat up straight and took a deep breath. 'Thanks, but I'd rather carry on. Take my mind off it.'

At that moment, their hostess entered the room. 'Is everything all right, Kylie?' she asked. She had a London accent. Wesley guessed there'd be a lot of incomers in

15

Little Rockington. Most locals couldn't afford anything so picturesque.

'Everything's fine, thank you, Mrs ... ' he said, hoping he sounded reassuring.

'Pugh. Linda Pugh.' She folded her arms. 'I haven't given a statement yet.'

'My officers are conducting house-to-house enquiries,' said Gerry quickly, detecting a note of veiled criticism of the police's efficiency. 'But I told them we'd call here ourselves to have a word with Ms Mountjoy.'

Kylie stood up, more composed than she had been when Wesley and Gerry first arrived. She was still wearing her cleaner's tabard. 'Thanks for the tea, Linda. I'm feeling a lot better now and I'd rather get back to work.'

Wesley accompanied her to the front door, where he watched her pick up her plastic box of cleaning equipment and walk off down the pretty front path lined with colourful blooms.

When he returned to the living room, Gerry had made himself at home, sitting back on the sofa, legs splayed. Wesley could hear the clattering of crockery from the direction of the kitchen, and guessed that more tea had been offered and Gerry, as usual, had accepted.

As he sat in the armchair vacated by Kylie, Linda Pugh entered the room again with a laden tray.

'Thanks, love, you're a lifesaver,' said Gerry, rubbing his hands together as he watched her pouring tea into mugs. 'We're hoping you might be able to help us. The man in the cottage opposite was called Barry Brown. Did you speak to him at all?'

'No. People come and go from the holiday cottages. They rarely want to pass the time of day.'

16

'Our doctor thinks he died sometime last night, and the lights were on in his cottage so it must have happened after it got dark. Did you see anything suspicious?'

She handed the mugs round and sat down before answering.

'I think I saw someone calling there.'

'At Mr Brown's cottage?'

She nodded. 'I'm not quite sure of the time, but it was probably between nine thirty and ten. It was getting dark, so I decided to draw the curtains, and when I looked out, everything was quiet because the tourists had gone home for the day, you see. They drive you mad in the summer months, coming up the path and staring in through the windows as though the village is some kind of museum. They don't seem to realise that some people actually live here all year round.' She gave a long sigh. 'Most of the houses are holiday lets, and it's a ghost village in winter. But in summer we're inundated. Coach tours stop here most days in the season.'

'I can imagine,' said Wesley with some sympathy. His own modern house in Tradmouth could hardly be described as quaint, but Gerry lived in a cottage on the picturesque waterfront, and he often complained about the influx of tourists in the warmer months. 'Can you describe the person you saw?'

'Like I said, it was getting dark, so I was drawing the curtains,' she gestured towards the floral drapes at the little lattice window, 'when I noticed someone at the front door of the cottage opposite – the one Mr Brown was renting. Of course I didn't know his name then. As far as I was concerned, he was just another holidaymaker. Although it struck me as a bit odd that he was on his own.

Usually it's couples. Or families. He didn't even have a dog,' she added, as though this was an unforgivable omission.

'You're sure it wasn't Mr Brown himself you saw?'

'Oh no. Every time I saw *him*, he was wearing a leather jacket, and this person didn't have one on. And they were tall, around six feet, I think. Mr Brown was smaller.'

'Could it have been a woman?'

She considered the question for a few moments. 'No. I'm sure it was a man.'

'Can you tell us anything else? What was he wearing?'

'Light-coloured trousers, I think. Some kind of jacket. Sorry, I wasn't really taking much notice?'

'Approximate age?'

She shrugged. 'I only caught a glimpse. And it *was* getting dark.' She looked crestfallen, as though she feared she'd let them down.

'Did you see this person actually enter the house?'

'No. I drew the curtains and settled down to watch TV. There was a good detective programme on.'

'Well if you like detective programmes, you'll realise the importance of every little detail,' said Gerry, looking her in the eye. 'The smallest thing could be important.'

She closed her eyes as though she was trying to envisage the scene. Then they flicked open and she shook her head as though the idea was too ridiculous to say out loud. 'It might have been a trick of the light. It was dusk and ... You're going to think I'm stupid.'

'Not at all. Just tell us, love,' said Gerry. 'It can't do any harm.'

'OK. I could only see his profile, you understand – he'd turned his head a little. And it was some distance away.'

She fell silent for a few seconds, and Wesley and Gerry waited with bated breath for her to continue.

'I can't be sure, but I got the impression he was wearing some sort of mask.' She gave a little laugh. 'Do you know, I think he looked a bit like the King.'

Diary of Flight Officer John Carmody

3 May 1943

There'll be a new moon tonight and plenty of cloud. Perfect. A clear night with a full moon makes you vulnerable. What we really need is a murder moon. A moon so dim that you can sneak in and out undetected. A moon that provides complete cover.

Tonight I'm to pick up my precious cargo somewhere in Normandy. I won't write any more, even though this diary is private – for my eyes only – and is kept safely in my locker. I know that careless talk costs lives, and in the unlikely event of somebody with bad intentions coming across it, I'd put certain people in jeopardy if I add too many details. And that's the last thing I want to do.

The landing site will be lit with torches as usual. Sometimes when I'm on the approach, I experience a moment of panic. What if it's a trap? What if we've been betrayed and the Nazis have captured the cargo and tortured the truth out of them? What if they're lying in wait for me, ready to burst out of the surrounding trees, guns blazing? It hasn't happened yet, thank God. But the possibility is always at the back of my mind whenever I see those two rows of dim lights set out in an isolated French field.

I'm flying out from Bolt Head tonight. It's a beautiful spot overlooking the sea, and on a fine day with the gulls crying and the waves sparkling you can almost believe we're not at war. On my return, I'll head back to my usual base further inland. Devon seems to be full of Americans at the moment, and it's just my luck that the girls can't resist them. There's a dance at their base on Saturday night, and I'll go provided there isn't another drop. Business before pleasure.

I wish I could tell Ma, Pa and Sis not to worry about me. If loose lips didn't sink ships – and bring down aeroplanes – I'd tell them that my kite is a little darling, painted all in black so hopefully the enemy will never know I'm there. I'd tell them I'm indestructible, and it's my cargo the enemy want to capture, not me.

4

Neil Watson was pleased to see that the students from the university had taken Michael under their collective wing.

Pam and Wesley had been keen to get their son away from his screen and out into the fresh air during the summer break, but Neil had hoped Michael wouldn't feel bored and out of place. He remembered that his own archaeological career had begun at a similar age, when his history teacher had encouraged him to volunteer at the excavation of a Roman villa. Even though he'd been the youngest there by far, he'd soon caught the archaeology bug, and after that he'd never looked back. He was nursing a hope that the experience would fire a similar lifelong enthusiasm in Michael. Neil had always been an optimist.

He'd watched Michael studying the geophysics printouts with the students, showing a genuine interest and asking questions. What kind of plane was it? How did it come to crash? Had it been shot down? Neil answered patiently. It was a Lysander, the kind of plane used to transport SOE agents and drop them off in France to embark on secret missions. This appeared to catch Michael's imagination, although he'd looked mildly disappointed that the crash had been due to an accident and not enemy action. According to contemporary reports, thick fog had descended suddenly over Dartmoor that night and the pilot misjudged the terrain; either that or his instruments malfunctioned. He managed to crawl from the wreckage and was found unconscious by locals and taken to the Gornay Arms, where he passed away from his injuries. His name was John Carmody, and he'd been buried in the local churchyard.

The incident was well documented, and there were accounts of locals going to the crash site to gather souvenirs after the RAF removed the bulk of the wreckage and before what was left was buried. As nobody had died in the plane itself, souvenir-hunting hadn't been regarded as disrespectful back then.

Neil had ordered three trenches to be opened where there'd been strong geophysics signals. He'd put the soldiers in charge of trench one, where they worked quietly and professionally. Dave, his second-in-command, was supervising the students and Michael, while a couple of postgraduate students had been placed with the enthusiastic members of the local archaeological society. Neil himself went from trench to trench dispensing advice and examining what had been found. A marquee had been erected to provide shelter during tea and lunch breaks, and a couple of Portaloos had been brought to the site to cater for any calls of nature. Neil looked upon his work and felt rather pleased with himself. It was a rare experience for one of his digs to be focused on such recent history, something there was a chance someone still alive might have witnessed, and he was looking forward to it.

When it was time for the tea break, he went round telling everyone to down trowels for a while. Sometimes people needed reminding. As everyone made for the marquee, he fell in beside Michael.

'Are the students looking after you OK?'

'Yeah. They're great.'

Michael seemed to be about to say something else, but then changed his mind. Neil stopped walking. 'Something the matter?'

He saw the boy glance towards the group from the local society, who'd already reached the marquee and were taking flasks of coffee out of their rucksacks.

'No. Nothing. I just thought I saw that man in the bucket hat wandering off over there.' He pointed to the big rock in the distance. 'He looked a bit ... shifty.'

'Probably didn't realise the Portaloos were in operation and was looking for somewhere private to have a pee. Did he say anything to you?' Neil asked, suddenly feeling protective towards his best friend's son, a side of his nature he hadn't known he possessed.

'No. Nothing like that. Just thought I'd mention it.'

Neil nodded. Panic over.

'What do you think?' Wesley asked as they were walking back to the car.

'Ms Pugh admitted that she was too far away to see properly. And it was dusk,' Gerry replied. 'Can you really see those jewellery robbers changing their MO and targeting holiday cottages? And don't forget the Rolex that was left in plain sight on the bedside table; that must be worth a couple of grand at least. Not that I know much about it. Can't afford that sort of thing on a policeman's salary.'

Wesley chuckled. 'Whenever Pam mentions my pay, I

point out that our financial position would have been a lot worse if I'd stuck to archaeology.'

'Your Michael's on a dig at the moment, isn't he?' Gerry asked as he opened the car door. 'Heard how he's doing?'

'No doubt I'll find out tonight.'

'It'll keep him out of mischief over the school holidays.'

'That's the plan.' Wesley returned his attention to their case. 'We need to know more about the victim.'

'The team are trying to track down his next of kin as we speak.'

He was about to start the car when his phone rang. After a short conversation, he pressed the speaker so Gerry could hear what was being said, and DS Rachel Tracey's voice filled the car.

'Thought you'd like to know right away,' she said. Wesley could hear the excitement in her voice. 'We've traced Barry Brown's next of kin – his sister. I've spoken to her, and she says he came to Devon a week ago on an assignment.'

'What kind of assignment?'

'She wasn't sure, but she says he's a freelance author and that he writes a lot about celebrities.'

'Thanks, Rach,' Gerry called over from the passenger seat. 'We'll be back with you in half an hour.'

5

The large window took up almost the whole of the far wall of the CID office and overlooked the Memorial Gardens with the sparkling ribbon of river beyond. It was a view that would add considerable value to any Tradmouth house or flat, but everybody who worked at the station had become so used to the stunning vista that they barely noticed it any more.

When Wesley and Gerry had arrived back in Tradmouth, they'd found the office humming with purposeful activity as officers spoke quietly into phones or typed on computer keyboards.

As they walked in, they were greeted by Rachel. 'Here are the victim's details,' she said, handing Wesley a printout.

Gerry plucked it from his fingers and began to read. 'Barry Steven Brown, aged thirty-five. Address in London. Your family's neck of the woods, Wes.' He thrust the paper under Wesley's nose. 'Know it?'

'Can't say I do. I was brought up in Dulwich. He lived in Docklands. New development, by the sound of it. It wasn't one of my childhood haunts.'

'Sorry, forgot you came from the posh bit. How does your dad like being "Sir Joshua"?' Gerry, the son of a Liverpool docker, could never resist the urge to tease Wesley affectionately about his classy upbringing by parents who had come over from Trinidad to attend medical school and went on to forge extremely successful careers in medicine.

Wesley gave the boss a modest smile before reading the address again. 'He must have been well paid. Those Docklands flats don't come cheap.'

'Nothing in London comes cheap, so I've heard,' Gerry said with a dismissive sniff. 'What else have we got on him?'

It was Rachel who answered the DCI's question. 'Naturally his sister's very upset, but I managed to have a good chat with her. She lives in Walthamstow with her family, and she said she didn't see Barry as often as she'd have liked because of kids and work.' Rachel, with her police career, a farm to help run and a baby who'd soon be celebrating his first birthday, understood what it was like to be a busy mother. 'She said he's ghostwritten books for celebrities and it paid really well. But she doesn't know any details.'

Wesley and Gerry exchanged a look. 'I expect it's too much to hope that she gave you the names of these celebrities,' said Gerry.

Rachel shook her head. 'No, but she's coming down here tomorrow, so it's something we can ask.'

'If he was here for work, I think we can assume someone gave him a commission. If we can find out who that was ...'

'Any clues found at his accommodation?' Rachel asked.

'The search is still ongoing,' Wesley answered. 'But it looks as though his laptop was taken, and there's no sign of a phone either. There were a few cardboard files lying about, but they were all empty.'

'His sister gave me his phone number, so the service provider might be able to give us a list of his calls. Although from experience, we know that could take time.' Rachel thought for a moment, smoothing her blonde ponytail, an unconscious habit. 'If the contents of his files were missing, it suggests that the killer was after his research. Whatever he was planning to write about, somebody might have been trying to stop him.'

'Sounds likely,' said Gerry, scratching his head.

'What time's the sister arriving?' Wesley asked.

'She's catching the train first thing and she'll let me know what time it's due in. I'll arrange for someone to pick her up from Neston station to take her to do the formal ID.' Rachel shuddered. 'Trish has booked a room for her in Tradmouth.'

Wesley could see DC Trish Walton sitting a few desks away, studying her computer screen with great concentration. Her fiancé, DC Paul Johnson, was sitting at the adjacent desk. They were due to get married in a few weeks' time, and Wesley hoped this latest case wouldn't drag on and put a damper on the proceedings.

'Don't suppose anything new's come in on the jewel robberies?' Gerry shouted across the room.

When DC Johnson replied that they were still in the process of gathering CCTV footage from premises around Parker's shop, the DCI thrust his hands in his pockets and slouched into his glass-fronted office.

'Boss isn't in a good mood,' Rachel commented to Wesley as she watched him go.'

'The chief super's expecting progress on the robberies. Trouble is, all the likely local candidates have been interviewed and eliminated, and now we've got this murder . . . '

'I think the jewellery gang are from outside the area. But when Rob checked whether any similar crimes had been reported in other parts of the country, he drew a blank.' She glanced towards the window, where DC Rob Carter was speaking on the phone. When Rob had first started in CID, he'd been keen and sharp, reminding Wesley of an enthusiastic sheepdog eager to please his farmer. But since his partner, Harry, had passed away after a long illness the previous winter, he had seemed subdued, as though he was overwhelmed by a cloud of grief. Recently, however, they'd begun to see small glimpses of his old self. And now, whenever he smiled at one of the DCI's awful jokes, Wesley's spirits rose a little.

When Rob ended his call, he turned to face Wesley and Rachel, his cheeks reddening slightly as though he realised they'd been watching him.

'The bad news is that there's no CCTV or door-cam footage from around the murder scene, and no witnesses.'

'And the good news?' Wesley asked hopefully.

Rob shook his head. 'There isn't any.'

Lunch break. Pam had packed sandwiches for Michael. Tuna – his favourite – along with crisps, an apple and a small carton of orange juice. He'd often heard his mother complaining that she hadn't time for anything more im-aginative because she was a busy woman: a teacher with a husband who worked long hours whenever there was a major case to investigate.

Then there was his mum's mother, Della, whose weird crazes and arty clothes proved a great embarrassment to her teenage grandson. Michael always offered up a silent prayer to the God he'd learned about at his Uncle Mark's Sunday school that his gran – she hated being called that – wouldn't turn up when he brought friends home.

He'd been sitting on his own, but Harriet came and sat beside him. He felt himself blushing and hoped she wouldn't notice.

'How's it going?' she asked.

'OK.'

'Want one of these cheesy things?' She held out a plastic box and he took one, muttering his thanks.

'I just wanted to ask you, is Dr Watson your uncle?'

'Sort of. He's a ... friend of my dad's. They were at uni together.'

Michael had known Neil all his life and he'd never given him much thought. He was a fixture, rather like his parents, his sister, Amelia, Uncle Mark and Auntie Maritia and the embarrassing Della.

'Someone told me your dad was a detective.'

'Yeah.'

'I heard on the news that a man's been murdered in Little Rockington. Is your dad working on that case?'

'I expect so.'

There was a short silence before Harriet spoke again. 'Must be exciting, having a dad who's a detective.'

'You get used to it,' said Michael, trying to sound nonchalant.

'Do you know anything about what happened? With that murder, I mean.'

'I haven't seen my dad since this morning. But he might mention it tonight,' Michael replied, mildly disappointed that he wasn't able to impress her with a spot of inside knowledge. 'Why?'

Harriet smiled. 'Everyone likes a good murder, don't they? Ever read an Agatha Christie book?'

Before Michael could answer, one of the other students

had joined them: a boy called Greg with fair hair and freckles. He gave Michael a wide grin.

'Hey, have you heard that the royal family are going round robbing jewellers' shops? It's all over social media.'

'You mean a gang dressed up as the royal family. Not the real ones,' Michael corrected. 'My dad's working on that case,' he added proudly.

Harriet stood up. 'See you later.'

'Where's she going?' Michael asked as he watched her disappearing back.

'Don't ask me. I think she's got a secret boyfriend. Maybe one of those hunky soldiers. I saw her giving one of them the eye before. A woman of hidden depths is our Harriet.'

Michael knew Greg was joking, but he couldn't help feeling a tiny pang of jealousy.

6

Ellie, one of the newest DCs in the team, knocked on the open door of Gerry's office. When Wesley looked round, he could tell from her eager expression that she had news.

'The car's been found, sir. The one used in the robbery at Parker's Jeweller's.'

'Where did it turn up?' Gerry asked, hoping the location might give them a lead. Up until now, the robbers had covered their tracks well, stealing cars and abandoning them once the job was done, leaving no forensic traces. Presumably they transferred to another vehicle, but so far they'd been careful not to choose a place covered by CCTV.

'A lay-by just outside Belsham. It's between Neston and Morbay.'

'I know where it is,' said Gerry, looking at Wesley. 'Inspector Peterson's sister lives there.'

Wesley nodded. His sister, Maritia, was married to the Reverend Mark Fitzgerald, the vicar of Belsham, so he knew the village well. Several years ago he'd even investigated a murder at the large Victorian vicarage that had later become Maritia and Mark's home.

'Please tell me the lay-by's bristling with CCTV cameras,' said Gerry, his chubby face full of hope.

'Sorry, sir. Nothing. It's just off the main road, and there are no houses nearby.'

'I don't suppose anyone saw another vehicle waiting there? A car they might have used after they'd abandoned the stolen one? No observant farmers driving past in a tractor first thing this morning, for instance?'

'The nearest farm is some distance away, so . . . '

'Pity, but it was worth asking.' Wesley was trying to sound encouraging. 'Is the car damaged at all?'

'No. It's just like the other raids. High-end car nicked nearby then abandoned in a deserted place. It had been thoroughly cleaned, just like the others. The patrol who called it in said it looked as though it'd just been valeted. The forensics people are going over it, but they're not holding out much hope.'

'Considerate thieves who clean up after themselves. At least the owners'll be relieved to get it back in one piece once the CSIs have finished with it,' said Wesley, who was well aware that many getaway cars ended up burned out, with all possible evidence destroyed.

Ellie hurried out, looking relieved. Gerry could seem intimidating at first to new officers who hadn't yet got to know him. But Wesley had discovered his softer side early on in their working relationship. It was Gerry who'd welcomed him into Tradmouth CID when he'd first transferred to Devon after serving as a detective sergeant in the Art and Antiques Unit at the Met, and Gerry who'd made it quite plain to everyone that any hint of racism towards the new arrival wouldn't be tolerated. Even so, the DCI didn't hesitate to put the fear of God into incompetent officers and uncooperative suspects whenever necessary.

Gerry let out a long sigh. 'Why the royal family masks?'

'Well I think we can take it as read that His Majesty hasn't taken up armed robbery in his spare time. In my humble opinion, I reckon our thieves have got a sense of humour.'

'I'm not laughing. And neither were those jewellers who were threatened with a gun.

'How widely available are those masks?'

'All the possible outlets in the south-west have already been investigated, and nothing's come up. The only place that stocks similar masks is in Morbay, and they say none have been sold since the coronation. All the people who bought them were interviewed and eliminated from enquiries after the first raid in Tavistock.'

'No anonymous cash sales?'

Gerry shook his head. 'A few. But they're untraceable, I'm sorry to say.'

'Parker said one of the gang had a Liverpool accent. What if their MO is to travel down here along the motorway network, carry out a few robberies, then hurry back to wherever they come from. Maybe we should widen the search. And check holiday accommodation for any likely candidates in case they're staying here. We're looking for four adults sharing.'

'Two couples on holiday. That's common enough.'

'The first one happened over a fortnight ago, and most people only stay one or two weeks, so it's worth looking for any groups of visitors who stayed longer.'

'OK, Wes. I'll leave you to organise that.'

'I'll put Trish on it.' Wesley thought for a few moments. 'Is there any chance the robberies are linked to Barry Brown's murder? Given that Ms Pugh thought the person she saw might have been wearing a mask.'

'She might have heard about the robberies and put two and two together to make five and a half. But you're right, Wes. It's something we ought to consider.'

The phone on Gerry's desk rang. He mouthed the word 'fingerprints' at Wesley, who sat down on the visitor's chair beside the desk, awaiting the news.

'You're sure,' he heard Gerry say. After listening to the reply, the DCI ended the call. 'Looks like our thieves have been more careless than usual. The BMW's been cleaned inside and out, but a partial fingerprint was found on the inside of the steering wheel.'

'The owner's?'

'That's what we need to find out. It isn't a match for anyone on record. Someone's gone over to take the prints of the owner and his family for elimination purposes.'

'So it's either the owner's, or the getaway driver's never been in trouble before. I guess we'll just have to wait to find out.'

'Patience has never been one of my strong points, Wes.'

Neil would be the first to admit that his private life had always been a little disorganised. His relationships with women tended to fizzle out, not dramatically but with dwindling interest as his partner realised that he prioritised archaeology over domestic stability and romance. He'd recently become engaged to Annabel Collins, an archivist he'd known and worked with for many years. Their relationship, once purely friendly and professional, had blossomed over the past year or so, although Neil himself wasn't quite sure how this change had come about. They came from completely different backgrounds, hers decidedly upper crust, and yet they seemed to understand each other. In her own way, Annabel was as dedicated to the old documents she cared for in the Exeter archives as Neil was to his archaeological investigations. Perhaps they would make a good pair. Only time would tell.

But however chaotic his non-digging life might be, he prided himself that his excavations were always well organised, with everything done by the book and nothing of interest missed. This was why he found it hard to conceal his annoyance when two newcomers arrived on the scene. They swaggered into the fenced-off area bearing metal detectors and, without a by-your-leave, made straight for the nearest trench, jumping down into the newly dug hole, ignoring the archaeology society group's feeble attempts to stop them. The postgrad student in charge was shouting something Neil couldn't quite make out.

Neil was talking to the soldiers when it happened, impressed by their methodical way of working as they uncovered a section of Perspex, probably from the Lysander's cockpit window. They'd also found fragments of black metal, and one of them told him that aircraft carrying out clandestine missions had been painted black for camouflage because they flew by night, hoping to be invisible to the enemy. The soldiers had done their homework, and Neil was just congratulating them when he spotted the new arrivals who appeared to be pulling pieces of twisted metal out of the earth.

He jumped out of the trench, noticing that Dave had done the same.

'What do you think you're doing?'

'You in charge?' The speaker was a large man with a bald head and a prominent beer belly. 'My name's Ian, and me and Lance here are aircraft enthusiasts. We heard you were trying to lift some wartime wreckage and we thought we'd lend a hand. Can we see what you've found?'

'It's a community dig, so anyone who's interested can join in, but we need to establish some rules. You can't just go jumping into trenches and taking things out of the ground.' Neil was amazed at how stern he managed to sound, and as he glanced over at the students' trench, he saw that Michael was watching him with surprise – and maybe even admiration. 'Dave,' he called to his colleague. 'Will you do the necessary?'

Ian and Lance looked as though they were about to object, but in the face of Neil's determination, they climbed out of the trench and followed Dave meekly to the marquee, metal detectors slung over their shoulders.

Neil watched as they listened to Dave's lecture on archaeological procedure, probably the same one he gave to any novice diggers who were about to begin work.

He hoped they weren't going to be trouble.

Michael squatted down beside Greg, who was uncovering a piece of Perspex with an expression of earnest concentration on his freckled face. Harriet still hadn't come back, and he wondered where she was, surprised at how much he missed her. Although he'd never have admitted this to anyone. Not in a million years.

He looked up and saw the man in the beige bucket hat emerging from one of the Portaloos. But instead of returning to the trench where his fellow archaeology group members were working, he picked up a spade and crept off, glancing behind him as though making sure he wasn't being observed. Michael wondered if he was going for a cigarette. He knew some teachers at school did that, with the same furtive look about them. But whatever the man was up to, it was none of his business. He had a plane to help uncover.

Diary of Edith Tallow

Sunday 16 May 1943

My husband Bram's brother Isaac and his wife, Florrie, are renting one of the manor cottages from Colonel Gornay. Bram says he doesn't want anything more to do with Isaac and Florrie, but I miss them a lot. When they lived here with us, Bram had to mind his Ps and Qs, but since they left, he's changed – and I'm frightened. Florrie said I can visit them at their new house whenever I want, and I'd like to confide in her, I really would. But she's always been a gossip, so can I really trust her with my secret? Her husband and Bram are brothers. Even though there's bad blood between them, they're still family. There are posters up everywhere saying careless talk costs lives. I'm sure Florrie thinks they don't apply to her.

Last Saturday, I told Bram I was going to stay the night with my sister in Exeter. It's not the first time I've lied to him, but if I told him where I was really going, I reckon I'd get a black eye at best. As for the worst, I don't dare think about it.

I packed my little suitcase, the one I brought with me when I came to live here after the wedding. Back then, I thought Bram was so good-looking; dark and brooding like the man in that book I used to love – Heathcliff, his name was. I liked books when I was younger – never had my nose out of one – and I always loved a romantic hero, the strong, silent and protective type who made the heroine feel safe. Maybe that's what gave me such a rosy view of men.

I met Bram at a dance in the village hall a few weeks after I arrived in Moor Barton to work as a land girl for the Southens at Home Farm, on the other side of the village. He was all charm when we were courting, and he told me he owned a farm. I thought it would be something like the Southens' farm. It was only later I found out it was just a run-down smallholding. And he never said that his mother, Dorcas, would be living with us.

Most importantly of all, he never told me that old Dorcas is a witch. She sits by the range in the kitchen, thin and dressed all in black like a giant spider. She only talks to me when she's ordering me to do something. And she watches me all the time. No wonder Florrie and Isaac got out as soon as they could.

I have to help out with the animals here as well as working at Home Farm five days a week because the Southens' farmhands went off to enlist and they need all the help they can get. I like working for the Southens, but being there has made me into a liar.

When we were milking one morning a few weeks ago, one of the other land girls, Marie, asked if I was going to the dance at the base. There'd be Americans there, she said. They were rich and handsome and ever so polite. A bus had been arranged and it would stop outside the Gornay Arms. I told her I was a married woman, but she said I looked as though I needed some fun. I knew she was right, so I gave in to temptation. I told Bram I was going to my sister's, but really I stayed the night with the other girls in the barn where I used to sleep before I was married. It was so good to laugh and be free again.

40

I really like Marie. Her dad's French and she was brought up over there. She's got a lovely accent, and we all get her to teach us how to say things in French. She seems so stylish and sophisticated compared to the rest of us, and I can tell her French ways impress the Americans, who flocked round her at the dance. I can't help wishing that I was as pretty as her, but I keep telling myself it doesn't matter. I'm married, and I shouldn't have been thinking that way.

Marie says she might be going away soon. She says a car's being sent to take her to a meeting to see if she's suitable for special war work, but it's all very hush-hush. I said she shouldn't have told me about it, but she said she knows she can trust me not to tell Hitler. If she does go away, I'll miss her terribly.

To my surprise, Marie wasn't the only one who attracted some attention at the dance. I met a really nice soldier there. His name's Hank and he wants to see me again. I don't really know what to do.

I've got to make sure I hide this diary. There's a loose floorboard in our bedroom, and I'm sure Bram won't think to look under there.

7

Gerry sat back and his leather swivel chair creaked ominously under his weight. 'I have a theory, Wes,' he announced, looking pleased with himself. 'If Linda Pugh was right about Brown's visitor wearing a mask, what if Brown was one of the jewellery gang and he stepped out of line? Maybe it was a punishment beating; a warning not to be a grass that went too far. What do you think?'

'I suppose anything's possible. When's Colin doing the post-mortem?'

'He'll fit it in first thing tomorrow. And the sister's arriving later that morning. Let's hope she'll be able to tell us something useful.'

Wesley stood up. 'Rachel's arranged for a constable to guard the crime scene in case the killer didn't find whatever it was he was looking for and decides to return. A forensic team are going over there first thing to carry on searching the cottage. With any luck, the killer will have left some trace behind.'

The DCI checked the time. 'I want all the neighbours interviewed again. They've already given statements, but there's no harm in trying to jog a few memories. But we can deal with that tomorrow. I vote we get home now and make an early start.'

Wesley felt unusually energetic as he trudged home up the hill leading out of the town, passing rows of pastel-painted cottages, many now occupied by holidaymakers or second-home owners who only used them a few times a year. It was still light, so curtains hadn't been closed, allowing him tantalising glimpses of the lives of others. TV-watching, dining, wine-drinking – things he couldn't wait to do once he'd arrived home. And he was impatient to find out how Michael had fared on the dig.

As soon as he opened the front door, Michael rushed into the hall to greet him, with Sherlock, the Petersons' dog of uncertain breed, at his heels. Sherlock wagged his tail enthusiastically, and the grin on Michael's face told Wesley everything he needed to know.

'I take it you enjoyed the dig?'

'It was fantastic. Neil put me with some archaeology students.' Michael suddenly seemed more grown-up, even though he looked exactly the same as he had that morning.

'They looked after you then?'

'I don't need looking after, Dad. I just did what the others were doing. We've already found some of the fuse-lage, but Neil said the RAF took a lot of the wreckage away after the crash.'

'Do they know what caused the accident?'

'A thick fog came down suddenly and the pilot probably got confused. Either that or his instruments weren't work-ing properly. Neil wants to find the altimeter – he says it'll prove it one way or the other. It was a Lysander – the type of plane they used to drop secret agents on the continent. It was painted black so the enemy couldn't see it when it flew at night and we've found lots of black metal. Neil's trying to find out about the missions the plane went on, but he says that might be difficult because it was all top secret.'

'Glad you had a good time,' Wesley said with some relief. He'd been afraid Michael would become bored by the inevitable painstaking slowness of an archaeological dig. But being treated as an adult seemed to be doing wonders. 'How are you getting on with the students?'

Wesley was half afraid that they might regard a thirteen-year-old-schoolboy as a bit of a nuisance and leave him out.

'Great. Harriet's teaching me a lot.'

'Harriet?'

The boy blushed and bowed his head. 'She'll be in her second year when the next term starts. She's really nice.'

Wesley wondered if he could detect the beginnings of a crush.

Michael said he was going to his room to do a bit of research about secret missions during the war. Wesley was grateful that the dig had fired his imagination. Much better for teenagers to be out in the fresh air than sitting in their rooms in front of a screen all day, he thought. Then he suddenly realised he was starting to think like his own parents. Perhaps it was a fate that came to everyone in time.

He watched as Michael headed up the stairs with Sherlock following close behind. When the dog had first arrived in the Peterson household, he hadn't been allowed upstairs, but under pressure from Michael and Amelia, that rule was soon relaxed. And any attempt to reimpose it would be like King Canute trying to turn back the tide.

Pam appeared at the living room door and told him his dinner was in the microwave, so he made for the kitchen.

When he turned his head, he saw that she'd followed him with two glasses of red wine in her hands.

'Thought you might need this,' she said, handing him the fuller glass. The latest jewellery raid was on the news earlier.' She sat down at the kitchen table, waiting while the food heated up.

'Not only that,' Wesley said once he'd finished his first mouthful, only just realising how hungry he was. 'We've also got a murder on our hands. A man was attacked in Little Rockington during a break-in.'

'It was on the news earlier, but they didn't give any details. I wondered whether you'd be working on it. Little Rockington's a tourist trap. I never had it down as a dangerous place. Was it a burglary gone wrong?'

'His laptop, phone and some files are missing, but they left other valuables: money, credit cards and even a Rolex watch.'

Pam raised her eyebrows. 'Perhaps the burglar was disturbed – or he panicked. What do you know about the victim?'

'According to his sister, he was an author. She's coming down here tomorrow to ID the body.'

Pam shuddered and reached over to place a hand on his knee. 'I worry about you having to deal with all this violence you hear about.'

Wesley gave her hand a gentle squeeze. 'Most criminals we encounter in CID are weak rather than wicked. We don't come across real evil very often. It's mainly uniform who have to sort out the violent stuff.'

Pam looked sceptical. 'Admit it, Wes. You've had your moments. Promise you'll be careful?'

'I promise,' he said earnestly. He knew that many police

officers' partners lived in dread of them being injured or even killed in the line of duty, but Pam had never expressed such misgivings before, and he wondered what had brought it on.

To his surprise, she changed the subject abruptly. 'Michael enjoyed his day at Neil's dig. He's talked about nothing else since he got home. I even caught him telling Amelia all about it.'

'That's good,' he said before he took another mouthful of chicken casserole. He'd tentatively offered to cook some Caribbean meals when his parents came to visit later that summer to give Pam a break. But if his new case dragged on, he knew he might not have the opportunity to redeem himself on the domestic front.

After he'd finished eating and the dishwasher was loaded, they made themselves comfortable in the living room and refilled their glasses. But that night Wesley didn't sleep well. He kept going over things in his mind, and when he did eventually fall into a fitful slumber, he dreamed of shadowy figures in distorted masks battering Barry Brown's lifeless body.

8

The following morning Gerry delivered his briefing to the team; what he jokingly referred to as his morning sermon. Wesley stood to one side, watching the performance. The DCI seemed to be fired up with enthusiasm for the new case; there hadn't yet been time for pessimism to set in. According to Gerry, Barry Brown's killer was going to be caught within the next couple of days – and they would arrest the jewel thieves while they were at it. The possibility that Brown's attacker might have been wearing some kind of mask opened up a promising line of enquiry, but every avenue needed to be explored.

Gerry was giving serious consideration to the theory that Brown was connected to the robberies. But Wesley wasn't sure whether this idea of thieves falling out held water. They needed to find out more about Barry Brown. Hopefully the arrival of his sister later that day would provide them with some useful leads.

Once the briefing was over and the officers had returned to their desks, Wesley followed Gerry into his office.

'Post-mortem at nine,' Gerry reminded him. 'Is it me, or is it hot in here?'

'It's hot.' Wesley had been so preoccupied by the case

that the climbing temperature outside had barely registered. 'Looks like it's going to be a lovely day. Good for anyone lucky enough to be on holiday.'

Gerry grunted. 'That means the tourists are going to be out in force, getting in our way. Kept me awake half last night, they did, chattering on the quayside outside the pub.'

'The perils of living on the waterfront.'

Gerry's frown turned into a fond smile. 'Alison loves being next to the water, watching the boats.' He picked up a sheet of paper lying on his desk. 'This has just arrived. The print found on the steering wheel of the getaway car doesn't belong to the owner or any of his family.'

'But it's not on record either, so it doesn't help us much,' Wesley pointed out.

'Until we pull someone in and get a match.' Gerry checked the time. 'Right, Wes. If we don't shift, we'll be late for the post-mortem. We need to get over to Morbay, so we'd better set off.'

They picked up a pool car and Wesley made for the car ferry. Later in the day there would be long queues of visitors, but at that early hour they managed to drive straight on, sitting in silence as the vessel chugged across the sparkling river. Yachts skimmed over the water and a cruise ship made its stately way upstream to moor in the centre of the river, guided by attendant tugboats. If they didn't have work to do, they would have enjoyed the view.

The mortuary at Morbay Hospital was state-of-the-art and the two detectives took their place behind the glass viewing screen. Wesley was glad of this; at Tradmouth Hospital they were positioned closer to the action.

Colin worked with his usual thoroughness, keeping

up a commentary into the microphone dangling above the stainless-steel table where the corpse lay. When it was over, they made for his office and waited for him to join them.

When the pathologist entered, now in his shirtsleeves, having discarded his green surgical gown, he put the kettle on. It was a ritual they'd become used to over the years they'd worked with him – and one they looked forward to, because Colin always provided the best sort of refreshment: leaf tea from Betty's and biscuits from the royal estates. He prepared the tea with great ceremony, and it was only when the porcelain cups were set before them and the biscuits offered that he got down to business.

'What about time of death?' Wesley asked.

Colin smiled. 'I thought I'd trained you not to expect an accurate answer to that one, Wesley. But if you want a guess: he was found on Monday morning, so I'd say he probably died between seven and midnight the previous night. He'd eaten around one to two hours before death, if that's any help.'

'And the cause was the head injury, right?' said Gerry.

'Well, gentlemen, I'm afraid that wasn't what killed him. In fact the wound's pretty superficial; not severe enough to cause any damage to the brain and certainly not enough to kill, unless the victim had a particularly thin skull – which our man definitely didn't.'

'So what did he die of?' Gerry asked, as though he wished Colin would come to the point.

'Vomit was found at the crime scene and it's being analysed. But from my observations, I can't rule out the possibility of poison.'

Wesley and Gerry exchanged a puzzled glance.

'Poison? Any idea what?' Wesley asked.

'We'll have to wait for the lab to tell us that, I'm afraid. But there was a distinct whiff of Scotch about his stomach contents.'

'We didn't find a bottle of whisky on the premises, but when we were in the cottage, I noticed two washed-up glasses on the draining board,' said Wesley.'

'I never noticed them,' said Gerry, a note of disappointment in his voice.

'That isn't surprising. At first we assumed it was a break-in and the burglar inflicted a fatal head injury. Now I'm wondering whether the killer hit the victim when he was dying or already dead to make it look like a burglary gone wrong.'

'That would certainly fit with my findings,' said Colin.

'Those two glasses suggest to me that either Brown knew his killer or he had no reason to suspect they posed any danger to him,' Wesley went on. 'He had a drink with them and then they washed up the glasses later to destroy the evidence.'

'And took away the bottle?' asked Gerry.

'Very possibly.'

'Which means we need to look at all his contacts. Pity we haven't got his phone. The service provider could take ages to track down.'

Wesley looked at Colin. 'How soon will the toxicology results come through?'

'They usually take a few days, but I'll emphasise the urgency.

'Thanks, Colin.' Wesley turned back to Gerry. 'I think this changes everything, don't you?'

On their return journey from Morbay Hospital, Wesley and Gerry made a detour and stopped at Little Rockington to see how the search of the cottage was progressing.

Hopefully Barry Brown's killer had missed whatever he'd been looking for when he turned the place upside down. If that thing was of value, Brown might have hidden it. Wesley wasn't normally a superstitious man, but he was keeping his fingers crossed.

They reported to the sergeant stationed at the entrance, then donned gloves and protective overshoes. As they walked in, the search was in full swing.

'Anyone found anything useful?' Gerry called out.

A young constable put his hand up. He was slightly plump, fresh-faced with a shaven head, which made him look like an oversized baby. 'Sir, we've made a thorough search of the bedroom and this was under the bed.'

Gerry grabbed the plastic bag containing the object like a starving man seizing a morsel of bread. He held it up for Wesley to see. It was a small notebook with a red cover.

'Have you looked inside?' Wesley asked.

The constable nodded. 'It's mostly names and phone numbers. Some addresses.'

Wesley gave the young man an encouraging smile. 'Great. This could be just what we've been waiting for.'

9

Neil's decision to put Michael with the students was paying off now that Harriet and the others had taken him under their collective wing. Michael had always been an amiable lad, but Neil wondered whether that would change as the teenage years rolled on. He hoped not, although he knew there were pressures on youngsters nowadays; pressures that he and Wesley had never had to deal with in their formative years.

He'd spent the previous evening on his laptop, searching for information about the plane crash they were investigating, but he hadn't come up with anything new; just the bare facts. The plane had been en route to Winkleigh airfield after making a brief stop at Bolt Head, probably to drop off an agent who'd returned from a clandestine mission behind enemy lines. The pilot wouldn't have been expecting a thick fog to descend so rapidly during that short journey. His luck had run out – just as it had for so many others at that time.

'Neil, can I have a word.'

He swung round. He'd been so deep in thought that Michael's voice made him jump.

'Hi, Michael. Everything OK?'

'There's a man over there who's been watching us for ages. Just thought you'd like to know. I saw him talking to that man I was telling you about. The lanky one in the bucket hat.'

Neil looked round and saw that the man in the bucket hat was now working alongside his fellow archaeological society members in their trench, ignoring the newcomer.

'He's probably a curious local asking about the dig. This might be the most exciting thing that's happened in Moor Barton since the crash itself.'

Neil was used to members of the public taking an interest in his work, and he could see the man standing behind the fenced-off area, watching intently. He was in his sixties, with neatly cut greying hair. He wore a linen jacket with a silk cravat at his neck. His silver-topped walking cane and the golden Labrador sitting obediently at his side made him look like the archetypal country squire.

It was a few moments before Neil remembered where he'd seen him before. He'd been sitting in the front row during the village hall meeting. Most of the people at the meeting had been supportive of the proposed excavation. But this man, dressed in a smart jacket over a shirt and tie, had asked whether the archaeologists considered it disrespectful to dig up a crashed wartime plane merely out of idle curiosity.

Neil's answer had been firm. Since nobody had actually been killed in the crash, it wasn't a case of desecrating a war grave. It was a useful training dig for the students and the amateur archaeologists taking part. Besides, some of the participants were former soldiers, some of whom were recovering from traumatic events they'd experienced during their years of service. He had explained that it was a win-win situation all round, and he'd seen the audience nodding in agreement. Only the man who'd asked the question hadn't seemed convinced by his enthusiastic words.

He waited until Michael had returned to the students' trench before walking over to the spectator, hoping this might be a chance to win him over. Establishing good community relations was part of his job, after all.

'Hello there,' he said, trying to sound cheerful. 'Would you like a tour of our trenches – see what we've found?'

The man drew himself up to his full height. 'Thank you, but no.' There was a moment of hesitation. 'Tell me, Dr, er ... '

'Watson.'

'Of course. I remember now.' A thin smile appeared on the man's lips. 'Like in Sherlock Holmes.'

Neil laughed, glad that they seemed to be establishing a rapport. 'Well, I do have a friend who's a detective, but ... What did you want to know?'

'Have you come across any ... bones?'

Neil smiled and resisted rolling his eyes. This was a question many members of the public asked when they saw archaeologists at work. 'Nothing like that. And we don't anticipate finding human remains, Mr ... ?'

'Gornay. Ralph Gornay. I just wondered.'

Gornay turned and walked away, his Labrador trotting obediently by his side.

The notebook found in Barry Brown's cottage sat on Gerry Heffernan's desk and the DCI stared at it as though he was willing it to give up its secrets. The constable had been right. It contained scribbled names and initials along with some phone numbers. On their return to the station, Gerry had ordered the pages to be copied, and a few were allocated to each officer in the team. Now they were busy calling the numbers.

'With any luck the killer will be in there somewhere,' said Wesley, trying to inject a note of optimism into the situation.

'Fingers crossed,' said Gerry.

'Brown must have dropped it and it got kicked under the bed accidentally.'

'Or he hid it.'

'Either way it's lucky. The killer obviously didn't search the place thoroughly enough.'

'You say *he*, Wes. What makes you so sure it's a man? If Colin's right about the cause of death, isn't poison traditionally supposed to be a woman's weapon?'

'You're right, Gerry. A woman could have done it.' Wesley looked at his watch, a present from Pam the previous Christmas. He'd never really got on with using his phone to check the time; Michael said it was because he was getting old. 'What time's Barry Brown's sister arriving?'

'Her train got into Neston at eleven and Trish has gone to pick her up. She's taking her to the hospital first to make a formal ID then bringing her straight here. She should arrive any time now.'

The DCI stood up and surveyed the busy main office, and Wesley sensed his impatience as he watched the team contacting everyone in Brown's notebook in the hope of finding a new lead. So far they knew frustratingly little about the victim. And he'd always believed in the old saying that if you wanted to know how someone died, you had to find out how they lived.

When Gerry's phone rang, it was the front desk to say that Barry Brown's sister had just arrived and Trish was taking her to the interview room; the comfortable one with sofas and coffee-making equipment reserved for witnesses and victims, rather than the grimmer alternatives near the cells in the basement. Gerry's eyes lit up at the news; now perhaps they'd get somewhere.

Lizzie Clivedon was small and dark, with unruly curls and freckles. She didn't resemble her brother in the least, but almost as soon as the interview began, she explained that they were half-brother and sister. Their mother had married again after Barry's dad walked out, and Lizzie was four years Barry's junior.

She was equally swift to point out that in spite of the family disruption, she and Barry had been close when they'd been growing up. He'd always been protective of his little sister, she said as her eyes filled with tears. It had been so upsetting to see him at the hospital, but everyone had been really kind.

Wesley had asked Rachel to conduct the interview with him. He trusted her judgement and he was glad of her reassuring presence. Now she sat beside Lizzie on the sofa and touched her arm in a gesture of support before passing her a tissue from the box on the coffee table.

Lizzie looked straight at Wesley, sitting opposite, and he noticed that her brimming eyes were a startling shade of blue. 'I was told it was a burglary.'

Trish Walton had obviously supplied her with a simplified version of events, but now it was time to clarify matters.

'That's what we assumed at first,' said Wesley gently. 'But since then, we've found evidence that your brother's death wasn't that straightforward.'

'What do you mean?'

'We think he might have been targeted. Do you know of anyone who might wish to kill him?'

'Absolutely not.' She picked up the mug of coffee on the table in front of her. 'Barry wasn't that sort of person. He was a good man. He hated anything . . . dishonest,' she said before taking a sip.

Wesley leaned forward like a doctor about to deliver bad news. Gerry had often remarked that, coming from a medical family, he'd inherited some of their bedside manner. 'You told us he was a writer.'

'That's right. Barry was gentle. Creative. He could get people to confide in him, that's why he was so good at his job. He was a lovely man.'

Wesley caught Rachel's eye. Up until now, Barry Brown had been an enigma. And there were thousands of Barry Browns on the internet, so it was proving difficult to find out much through the usual channels. The landlord of his Docklands flat had been unable to provide any useful information, and there was no trace of him on any police records. They were still trying to contact his bank for details of his financial dealings.

'What kind of books did he write?' Wesley asked.

'Mostly ghostwriting for celebrities. That's why nobody's ever heard his name. I told him he should write stuff of his own, but what he did was very well paid and he said he needed to make a living. Although he did say he wanted to branch out into true crime or unsolved mysteries. I think that's where his interest really lay.' She smiled fondly. 'He said he was looking for a perfect tangled web. Though I'm not quite sure what that meant.'

'Do you know which publishers he dealt with? And did he have an agent?'

'I'm sure he had one, but I don't know the name. Sorry. But I do know he was doing well. All his correspondence about his work will probably be at his London flat.'

Wesley nodded. He'd either have to trust the Met to do a thorough job or send someone on a trip to the capital.

A smile appeared on Lizzie's lips. 'Barry was a brilliant uncle to my kids.' The smile suddenly vanished. 'Oh God, how am I going to tell them he's dead?'

It was a question Wesley couldn't answer, and he suddenly felt helpless. This was reality. The dead weren't the only victims. Their families served a life sentence too, he thought. He saw Rachel lean over and give Lizzie's hand a comforting squeeze.

'Do you know what he was currently working on? Was it something down here in Devon?'

She shook her head. 'Sorry. All he said was that it was a new project. Something exciting, he said.'

'His perfect tangled web?'

Lizzie raised her head as though she'd suddenly remembered something. 'I think he said someone had asked him to write a book about some mystery connected with the war and he was going to get paid well for it. I wasn't giving him my full attention at the time because I was busy with the kids.' She put her hand on her forehead as though she was frustrated by her lapse of memory. 'Oh, what were the exact words he used?' She thought for a few moments. 'I think it was something to do with secret agents.'

10

As soon as the interview was over, Trish took Lizzie Clivedon to the accommodation she'd booked for her. It hadn't been easy to find somewhere at such short notice at the height of the tourist season, and the B&B on Albert Road was hardly luxurious, but it was reputed to be clean and relatively comfortable. Besides, the owner was a good friend of Trish's cousin, something she seemed to regard as a guarantee of quality.

Wesley and Rachel returned to the CID office in silence, each lost in thought. The conversation had given Wesley plenty to think about. Before his death, Barry Brown had begun to follow a new path in his writing career: he'd branched out into working on a wartime mystery, and according to Lizzie, someone was going to pay him well for researching and writing a book about it. The empty folders found at the crime scene suggested the killer hadn't wanted that book to be written, which was mystifying in itself. World War II was a very long time ago.

As Brown had travelled down to Devon, it was reasonable to assume that whatever he was researching had a local connection, and Wesley hoped that if they went through the notebook they'd found underneath the victim's bed methodically, sooner or later they'd strike gold. But so far all the numbers they'd called belonged to people who'd worked with Brown in the past on ghostwritten autobiographies, and various other contacts he'd made during his professional career. Frustratingly, none of them were aware of any links to the West Country.

It was Rob Carter who eventually came up with a promising lead. A phone number on the back page of the notebook, underlined twice, belonged to a man called George Melling, who described himself as a local historian. When Rob had spoken to Melling, the man had told him that he'd found Barry Brown's details through his London agent and had contacted him with an idea for a book about an unsolved missing persons case. He'd proposed a collaboration; he'd provide the ideas and the information and Brown would carry out further research and do the actual hard work of writing the thing.

'Well done, Rob,' Wesley said, hoping this would be the breakthrough they were waiting for.

Rob gave a weak smile. 'Melling lives in Neston. I told him someone would be round to interview him this afternoon.'

'Perfect. I'd like to speak to him myself. Do you fancy coming with me?' He was standing at Rob's desk by the window, and he glanced towards Gerry's office, where he could see the DCI talking on the phone. The look of pent-up frustration on his face suggested that he was discussing something tedious like the previous month's crime reports. If this was the case, he'd probably be tied up for some time.

Neston was eight miles from Tradmouth. Rob drove, and in spite of Wesley's attempts to initiate a conversation, the younger man barely said a word. Before Harry's death,

Rob had been talkative, sometimes even cocky. But now the silence hung between them like a barrier. It was a barrier Wesley wished he could demolish.

George Melling lived in a small whitewashed terraced house in a side street running parallel to Neston's ancient main thoroughfare. Fortunately there was a free parking space outside, and as Rob drew up by the kerb, it crossed Wesley's mind momentarily that Melling might even be the killer. After all, Brown's computer had been taken along with files that had presumably contained his research notes. Maybe Melling had taken them for some reason. Professional jealousy, perhaps. Or a disagreement about how their mutual project should progress. Or maybe Brown had made an unwelcome discovery, something Melling might want to keep hidden.

According to Rob, Melling had seemed keen to co-operate with the police. But Wesley had discovered early on in his police career that people weren't always what they seemed.

The man who answered the front door was tall, with a shock of white hair and a matching beard. Wesley was struck by the inappropriate thought that he looked rather like Father Christmas. Although his solemn expression hardly exuded festive bonhomie.

'Mr Melling?' he said, showing the man his ID. 'I'm DI Wesley Peterson and this is DC Rob Carter. I understand you spoke to DC Carter on the phone earlier.'

The man nodded and stood aside. 'You'd better come in. Barry's death has come as a terrible shock.' He shuddered. 'I heard it was a burglary gone wrong.'

Wesley said nothing as they were led into a gloomy back room and invited to sit on armchairs protected by shabby crocheted blankets. The walls were covered with faded cuttings from newspapers and magazines. Between the cuttings he glimpsed stained wallpaper that was probably decades old. Interior decoration clearly wasn't George Melling's main priority.

'I was talking to him only the other day. I can't believe he's dead,' Melling went on as he sat on a hard dining chair opposite. 'You're not safe anywhere nowadays, I mean, Little Rockington's the quintessential chocolate-box village, isn't it,' he added, looking at Wesley and Rob accusingly, as though he judged them solely responsible for the outbreak of violent crime. 'And these jewel robberies you keep hearing about on the news. I don't know what's the world's coming to, I really don't.'

'We're pretty sure Mr Brown's death wasn't due to a random attack,' said Wesley, ignoring the implied criticism. 'We think he was targeted and we're trying to find out why. We're hoping you can help us.'

'I don't see how. Unless . . . '

'Unless what?' Rob said. He sounded impatient, more like his old self.

'Unless he'd stumbled on something that someone was desperate to cover up. Maybe even after all these years the secret service will stop at nothing to hide the truth about what happened.'

Wesley couldn't help wondering whether Melling was being overdramatic. 'Why don't you start at the beginning? Tell us about your connection with Barry Brown,' he said, glancing at Rob, who was perched on the edge of his seat, listening intently.

George Melling took a deep breath. 'I'm a local historian with a particular interest in the history of this area in wartime, and I contacted a number of literary agents in London asking whether they could recommend an author who'd be willing to investigate a rumour about a spy who went missing after an unexplained plane crash and possibly help me write a book about it. One of them suggested Barry Brown because of his extensive experience in collaborating with other people; ghostwriting, the agent called it. She said Barry was keen to take on a fresh challenge and branch out into other things, historic cases he could investigate. He sounded ideal, so the agent put us in touch.'

'When did you last speak to Mr Brown?'

'I called him on Sunday night around half past eight to see whether he'd made any progress. I assure you he was alive and well when I spoke to him.'

Wesley glanced at Rob. If this was true, it would help them pin down a more accurate time of death.

'Tell us about the rumour you wanted him to investigate.'

'The crash was up on Dartmoor. A Lysander. One of the ground crew at the airbase it flew from saw a young woman getting on board with the pilot. The pilot, Flight Officer John Carmody, managed to escape from the wreckage but died later from his injuries. However, there was no sign of the woman. Her body wasn't found and there was no trace of her in the vicinity.'

'Maybe the person who said he saw her board the plane was mistaken,' said Rob.

A flash of outrage appeared on Melling's face. 'I doubt that very much. That person was my father. He was ground crew at Bolt Head airbase and he wasn't in the habit of lying.'

'I'm sure he wasn't,' said Wesley, trying to smooth the situation.

'Anyway, the incident stayed with him all his life. He passed away a few years ago at the ripe old age of ninety-seven, and before he died, I promised him I'd try to discover the truth about what happened.'

'Perhaps the woman got on board because Carmody wanted to show off his plane to her – a bit of flirting, maybe. Your father might not have seen her disembark before he actually took off.'

'My father watched him take off. She was on board all right.'

'Did he tell anyone this at the time?'

'I can't be sure. You have to remember that there was a veil of secrecy surrounding all the Lysander operations, so he might not have liked to say too much.'

'Where did the plane come down?' Wesley asked, though he suspected he already knew the answer.

'Outside a village called Moor Barton.'

He wondered whether to mention Neil's dig but decided against it. He didn't want to distract Melling from his narrative.

'Do you know who the woman was?'

'SOE agents used to be flown into occupied Europe from Bolt Head. It was top-secret work and extremely dangerous, and the people who undertook it must have been remarkably courageous. This woman was one of them. Her name was Marie Leon and she was bright, vivacious and very pretty. Someone I spoke to told me they'd heard that Carmody said the name Marie before he passed away, although whether this was true or not, I don't know.'

'So you commissioned Barry Brown to find out what happened to her?'

'That's right. It preyed on my father's mind until his

death.' Melling paused. 'One thing I haven't mentioned is that Marie was my father's cousin. My grandmother's sister, that's my father's aunt, married a Frenchman called Pierre Leon, and Marie was brought up over there. She obviously spoke the language fluently, so I presume that's why she was chosen for the work. She must have been a very brave young woman.'

He walked over to a bureau in the far corner of the room and took something out of a drawer. He handed it to Wesley. It was a photograph of a pretty young woman with a heart-shaped face, intelligent eyes and full lips. Her dark hair was arranged in a classic 1940s style.

'This is Marie,' he said. 'In a way, I envisaged the book would be a tribute to her.' He bowed his head briefly before continuing. 'I tried to interest a TV company in the story, without any success, and I thought a book might move things along. Barry and I had agreed that he would write it, and I was going to pay him well out of money I've inherited recently. He seemed very keen on the project and he said he intended to go up to the village and make enquiries. He hoped someone there would know something.'

Wesley sensed that for George Melling, solving the puzzle that had baffled his father and at the same time paying tribute to a distant cousin he'd never known had become an obsession. Perhaps he'd even fallen a little in love with the girl in the photograph. But could it possibly have any connection with the death of Barry Brown?

'Can you think of any reason why someone would want to cover up the truth about what happened to Marie? After all, the war was over a long time ago and the activities of SOE agents are now in the public domain. People who did secret work at that time, like the codebreakers at Bletchley

Park, kept silent for years, but now we know all about them, and they're regarded as heroes.'

'Yeah,' agreed Rob. 'What would be the point of covering anything up now?'

Melling hesitated. 'I wondered whether Marie was murdered and someone in the village wanted to hide what really happened.'

Wesley took a deep breath. Would someone have resorted to killing Barry Brown to conceal a murder from over eighty years ago? He knew stranger things had happened.

'Do you know whether Barry ever got round to visiting Moor Barton?'

'He said he was going up there, but I don't know whether he managed to discover anything,' said Melling, before returning to the bureau, where he scribbled something on a small piece of paper.

'You might want to have a word with this gentleman,' he said as he handed the paper to Wesley. 'Craig Parker. His grandfather worked with my father at the airbase. They were good friends and he was with my father when the plane took off. I told Barry that Craig's grandfather might have said something or left some clue before he passed away. Last time I spoke to him, he said he'd seen Craig but hadn't learned anything new.'

'Apart from the wartime case, were you aware of Mr Brown undertaking other work in the area?'

Melling hesitated, frowning as though he was making a great effort to remember. 'He didn't say in so many words, but he did become a little elusive. A couple of times over the past week he said he couldn't meet me because he was busy.'

'Perhaps he was investigating your case?'

'That's not the impression I had.' He hesitated. 'If you must know, I was becoming rather irritated. I was paying him to investigate the mystery of my missing cousin, not to go haring off doing other things.'

'Tell us what you can about Barry.'

Lizzie Clivedon had described the victim from a sister's point of view, but so far Wesley's image of his professional life was only half formed; a vague blur he needed to bring into focus.

'In his thirties. Leather jacket. Tattoos. An earring. He didn't say much about himself, but he was a good listener; I suppose he needed to be in his job. He told me he'd ghostwritten biographies for various footballers and celebrities and that it's always important to take notes and listen carefully to what a subject has to say.' There was a pause. 'Have you got the notes he made about Marie? He made a lot while he was here.'

Wesley looked at Rob. 'We believe his work papers were taken from the premises when he was killed. Sorry.'

'That definitely means he'd discovered something someone didn't want to come to light.'

There was a fresh excitement in Melling's eyes, as though this was the evidence he'd been waiting for; the missing link that would solve the mystery that had preyed on his father's mind and was now consuming his. But Wesley was determined not to leap to conclusions at this early stage.

'He promised to give me a full briefing once he'd made more enquiries but I thought he sounded a little vague when he said it, as though his mind wasn't completely focussed on the task I'd set him. I couldn't help suspecting that he'd become distracted by something else and was in danger of losing interest in Marie's disappearance.'

'You've no idea what this might have been?'

'I'm afraid not.'

'If anything occurs to you, you will let us know, won't you,' said Wesley, handing the man his card.

'Of course, Inspector. Anything to help the police.'

'Thank you. If we have any information, we'll be in touch,' he said as he stood up, catching Rob's eye. 'Just one more thing. Where were you on Sunday evening?'

'Immediately after I spoke to Barry, I went out to my quiz night.' A smile played on Melling's lips. 'My team's called the Dartmoor Demons. The pub's called the Dartmoor Arms, you see. After closing time, I went back to one of my fellow team members' place for a nightcap and to plan next week's strategy. We take the quiz very seriously, and we only came second so we really need to pull our socks up.'

'You didn't go to Little Rockington?'

He raised his eyebrows. 'Good heavens, no. It's five miles away, so how would I have got there? I don't have access to a car, and even if I did, I'd been drinking,' he added self-righteously.

Wesley thanked him for his time and he and Rob took their leave. George Melling was fixated on one particular mystery, which in the chaos of wartime might not even turn out to be a mystery at all, because his father might have been mistaken. Marie could have left Carmody's plane without him seeing and embarked on a mission soon afterwards from which she failed to return. But even if Barry Brown had given him disappointing news, Wesley found it hard to see Melling as a killer. His alibi would be checked as a matter of routine, but it seemed pretty solid.

'What do you think?' he asked Rob as they climbed into the car. 'I can't really see him as a murderer, can you?'

'He seems obsessed with that wartime case, and if he thought Brown was neglecting it, he might have lost his temper and lashed out at him.'

'It's a possibility, I suppose. My friend Neil's excavating a wartime aircraft near Moor Barton.'

'The plane Melling was going on about?'

'I think that's highly likely, don't you?'

'Maybe he'll find this Marie's body.'

'There's been no sign of anything like that so far. And even in those days the authorities were pretty hot on retrieving bodies to give them a proper burial.' Wesley thought for a moment. 'Poison suggests premeditation, don't you think? Melling said that over the past week Brown kept making excuses not to meet him. That could mean he was getting fed up with his interference – or it could mean Brown had become mixed up in something else.'

'What?'

'That's what we need to find out,' he said before Rob started the engine. 'Perhaps Craig Parker will be able to throw some light on the matter.'

The dig was going well, but Neil Watson couldn't get Ralph Gornay's question about bones out of his head.

He did the rounds of the trenches, helping out with his trowel when needed. The soldiers were meticulous, recording all the finds, however small, and when he moved on to the students' trench, he was pleased to see Michael was still engrossed in the work. He didn't even glance up from the object he was uncovering, something that looked intriguing from where Neil was standing.

'What have you found?'

Harriet was hovering, allowing the boy his moment of glory. 'It looks like leather,' she said.

She squatted down and began to help. Eventually, as Neil watched, the object emerged. It appeared to be the rotted remnants of a boot.

'The pilot might have lost it when he managed to scramble out,' said Michael, excited.

'That's very possible. Well done, you two.'

He turned and saw one of the women from the local archaeology society, a tall and wiry retired headmistress with sensibly short grey hair and an air of confident authority. She was standing perfectly still with a puzzled look on her weather-tanned face. Neil leapt out of the shallow trench and strolled over to her.

'Something the matter?'

'I'm not sure,' she replied. 'I've just taken a walk up to that big rock over there. I needed to stretch my legs after kneeling in the trench for so long.' She waved her hand in the direction of a sheep-shaped boulder about a hundred yards from the dig site. 'I thought we were confining ourselves to the area of the crash.'

'That's right. We're only digging in the fenced-off area,' Neil said, wondering whether the gung-ho aircraft enthusiasts, Ian and Lance, had decided to branch out on their own. They were working in trench three under Dave's supervision, the picture of innocence. But he couldn't forget how they'd behaved when they first arrived.

'The ground's definitely been disturbed over there,' the woman said. 'Of course it could be so-called wild campers. I believe there's been a lot of that sort of thing recently.'

'Well, if someone's been digging there it has nothing

to do with us,' Neil told her, impatient to get back to work. He looked round and saw that one of the archaeology group was listening with a worried look on his face. The quiet man who always wore a bucket hat. His name, Pelham Jenks, had stuck in Neil's mind because it was so unusual.

'I think you should take a look,' the woman said with determination. 'Follow me.' The words sounded like an order.

Neil felt he had no choice. If Ian and Lance had gone off piste, he needed to clear up the matter once and for all. He followed her meekly until they came to a halt in front of the boulder. Sure enough, a patch of ground had been disturbed, and that disturbance looked recent.

'Could be hikers,' he said with a certainty he didn't feel. 'Or . . . ' He was about to suggest wild animals, but he could see spade marks in the soil.

'I just thought you should know,' the woman said.

'Thanks. You did the right thing.'

She returned to her trench, and Neil waited until she was some way away before examining the site more closely. A rectangle of red earth was dotted with small stones that looked as though they'd been placed there deliberately. Eventually his curiosity got the better of him, and he yielded to temptation and took his trowel from one of the many pockets of his combat trousers, the uniform he always wore on a dig.

The spot was in a dip in the landscape, and he squatted down and began to scrape at the soil. The woman had been right: someone had been digging there recently in a rather haphazard way. And he wanted to find out why. Then he remembered that Michael had mentioned seeing Pelham Jenks wandering in this particular direction, and he couldn't help wondering whether he had anything to do with this new discovery.

He'd only gone down about four inches when he stopped. And what he saw there against the dark soil made his heart beat faster.

Diary of Flight Officer John Carmody

14 June 1943

They call us the Black Squadron – or the cloak-and-dagger boys. Pity we have to keep quiet about our hush-hush missions, because all the mystery might impress the girls and give us an advantage over the Yanks, who can offer nylons and sweets they call candy. I've heard some girls say the Yanks are all millionaires and live like Hollywood film stars back home. How can you compete with that?

In the meantime, our drops continue. Flying to France on dark nights with only a map and compass to find the way. Sneaking in and out by night without the visible heroics of our Spitfire boys. I sometimes wonder whether anyone will know we even existed once this war's over, whenever that will be. We keep dropping our cargo in those French fields and only half of them seem to make the return journey. I often wonder what's happened to them. Are they still living safely among friends in the Resistance, or has their cover been blown? Have they been betrayed and captured? Are they still alive? Are the Resistance members they were supposed to meet all they seemed? Or are there secret collaborators and traitors

73

in their midst? My admiration for my brave passengers knows no bounds. I merely offer a taxi service to get them behind enemy lines, so my sacrifice seems paltry in comparison to theirs.

11

When Wesley returned to the station, he made straight for Gerry's office and told him about his meeting with George Melling.

'A missing person from the 1940s is hardly our concern. Unless this Melling is so bent on solving the puzzle that he was happy to dispose of Brown if he showed signs of losing interest.'

'Stranger things have happened. If you ask me, he's pretty fixated on the case.'

'So what if Brown found out that Melling had got it all wrong and there was no mystery after all? How would he react?'

'I think he'd be disappointed, but I can't see him resorting to murder. Neil's digging at the site of the air crash. When I saw him at the weekend, he told me that the plane that crashed was used to ferry members of the SOE, the Special Operations Executive, into occupied Europe. The agents were dropped there to help the Resistance and send information back home. And maybe do a spot of sabotage as well. If they were caught, they faced death.'

'Do we know what happened on the night of the crash?'

'The pilot flew to France, picked up an agent and

delivered them to Bolt Head airbase safe and well. When he crashed, he was on his way back to the base at Winkleigh, just a short hop over Dartmoor. But he didn't make it.'

'And Neil hasn't come across the skeleton of any missing woman?'

'Not as far as I know. And I'm sure he would have been in touch if human remains had turned up.'

'Melling's dad could easily have made a mistake, and that would put paid to his precious book.' Gerry thought for a moment. 'Come to think about it, Brown would hardly expect Melling to slip something nasty into his whisky, would he?' He sighed. 'We're still waiting on that tox report. Until we get the results, we don't know what poison we're dealing with.'

'I want to have a word with Craig Parker. His grandfather served with Melling's dad at the airbase. Melling told us Brown paid him a visit, so he might have something to tell us.'

Before the DCI could answer, the phone on his desk began to ring. He rolled his eyes and picked it up with a muttered 'No rest for the wicked.' Then Wesley watched his expression change from bored resignation to excitement.

'You're sure?' Gerry hit the phone's speaker key and Wesley heard Colin Bowman's distinctive voice.

'According to the tox report, Brown was poisoned with cyanide.'

'How do they think he was given it?'

'Orally. Probably in the whisky I found in his stomach contents.'

'Let's work on the theory that the killer inflicted the head injury hoping we'd assume that was the cause of death. Maybe he didn't expect us to consider poison. But no one can pull the wool over your eyes, eh, Colin,' Gerry said cheerfully.

'I like to think not.'

Gerry thanked him before ending the call.

'Cyanide,' he said, sinking back into the executive leather chair, which creaked loudly under his weight. 'Where would you get hold of that?'

'It has industrial uses and you find it in some laboratories,' said Wesley. 'It used to be used by gardeners and farmers to get rid of pests, and you can make it from laurel leaves and various pips and fruit stones if you know what you're doing.'

'So it's not that hard to get hold of.' Gerry rolled his eyes. 'That's all we need.'

Trish hurried over. Wesley knew she'd taken Lizzie Clivedon to the B&B where she was staying that night. He'd expected the contact with grief to dampen her spirits, but he saw that she was looking pleased with herself, as though she'd had some good news.

'I've spoken to Craig Parker. You're not going to believe this, but he's only over the road. He's a blacksmith – works in that forge at the back of the pub.'

Wesley knew the place. Pam had dragged him in there once to look at garden ornaments. The forge, which had once catered for local everyday needs, now relied mainly on the custom of wealthy incomers and tourists, and the beautifully created garden items had been out of their price range. However, the blacksmith's skill hadn't diminished because of the change in clientele, and they'd watched, fascinated, as he'd hammered the metal into elaborate shapes. To Wesley, the process had seemed almost magical.

He could have delegated the task of speaking to Parker

to someone else, but the forge was so close to the station he decided to go himself. Gerry, who was clearly restless being confined to the office, practically leapt out of his seat and followed him to the door.

When they arrived at the old single-storey stone forge, the first thing that hit them was the heat from the furnace in the corner. Craig Parker, a large, muscular man with curly dark hair and wearing a leather apron, looked up from his work and told them he'd be with them in a minute.

When he'd finished his mysterious task, he turned to them. 'Afternoon, gentlemen. How can I help you?'

When they introduced themselves and showed their ID, Parker led them into a small, cluttered office at the end of the building.

'Yes, I had a visit from Barry Brown, but I couldn't tell him anything,' he said once they'd explained why they were there. 'My grandad never spoke much about the war. Of course George Melling's dad might have made a mistake about seeing the woman board the plane. I expect there were lots of comings and goings at the airbase and things got confusing.'

'Have you heard about Mr Brown's death?'

'Death? No.' Parker sounded genuinely surprised. 'I've been so busy here that I haven't had time to catch up with any news this week. How did he die? Was he involved in an accident?'

'We think he was murdered.'

The surprise turned to shock. 'No way. Who would want to . . . ?'

'Where were you on Sunday night?'

'At home. My wife will confirm it. It's the tourist season,

so it's been a frantic few weeks. I think I was asleep by nine-thirty.'

As far as Wesley could tell, the man was telling the truth. But they'd get his alibi checked anyway.

'Did Mr Brown say anything else to you?'

'He asked if I had any other relatives who might be able to help him, and I told him about my cousin Bella. Funnily enough, Bella's mum used to live in Moor Barton, the village where the plane came down.'

'Where can we find Bella?'

'She lives on that new estate on the way into Tradmouth, right at the top of the hill. But you might find she's away at the moment. Last time I spoke to her, she said she was going on holiday to Tenerife. Don't know when she's due back, but I don't think she'll be there long. Just a short break, she said.'

'We'll need her address anyway.'

'Sure.' He scribbled an address and phone number on the back of one of his business cards and handed it to Wesley. 'Brown might have had more luck with her because she's really into local history and anything to do with the family. We call her the keeper of the archives. If anyone's got any of my grandad's old diaries and things like that, it'll be our Bella,' he added as Wesley tucked the card into his notebook. 'She's been doing her family tree and she told me she traced her mum's side of the family back a few generations. Said it wasn't difficult because Moor Barton's only a small place.'

'Do you know if Mr Brown paid her a visit?'

'Sorry. No.'

'By the way, do you ever use cyanide in here?' Gerry asked before Craig could say any more about his cousin's genealogical research.

'No. But before I trained as a blacksmith, I worked some-where they did metal finishing, and they used it there. Why do you ask?'

'Because Barry Brown was poisoned with the stuff.'

There was no mistaking the shock on Parker's face as he swore under his breath. 'Poor bloke,' was all he could think of to say.

On their way out of the forge, Wesley paused to admire a wrought-iron garden ornament in the shape of a butterfly, making a mental note that it would be a good present for Pam's birthday. But that would have to wait for another day.

As soon as they returned to the station, Gerry hurried to his office to check his messages and Wesley asked Trish to contact Parker's cousin Bella, but there was no reply.

When he returned to his own desk, his phone rang and he saw Neil's name on the caller display. He was tempted to kill the call, then he remembered that Michael was with him and his imagination conjured a terrible accident: a broken leg, or worse still, a blow from a mattock. His hand was shaking as he answered.

'Wes,' Neil said before he had a chance to speak, 'I think I've come across human remains. It's some distance from the site of the plane crash, but one of our local volunteers noticed that the ground had been disturbed as though someone had been digging there. I found a bone that looked human not far from the surface. A shallow grave. I've done everything by the book – sealed off the area and called in a patrol car – but I thought you'd want to take a look. Wes? Are you there?'

'Yes, Neil, I'm here,' said Wesley, wondering whether George Melling's mystery of the missing woman was about to be solved. Perhaps she'd been lying there buried on the moor all along.

'He or she obviously didn't bury themselves, so it must be suspicious. And another thing, from the size of the bone, I'd say it was a child.'

'A child? Are you sure?' Wesley felt his new theory crumbling to dust around him.

'Absolutely.'

'OK, Neil. I'm coming over.

Pelham Jenks was uncovering what looked like part of an aircraft wheel with Dave, the professional archaeologist, whose thinning hair was shielded from the sunlight by an Indiana Jones hat. Pelham had never seen him without the hat, and he couldn't help wondering whether he ever took it off.

Over the past hour or so he'd been aware of the whispers between the professionals, and there'd been no sign of Dr Watson for a while. Something was going on near the boulder shaped like a recumbent sheep, and he knew they must have found it. He'd watched Watson walk over in that direction with his fellow volunteer, the rather bossy ex-headmistress. He wished he'd made a better job of covering his tracks.

The previous night a vivid dream had disturbed his sleep. He was running across the moor with his big brother, Norman, and when they reached the wall surrounding the manor house, they climbed over. Then the world exploded and he saw Norman lying on the ground, dead-eyed and covered in blood. He'd started to run for his life, and at that point he'd woken up with a start, sweating and tangled in his sheet.

He was tempted to sneak over to the boulder to see what was going on, but he knew he needed to leave it to the experts. He consulted his watch. If he didn't leave now, he'd be late for his appointment. He'd waited long enough to find out the truth about what had happened his brother. A little while longer wouldn't hurt.

12

'This is all we need,' Gerry said when Wesley told him about Neil's call. 'Brown's killer's on the loose, not to mention these jewel robbers.'

'I'm well aware of that, Gerry.'

Wesley had watched the late TV news the previous night, and when the presenter announced solemnly that a group of masked robbers nicknamed the Royal Family had carried out yet another raid, he and Pam couldn't resist laughing at the mental picture the statement conjured up.

The DCI put his head in his hands for a few seconds. Then he looked up. 'What's the latest?'

'We're following up those leads George Melling gave us about Barry Brown's research into a possible wartime missing persons case, and we've got people speaking to Brown's associates in London and his agent.'

'Anything else?'

'I've given Paul Johnson the job of contacting a couple of Premiership footballers who worked with Brown on their ghostwritten biographies.' Wesley grinned. 'He seems quite star-struck.'

'Nice little pre-wedding present for him.' Gerry gave a long sigh. 'We need this case cleared up before the wedding. We don't want Paul and Trish interviewing suspects on the way to the church.'

'In that case we'd better pull out all the stops.' Wesley hesitated. He could hardly ignore Neil's call. If a skeleton had been found, possibly that of a child, he needed to find out what was going on. 'I should go and check out Neil's discovery.'

'Think these bones could be linked to the Barry Brown investigation?'

'That's what we need to find out.'

Gerry sat back and frowned. 'Let's hope it's a medieval peasant. If it turns out to be recent, we'll have to call in reinforcements from Neston and Morbay.'

'I'd better get going then.'

But before he could move, Gerry's phone rang and he rolled his eyes, muttering, 'What does she want this time? The budget for my weekly shop?'

But it wasn't the chief super on the other end of the line. Gerry pressed the speaker so that Wesley could hear. The detective constable ringing from the Met had a London accent. And he sounded excited.

'Is that the SIO in charge of the Barry Brown case? The guy who's been found murdered on your patch?'

'It is. DCI Heffernan speaking.'

'This is DC Norris, sir. You requested a search of Brown's address in Docklands. We've just completed it and ... well, we've found some interesting stuff.'

'How interesting?'

'Very. Stuff the tabloids would pay good money for. All set out neatly in a number of notebooks. I'll have the originals sent over to you if you like. There's too much to scan and email across.'

'Understood. Can you get it to us sooner rather than later?'

'Do couriers deliver to your neck of the woods?'

'The occasional horse-drawn cart finds its way up rough tracks to drop off essentials to the tiny thatched cottage belonging to the village constable. Of course we have bloody couriers. How soon can you arrange it?'

'Tomorrow morning OK, sir?' The young man didn't sound quite so cocky. Being on the receiving end of Gerry's sarcastic wit had that effect on people.

'Are you going to give us a clue?'

'Clue?'

'About what the tabloids would pay good money for.'

'Er ... let's just say it concerns a certain squeaky-clean national treasure.'

'And would someone commit murder to keep it out of the headlines?'

'I'd say so, sir. If what's in those notebooks is true, it'd finish him.'

Intrigued as Wesley was by the call from the Met, he needed to see what Neil had found. Neil wasn't usually fazed by human remains turning up during a dig, but he'd sounded as though this particular discovery had disturbed him. Wesley knew how he felt. A child going missing, or worse still, being found dead, tore at his heart as his mind was flooded with thoughts of his own children. He usually tried to hide these feelings behind a facade of professionalism. It wasn't easy, but he told himself that succumbing to emotion never helped find a missing child – or brought a killer to justice.

Before he left the office, he carried out a quick check to see whether any children had gone missing in the area in recent years. Fortunately, most had been found safe and well. The only two who were still missing dated back decades. Even so, he still couldn't bear to contemplate what the parents had gone through.

It was a bright day when he arrived in the village of Moor Barton and parked, as Neil had suggested, in front of the Gornay Arms, a squat whitewashed pub next to the medieval church. Neil had also instructed him to bring his Wellingtons. There might be a bit of walking to do on rough terrain.

He followed the directions he'd been given and made his way out of the village towards the open moor, pausing to take in the view over undulating fields. Eventually he spotted the dig, with its marquee, temporary fences, spoil heaps and trenches. He scanned the scene for his son, and soon caught sight of him working busily in one of the trenches with a group of young people. He watched as Michael deposited a bucket of soil in the spoil heap. When the boy noticed him, he waved and resumed his place in the trench, squatting down beside a girl with auburn plaits; Harriet perhaps. She kept glancing up, looking in Wesley's direction as though she was wondering what he was doing there.

One of the diggers told him that Dr Watson was with the forensic people up by the big rock, and when he finally reached the spot, he found his friend looking unusually serious.

A local constable was guarding the area, which had been cordoned off with blue and white crime-scene tape. The proceedings were being photographed and videoed. When Wesley showed his ID, he was allowed to cross the barrier, and Neil came forward to greet him.

'What can you tell me?' Wesley asked as the two of

them stood watching the CSIs working with intense concentration. He could see that more of the body had been
uncovered, including the skull.

'It's a child aged around ten, judging by the bones and
teeth. It's a shallow grave and I think someone's been digging there recently.'

'Looking for the body?'

Neil shrugged.

'While you've been here, have you seen anyone taking a
particular interest in this spot?'

Neil hesitated. 'Your Michael saw one of the local archaeology society walking over here yesterday. I said he
was probably just looking for somewhere private to relieve
himself, but now ... '

'Where is this man? I'd better have a word.'

'He went off early – said he had a dentist's appointment.
He should be back tomorrow.' Neil thought for a moment.
'Funny, someone from the village asked whether we'd
found any bones.'

'You think he was trying to draw attention to the grave?'
said Wesley, suddenly suspicious.

'Not necessarily. It's something you often get asked, isn't
it. People are attracted to the macabre.'

'Who was it doing the asking?'

'His name's Ralph Gornay. Lord of the manor, no less.
The local pub's named after his family. He lives in the
manor house on the other side of the village. Well, it's
called a manor house, but it's not that big. Interesting,
though. Seventeenth century.'

Wesley resisted the urge to smile. Even the grimmest of
discoveries couldn't dampen Neil's enthusiasm for historic
buildings.

'Like I said, people often ask if we've found any skeletons, so I wouldn't read too much into it. Although at the meeting we held at the village hall, he didn't seem too keen on the dig taking place.'

'I'd better have a word with him,' said Wesley, wondering if Barry Brown had spoken to Gornay during his visit to the village. If he wanted to know about the history of Moor Barton, it would be as good a place as any to start.

Before he began to walk back towards the village, Wesley had a word with the CSIs and asked whether anything had been found in the grave beside the bones.

'We found the remains of what looks like a catapult. And some buttons that haven't rotted away,' the CSI said, scratching his head. 'Skull seems to be intact, so we can rule out a blunt instrument as the cause of death.'

'I'd like Dr Bowman to take a look. I'll arrange that.'

He rang Colin's number and was told that he was busy conducting a post-mortem, so he left a message. Then he called Gerry to ask for an update. The news was that there was no news. As he made his way past the dig, he saw the girl he assumed was Harriet watching him. After a few moments she whispered something to Michael, who looked up from his work and gave him a smile that warmed his paternal heart.

13

The sun was shining when Wesley set off for the manor house. Michael was happily occupied, the landscape was breathtakingly beautiful and the officers from the Met would soon send through information that would result in Barry Brown's murderer being brought to justice. Just for a moment he felt optimistic.

He stopped at the car to change his footwear; muddy Wellingtons were hardly suitable attire for calling at a manor house. Then he walked on through the village. Most of the pretty pastel cottages were terraced and their front doors opened straight onto the main street. At the end of the street stood a small white-walled village hall next to a lychgate guarding the winding tombstone-lined path to the church porch. Exploring old churches was one of Wesley's secret pleasures, but this time he resisted the temptation. He was supposed to be working.

The manor house stood at the end of a narrow lane to the right of the lychgate. It was a low granite building with mullioned windows and a date carved above the porch. 1670. The reign of King Charles II.

He tugged at the bell pull, wondering if the door would be answered by a butler who would try to steer him round to the tradesmen's entrance. But it was Ralph Gornay himself who opened the heavy oak door, a golden Labrador by his side. His initial reaction to seeing Wesley was suspicion. But his expression changed once Wesley had introduced himself and shown his ID.

'How can I help you, Detective Inspector?'

'I don't know whether you're aware that human remains have been found near the site of the archaeological dig.'

The man had been stroking his dog, but his hand suddenly froze. 'Human remains?'

'They appear to belong to a child aged around ten. I understand you expressed reservations about the dig taking place during a meeting at the village hall.'

'Dartmoor's a precious environment. Any excavation might disturb wildlife. Besides, I considered the excavation a little ... disrespectful.'

'I understand that nobody actually died in the aeroplane.'

Gornay shook his head. 'Even so, the pilot passed away shortly after the crash. Another young man who gave his life for our freedom. In my opinion, that site should be respected.'

The explanation didn't sound convincing, so Wesley carried on. 'You asked the archaeologist in charge whether they'd found any bones. Was respect your only concern? Or did you know that human remains were buried up there? Remains that had nothing to do with the plane crash?'

The colour drained from the man's face and there was a lengthy silence, as though he was making a decision. After a while, he said, 'You'd better come through to the drawing room.'

'Do you live here alone?' Wesley asked as he followed him into the house.

'Yes. Although a woman from the next village comes in a couple of times a week to clean, and my daughter visits quite often,' Gornay added, his expression softening at the mention of his child. 'I inherited this house from my father. He lived to a ripe old age – ten years off making his century, to use a cricketing term. You a cricket fan, Inspector?'

'My grandfather used to take me to the Queen's Park Oval in Trinidad when I visited him as a child,' Wesley said, hoping the subject would help him to build a rapport with the man.

'How wonderful,' said Gornay with a faraway look in his eye, as though he was imagining the sun-drenched scene. He invited Wesley to take a seat, then drew a deep breath. 'I have a confession to make. It's probably time I got it off my chest. But where to start?'

'Why don't you start at the beginning,' said Wesley.

'Very well. My family have lived in this house for generations. There are a lot of Gornays buried in the parish church, and we've always been regarded as the lords of the manor, although nowadays deference is a thing of the past, of course. I was a rebellious young man, and I left home in my teens to build a life in London. I never came back to see my father because when I left he swore he'd never speak to me again. However, we had a sort of uncomfortable reconciliation when his eyesight faded and he developed dementia, which meant he was too ill to manage by himself. I came back to live here, thinking the move would be temporary, but when he passed away nine years ago, I ended up taking the place over and leaving my London life behind.'

Wesley nodded, but he didn't interrupt, knowing there was more to come.

'I'm divorced and my daughter stayed with her mother,

91

so I rattle around this old place on my own. Pity.' Gornay gave a rueful smile. 'My late mother used to enjoy the role of lady of the manor, you know. Organising the village fete and arranging the church flowers and all that. Not that I remember much about her. She died when I was fifteen, a couple of years before I left for London.'

Wesley wished he'd come to the point. He guessed the man was glad of someone to talk to, but he wasn't there to provide a sympathetic ear. 'You said you had a confession to make.'

Gornay let out a sigh. 'Now that the remains have finally been found, the truth might as well come out. After all, he isn't here to take the consequences.'

'Who isn't?'

'My father. Before he passed away, he made a deathbed confession, though it was one I'd rather not have heard.'

He fell silent, as though he was contemplating how much to divulge.

'You were saying, Mr Gornay?' Wesley prompted.

'Ralph, please. My father wasn't a nice man, Inspector. He did a lot of bad things in his life, but this particular dark deed had been on his conscience for many years, and he said he needed to get it off his chest. In the late 1950s, when I was very small, he caught a boy in the grounds, probably scrumping apples as the local children sometimes did. He had his shotgun with him and he fired in the boy's direction. He swore he'd just intended to frighten the lad off, although I wasn't sure whether to believe him.'

He paused for a few moments, then began to speak again, lowering his voice as though what he was about to say was so dreadful it hurt him to utter it.

'My father said the boy changed direction unexpectedly

and ran straight into his line of fire. He saw him fall over, and when he went to him, he found the lad was dead. He said it was an accident, but he didn't want the servants to know what had happened, so he carried him into the garden shed. The gardener was away at the time, so he knew nobody would be going in there for several days.'

'He didn't get help?'

'He claimed he panicked.'

'Do you know who the boy was?'

'His name was Norman. His father was a labourer on one of the tenant farms nearby and his mother cleaned for us occasionally. I don't think I ever knew his surname. The boy was known in the village as a bit of a rascal, and it was assumed that he'd run away from home. Either that or he'd fallen into a disused mine shaft – or even wandered into a bog. People don't realise how treacherous Dartmoor can be.'

Wesley was about to say that he knew because *The Hound of the Baskervilles* had been one of his favourite childhood reads. But the comment seemed flippant, so he stayed silent.

'Needless to say, there was a big search for him,' Gornay continued. 'The whole village, including my father, turned out, but of course it was futile. Then the following night my father went out and buried the body near the Sheep. That's the big boulder not far from the site of the air crash; they call it that because of its shape. My father never told anybody what happened until the very end, when he made his confession to me.'

Wesley wondered how on earth the man could have joined in the search and acted normally, knowing what had really happened. But he'd heard that generation and

93

social class had been adept at hiding their true feelings; the British stiff upper lip that people sometimes talked about. Either that or he'd been so emotionally cold that the terrible event had had little impact on him.

'A pile of stones was found on the grave, as though someone had marked the spot,' he said.

Ralph Gornay raised his eyebrows. 'Really? I didn't put them there, and I'm sure nobody else knew about it, so perhaps my father had some feelings after all.' The words sounded bitter. 'In a way, it's a relief the child has been found. I was dreading the archaeologists coming across him. That's the true reason I raised objections at the meeting. But now it's happened, I suppose everything can come out in the open. Closure, they call it, don't they.'

'Why didn't you tell the police after your father died?'

Ralph hesitated. 'As I said, he'd developed dementia and was on some pretty strong medication before his death, so to be honest with you, I wasn't sure it was true. If he'd been having delusions, I would have been wasting police time, wouldn't I.' He swallowed hard. 'And I confess to feeling a little ashamed too. It was easier to ignore it and let sleeping dogs lie. But now that the situation has changed, I'll cooperate in any way I can.'

'Did you try to dig at the grave site?'

'Of course not.' He sounded horrified at the suggestion.

'Somebody's been digging there recently. And it wasn't the archaeologists.'

Gornay shook his head. 'It certainly wasn't me. All I knew was what my father told me. He said he'd buried the child somewhere near the Sheep, but he didn't specify the exact location.'

'Are the boy's family still around?'

'I understand they moved away after he disappeared, and I'm afraid I've no idea what happened to them. The parents are probably dead by now, of course.'

'Did he have any brothers or sisters?'

'I seem to remember he had a younger brother, but I can't recall his name. It was a long time ago.'

'If there are any relatives, they should be found and informed if possible.'

'I understand, but I would ask you to be discreet. My father's dead, but something like this can leave a stain on a family. And I do have a daughter.'

'I'm not a great believer in the sins of the fathers being visited upon the children,' said Wesley softly. It was time to ask the question he'd been wanting to ask since his arrival. 'There's something else I'd like to speak to you about.'

'What's that?'

'A man called Barry Brown may have come to Moor Barton to ask questions about the air crash. He was an author and had been commissioned to write a book about it.'

Gornay's eyes lit up with recognition. 'Yes, he called here, but I couldn't tell him anything. I have his card somewhere.' He stood up and walked over to the bureau in the far corner of the room. After a few moments, he returned and handed Wesley a business card belonging to Barry Brown, freelance author and journalist.

'What can you tell me about Mr Brown's visit?'

'He turned up out of the blue last Friday afternoon, just after I'd eaten lunch. A frozen meal for one, I'm afraid,' Gornay added with a note of sadness. 'He said he was an author and was interested in the history of the village. He seemed a nice enough chap, so I invited him in. I asked him how he'd got my name and he just said he wanted to interview people who had roots in Moor Barton and he thought the manor house would be a good place to start.'

'And what did you talk about?'

'He asked me what I knew about the plane crash, but all I could tell him was that I'd heard the plane was the kind that used to drop spies behind enemy lines.' He paused. 'I've actually always wondered whether there was some mystery about that crash.'

'Why's that?' Wesley asked, intrigued.

'It was something I remember people saying when I was a child. There was talk of clandestine night-time missions, and some people said there'd been a cover-up because it was all hush-hush. Maybe the plane had been sabotaged, or it was carrying secret equipment. All sorts of things went on at that time, didn't they, things they still don't want people to know about. He asked me one thing I thought was unusual.'

'What was that?'

'He asked if I'd heard about a woman being aboard the plane and going missing, but I said I wasn't aware of anything like that.'

'You didn't mention your father's confession?'

Gornay looked puzzled. 'Of course not. Why would I?'

'I had to ask, that's all,' Wesley said with an apologetic smile. 'No stone unturned and all that.'

'Of course, Inspector, I understand, but as I've already said, I couldn't even be sure my father was telling the truth. And it's hardly something I'd have mentioned to a stranger.'

'Did anybody else know about his confession?'

'No. He and I were alone when he dropped his bombshell, and I mentioned it to no one.'

Wesley tried to hide his disappointment, telling himself that at least they'd solved the mystery of the child on the moor. But he suspected that Barry Brown's murder was going to prove more difficult to crack.

'Did Mr Brown ask anything else?

'He asked about families who'd lived in the village in the 1940s and I told him that was before my time. I was a child of the fifties. But I did say that Moor Barton has changed beyond recognition since that time and most of the old families are long gone. I suggested a couple of people he might try but told him not to get his hopes up.'

'Can you let me have the names you gave him?'

'I couldn't think of anyone apart from a family called Tallow; they've been here for generations. They have a smallholding just outside the village – a scruffy old place. I also suggested he try the vicar.'

Wesley checked the time. He needed to get back to Tradmouth, so that would have to be a job for another day.

Diary of Edith Tallow

Saturday 5 June 1943

There's another dance at the base tonight. While I was help-
ing with the sheep at Home Farm yesterday, Marie asked
me whether I was going, but I told her that staying away
two Saturdays in a row would make Bram suspicious. And
sometimes he scares me. Marie said she understood, but I
don't see how she can.

When I got back from the farm yesterday, Bram's mother,
Dorcas, was waiting for me. When I was little, the story of
Hansel and Gretel gave me nightmares, and the picture of
the witch I had in my head looked just like my mother-in-law.
There's one cupboard in the corner she keeps locked, and
when I asked Bram about it, he said it was her cupboard
and nobody else was allowed to look in there. Not even him.

When I walked into the kitchen, I noticed the cupboard
door was open, and I saw rows of bottles and jars lined up on
the shelves inside. I only caught a glimpse before Dorcas shut
it and dropped the key into her apron pocket, but I couldn't
help wondering what the bottles were for and why she never
let anyone else touch them. Could the rumours be true about
her poisoning people's cattle and sheep? Can she really cast

spells? Some people in the village say that bad things happen to those who cross her. They say she never sets foot in the church because she's made a pact with the Devil. I used to think that was just superstitious nonsense, but I'm beginning to think there might be some truth behind it.

She often disappears into one of the outhouses for hours on end, and Bram says that's where she makes her medicines and potions. He says she cooks up plants and other things in there, but I've never seen inside because she keeps that door locked too.

Bram says we have to plant more potatoes. Dig for victory, the government say. But the ground's muddy and my hands are red and rough. I keep thinking of that nice American I met at the dance. Hank. But like my mother used to say, I've made my bed and now I have to lie in it.

14

Gerry Heffernan had never had much to do with celebrities. His cousin had once known somebody whose dad used to hang out with one of the Beatles, but that was as far as any tentative connection went. The cocky young DC he'd spoken to from the Met – or at least Gerry had formed the impression that he was young – had promised that the notebooks found in Brown's Docklands flat would be delivered to them by courier the following morning. Gerry couldn't wait to discover the identity of the individual the DC had referred to as a national treasure, and he knew the speculation would probably keep him awake all night as he went through the possible candidates in his head.

He'd had a call from Wesley to say that he might have identified the child whose bones had been found near Moor Barton. He'd also mentioned a development in the Barry Brown case and said he'd fill Gerry in as soon as he returned to the station. The DCI was frustrated by the delay. His late wife, Kathy, used to tell him that patience was a virtue, but he'd never been able to bring himself to believe her.

In the meantime, he occupied himself by going through witness statements from the Brown murder in the hope of spotting something that had been missed. But he was interrupted by his phone ringing. He picked it up and barked his name into the mouthpiece.

'Another one? When? Where?'

When the call was ended, he dashed out into the main office and called for attention. 'The Royal Family have struck again. This time they've turned over a jeweller's in Neston. I'd better get over there.' He looked at Rachel, who was sifting through a heap of paperwork. 'Rach, are you coming?'

She stood up eagerly, keen to be out on the trail. 'Think these robberies could be linked to Barry Brown's murder, sir? That neighbour thought she saw—'

'She's on the opposite side of the village green. She could easily have made a mistake at that distance.' Gerry saw the disappointment on Rachel's face as her theory was shot down in flames. 'But we'll bear it in mind,' he added kindly. 'Right then, let's go. We've got villains to catch.'

Rachel was making the most of the opportunity to get out of the office. Paperwork had never been her strong point, a trait she shared with the DCI.

She'd already told her husband Nigel that she'd be late home, and he'd accepted the news with his usual resignation. Nigel was a busy man, with a farm to run, and they were both confident that their baby son Freddie was being well looked after by his doting grandparents. Even so, Rachel worried that one day soon he might begin to resent the long hours she worked during a major investigation. The possibility had nagged at the back of her mind since her return to work. But she couldn't imagine life without her job.

Once in the station car park, she climbed into the driving seat. The DCI never drove on dry land, reserving his navigational skills for his thirty-foot yacht the *Rosie May*, moored on the river. Wesley had once told her that he suspected that Gerry's late wife's death in a hit-and-run accident had something to do with his aversion to getting behind the wheel. But Rachel didn't mind doing the honours.

When they reached the pretty Elizabethan town of Neston, she parked on the street outside the shop, narrowly avoiding a gawping crowd of onlookers.

'What's that ambulance doing here?' Gerry asked as they approached the scene.

'Looks like someone's been hurt this time.' Rachel felt worried. So far the robbers had only threatened violence. The last thing they needed was an escalation.

The area around the shop had already been taped off and the CSIs had arrived. The shop window had been smashed, and two paramedics were wheeling a woman out of the premises. Her face was ashen and she was swathed in a blanket.

'What's happened to her?' Gerry asked one of the uniforms after showing his ID.

'Someone fired a gun and the assistant collapsed, sir. According to the paramedics, she wasn't hit. They think she's suffering from shock.'

'What can you tell us about the raid?' Rachel asked.

'Sounds the same as the others. Three clowns in royal family masks burst into the shop and threatened the staff. Helped themselves to anything they could grab, then got away in a flashy car. A passer-by took a note of the number and we ran it through the system. The vehicle was reported stolen in Morbay first thing this morning. Traffic are checking their cameras as we speak. We'll get 'em this time,' the constable said smugly, as though he was confident of succeeding where the whole of Tradmouth CID had failed.

Rachel put on a pair of overshoes and crime-scene gloves before entering the shop to have a word with any witnesses. Gerry did likewise and followed her.

Inside, the CSIs were hard at work searching for finger-prints, and when Gerry asked where they could find the owner, they were directed to a small office behind the counter. There they found a woman being comforted by a young constable. She was in her fifties, slim, with dark hair cut in a neat bob. She was dressed simply in black, as though she was attending a fashionable funeral, and there was a Parisian elegance about her that in other circumstances Rachel would have envied.

When the DCI made the introductions, the woman looked up, and it was obvious she'd been crying.

'What's your name, love?' he asked. The constable stepped back, and Gerry took a seat beside the woman while Rachel made herself comfortable on a hard dining chair opposite.

'Emma Grey,' she said with a slight quiver in her voice.

'You must have had a terrible shock,' said Rachel. 'Do you feel up to telling us about it?'

Emma nodded. 'I'd just told Penny – that's my assistant – to start locking up when we heard glass smashing. It was the front window, and someone was grabbing the rings that were on display there. I pressed the panic button, but as soon as the alarm started to sound, they burst in. Three people wearing those rubber masks – the royal family. If it hadn't been so frightening I would have laughed, because they looked rather ridiculous.'

'Did they speak?' Rachel asked.

'Once of them – the one in the King mask – said something like "Don't move", then they started smashing the glass cabinets and shoving everything into a holdall. Penny and I were terrified, but he said that if we did what we were told, nobody would get hurt.'

'But Penny did,' said the DCI, impatient to know what had gone wrong.

Emma Grey sighed. 'I always told her that if anything were to happen, nobody was to play the hero. The insurance would take care of everything and it wasn't worth risking your life.' She tore a tissue from the box on the table and wiped her eyes. 'But Penny came over all gung-ho and launched herself at the man in the King mask. Then I heard a massive explosion. It was a few seconds before I realised that the one in the Queen mask had fired a gun. When Penny collapsed, I thought she'd been shot. After they ran out, I checked her over, but I couldn't see any wounds. Then I called the police and the ambulance. How is she? Have you any news?'

'Not yet, I'm afraid,' said Rachel. 'But the officer we spoke to thought she was suffering from shock.'

Emma took a deep breath. 'That's a relief. I'd never have been able to forgive myself if ... '

'Did the robber fire the gun deliberately?'

'Everything happened so quickly. But even if it was an accident, does it make any difference? They were armed. They might have killed us.' Her voice was shaky, as though the potential gravity of the situation had suddenly hit her. 'I should have done more to protect my staff.'

'I'm sure Penny will be all right,' said Rachel, reaching out a comforting hand.

'DS Tracey's right, love,' said Gerry. 'No need to blame yourself.'

'But I do, Chief Inspector. If I'd installed better security ... But you don't expect that sort of thing in Neston. It's just not that sort of place.'

'You're right, love,' he agreed. 'It's a hippy paradise full of crystal healing shops and vegan cafés. It's hardly the mean streets, but villains are mobile nowadays, and this gang like to pick on easy targets. Low-hanging fruit, they call it, don't they?'

Rachel nodded. 'And next time someone might get killed.'

'Is there anything else you can tell us?' said Gerry. 'Anything at all?'

Emma Grey retrieved something from the pocket of her dress. 'I was going to give this to the officers outside, but they seemed so busy.' She passed him a colourful business card decorated with two masks – comedy and tragedy. Ancient symbols of the theatre. 'I found this on the floor when the robbers left. I think one of them must have dropped it.'

'Careless of them.'

He fished in his pocket for an evidence bag. He didn't find one, but Rachel had one in her handbag, and Gerry dropped the card into it.

She held the card up to examine it. 'The TR Theatre Company. They've got a website.'

'Then we'd better have a look at it,' said Gerry.

15

The TR Theatre Company's website stated that TR stood for Truly Radical and that they specialised in 'experimental, ground-breaking performances intended to rattle the establishment'. There was no information about the members of the company; only that they all came from the north-west of England.

'Which includes my own home city, Liverpool,' said Gerry as they drove back to Tradmouth. 'And the jeweller from their last job said the leader had an accent like mine.'

Rachel smirked. 'According to Inspector Peterson, he virtually accused you of being involved. Weren't you in the shop the previous week buying a bracelet or something?'

'It was a necklace for Alison. It's her birthday next week. And I promise you I haven't taken up armed robbery in my spare time.' He smiled. 'How's your little lad?'

'He's great, thanks. Spoiled by an army of doting grandparents. Nigel can't wait till he can help round the farm.'

'Thought child labour was illegal.'

Rachel laughed. 'I used to love helping with the milking and the feeding when I was little. It seems like a load of fun when you're a kid. It's only when you grow up and you need to do it day in, day out and get up at silly o'clock in the morning plus holding down your day job that the novelty wears off.'

Gerry thought he could detect a note of bitterness behind her words. 'Look, Rach, if it's getting too much for you, I can—'

'I'm fine. Coping well,' she said with determination.

Something told him that wasn't the whole truth, but he knew the time wasn't right to delve further.

As soon as they arrived at the station, they climbed the stairs to the CID office and Gerry shouted out his instructions as he walked in.

'I want to know everything there is to know about a theatre company based in the north-west. The TR Theatre Company. There's a website, but it isn't much help. A free pint for anyone who can bring me chapter and verse on them. Is Inspector Peterson back from the wilds of Dartmoor yet?'

'Not yet, sir,' DC Paul Johnson called over.

'Trish, will you go to Morbay Hospital and have a word with a woman called Penny Pleasance. She was taken there after the latest Royal Family robbery, suffering from shock. See what you can find out. You never know, she might have noticed something Ms Grey missed.'

'Will do, sir.'

The CID office descended into hushed activity. Half an hour later, Rob Carter knocked on Gerry's open door.

'Barry Brown's phone records have come through.' He passed a list to the DCI. 'We've identified most of the numbers he's contacted over the past couple of weeks, including Craig Parker and his cousin Bella Renolds. He spent a lot of time talking to George Melling, but the rest of the calls are to his sister, Lizzie, or his agent. He received a call from

Melling at eight-thirty on the night he died, which fits with what Melling told us. There are only a couple of numbers we've not been able to trace. Pay-as-you-go.'

Gerry rolled his eyes. Perhaps it had been too much to hope that the phone records would hold the answer to everything.

Before Wesley left Moor Barton, he returned to Neil's dig. Pam would never forgive him if he didn't offer Michael a lift home to save him relying on trains. He stood behind the fence for a while watching his son, pleased to see that he looked as though he was enjoying himself working next to his new friend, Harriet. He hoped the girl wouldn't get bored playing big sister to a thirteen-year-old.

Neil spotted him and waved him over. 'Wes. Want to see what we've found?'

As Wesley walked onto the site to join Neil, Michael looked up, but this time he didn't acknowledge his father. Perhaps, Wesley thought, the boy was afraid of appearing childish in front of Harriet. At his age parents could be a terrible embarrassment.

'I thought you'd be helping to lift the bones.'

'I was. But I had to come over to check on things here.' Neil lowered his voice. 'I must say I'm impressed with the soldiers. They've really taken to it.' He glanced admiringly at them. 'I could do with them on a few more digs.'

'I'm sure that could be arranged.'

He nodded towards two men who were digging in the archaeological society's trench, laughing as they worked. 'That's Ian and Lance. Aircraft enthusiasts and metal detectorists. I'm attempting to teach them the rudiments of archaeology, but I'm not getting my hopes up.'

'How's Michael doing?'

'I think he's enjoying himself. Between you and me, I think he's got a bit of a schoolboy crush on Harriet.'

Wesley laughed. 'He's growing up, Neil. How did that happen?'

'Don't ask me. Doesn't seem that long ago that he was digging in the sandpit in your garden. Let's see how the CSIs are getting on.'

Wesley didn't need asking twice. He walked beside Neil towards the sheep-shaped rock.

'I don't know whether I should be telling you this, but it looks like I've already got an ID for the body.'

'Who is it?'

'A kid called Norman – don't know the surname yet. I've just been to visit Ralph Gornay at the manor house, and he told me the boy was shot accidentally by his father, who apparently confessed to the killing on his deathbed.'

'So that explains why Gornay wasn't happy about us digging in the area. And he never thought to tell the police?'

'His father had dementia and was on strong medication when he confessed, so Ralph thought he was probably hallucinating. To his credit, now that the bones have turned up, he's been quick to come clean.' Wesley thought for a moment. 'If you ask me, he's been uneasy about the whole thing since his father made his confession, and now he's glad to have got it off his chest.'

'So maybe I've done him a favour.'

'I'll make a report as soon as I get back to the station, but the perpetrator died some years ago and Gornay's explanation about why he failed to contact the police makes sense, so there's nothing we can do. According to Gornay, the boy's family left the village after he disappeared. He thinks there might have been a brother, but he's not sure.' There was a short silence while Wesley decided how to phrase his next question. 'Have you found anything to suggest there was more to the air crash than a tragic accident?'

Neil shook his head. 'Absolutely not. But people love a good conspiracy theory, don't they.'

'That's exactly what I thought. Thanks for confirming it.'

They'd arrived at the spot where the CSIs were still working, and Wesley could see the small skeleton lying exposed. Ralph Gornay's father had laid the boy out respectfully, hands crossed across his chest. Wesley stared at the bones for a few moments, suddenly feeling sad. Norman might have been a scallywag, but he hadn't deserved his fate.

As Neil grabbed his trowel and kneeling mat, Wesley looked round. To his surprise, he could see somebody watching from some distance away, half hidden by the rock known as the Sheep: a tall, thin man wearing a bucket hat. But before he had a chance to investigate, the figure stepped back into the shadows as though he didn't want to be seen.

16

Michael had been reluctant to accept his dad's offer of a lift at first, but after weighing up the options, he'd decided it was preferable to public transport.

During the journey he hardly said a word. But Wesley hadn't expected too much gratitude from a boy who'd just embarked on his teenage years. When he'd asked him how he was getting on with the students, Harriet in particular, the answer had been a non-committal 'OK', followed by silence.

He dropped Michael off in town, and it was almost six by the time he reached the station, where the CID office was still buzzing with activity. He entered Gerry's domain and took a seat.

'Have I missed anything?'

'Not really. We're busy following up the theatre company lead. And forensics found no sign of a bullet at the jeweller's, so I'm wondering whether their gun was loaded with blanks.'

'Which suggests they're more interested in scaring people than actually inflicting injuries.'

'If that's the case, they've certainly succeeded. What about you? When you rang, you said you'd identified the killer of the child buried near Neil's dig. That was quick work.'

Wesley told Gerry everything he'd learned from Ralph Gornay.

'So the child was killed by Gornay's late father,' Gerry mused. 'Could Brown have found out about it and Gornay killed him to cover it up?'

Wesley shook his head. 'Once the bones were found, Ralph was only too eager to tell all, so I don't think that theory holds water. Besides, the killer's long dead. And it can't be connected to the plane crash Brown was investigating, because the killing happened in the late 1950s.'

'No hope of a prosecution then. Case closed. Pity. I don't like the idea of someone shooting a kid and getting away with it.'

'Ralph Gornay said his father was a bad man. But sadly, he's beyond earthly justice now.' Wesley sighed. 'Colin's promised to have a look at the child's bones, and if everything fits with Gornay's version of events, I think we'll have to put that one on the back burner. Agreed?'

'Agreed. But there's a call I'd like to make first.'

Wesley returned to his desk, where messages and paperwork had piled up in his absence and covered the surface of his desk like an unwelcome fall of snow. He punched in George Melling's number. He had a question to ask. Just to make sure.

Melling picked up right away. He sounded a little confused as he confirmed what Wesley had suspected. Never in his dealings with Barry Brown had a missing child been mentioned. Wesley called Craig Parker, who said the same.

Once he'd finished the calls, he let Gerry know. The

DCI's reaction was to shrug his large shoulders. 'Looks like we can put that one to bed once relatives have been traced. One case solved.'

It was almost eight by the time Wesley arrived home. To his disappointment, they had a visitor. Pam's mother Della had installed herself on the sofa in the living room with a bottle of wine; one of the good bottles Wesley had been keeping for him and Pam to enjoy with a nice meal one Saturday night. It was already half empty.

'Don't mind me,' she said as soon as he poked his head round the door. 'I just came to bring Pamela up to date with my publishing news. My agent's been in touch.'

'Let me guess. You've been told it's going to be a massive bestseller.'

She pursed her lips. 'There's no need for sarcasm, Wesley. She actually said that I've had an offer. It's from a very small press, but they do have a good reputation.'

'And the advance?'

'Well, er ... there isn't one. But as I said, they do have a reputation.'

'For what?'

'Now if you're going to be like that, I won't invite you to my launch.'

In his head, Wesley uttered the words 'Is that a promise?' but he stayed silent and smiled.

'I also came to see my grandchildren, but it seems they don't want to see me. Pamela said they went straight up to their rooms after they'd eaten. Is it true you've had poor Michael digging?'

'That's right. Neil's allowed him to take part in a dig up on Dartmoor. He's enjoying it.'

'Sounds like child labour to me,' she muttered. 'Is that sort of exploitation even legal these days?'

As Wesley was preparing to make his escape and rescue his congealing dinner from the microwave, Della called him back.

'I've also got some information for you. Not that I usually help the forces of oppression, but as you're my son-in-law, I thought I might do you a little favour.'

Wesley took a deep breath and turned round. He was hungry now. He just wanted to eat, go upstairs to say hello to his kids, and spend the rest of the evening quietly in front of the TV with Pam. But he curbed his impatience in the hope that once Della had said her piece, she'd decide to go home.

She took out her phone and patted the vacant place on the sofa beside her. Resigned, Wesley obeyed and sat down. She thrust her phone under his nose.

'You know these Royal Family raids. Well, a friend of mine took a video on the day of the coronation.'

'Very nice. What about it?'

'It shows a group of people in Neston with banners saying "Ban the King". And my friend said they were all wearing masks; rubber royal family masks just like those jewel raiders.'

'Do you know who these people were?'

'Not yet. But I might be able to find out,' said Della, sounding unbearably smug.

17

Wesley wasn't sure whether to take Della's statement seriously. He had a nasty suspicion that her claim regarding the identity of the so-called Royal Family was an example of her own peculiar brand of mischief. Teasing a member of the police force would appeal to her misguided sense of humour.

She'd promised to make enquiries and let him know if she discovered anything useful. Not that she was a grass, she'd added, much to Wesley's irritation. She hadn't seen the fear in the eyes of the shopkeepers. It hadn't been a game to the people who were trying to go about their daily lives and keep their businesses afloat – or to Penny Pleasance, who'd endured a trip to hospital. She was uninjured, but was by all accounts still in a state of shock.

As he walked down the hill into town the following morning, he experienced a frisson of excitement. The file from the Met was due to be delivered that day. And, according to the officer they'd spoken to, it contained interesting information.

When he arrived at work, he stood beside Gerry, listening to his morning briefing, beginning with Barry Brown's murder and concluding with the Royal Family raids.

Wesley's contribution was to go through everything he'd learned during his trip to Moor Barton the previous day, including Gornay's revelation about his father's deathbed confession. There was no evidence at this point that this was connected to Brown's murder, but it was always wise to keep an open mind. He couldn't forget the fact that someone had obviously been digging in the area around the grave, and he'd have liked to follow this up. But Gerry insisted they had more urgent leads to concentrate on. As the case of the child's bones appeared to be solved, it had been moved down their priority list, although someone had been given the job of tracing the next of kin, so far without any success.

When Wesley consulted his notes, he was reminded that Ralph Gornay had given Barry Brown the name of a local family, the Tallows. If there was a chance that Brown had contacted them, they needed to be spoken to.

'It looks as though Brown was being thorough about the research he was doing for George Melling's book,' he said.

'If he was interested in that air crash, I'm surprised he didn't talk to your mate Neil,' Gerry chipped in.

Wesley nodded. 'I was thinking about that. Perhaps he didn't know the dig was planned. Or maybe he was intending to get round to it later to see whether they'd found anything connected to this allegedly missing woman, Marie. Although I can't help thinking that Melling's father might have been mistaken and she wasn't on the plane after all. Her missions would have been shrouded in secrecy, so who can know what really happened? Have we eliminated Melling as a possible suspect?'

'His alibi checks out,' said Rachel, who was listening carefully.

'But alibis can be broken,' said the DCI with a grin. 'I want it double-checked.'

They moved on to talk about the jewellery raids, but Wesley decided not to mention that his mother-in-law had offered to provide a possible lead. Della was unreliable, and until she proved otherwise, he didn't quite trust her. But in the back of his mind, he still nursed a hope that she would come up with something useful.

It wasn't until eleven o'clock that a courier entered the building and deposited a package on the station's reception desk. It was addressed to DCI Heffernan and marked urgent.

As soon as Gerry learned of its arrival, he rubbed his hands with glee and sent Rob Carter down to fetch it. Wesley waited with Gerry in his office and watched the DCI pacing up and down like an expectant father in an old black and white film. Rob's return seemed to take an inordinately long time. When he eventually appeared in the doorway, Gerry bounded over to him as fast as his bulk would allow and snatched the package from his hands.

He cleared a place on his desk and set it down in the middle. 'You do the honours, Wes.'

Wesley hesitated for a split second before tearing at the tape. The package had been well wrapped, so frustratingly it took a while to get at the contents. But once the layers of cardboard were breached, he could see three lever-arch files inside the box. He was about to pick the topmost one out of the debris, but Gerry got to it first.

'Let the dog see the rabbit,' he said as he grabbed it and flicked through the pages, some handwritten, some printed.

Wesley picked up another file and found that it was full

of notes concerning the life and times of a well-known Premiership footballer. Brown had interviewed him extensively, making copious jottings. Wesley imagined that forming these into a coherent narrative for his 'autobiography' would take considerable skill.

'What's in yours?' he asked Gerry.

'An international cricketer. And an American film star. Big names. So what made Barry accept a job from the likes of George Melling?'

'According to Melling, he was intrigued by the case of the missing spy.'

'Do you really believe that? Melling could hardly pay him what these celebrities could.'

'He said he was spending an inheritance on his pet project. And if Brown wanted to branch out into writing about real-life mysteries, he might have thought it was a good place to start.'

'Are there any notes about the air crash in that file?'

'I haven't seen any, but I presume if he'd had any material about it, he'd have brought it here with him.'

'And whoever killed him must have taken it. But who would want to stop him investigating a wartime case like that?'

'If the missing woman was murdered, maybe the murderer's descendants might not want it to come out.'

'Anything's possible, I suppose,' said Gerry. 'But to go as far as poisoning someone to cover up a murder that happened eighty years ago ...'

'I agree. We haven't spoken to Craig Parker's cousin Bella yet. According to Craig, she's the family historian. Someone checked, and she'd definitely flown off on holiday by the time Brown was killed, so we can cross her off our suspect list. But if Brown did get round to calling on her, she might have told him something interesting. We've got her contact details and we've been trying to get in touch. No luck so far. She might be somewhere with no phone signal.'

'We need to find out who else features in these files,' said Gerry. 'We're looking for a national treasure. Would you describe a footballer as a national treasure?'

'Possibly. But only someone really famous, like David Beckham or the late Bobby Charlton. Not the one in this file, that's for sure.'

'I agree. Let's have a shufti at the last one.'

Gerry opened the third file and began to read. After a while, he gave his verdict. 'Well, there's a well-known actor. A soap star. And a tennis player. But I can't see anything they'd take exception to in here.' As he carried on flicking through the pages, he fell silent, and Wesley saw a smile spread slowly across his face.

'Well, well. Who's been a naughty boy then?' He pushed the open file towards Wesley, his finger jabbing at a name. 'Who would have thought it? Drugs and call girls.'

Wesley scanned the page. After a while, he looked up. 'Wow. Well he certainly wouldn't want this mentioned in a book.' He tapped at his phone. 'I'm looking him up online. He did mention on a talk show last year that he was writing an autobiography.'

'You mean he was getting someone else to write it for him.'

'Nothing's been published so far.'

'If there's any truth in these notes, I'm not surprised. He's always played on his squeaky-clean image and something like this would keep the tabloids happy for weeks. Harvey Pottinger, eh? My old auntie thinks the sun shines out of his backside, but if this anonymous source of Barry Brown's is to be believed, he's been attending some very dodgy parties. The notes even mention that a woman died at one of them.'

'Where did this take place?'

'Banbury, near Oxford, at the home of someone called Lenny Brice. We'd better get someone to contact the local station and ask for details of the incident. What else can you find out on that little phone of yours?'

It didn't take Wesley long to discover more details about the TV presenter and quiz show host whose face was so familiar to so many viewers.

'He lives in Oxford,' he read, 'but he loves spending time in his holiday home in rural Devon, where he is able to escape the pressures of his busy life and relax with his beloved wife of twenty years, Donna, and their dogs, Julius and Tiberius.'

'Does it say where in Devon?'

'No. Apparently he treasures his privacy, although he likes to feel he's part of the community down here and he particularly loves his local artisan bakery.'

'Wonder if that's true.'

'We need to speak to him. And find out where this second home is. If he was in Devon at the time of Brown's death ... '

'Then he shoots to the top of our suspect list.'

Wesley hesitated. 'You've read the notes in that file. Is anything Harvey Pottinger got up to actually illegal?'

'Well even if it isn't technically illegal, it's an item of dirty linen someone who makes their living by being Mr Nice Guy wouldn't want washing in public.'

A thick blue-grey cloud had suddenly descended on Dartmoor, bringing with it thunder and heavy, pelting rain. Neil ordered the trenches to be covered with tarpaulins before the diggers took shelter. They crowded into the marquee, jostling for space and trying to avoid disturbing the finds set out on trestle tables in the middle. Neil checked his phone for the weather forecast and was relieved to learn that the storm was due to ease up within the hour.

He suddenly remembered the little grave. The bones had been taken away, but the hole hadn't been filled in because the CSIs said they'd need to take further samples from the soil. He knew that if he didn't act immediately, it would fill up with water, and as it was on a slope, there was a risk the sides would collapse.

After asking Dave to keep an eye on things in the marquee, he donned the waterproof overtrousers he kept in his rucksack and zipped up his coat before dashing out to grab a spare tarpaulin from the university minibus parked on a nearby track. Struggling against the driving rain, he made his way to where the crime-scene tape was blowing to and fro in the Dartmoor wind. He wondered fleetingly when somebody would come and remove the blue and white plastic ribbons that looked so out of place in the green landscape, but he didn't have time to think about that now. The little grave needed protection.

He trudged over the now muddy ground towards the sheep-shaped boulder, head down and using the tarpaulin as a cloak to protect him from the elements. Eventually he reached the sad little grave, now filling rapidly with rainwater. As he had feared, the sides had caved in, and earth from further up the slope was tumbling into the open hole. He hauled the tarpaulin off his shoulders and tried to spread it over the top, hoping to prevent further damage. But the action only caused further disturbance, and when a whole section of earth fell away, he swore under his breath.

The rain was easing off a little, and once he'd managed to arrange the tarpaulin in place, he looked up and saw two dark figures a hundred feet or so from the rear of the marquee, out of sight of the sheltering diggers. They were sweeping the ground with metal detectors, and every so often one squatted down to dig something out of the earth.

Neil marched towards them shouting, 'What do you think you're doing?' The pair looked round guiltily, and he recognised them as Ian and Lance, the aircraft enthusiasts, who'd taken advantage of the break in the digging to do some sly investigations of their own.

'OK, keep your hair on, Dr W,' said Ian. 'We thought we'd do you a favour and see if any of the wreckage found its way over here.' He held up a small object. 'But we've only found some of these – buttons off a uniform. Could be US Army. See the eagle?' He pointed to where they'd dug in the ground. 'And there's something else in there with them.'

Neil took a deep, calming breath and bent to peer into the small hole. Sure enough, there was a pale, slender object buried a couple of feet down. He'd seen enough bones during the course of his career to recognise that this was another.

'Is it a bone?' Lance asked with relish.

'Probably an animal,' Neil replied, trying to dampen the men's excitement. 'Some farmer might have buried a sheep on the moor.'

'I've never seen a sheep wearing a US Army uniform,' Lance snorted.

Neil ignored the remark. The rain had diminished to a light drizzle, so he reckoned it would do no harm to investigate a little further. He took his trowel from his coat pocket and began to scrape away the muddy earth very carefully, expanding the hole a little and removing the soil gently from the bone, disturbing another button as he worked. There was another bone parallel to the first. A ribcage, perhaps.

But the sky was growing darker, and soon the rain began to pelt down again.

'We'll leave this for now,' Neil said firmly. 'Go and tell Dave I need a tarpaulin, will you.' He looked the men in the eye. 'And if I arrive tomorrow morning and find that someone's been digging here, I'll know who's responsible and you'll be banned from the site – and I might even have to notify the police. OK?'

'Yes, boss,' the men muttered, before hurrying off to the marquee.

Neil began to fill in the hole. Whatever it was needed to be protected. But he had an uneasy feeling that young Norman hadn't been the only one to end up buried out there on the moor in the cold earth.

Diary of Flight Officer John Carmody

Two more successful missions. At least I hope they prove successful. The young man I dropped off the night before last didn't look more than nineteen years old, and he appeared to be seeking divine protection, passing his rosary beads through his fingers as his lips moved in prayer. I reckon he'll need all the help he can get.

Last night I picked up another agent and everything went smoothly. But it was a relief to be back in the air, heading home to Devon. The man I picked up has been living with a farming family as their 'uncle' from Honfleur come to help out with the animals. He'd been there six months and managed to fool the enemy all that time, although he said there'd been some sticky moments when his forged papers were inspected. But he got away with it. I told him he was very brave, but he said he was doing what he has to do for King and country, just like the rest of us. I asked him if he was ever afraid, and he confessed that sometimes he was. He said you wouldn't be human if you weren't.

I wished him the best of luck for his future missions. It was all I could do.

18

Wesley could tell that this fresh twist in the Barry Brown case had fired up the boss's enthusiasm. Harvey Pottinger, the man who'd been voted the People's Favourite TV Personality for several consecutive years, had, if Brown's notes were to be believed, a dark side to his outwardly genial nature.

Wesley and Pam had always found the perma-tanned, self-satisfied game show host, presenter of travel programmes and numerous shallow documentaries, smug and irritating. Pam had never liked the way he patronised elderly contestants, and his sickly references to his perfect domestic life once caused her to misquote from *Hamlet*. 'The gentleman doth protest too much, methinks,' she'd uttered in disgust before changing the channel.

It was an exciting lead, but Wesley didn't want it to distract them from the more routine aspects of the investigation. He wanted to speak to the Tallows in Moor Barton to ask whether they'd received a visit from Barry Brown. In addition, he'd asked Ellie to attempt to trace any of Norman's surviving relatives. If possible, the child should be given a decent burial.

But for the moment, Gerry seemed starstruck, eager to

brush shoulders with a celebrity, even if he had to be considered a suspect. What they'd read in Brown's notes could scupper Harvey Pottinger's stellar career for good if it was made public. And people had killed for a lot less.

Rachel had taken on the task of discovering Pottinger's current whereabouts, and judging by her expression when his name was mentioned, Wesley guessed she shared his own opinion of the man. He'd always been able to rely on Rachel's judgement.

It didn't take her long to come up with an answer. 'According to his agent, Harvey Pottinger's currently at his home in Oxford. Shall I contact his local police and ask them to send someone round for a word?'

Gerry appeared at his office door, stretching like a bear emerging from hibernation. 'Hold on, Rach. Did you ask this agent of his where Pottinger was at the time of Barry Brown's murder?'

'Yes. He was here in Devon. He's got a holiday home in Millicombe, and he was there until yesterday.'

'If he was in Millicombe, it means he wasn't far from the scene of Barry Brown's murder at the relevant time, so I want to speak to him myself. I want to look him in the face so if I can tell if he's lying.'

'Did you ask Oxford police about the death of the woman at Lenny Brice's party?'

'Ellie spoke to them and they confirmed that a woman called Suzie Dix died of a drugs overdose, but there's no record of Harvey Pottinger being present.' Rachel gave Wesley a meaningful look. 'Mind you, he could have made himself scarce before the officers arrived on the scene.'

'You could be right there, Rach,' said Gerry. 'Can you tell Oxford we're on our way? It's only good manners to let them know we'll be invading their patch. Wes, we'll set off first thing tomorrow. It might mean a night away from home. Unless we can make it there and back in a day.'

Wesley hesitated. It was the school holidays, so Pam didn't have to be at work. Michael would be at Neil's dig and Amelia didn't need much entertaining these days. 'Fine. I'll let Pam know tonight.'

'She'll be glad of a bit of peace and quiet,' said Gerry.

'Unless her mother turns up to drink all our wine,' Wesley said with a grin.

When he glanced at Rachel, he saw a look of disappointment on her face, as though she wished Gerry had asked her to go with him. Wesley suspected that the DCI, being somewhat old-fashioned, had taken it for granted that she wouldn't want to be away from little Freddie for too long. He gave her an apologetic smile before telling her that they needed someone reliable to take charge in their absence and arrange for someone to visit the Tallows' premises in case Barry Brown had spoken to whoever lived there. She didn't look convinced.

Wesley's mobile phone rang and he saw Neil's name on the caller display.

'Wes. You're not going to believe this. I've just caught our two aircraft enthusiasts doing a spot of unauthorised metal detecting on the moor while everyone else was sheltering from the rain.'

Wesley could hear the disapproval in his voice. 'I'm afraid that's not a police matter, unless—'

'I'm not asking you to arrest them. I think they might have uncovered some bones. Not sure whether they're human or animal yet, but I thought I'd better let you know. It's pouring with rain here, so I've protected the spot with a tarpaulin, and I've warned our metal detectorists to keep quiet about it for now. I haven't told anyone apart from you and Dave.'

Wesley's heart sank. The last thing they needed was another body turning up.

'If the bones turn out to be human, we'll have to follow the usual procedures,' he said. He couldn't help wondering whether they belonged to George Melling's missing relative, but he told himself not to jump to conclusions just yet. It was early days.

'Of course,' Neil replied. 'I know the routine, but because of the weather, I won't be able to have a proper look till tomorrow. Like I said, I've protected the site as best I can, and whatever it is isn't going anywhere. I've got to set out for the station with Michael soon, so I'll deal with this first thing tomorrow. If the bones do turn out to be human, I'll let you know at once.'

'I'm off to Oxford tomorrow – not sure when I'll be back.' Wesley was intrigued by Neil's possible discovery, and he suddenly wished he was staying in Devon so he could find out more. But duty called.

'A jolly. Lucky you. Give my love to the Ashmolean.'

'Don't think we'll have time to browse around museums. It's strictly business.'

'I'll keep you posted then.' Neil paused. 'I could be wrong, of course. It could be a sheep.'

'Let's hope,' Wesley said with some sincerity, crossing his fingers.

Pam took the news of her husband's Oxford trip philosophically, saying she wished she could go with him because she fancied a couple of nights staying in luxury at the

Randolph. Last time they'd visited Oxford, they'd stayed in Maritia's college; basic student accommodation. Maritia had been studying medicine there, and it was where she'd met her husband, Mark, who'd been studying theology. They'd married and had a son, Dominic, who was now at school. Initially Wesley's parents had expressed surprise at both their children embarking on mixed-race marriages. But they soon accepted their children's choice of partner. They got on well with Pam and had become particularly close to Mark, who was an impossible man to dislike.

Wesley had decided not to mention Neil's call about the bones to Gerry until he knew more. It was still possible that it was a false alarm, and the last thing they needed was another distraction.

The local police in Oxford had informed Harvey Pottinger of the detectives' imminent arrival. But they hadn't said how he'd taken the news that they were travelling all the way from Devon to speak to him.

The sat nav took them straight to Pottinger's address. Summertown was one of Oxford's most prestigious districts, and his house stood on one of its most exclusive roads. It was an impressive Victorian red-brick pile, double-fronted with pristine sash windows and a front door inset with decorative stained glass that wouldn't have disgraced a modest parish church. The neat gravel drive swept round in a graceful circle to a second gate so there was no need for vehicles to back out awkwardly onto the road. The circular front lawn was lush and weed-free, and the entrance was flanked by an impressive pair of stone urns planted with a colourful display of summer flowers. Not a thing was out of place. It reminded Wesley of a film set – or a home featured in a glossy magazine.

Gerry hung back while Wesley rang the doorbell. The DCI usually left him to deal with the moneyed classes because he'd attended a public school and was well-spoken. Wesley wondered whether the boss had a chip on his shoulder about his own humble background. But as Harvey Pottinger always adopted a man-of-the-people persona, he wasn't sure Gerry's misgivings applied in this particular case. Even so, he resigned himself to doing the talking, at least initially.

As soon as the bell rang, they heard dogs barking somewhere within the house. But when the door was answered by a young woman in a tracksuit, there was no sign of the animals. She looked too young to be Pottinger's wife, and Wesley's research had told him that the couple had no children.

'Yes?' The girl tilted her head to one side, eyeing them suspiciously.

Wesley held up his ID. 'We're here to see Mr Pottinger. I believe he's expecting us.'

'Come in. Please.' Her accent was European. Polish, perhaps.

'And you are?'

'Yolanda. I am au pair.'

'Did you go to Devon with Mr and Mrs Pottinger recently?'

'Yes. I go there. It is nice.'

'It's a beautiful county,' said Wesley, smiling to put her at her ease. 'Do you often go there with the Pottingers?'

'Yes. I look after the dogs,' she said warily.

He decided to leave it there. Yolanda might turn out to be a witness, but he didn't want to interrogate her at this early stage. Instead he allowed her to lead the way into the house. He noticed Gerry looking round admiringly. The lofty hallway was decorated in the best of taste with subtle but expensive wallpaper, an elaborate Murano glass chandelier, and antique furniture polished to a soft glow. A wide, thickly carpeted staircase swept up to the first floor, and when Wesley glanced upwards, he saw a woman watching from the galleried landing. As soon as she saw him looking, she darted back as though she didn't want to be seen.

They were shown into an elegant drawing room with rich drapes at the tall sash windows, a marble fireplace, and thick rugs on the polished parquet floor. The place almost smelled of affluence and good taste. Wesley knew Pam would love it.

They recognised Harvey Pottinger at once as he rose to greet them. His expression of puzzled co-operation suggested that he was a law-abiding, decent citizen, anxious to help the police in any way he could. Wesley couldn't help remembering that according to his biography, he'd started out as an actor. He suspected it was a skill he'd never lost.

Pottinger wore red chinos and a pink polo shirt, and his immaculately cut brown hair was thick and peppered with grey at the temples; someone in the office had mentioned that the news of his hair transplant had made the tabloids. His skin had the golden glow Wesley had noticed before in very wealthy people and his lips turned slightly upwards at the corners, giving him a permanently good-natured look. But from time to time his bright blue eyes flickered warily. He wasn't as relaxed as he appeared.

'I confess I'm a little confused, gentlemen. How do you imagine I can help you?' he said before inviting them to take a seat on a soft leather sofa set at right angles to the fireplace. 'The officer who called me mentioned a murder,' he continued as he reclaimed his seat on the matching sofa opposite. 'I'm sorry to disappoint you, but I don't know anything about any murder, so I suspect you've probably had a wasted visit. Still, you're here now, so would you like tea? Coffee? I don't suppose you're allowed anything stronger when you're on duty, eh!'

'Tea for me if it's not too much trouble. Ta,' said Gerry. It was the first time he'd spoken, and Harvey treated him to one of his trademark dazzling smiles.

'Ah, you're a Liverpudlian. It's a beautiful city; the waterfront and all that stunning Georgian architecture. I went there when I was filming my last series, *Harvey's Cream of British Cities*. Did you watch it?'

'I'm afraid not,' said Wesley. Because of Pam's aversion to Pottinger's patronising interviews, it hadn't been on their viewing list.

'I watched that episode with my daughter,' said Gerry. 'We enjoyed seeing some of my old haunts.'

Wesley looked at the DCI, wondering if he was falling under Harvey Pottinger's spell.

'I'm so glad you liked it,' Pottinger said, rising from his seat and pressing a bell by the fireplace; a relic from the days when the house would have been staffed by a team of servants. Wesley found himself wondering whether the bells had never been removed, or whether Pottinger himself had had them reconnected.

Yolanda entered carrying a tray of crockery, as though she'd anticipated their requirements.

'Tea for three, Yolanda, if you'd be so kind. And some of that delicious cake you made this morning.' He looked from Gerry to Wesley. 'Yolanda's cake is very good. Your grandmother's recipe, isn't it?'

132

Yolanda nodded before hurrying from the room, leaving Harvey to set out the cups on the coffee table in front of them. When she returned with the teapot, he made a point of pouring and handing round the cups and the slices of cake, as though he wished to demonstrate that he was happy to carry out his own domestic duties. The man of the people again.

Once the refreshments had been served, and Gerry had accepted the offer of a second helping of cake, Wesley posed the question that had been on his mind since their arrival.

'Tell me, Mr Pottinger ... '

'Harvey, please. I can't stand formality.' They were treated to the sincere smile again. Wesley and Gerry had seen the same sort of smile on the faces of expert scammers and con men.

'Tell me, Harvey, where were you last Sunday evening?' Wesley kept his tone casual, as though it was a friendly enquiry.

Harvey took a sip of tea. 'Why do you want to know?'

'Are you familiar with the village of Little Rockington, near Morbay?'

Gerry took over. 'It's a pretty village. Bit of a tourist trap. Ever been there?'

'I think Donna and I visited a few years ago when we first bought the Millicombe house and were exploring the area. As you say, it's a pretty village. Very ... chocolate box. We haven't been there since, though. Once was enough, I suppose.'

'So we won't find your car number plate on any of our traffic cameras in that area?' Gerry's question was sharp. Wesley's fear that he had been taken in by Harvey's charm was quite unfounded.

'No. Of course not.'

'You're familiar with the name Barry Brown?'

There was a moment of hesitation before Pottinger answered the question. 'Yes. He's been helping me with my autobiography.'

Gerry couldn't resist reaching for a further slice of cake, so it was up to Wesley to break the news. 'Barry Brown was found dead at his rented cottage in Little Rockington on Monday.'

'That's terrible. What happened?' Pottinger's look of wide-eyed innocence would have convinced most people. But years in the police had made Wesley cynical. He watched the man's face carefully.

'He sustained a head injury, but that's not what killed him. It turned out that he'd been poisoned. And we think he knew his killer.'

'That's awful, but I'm sorry, I really can't help you. I was in Millicombe all that day. That's twenty-odd miles away.'

'Can anyone confirm that?'

'My wife. She's somewhere around if you want to ask her. And Yolanda too, I suppose.' He frowned as though he was trying to retrieve an elusive memory. 'Although actually, I think she had the evening off. I'm sure that was the night she went into Millicombe. Yes, that's right. She came roaring home on some young man's motorbike, as I remember. Thing made a terrible racket.'

'You say Barry Brown was working on your autobiography, but it appears he was pursuing a new project at the time of his death. Any reason for the change of plan?'

'That's simple. A few weeks ago, he said he wanted to put my autobiography on hold.' He hesitated. 'I don't like to speak ill of the dead, but I found him a bit ... unreliable.

He didn't always turn up on time for meetings, and I'm a busy man, as you can appreciate.'

For the first time Pottinger showed signs of irritation, there for a moment then swiftly concealed behind his usual expression of bonhomie.

'He said he'd been approached to write about an old missing persons case and did I mind shelving our book for a while. I wondered if it was something that interested him more – or paid more – than helping me tell my life story. Barry was used to working with sportsmen and women, and I got the impression he didn't have much enthusiasm or empathy for the world of TV and entertainment.' He gave a modest smile. 'Or maybe my ramblings bored him.' He shook his head as though he found this hard to believe. 'When I told my agent, she said it was probably for the best to wait until we were both ready to resume the project.'

'You said on a talk show that your autobiography would soon be out. The delay must have been embarrassing,' said Wesley.

'Not particularly.' In spite of his relaxed appearance, Pottinger was fidgeting with one of his shirt buttons.

'He didn't postpone your arrangement with him because he'd discovered something about you? Something you'd prefer the world didn't find out about?' Wesley asked the question with devastating charm, tilting his head to one side inquisitively as he awaited the answer.

'I assure you, Inspector, my life is an open book.'

As if on cue, two French bulldogs bounded in and made straight for their master, who made a great fuss of them. After a few moments, he looked up. 'Meet Tiberius and Julius. Our fur babies.'

The dogs were followed by their mistress. The first thing

Wesley noticed about Donna Pottinger was that she was tall, slim and elegant. He remembered reading somewhere that she was a former fashion model.

'Darling, these officers want to know where I was last Sunday night. We were at the Millicombe house and I was at home all evening, wasn't I?'

It was a leading question, but Wesley let that pass for the moment.

'Of course you were, darling. Yolanda went out with some boy on a motorbike and we had a cosy night in.'

'Can anyone else confirm that, love?'

Donna looked at Gerry as though he was something unpleasant she'd found stuck to the sole of her shoe. 'No. But we weren't aware that we'd need an alibi. I think you'll find that innocent people aren't.'

'Did you ever meet Barry Brown?'

'Who?'

'That man who started to help me with my autobiography several months ago. Remember?'

Donna shook her beautiful head. 'I vaguely remember someone coming round to the house, but ... I'm sorry. I can't help you.'

'He was found murdered in a cottage near Morbay,' Gerry said. 'He'd been poisoned. You might have heard about it on the news.'

'We never watch the news. And I really don't see what his death has to do with us. Come on, Julius, Tiberius. Walkies.'

The dogs snuffled after her eagerly, and Wesley was glad she'd left them alone. He needed to drop his bombshell.

'Mr Pottinger. Harvey. Do you know a man called Lenny Brice?'

Harvey's eyes widened for a split second. 'Who?' The word came out in a squeak.

Wesley repeated the name.

'I think I might have met him at a charity event. Why?'

'Officers from the Met searched Barry Brown's London flat and found some notes he'd made for your autobiography. Those notes say that an anonymous source told him that a man called Lenny Brice organised ... parties at a house near Banbury. That's not far from here, is it? Apparently you were a regular guest at these parties.'

Pottinger looked away. 'I'm afraid this anonymous source got it wrong. You've been misinformed.'

In spite of the denial, Wesley continued. 'There was an incident at one of Mr Brice's parties. A young woman died; something confirmed to one of our colleagues by Mr Brice's local police. The subsequent investigation found that drugs were involved. Were you present at that party?'

'Of course not. That's a ridiculous suggestion.'

Pottinger rose to his feet, and Wesley could tell their questioning had hit a raw nerve. 'Look, I've told you everything I know and I'm afraid I have things to do. You can find your own way out, can't you.'

His agreeable expression had vanished and they could tell he was rattled. They knew they were unlikely to get any more out of him that day, so they left the room. As they reached the front door, Yolanda appeared. She looked as though she wanted to say something, but kept glancing nervously towards the drawing room door. Wesley approached her and pushed his card into her hand.

'If you want to get in touch with us, this is the number to ring,' he said quietly. She nodded and hurried away.

As they crunched their way down the gravel drive, Gerry

broke the silence. 'Well, the mention of that party certainly shook him. If you ask me, he was there all right. And if what Brown's notes say is true, it gives that old nursery rhyme "Ride a cock horse to Banbury Cross" a whole new meaning, doesn't it.'

Wesley couldn't resist laughing at the boss's off-colour joke.

'You gave Yolanda your number. Think she knows something?'

'It wouldn't surprise me. We'll have to wait and see.'

As they reached the car, his phone began to ring. He mouthed, 'Neil,' and Gerry rolled his eyes.

A couple of minutes later, Wesley broke the news. 'Neil called me last night to say that he might have found some more bones. I decided not to mention it because he was hoping they belonged to an animal.' He hesitated. 'But he's just told me that they're human. There's another body buried on the moors.'

19

Earlier that day, Neil had made sure Ian and Lance were kept busy helping the archaeology society, then he and Dave had removed the tarpaulin they'd placed over the grave the night before. Neil could see the two aircraft enthusiasts watching as though they were yearning to be in on the excitement. But he was determined to be firm. If his suspicions proved correct, this was a job for the experts.

'That's definitely human,' Dave said as he watched Neil scraping the soil from the ribcage. 'Could there be a serial killer on the loose? The Dartmoor Strangler?'

'Let's not get ahead of ourselves. Ian and Lance found some metal buttons in the hole – thought they were US military because they had eagles on. I looked them up on the internet last night and it seems they're right.'

'Is Wesley on his way?'

'He's gone to Oxford today, so if this turns out to be what we suspect, we'll have to make do with some plod from the nearest station who'll trample over the site like a herd of elephants.'

Dave nodded and arranged his kneeling mat opposite Neil before lowering himself down. After a few minutes of careful scraping, more of the object had been revealed. And their worst fears were realised.

'It's time to notify the police and the CSIs,' Neil said, 'but let's keep this between ourselves for the time being. Agreed? I've told Ian and Lance not to mention it to anyone. I'll call Wesley; he'll want to know what's going on.'

Dave stared at the ground. 'You don't think we've come across a cemetery, do you?'

'I doubt it. But it's a perfect place to bury a body if you don't want it to be found.'

'There was some opposition to us digging around here when we had that meeting in the village hall.'

'You mean the lord of the manor?' Neil thought for a moment, considering the possibilities. 'Maybe the child's skeleton wasn't the only thing he wanted to hide. Pity Wesley's not available today,' he added, as though his friend had no right to be away when he needed him.

He resumed scraping the earth away delicately with his trowel. He was only doing what the CSIs would have to do later under his guidance, so he might as well make a start.

Rachel received a call from Wesley. He said his journey back from Oxford would take at least three hours, so could she go up to Moor Barton to find out what was going on at the dig. Neil had found some more bones during his excavation and they looked human. She heard a note of disappointment in his voice. This was a job he'd have liked to do himself.

He also asked her to make a couple of visits while she was up there, and she readily agreed. If Barry Brown had got round to contacting the people Ralph Gornay had mentioned, she might even find the elusive lead they'd been looking for, which would impress Wesley, the DCI and, most importantly, the chief super. She'd been a detective sergeant for a while now, and since returning from her maternity leave, she'd been thinking that maybe it was time she moved up to the next level. Although she knew Nigel wouldn't be altogether keen if she gave even less of her attention to Freddie and the farm.

She saw Rob Carter staring out of the office window at the busy scene outside the station. The holiday season and the sunshine had brought out strolling crowds in the Memorial Gardens, and the river teemed with boats, big and small. When she called Rob's name, he looked round guiltily.

'Fancy a trip out to Moor Barton? The DI's asked me to look in at that dig. His archaeologist friend thinks he might have found some more human remains.'

She saw Rob raise his eyebrows in surprise.

'And there are a couple of people Barry Brown might have visited up there – the vicar, and a family called Tallow. I thought we could call on them while we're in the area.'

Rob's eyes lit up at the prospect of escaping the office – and the pile of paperwork on his desk.

Rachel did the driving, as she usually did. She'd learned to drive on her parents' farm, then passed her test first time soon after her seventeenth birthday. She was used to Devon's single-track hedge-lined lanes and negotiated them at a speed that made Wesley Peterson grab the sides of his seat with terror. It wasn't long before they arrived in Moor Barton, where they parked outside the pub. From there she could see the dig in the distance. Rachel's feelings about Neil Watson were ambiguous. On one hand her instincts told her that any friend of Wesley's could be trusted. On the other, she was used to the ordered worlds of farming and the police, and there was something anarchic about Neil and his passion for digging up the past that made her slightly uncomfortable.

She decided to delay their visit to the dig and make the calls in the village first. The murderer of Barry Brown was still at large, and finding him or her needed to be their priority.

The Old Vicarage was a substantial Georgian house next to the church. The immaculate building looked as though it had undergone a recent programme of renovation, and it resembled no working vicarage that Rachel had ever come across. And indeed, the well-dressed middle-aged woman who answered the door turned out not to be the vicar – or the vicar's wife. Rather, she explained that the house had been sold by the diocese a decade ago. She'd moved there from London with her family when her husband, who'd been in finance, had taken early retirement. When Rachel asked about Barry Brown, the woman told her that a man answering his description had called the previous Saturday morning looking for the vicar, and she'd told him that the reverend now lived in a modern house a few miles away. When Rachel showed her a picture of Barry Brown, she recognised him at once.

'I told him to try a lady called Miss Gabriel in the village. Someone told me she's lived in Moor Barton all her life, and she used to run the post office.'

Rachel caught Rob's eye. Village postmistresses tended to know everything that went on. 'Can you tell me where she lives?'

'In a pink cottage opposite the Gornay Arms. You can't miss it.'

'Do you know a family called Tallow?'

'I've heard the name, but I've never met them. I think they have that run-down farmhouse on the edge of the village They keep themselves to themselves.'

'You want to try this Miss Gabriel first?' Rob asked as they walked back down the vicarage path.

'Why not? Then we'll try the Tallows,' Rachel replied. 'If Ralph Gornay told Brown about them, it's highly likely he would have paid them a visit.'

Miss Gabriel's pink cottage was easy to find, and the door was opened by an energetic lady in her seventies. She wore cord trousers and sensible shoes and her grey hair was arranged in a flyaway bun. She confirmed that she was indeed Miss Jane Gabriel, and that Barry Brown had turned up on her doorstep the previous week.

Rachel had met the likes of Miss Gabriel before – country ladies who possessed an encyclopaedic knowledge of their communities. When she asked if they could talk inside, she saw a sceptical look on Rob's face. To the young, people like Miss Gabriel were often dismissed as out of touch, but a lifetime spent in a close farming community had taught Rachel that they usually had their fingers on the pulse of life; younger people, preoccupied with their own work and lives, often lacked their well-honed powers of observation.

'So you received a visit from Barry Brown?' said Rachel after they'd been invited into a neat little front parlour.

'That's right. He was wearing a leather jacket like one of those . . . ' Miss Gabriel searched for the right word, 'motor-bike riders. And he had tattoos as well. And one earring,' She gave a little giggle. 'Like a pirate. But he was very well-spoken. He said he was a writer and that he was doing research for a book he was working on. He told me that Mrs

Blount from the vicarage had suggested he speak to me. She's a nice woman – helps out at the local playgroup and does the church flowers. Not like some blow-ins,' she added with a roll of the eyes. 'It's not the village it was years ago. It's mostly incomers now. There are some holiday homes and quite a few arty people – artists, potters and the like – who bought up cottages here when the old folk moved out or passed away. And there are some city people doing this working from home they all talk about. Things are very different from what they used to be. That's what I told the man you're asking about,' she said with a note of sadness. 'You won't find many of the old villagers here nowadays.'

'I'm sorry to tell you that Mr Brown was found murdered in Little Rockington, near Morbay, last Monday morning. We think he died sometime the night before.'

Miss Gabriel had been standing, but now she sank into the nearest chair. Rachel knelt down beside her and took her hand, turning her head to whisper to Rob, 'Go into the kitchen and make a cup of tea, will you.'

Rob hesitated for a moment, then did as she asked.

'I'm sorry if it's come as a shock,' she said gently.

Miss Gabriel straightened her back. 'Poor man. Do you know who killed him?'

'That's what we're trying to find out.'

She shook her head. 'I'm sorry, maid,' she said, using the old Devon form of address that had been so familiar to Rachel while she was growing up, 'I don't think I can tell you anything.'

'What kind of questions did he ask you?'

'He wanted to talk about the plane crash. Had I heard anything about a woman on the plane going missing? Said someone had spotted her getting on but she was never seen again afterwards. I said I'd never heard about anything like that. Then he asked me about families who lived here during the war.'

'And you were able to tell him what he wanted to know?'

'I was born here, maid. Lived here all my life, so there's not much I don't know about the old Moor Barton. I wasn't even born when that plane crashed, but things like that pass into local folklore, don't they. That poor young pilot.'

Rachel nodded, convinced she'd come to the right place.

At this point, Rob returned with the tea. He'd made a pot, and he set down the tray and poured, enquiring about everyone's sugar requirements. Rachel was impressed. For some reason she hadn't expected him to be so domesticated.

'Thank you, my lover,' Miss Gabriel said as he passed her a cup and saucer. She nursed it on her knee and carried on speaking. 'I told Mr Brown I remembered my mother talking about the crash. The pilot escaped, you know, but he was so badly injured that he died soon afterwards. He's buried in our churchyard. The village made sure he had a proper hero's funeral.'

'Did he ask you anything else?'

'Not really. No.'

'You say he was keen on finding out which families were here in the village during the war.'

'Yes, but like I said before, they're mostly incomers these days – apart from the Gornays, of course.'

'What about local farming families? We passed a farm on the way into the village – Home Farm, the sign said.' Rachel, with her farming background, tended to notice these things.

145

Miss Gabriel shook her head. 'It used to belong to the manor. The Southens were tenant farmers there for years, but they left the village a long time ago. Mr Gornay sold the house to a lawyer from Exeter and the land's rented out for grazing to a farmer from the next village.'

'Do you know if Mr Brown intended to trace the Southens?'

'He never said so. Anyway, I heard the last of them passed away some years back.'

'Any other families you can think of?'

She shook her head again. 'The old ways and the old people are gone. It's the way of the world now,' she added sadly.

'Can you remember any families who used to live here? Maybe ones we can contact?'

'There were a few, but I wouldn't know how to get in touch with them.' Miss Gabriel thought for a moment. 'I remember a very nice family called Cregan who'd lived here for generations. They had a little girl, but again, they moved away and incomers bought their house. Built a pottery studio round the back, so I've heard.'

'Mr Gornay mentioned the name Tallow,' said Rob. 'Does that ring a bell?'

'Now *they're* still here. And they would have been here during the war. They own a farm – more of a smallholding really – outside the village to the south. They've always been a strange lot. My mother never allowed me to play with the Tallow boy.' A mischievous grin spread across her face. 'There was talk in the village about them.'

Rachel knew from long experience that gossip could solve cases. 'What kind of talk?'

'Well.' Miss Gabriel looked round as though she

146

imagined someone might be listening in. 'They said the father was a nasty brute who threw his own brother out of the house and made his poor wife's life a misery. Never darkened the door of the church, they didn't. Even the vicar wouldn't venture out there in the end.'

'That bad, eh?' There was mockery in Rob's voice, and Rachel gave him an admonishing look.

'You said they still live here?' she said. 'Might Mr Brown have called on them?'

'The old man died many years ago, but last I heard, Edith, the mother, was still alive, although I haven't seen her for years. I haven't heard that she's passed away so she'll be almost a hundred now by my reckoning. The son's sometimes seen driving through the village in a battered old pickup.' Miss Gabriel sighed. 'The village grapevine isn't what it used to be. We even have to share a vicar with six other parishes. We used to have our own, and he knew everyone in Moor Barton, but he retired a long time ago. He was a lovely man,' she added wistfully.

'Is he still alive?' Rachel asked hopefully.

'I believe he passed away last year. There's a new one; a young woman,' Miss Gabriel added with a hint of disapproval.

Rachel checked the time. She should really get over to the dig. She thanked Miss Gabriel for the tea and stood up, giving Rob a nudge. It would be a nice gesture to return the cups to the kitchen. He took the hint, and five minutes later, their hostess showed them out.

'If I were you, I'd be careful if you go up to Tallow Farm.' She paused. 'It's always been known as a bad place.'

'Fancy paying the Tallows a visit?' said Rob as they walked away.

'Not really, but we should. And after that, we need to have a word with Neil.'

According to Miss Gabriel, the Tallow place was more than half a mile outside the village. Rob wanted to take the car, but Rachel preferred to walk. That way she could get a better idea of the lie of the land. And she might notice things she wouldn't see cocooned inside a vehicle. Besides, it was a glorious day with no sign of the previous day's thunder and torrential rain.

As she walked along the lane leading out of the village, she couldn't get Miss Gabriel's warning out of her mind. Eventually they reached the isolated smallholding. It was a low stone building, very old; even perhaps an ancient Devon longhouse where a family lived at one end of the building and kept their animals at the other. The paint on the window frames and front door was flaking off and the windows were opaque with grime, and Rachel wondered whether anybody still lived there. The lace curtains at the windows were discoloured with age and mildew. There was no sign of life.

'Looks like something out of a horror film,' Rob said in a low whisper, as though he feared being overheard by any resident zombies.

Rachel felt the same, although she wondered whether these feelings had been influenced by Miss Gabriel's opinion of the place. In the end, she decided to take the bold approach and banged on the front door. But the only sound they could hear was the cry of a pair of buzzards wheeling overhead and the distant bleating of sheep.

'Nobody at home,' said Rob. 'Let's get out of here.'

'We should have a look round the back,' Rachel said. There were bound to be a lot of outhouses, and as they'd come this far, she wasn't going away without checking them.

Sure enough, the back of the building sprouted various low extensions: empty, dilapidated pigsties, laundries, storerooms. She wandered from one to another, glad that Rob was with her, because the place made her uneasy. The only life she could see was a colony of spiders that had decorated everywhere with their finely spun webs.

On one outhouse door hung a rusted padlock. When Rachel pushed at the splintery wood, the lock gave way and it opened with an ominous creak. Inside, she was surprised to see what appeared to be a rudimentary laboratory draped in cobwebs and thick dust. She closed the door quickly. Nobody had been in there for years – and the sight of that strange equipment made her flesh crawl.

'There's nobody here,' said Rob.

Rachel didn't argue. The place looked semi-derelict. Perhaps, she thought, the Tallow family had deserted it long ago. Although Miss Gabriel had said that one of them had been spotted driving through the village.

She was glad to walk away, but when she reached the edge of the cobbled yard, she couldn't resist turning round. That was when she saw movement at one of the windows; a shift in the position of one of the filthy curtains, as though someone was standing behind it, watching.

She nudged Rob's arm and whispered to him. But by the time he'd turned round too, the curtain was still again.

'You must have been imagining it, Sarge. It's that sort of place. Shouldn't we be getting to that dig?'

Rachel didn't argue. She was only too glad to get out of there.

*

Wesley had told Neil he would send somebody experienced and responsible to have a look at the bones he was uncovering so he wouldn't have to keep explaining things to some callow young patrol officer. Even so, he hadn't expected Rachel Tracey to turn up. But he was relieved, because Wesley always spoke highly of her. There had been times he'd almost wondered whether there was some attraction there. But he'd soon dismissed the idea. Wesley and Pam were solid.

He was pleased to see that Rachel was wearing sensible green Wellingtons, suitable for the terrain. Unlike her companion, whose expensive trainers obliged him to pick his way gingerly over the damp ground to avoid any damage.

'What's the verdict?' she asked as she approached the large and expanding hole in the ground some distance from the main dig.

'You know we found the child's skeleton?'

'Of course. I believe you told Wesley that you've discovered something else.'

Without another word, Neil beckoned her over, and she made her way to where Dave was painstakingly scraping at the ground.

'Some idiots with metal detectors decided to try their luck away from our dig site and found some military uniform buttons. When they dug down a bit further, they came across a bone. I hoped it was an animal at first, but I came back this morning and expanded the hole further, and this is what I found.'

A ribcage, a left arm and a skull with empty eye sockets stared up at Rachel from the hole. She looked away.

'Shouldn't you have waited for the forensics people?'

'They usually rely on me and Dave to do the digging

anyway, so we thought we'd make a start. I have done this before, you know – helped the police with their enquiries,' he added with a grin.

'How long do you think it's been buried?'

'I think the buttons are from a US military uniform, and the only time I can think of when the country was swarming with American soldiers was during the Second World War.'

Rachel made the call, asking for a CSI team to be sent over to Moor Barton. 'What about your dig?' she asked Neil once she'd finished.

'I've got people from my unit helping out along with some postgrad students, so they'll manage fine without us for the moment. Wes's Michael's giving us a hand too. I must say, he's a natural. Wouldn't be surprised if he didn't follow in his dad's footsteps.'

'Joining the police?'

Neil laughed. 'No. I meant studying archaeology at uni.'

After the two officers had left, Neil and Dave continued their work, preparing the site for the CSIs' arrival. But once they'd expanded the hole a little, Neil spotted something he hadn't expected. 'Have a look at this, Dave,' he said, his trowel frozen in mid-air. 'Bloody hell, I think there are two of them.'

20

Wesley and Gerry decided that while they were in the Oxford area, they might as well visit Lenny Brice, whose name featured prominently in the notes Barry Brown had made for Harvey Pottinger's autobiography – heavily underlined and starred. They contacted the local police, who provided the address and asked if they needed any help.

'Why?' Gerry asked the officer on the other end of the line. 'Do you think we'll need it? Is this Brice character dangerous?'

After a long silence, the officer spoke again. 'Not dangerous exactly, not in a violent way, but he has some very unsavoury contacts. Let's put it this way – he provides services for the wealthy and influential. A sort of Mr Fixit.'

'Are you aware of any connection with Harvey Pottinger?'

The officer laughed. 'Harvey? Surely not.'

'So Pottinger wasn't on the guest list when that girl died of a drugs overdose last year at one of Mr Fixit's get-togethers?'

'Not that we're aware of. Look, let me call Brice. You've come a long way and I wouldn't like you to have a wasted journey.'

Gerry's answer was definite. 'Thanks for the offer, but we'd rather you didn't warn him we're on our way. We don't want to give him time to dream up any fairy tales, do we,' he added before ending the call.

'We certainly don't,' said Wesley with a knowing smile. 'The DC you spoke to sounded like a Harvey Pottinger fan.'

'There are a lot of them about. But let's keep an open mind.'

'Fine by me.'

Lenny Brice lived in an impressive house in the countryside just outside the town of Banbury. The first obstacle they faced was a sturdy pair of gates and an entry system that meant they had to announce themselves into a speaker. For a few moments Wesley wondered whether the gates would fail to open, but after a while they began to part at a stately pace. The drive was long, and when they reached the house, Wesley parked between a brand-new SUV and an equally new sports car. The house itself was angular and ultra-modern, all glass and cedar cladding, surrounded by trees and extensive gardens. It must have cost a packet, and he couldn't help wondering what Brice did for a living.

Brice opened the front door before they had a chance to press the bell. He was a small, wiry man in his forties with blonde hair that looked dyed and a tan to match Harvey Pottinger's. His arm was a gallery of tattoos and he wore chunky gold chains around his neck and an expression of wry amusement on his face.

'What can I do for you, officers? You're a bit off your patch, aren't you? All the way from Devon. Nice county. Not that I've ever been there myself. Missus prefers the Maldives.' His accent betrayed his London origins.

153

'We're investigating a murder that took place near Morbay in Devon on Sunday night,' Wesley said.

'The victim made some notes,' added Gerry. 'And you got a mention.'

'I'm a popular man. I was nowhere near Devon on Sunday night. What's this geezer's name?'

'I didn't say it was a man,' Wesley said quickly.

Brice rolled his eyes. 'Silly me. This bird then, what's her name?'

'It might be better if we discussed this inside,' Gerry said, fed up of being kept standing on the doorstep.

Wesley was half expecting Brice to refuse, but he shrugged and stood aside. They walked into a lofty atrium dominated by a huge chandelier that wouldn't have looked out of place in Versailles. The living room was equally impressive, with massive white leather sofas and a mock inglenook fireplace. Through the folding glass doors that dominated one end of the room, they could see a massive conservatory housing a swimming pool. The place reminded Wesley of a Bond villain's lair.

'I understand Harvey Pottinger has attended parties here?' he began.

'I know Harvey, yes. Great bloke. Does a lot for charity. And he might have been here when I had guests over. What's the harm in that?'

'That depends,' said Gerry. 'You have girls at these parties of yours.'

'They're not men only,' Brice said with a smirk.

'I'm talking about girls you hire. To entertain your male guests. Don't bother denying it, because it's a matter of record. When that poor girl died ... What was her name?'

154

The smirk vanished. 'Suzie. Suzie Dix. It was a terrible accident. She'd got hold of some drugs somehow and overdid it. Not that I agree with that sort of thing, but if someone sneaks the stuff in ... We were all gutted.'

'Suzie Dix was a working girl, wasn't she? That's a matter of record too. Caused a bit of a scandal at the time. Some of the great and good were caught with their trousers down. Was Harvey Pottinger here? '

When Brice shook his head, Wesley took over. 'Did a writer called Barry Brown interview you for the autobiography of Pottinger he was ghostwriting?'

'I don't know what you're talking about. Who is this Barry Brown?'

'He's the man who was murdered. And someone stole his laptop and notes. But the thing is, most of his material about Mr Pottinger had been left at his London flat. We've seen that material and it's been very helpful.' There was a hint of threat behind Wesley's last statement.

'I remember some writer did turn up a while ago, but I can't remember the name. Wanted to talk about Harvey's charity work, and I just told him how much we made at the last charity auction. Harvey was the auctioneer and he did a brilliant job. Look, that's all I know. Sorry I can't help you.' Brice folded his arms and Wesley knew they'd get nothing more out of him. 'Now, I'm a busy man.' He made a show of examining the Breitling watch on his left wrist. 'You can find your own way out.'

They had no choice but to leave, so they made for the front door. But as they were about to open it, they heard a woman's voice calling out in a whisper. Wesley turned and saw a slender woman with long blonde locks and im-maculate make-up standing at the other end of the hall, beckoning frantically. She wore a short leopard-print dress that looked eye-wateringly expensive and high heels that added several inches to her already considerable height.

Wesley and Gerry followed her into a cavernous kitchen filled with gleaming appliances that looked unused. She shut the door and looked round as though she was afraid of being overheard.

'I didn't tell the police at the time because I was scared to say anything, but it's been on my mind ever since it happened.'

'Since what happened, love?' Gerry asked.

'The girl who died, Suzie, was one of the regulars. They found her by the pool the morning after the party.'

'How do you mean, regulars?'

'Call girls. There are always a few at Lenny's parties. I just serve the canapés. Lenny likes to show me off,' she said with a hint of bitterness. 'He doesn't think I see things, but I do.'

'And you are?'

'Tiffany. Tiffany Rhodes. I'm Lenny's partner.' The way she said it told Wesley that the partnership might not last much longer.

'Tell us about these parties,' Gerry said. 'Who turns up?'

'Lenny usually invites the great and good of the area, particularly MPs and local councillors. He's a property developer and he likes to have friends in high places, if you get my meaning. He thinks his money buys my silence, and I suppose it did for a while when I was dazzled by all this.' She looked around the opulent kitchen. 'But now it's got to the stage where I'm fed up of being his eye candy. I was brought up to know right from wrong.'

'You're doing the right thing, Tiffany.' Wesley wished

156

she'd get to the point before they were discovered. 'Tell me about the night Suzie died.'

'He was ... with her. I saw them together. I don't think his name was ever given to the police. And Lenny told me to keep my mouth shut about it.'

'Who are you talking about?'

'Promise you'll keep me out of it. Lenny mustn't know I've spoken to you. Please. If he thinks—'

'He won't find out from us, love,' said Gerry. 'You were going to give us a name.'

There was a moment of hesitation before she spoke again. 'It was that man off the telly. Harvey Pottinger. Off his head on coke, he was. I heard Lenny say he had his own supply and I saw him give some to Suzie. As far as I could see, they were together most of the night. All over her, he was. He isn't the Mr Clean he likes everyone to think he is.'

'Did you ever speak to a writer called Barry Brown?' Wesley asked, suspecting they'd found Barry Brown's anonymous source.

She glanced towards the door and lowered her voice to a whisper. 'A writer called one day and I couldn't help overhearing what was being said. He was asking Lenny about Harvey Pottinger and Lenny was giving him all this crap about what a great bloke Harvey was and how he did so much for charity. He'd hung his jacket up in the hall and I ... I scribbled a note asking him to meet me in a café in Banbury. When we met, I told him what I've just told you. I asked him to keep my name out of it and he promised he would. Like I said, if Lenny knew I'd been talking to you ...'

'When was this?'

'About six weeks ago. He didn't let on to anyone that it was me who told him, did he?'

Wesley gave her a reassuring smile. 'Don't worry. He kept his promise.'

They sneaked out of the back door, careful not to be seen. Tiffany had put her safety on the line. The last thing they wanted to do was betray her.

'So Barry Brown knew all about Harvey Pottinger's double life,' Gerry said as they returned to the car.

'Pottinger has an awful lot to lose, which would give him a massive motive for silencing Brown for ever.'

'You're not wrong there, Wes.'

They found a café in Banbury, where they had a quick late lunch before setting off on the long drive home.

'I feel sorry for that Tiffany,' Gerry said once they'd finished eating. 'Don't know why she doesn't ditch Brice.'

Wesley sighed. 'Why do people stay in toxic relationships? Habit? A hope that things will change? Fear of stepping into the unknown? Or in Tiffany's case, she might be reluctant to give up the luxurious lifestyle she's become used to.'

Gerry shrugged. 'You could be right.'

'So now we know that Pottinger lied to us,' said Wesley.

'I wouldn't trust him to tell me the time even if he had an armful of watches. In my humble opinion, he's a slimy bugger.'

'But did he kill Brown to stop his secret coming out? We need to speak to him again, though maybe we should wait until we've gathered more evidence.'

'Agreed, Wes. The first thing I'll do when we get back is put a bomb up Traffic's backside. We need to know if

Pottinger's vehicle was caught on camera the night Barry Brown was murdered.'

Wesley's phone rang. It was Rachel, with news of her visit to Moor Barton and Neil's new discovery. She also mentioned her abortive visit to Tallow Farm. Before ending the call, she offered to stay at work until they got back, but Gerry was listening in and he told her to get off home, saying there was nothing she could do until the following morning and she had little Freddie to think about. She sounded reluctant to obey his instructions, but by the time they arrived back in Tradmouth, she was gone.

The early start and the lengthy drive meant that Wesley was longing to get home, put his feet up and have an early night. But the call he received as soon as he arrived back in the CID office told him his working day wasn't quite over yet.

'We've found more bones at the dig,' Neil began.

'I know. Rachel called when we were on our way back from Oxford.'

'But you don't know what turned up after she left. We thought we had one skeleton, but we found another buried in the same grave. Two articulated skeletons. A male and a female.'

Wesley's heart sank. 'I hope they're historic.'

'Items we found in the grave suggest they date to the middle of the twentieth century.'

'You say one's female?'

'That's right. Dave and I helped the CSIs lift the bones, and they've just been taken off to Colin Bowman's mortuary. The CSIs are coming back first thing tomorrow morning to re-examine the grave, and I'm going to give them a hand. Fancy coming up to help?'

159

'I'd love to, Neil but I've got my hands full at the moment.'

'Pity.' Neil sounded disappointed as he ended the call.

Wesley hesitated for a few moments, getting things straight in his mind, before walking over to Gerry's office to break the news.

'Can't you tell your mate to stop making work for us? I feel like confiscating his trowel.' Gerry blustered for a while, pacing his office, letting off steam. 'Mid-twentieth-century.' His eyes filled with hope. 'If that's true, the perpetrator's probably dead, so we'll be wasting valuable time.'

'Agreed. But we have to ask ourselves whether he's just dug up the missing woman Melling asked Brown to find.'

'But if it's her, who's the male?' Gerry sank back in his chair. 'We've got far too much work on to have people digging around in old records just in case.' He paused. 'But if you really think there's a link between Brown's murder and what he was doing in that village ... '

'He obviously went there to ask questions, but did he stumble on something that got him killed? A double murder, perhaps?'

'My money's still on Harvey Pottinger. If Brown uncovered his nasty side and refused to keep quiet either out of honesty or because of a lucrative offer from the tabloids, it would have been the end of Pottinger's sparkling career. That's the trouble with having a squeaky-clean image – if there's something mucky in your background, it's bound to float to the surface eventually.'

Wesley knew Gerry was right. But how far would Harvey Pottinger go to protect his reputation? Would he resort to murder?

The puzzle churned in his mind as he walked home. It was still light, and warm enough for him to take off his jacket as he trudged up the hilly streets. When he arrived, he heard the sound of excited barking, and Michael rushed out to greet him with Sherlock trotting beside him wagging his tail enthusiastically. Wesley bent down to pat Sherlock's head, wondering how the household had managed without a dog for so long.

'Dad, we found an instrument today. An altimeter. Harriet wondered if it had malfunctioned and that's what caused the plane to crash.'

'That's possible,' said Wesley. He knew virtually nothing about aircraft instruments, but he thought he'd better sound knowledgeable.

'I showed it to Neil and he said it seemed to be stuck but it had been buried so long that it was hard to tell. Oh, and Della's here.' These were the last words Wesley wanted to hear after a long and stressful day.

As soon as Michael had disappeared upstairs with the dog following faithfully at his heels, Wesley took a deep breath and opened the living room door. Sure enough, Della was sprawled on the sofa, shoes off and feet up, with the cat, Moriarty, curled up on her lap and a glass of wine in her hand. She looked as though she intended to stay there for the duration. Pam was nowhere to be seen.

'Where's Pam?'

'Picking Amelia up from her friend's house. If you did your job properly, your daughter would be able to walk home on her own. As it is, the streets of Tradmouth aren't safe.' She sniffed and took another sip of wine. 'She said your dinner's in the dog, by the way – or was it the microwave?'

'Thanks.' He started to make for the kitchen, but Della called him back.

'Remember I mentioned those demonstrators in royal family masks?'

Wesley remembered all right, and officers had been making enquiries that had come to nothing. He hadn't expected Della to come up with anything useful. Not only was she notoriously unreliable, but she wasn't a great fan of the police either, something he had never fully understood, because she'd never been in trouble of any kind.

'I made a copy of my friend's video. Want to see?'

Before he could answer, she thrust her phone in front of his face. Sure enough, the recording showed a group of people in royal family masks dancing around with banners. He asked Della to send it to him. It was the best lead they had, and Gerry would want to see it.

'I've got a name,' she said.

'And are you going to share this name?'

'What's in it for me?'

'The satisfaction that you've been a good citizen and helped to keep armed robbers off the streets.'

She snorted dismissively. 'The people in that video aren't armed robbers. They were just exercising their democratic right to protest.'

'In that case they have nothing to fear. We just need to find out where those masks came from. A woman ended up in hospital. You wouldn't want anyone else to get hurt, would you?'

At that moment Pam opened the door. 'Oh for heaven's sake, Mother, just tell him.'

Della, realising she was outnumbered, meekly recited a name, claiming she didn't know where the individual could be found. She said she didn't know who the others were, but she thought they were local. Wesley wasn't sure whether to believe her, but at least the one name gave him somewhere to start.

And it was a name he'd heard before.

Diary of Edith Tallow

Friday 18 June 1943

Bram's mother sleeps in the next room to ours and the walls are thin. Bram says that knowing she's there, snoring away, puts him off you know what. I suppose that gives me something to thank her for.

One of the Southens' land girls has had to go home because her mum's very ill, so today I stayed on late to help. Bram moaned a bit, but I told him it was for the war effort. He couldn't argue with that, especially when I told him we've all got to do our bit or Hitler will come marching in to take over his farm. I could tell that got him rattled, and he didn't say any more. I wonder if I can dangle that threat in front of him to get my own way. If you don't let me go to the dance with the Yanks, you're a traitor and Hitler will come and pinch everything you've got. It's a stupid thought, but it's sometimes fun to imagine silly things. Imagining what it'd be like to kiss Hank isn't silly. But it might be dangerous. Bram has a terrible temper, something I never knew before I married him. And if he ever found out . . .

Marie's egging me on. She knows how miserable I am and she says she wishes she could have stopped me marrying

Bram. But would I have listened? I didn't know what he was like back then and I'd never met his mother. He kept that side of his life well hidden until it was too late.

Marie says she's going to see someone on Monday but it's top secret. She says it's because she speaks French, but that's all she can say. There's another dance tomorrow night and she says I should tell Bram I'm going to Exeter to stay at my sister's again. She says I could say my sister's not well and she needs me to help out. She'll write a letter I can show him. She knows Bram's never met my sister and doesn't know her writing, so she's sure we can get away with it.

The idea of it makes me excited, and I feel as though I'm going off on some secret mission of my own. I really want to see Hank again and I'm willing to throw caution to the wind. How did I ever get into such a scrape?

21

Della didn't stay late. Wesley made sure of that by offering to walk her home, and fortunately she took the hint. Her flat was in the centre of Tradmouth, so it meant another trudge up and down the hill. He tried to convince himself the exercise would keep him fit.

As they walked, he attempted to wheedle more information out of her. Where did the protesters live? What did they do for a living? Della said that as far as she knew, they lived in squats or caravans near Neston and they regarded protesting as their vocation so they had no time for conventional jobs. But that was only hearsay. She didn't know anything for definite.

That night Wesley lay awake wondering whether the Jay Tallow named by Della could be related to the Tallows who owned a smallholding in Moor Barton. When Rachel and Rob had called at the Tallow property, they'd found nobody at home. Perhaps Jay lived there and he'd been out protesting somewhere. But finding out would have to wait until the following day.

As soon as he arrived at work the next morning, he hurried into Gerry's office to show him the video and tell him about the new lead.

'My mother-in-law might have come up with something useful for once.'

'Wonders will never cease. What exactly did she say?'

'She says there were a few people in royal family masks protesting against the monarchy during the coronation celebrations in Neston. From the sound of it they were the usual ragbag of people who protest about anything as a matter of principle.'

'Could they have branched out from protesting to armed robbery?'

'She didn't think so.'

'Did she give you any names?'

'Just one. Jay Tallow.'

Gerry raised his eyebrows. 'Tallow. That name's familiar.'

'Rach went to the Tallow place in Moor Barton yesterday because the name came up in connection with the Brown case. There was nobody at home and she said the place looked semi-derelict. Apparently the family have always been reclusive. Jay Tallow might not be related to the Moor Barton Tallows, but it's worth checking out.'

'Too right, Wes. If this Jay character's a professional protester, he might have come to the attention of uniform at some point, so let's track him down and speak to him.' Gerry looked pleased with himself. 'With any luck we'll have both our cases wrapped up by the end of the day and we'll all be able to go home and put our feet up.'

'Hopefully.' They both knew this was a fantasy, but it was a nice thought.

The DCI checked the time. 'Colin left a message to say he's going to have a look at these new skeletons of Neil's this morning.'

'I'd like to hear his verdict.' Wesley suddenly felt curious about the mysterious appearance of two bodies buried on the moor. Three if you counted young Norman, although they already knew his tragic story.

'He's examining the child's bones as well, just in case something doesn't tally with Ralph Gornay's version,' Gerry said as though he had read Wesley's mind. 'Maybe you should get over there. Until we know for sure that these new bones are historic, we'd better assume the worst. Colin said ten o'clock.'

'What about you?' It wasn't like Gerry to pass up the offer of Colin's biscuit selection.

'The chief super wants to see me. She wants to know what progress we're making on the Brown murder – and an update on the jewellery raids. At least I've now got something new to report on that one.'

'Rather you than me,' Wesley said, giving Gerry a sympathetic look.

As soon as he returned to the main office, he asked Ellie to check whether Jay Tallow had a police record. He also asked whether she could trace a family called Cregan who used to live in Moor Barton – if Miss Gabriel had mentioned them to Barry Brown, it was possibly he might have tracked them down. He believed in being thorough. Every avenue had to be explored.

As he sat down, his phone began to ring. It wasn't a number he recognised and he answered cautiously. The woman on the other end of the line sounded nervous. 'Is that Inspector Peterson?' she said, so quietly that Wesley had to press the phone to his ear.

'Speaking.'

'This is Yolanda. We met yesterday in Oxford. I work for Harvey Pottinger.'

'What can I do for you, Yolanda?' he said as he retraced his steps to Gerry's office. He closed the door behind him, made a show of pointing at the phone to get the DCI's attention and mouthed, 'Yolanda,' before switching on the speaker. 'Can you speak up a bit, please?'

'I do not want them to hear me. I hear what he tell you yesterday, but he lie. He went out on Sunday night. I hear his car start and I look out of window. I see him drive away. He tell you he stay at home, but is not true.'

Wesley looked at Gerry, who was now listening intently.

'Are you sure this was on Sunday? It wasn't another night?'

'No. It was Sunday.'

'Mr Pottinger said you were out on Sunday night, with a boy on a motorbike?'

'That was Saturday. We go to bar in Millicombe. You ask my boyfriend. Harvey tell you wrong. I was at the house on Sunday.'

She went on to recite the boyfriend's number. It would be checked out by one of the team, but Wesley was inclined to believe her. As far as he could see, she had no reason to lie.

'Is there anything else you'd like to tell us?' he asked gently.

He heard a female voice in the background. Then barking. Julius and Tiberius. 'I must go,' Yolanda said in a frantic whisper, and ended the call. She'd sounded frightened.

'What did you make of that?'

Gerry took a deep breath. 'Let's bring Pottinger in for questioning.'

*

169

Wesley called Oxford, and the officer he spoke to promised to send someone over to Harvey Pottinger's home. But he knew it might be some time before they could speak to their suspect again. He also knew that patience didn't come naturally to Gerry. However, on this occasion he had no choice. The DCI managed to postpone his meeting with the chief super, saying something urgent had come up. The truth was that he'd decided to accept Colin's invitation to attend the post-mortem on the Dartmoor bones. He admitted to Wesley that he needed the distraction.

Their progress to the mortuary was slowed by the crowds of tourists strolling along the embankment next to the river, enjoying ice creams and the view over to Queenswear on the opposite bank, with its terraces of colourful houses perched on the hillside. The yachts were out in force, making the most of the fine weather, and crowded tourist boats plied to and fro, their amplified commentary clearly audible from dry land. Wesley knew that Gerry found the tourist season irritating, but he didn't mind seeing the port come to life in the summer months.

When they arrived at the mortuary, Colin greeted them with the news that Margaret, Neil's tame bone specialist from the university, had agreed to assist him. Wesley, who usually viewed post-mortems with trepidation, found that he was quite looking forward to this one. There'd be no blood and guts this time, just dry bones.

Colin and Margaret dealt with Norman first. They found shotgun damage to the face, and Colin pointed out that numerous lead pellets had been found in the soil with the body. Their findings tallied precisely with everything Ralph Gornay's father had told him on his deathbed.

They then turned their attention to the two mystery

170

skeletons. Samples were taken and teeth extracted for DNA and other tests. Margaret was hoping to discover through isotope analysis where the pair were brought up, which might aid their identification.

'What killed them?' Wesley asked.

She turned round. 'Come and have a look.'

This was Wesley's first opportunity to get a close look at the skeletons, and as Margaret stood aside, he saw that the cause of death was obvious, at least for the male.

'He was shot in the shoulder then in the head,' said Colin. 'No sign of the bullets. Must have gone clean through, so I can't specify the weapon. But I can tell you for certain that it wasn't a shotgun like that poor child over there. Probably a revolver or possibly a rifle.'

'What about the woman?' Gerry asked, coming closer to get a better look at the remains. The rotted scraps of material clinging to the bones suggested that both individuals had been buried fully clothed.

'She was shot too, probably from further away, and the damage to her spine suggests that she was shot in the back. Again, no bullet was found in the grave, so it probably went straight through her body.'

'How long had they been there?' There was a note of anxiety in Gerry's question.

'Quite a few items were found in the grave, and Neil's taken them away to be cleaned up and, hopefully, dated,' said Margaret. 'He found fly buttons on the man's pelvis, which indicates that his trousers didn't have a zip. And there were uniform buttons in the grave, probably US military.'

'So the man might have been an American soldier?' Wesley asked.

'That's very possible. Unless someone got hold of a uniform jacket sometime after the war and wore it as a fashion statement.' She smiled. 'I like to consider all possibilities. As for the woman, Neil said he found the remnants of a metal zip. They had those on dresses in the 1940s, I believe. And the remains of a leather shoe.' She paused. 'You've no idea who they might be?'

'It was said that the pilot who crashed in 1943 might have had a female passenger, but no body was found in the wreckage.'

'You think it could be her?'

'It's a possibility we have to consider. If it is her, her name's Marie Leon. But why she would be buried with an American soldier, I've no idea.'

As expected, Colin invited them all back to his office for tea and biscuits. 'Any progress on the Barry Brown murder?' he asked once they were settled.

'We're still working on it,' said Gerry quickly.

'Not a nice death, cyanide,' said Colin. 'Convulsions, gasping for breath, headache, dizziness. It prevents the red blood cells absorbing oxygen.'

'Poor man,' said Margaret.

Gerry put his cup down. 'We'd better be going, Wes. Things to do. People to arrest.'

Wesley followed him out. 'Something wrong, Gerry?'

'I don't like to be reminded of my failures, that's all.' It wasn't like Gerry to sound so despondent.

'We haven't failed yet. We've got that lead on Harvey Pottinger, don't forget.'

'That's what worries me, Wes. Pottinger's bound to have an army of expensive lawyers who'll help him wriggle out of it and make us look bad.'

Wesley considered it his duty to inject a note of optimism. 'According to Yolanda, he lied about where he was on the night of Barry Brown's murder – and that gives us an advantage, don't you think?'

Gerry didn't reply.

22

When they returned to the station, Gerry found a message waiting on his desk. The local officers who'd called at Harvey Pottinger's Oxford home reported that he'd left that morning to film an episode of a new travel series. His wife claimed he'd gone up to the north-east to film an episode about Alnwick. She said she wasn't sure when he'd be back, but the officers thought her vagueness might have been deliberate.

Wesley suspected their instincts were right and Donna Pottinger had been lying to protect her husband. Gerry wondered whether their visit the previous day had shaken him and now he was doing his best to avoid them.

'But he can't keep it up for ever,' said Wesley with a confidence he didn't really feel. 'I'll ask someone to get on to his agent and production company. See if they can tell us when he's due back. Surely sooner or later he'll realise it's better to come here of his own accord; at least that way he can be discreet, rather than having patrol cars crunching across his gravel drive with sirens blazing to drag him in for questioning. That wouldn't look good in the tabloids, would it.'

Before Gerry could reply, Ellie knocked on his open

office door. 'Sir. I can't find any trace of a family called Cregan in the area with links to Moor Barton.'

'OK. Any good news?' asked Wesley.

'Yes, sir. As a matter of fact, there is. I've been looking up Jay Tallow's police record like you asked.'

Gerry glanced up. 'Come in, love. What have you found out?'

Ellie stepped across the threshold. 'He's got form for breach of the peace. Seems like he's a professional protester who doesn't really care what he's protesting about as long as it's against the establishment. He was arrested after that animal rights protest at the chicken farm. Criminal damage.'

'Anything else?' Wesley sensed that she had more to say.

'He did twelve months for burgling second homes in the Millicombe area. Claimed it was a political protest.'

'Was any video footage taken of that coronation protest?'

Ellie shook her head. 'No, but I had a word with my brother, who was in Neston at the time. He works in a pub there and it was open all day. He went out during his break and got a good look at the protesters. He said there were about five of them, chanting "Not my King"; said they looked pretty pathetic because everyone else was having a good time. He confirmed they were all wearing royal family masks. The rubber kind the robbers wore.'

Gerry gave the young DC a wide smile, showing the gap between his front teeth he'd always claimed was a sign of luck. 'Good work, Ellie. Do we know where we can find Jay Tallow?'

She gave him a nervous grin. 'Apparently he lives in a yurt in Tradington.'

'A yurt?'

'So I'm told.'

'Well let's go and rattle his cage. Or should that be shake his yurt?'

Ellie laughed dutifully before returning to her desk.

'What do you think, Wes? Should we go over to Tradington?'

The phone on Gerry's desk began to ring. From the look on his face, Wesley guessed the call was unwelcome. He heard him say, 'Sorry, ma'am, something important's just come up and I've got to go out again. Can it wait?'

When he ended the call, he looked at Wesley and winked. 'Auntie Noreen wants to discuss the budget for the investigation.' His use of the cosy nickname made the chief super seem less formidable, but it was one they only used between themselves. 'I really shouldn't keep putting it off.' He thought for a moment. 'On the other hand, this is a murder investigation.' He raised his hand. 'And in case you're tempted to point out we could easily give the job to a couple of DCs, let me remind you that the name Tallow has already cropped up in the Barry Brown investigation.'

'That's exactly what I was thinking,' said Wesley, amused. 'If we can connect Tallow to the robberies *and* the murder, we'll be killing two birds with one stone, in which case it's a sensible use of resources, don't you agree?'

Gerry stood up. 'It's another lovely day. Let's get some fresh air.'

Before they could escape the office, Gerry received another call, on his mobile this time. When he answered, his expression softened, and Wesley guessed it was Alison on the other end of the line.

'Hello, love. Everything OK?'

Wesley watched as the DCI returned to his desk and

picked up a pen. 'Can you say that again?' he said before scribbling something on a sheet of paper in front of him. 'Thanks, love, that might be really useful. Not sure what time I'll be back. We'll pick up some fish and chips tonight, eh?'

He killed the call and turned to Wesley. 'Alison's spoken to someone she knows up in Liverpool about the TR Theatre Company. She says they're very political and they've got a reputation for carrying out crazy stunts. She also heard that they were thinking about doing a tour of the south-west.'

'Would a theatre group go in for armed robbery?'

'Stranger things have happened, Wes. You mark my words.'

The yurt was easy to find. It was at the centre of a small enclave of scruffy caravans near Tradington Hall Arts Centre, and it sat in the shadow of a repurposed double decker bus. Pam had attended a literature festival once where a similar yurt had been used as a green room for the authors to relax in before their event. But the walls on Jay Tallow's yurt were mildewed and frayed in places, so Wesley guessed he'd acquired it cheaply somehow. Although he wasn't quite sure how someone went about buying a second-hand yurt.

There was no sign of life, but this didn't put Gerry off. He marched over to the yurt, then hesitated. 'Do I knock or what?' he whispered to Wesley, who was standing behind him.

'I'd shout if I were you.'

Gerry did just that, and Wesley heard something stirring inside the yurt. 'I think he's at home,' he whispered.

'Who is it?' a voice called out.

'Is that Jay?' said Gerry. 'Can I have a word?' He left it at that, hoping curiosity would make Tallow show himself.

They waited a while, and eventually the flap of the yurt twitched open and they found themselves face to face with a thin, freckled man with a shaved head, heavily tattooed arms and small bright blue eyes. He wore jeans that looked as though they were ripped by wear rather than design, and a grubby T-shirt. As soon as he saw Wesley and Gerry standing there, holding out their ID, he retreated back into the tent, letting the flap fall.

'We only want a word,' Wesley said reasonably. 'We'd like to ask a few questions about your family. Nothing to worry about.'

The flap opened again and Tallow stuck his head out. 'What about them?'

'We just wanted to know whether you're related to a family called Tallow who have a smallholding up on Dartmoor – place called Moor Barton.'

Tallow looked unsure of himself. 'I don't usually talk to the pigs.'

Wesley gave him an unthreatening smile. He had a plan. Start with the easy stuff, then move on to the masks when his guard was down.

'Like I said, I only want to ask about your family, that's all.'

'My mum and dad are in Spain. There's only me and my nan now.'

'No cousins? Uncles? Aunts?'

'I think there are some up on Dartmoor – she mentioned a place called Moor Barton. I never met them, but my nan told my mum they were bad news. Devils, she called them.'

Wesley glanced at Gerry and saw him raise his eyebrows in surprise.

'How are you related to these devils?' Gerry asked.

'One of them was my great-grandad's brother, but they never spoke as far as I know.'

'Why was that?'

'I think something happened.'

'Any idea what?'

'Don't know, but it must have been something bad.'

'Have you ever spoken to a man called Barry Brown? He might have been asking about your family too.'

Jay shook his head, and one look at his face told Wesley he was telling the truth.

'Well, thanks for your time. We'll be off now.'

Gerry looked as though he wanted to interrogate the man further, but Wesley gave him a slight shake of the head and a look that said, 'Leave it for now.'

Tallow emerged from the tent stretching and scratching his bald head. Wesley noticed that he was painfully thin.

Gerry began to walk off and Wesley moved to follow. But then he came to a sudden halt and retraced his steps. Gerry did likewise.

'Just one more thing before we leave you in peace,' Wesley said, looking Tallow in the eye. 'You were seen protesting about the coronation. Have you still got those masks you were wearing?'

'No. We didn't need them no more, so we gave them away.'

'Who to?'

'Dunno. Someone. Look, why don't you bugger off. If anyone saw me talking to a couple of pigs—'

'It wouldn't do your reputation any good,' said Wesley. 'We understand.'

'I thought we were going to ask him about the jewel robberies,' said Gerry as they returned to the car.

'If we had, he would have clammed up right away and claimed police harassment. I think we're better off using the softly-softly approach.'

'You could be right, Wes.'

Wesley was about to start the engine when Gerry put his hand out to stop him. A battered Transit van had just driven up, and they saw Jay Tallow climb into the passenger seat.

'Give it a minute, Wes.' They waited until the van had driven off. 'Do you need a warrant to break into a yurt?'

Wesley considered the question. 'Technically we probably do. But on the other hand, it's not locked, is it. And this is a murder inquiry. I don't suppose a quick look will do any harm.'

They exchanged a conspiratorial grin and left the car, checking that there was nobody about.

The interior of the yurt smelled rank. Sweat, dirty clothes and something else Wesley couldn't quite put his finger on. Gerry held his nose. 'He's not going to win a good housekeeping award, is he?'

'Not even a good yurt-keeping one.'

In spite of the sunlight outside, the inside of the yurt was dark, and Wesley turned on his phone torch. As he flashed the light around, the beam rested on a filthy, rumpled sleeping bag, but there was no sign of anything resembling a mask. Maybe Tallow had been telling the truth. Or maybe the masks were kept elsewhere.

'Let's get someone over here to make a proper search. And they can have a look at his mates' accommodation while they're at it,' said Gerry. He sounded disappointed.

*

When Ellie and Rob arrived to make the search, they found nothing apart from a small quantity of cannabis. No firearms, no stolen jewellery. But they did find something of interest – a couple of business cards tucked beneath a sleeping bag in the old bus. The TR Theatre Company. Just like the one the robbers had dropped during their last raid.

23

Bringing Jay Tallow in for questioning was easier said than done. When officers attempted to track him down, it was as though he'd vanished off the face of the earth. Wesley concluded that his comrades had told him about the police search and this had scared him off. Even so, they'd discovered nothing incriminating apart from the business card. Nothing of value was found among the group's meagre possessions. But if they'd been responsible for the robberies, the stolen goods might have been kept elsewhere.

Officers spoke to the residents of the caravans and the ancient bus, and at first their enquiries were met with a wall of silence. However, once the raids were mentioned, one of the bus's occupants, a girl with blue hair and harem pants, became quite talkative and insisted that they had nothing to do with her or her friends. They'd protested, as was their democratic right. They'd made a nuisance of themselves to the hated establishment, but they'd never robbed any jewellers.

When asked about the masks, she'd backed up Jay Tallow's story. They'd given them to someone who'd come down from up north. Possibly Liverpool. When asked who the police should talk to if they wanted to find out more, she refused to say. She wasn't a grass.

On Gerry's instructions, the officers also asked about the TR Theatre Company. Did anyone know anything about them? The question was again met with silence. But Gerry took the news cheerfully and reminded Wesley about Alison's friend who'd said they intended to tour the south-west. Theatre companies didn't tend to operate in secret. What would be the point? Sooner or later they were bound to seek an audience somewhere.

'We'll just have to wait until Tallow turns up,' he said with a sigh when they returned to the station.

'We've got patrols out looking for him.' Wesley hesitated. 'What do you think he meant when he said the Tallows up in Moor Barton were devils?'

Gerry shrugged. 'Rach said the smallholding looked unoccupied, so maybe the devilish Tallows are long gone.'

'One of them was seen driving through the village.'

'Someone could have got that wrong. We might be chasing shadows.'

'I disagree, Gerry. I think it's worth following up. If Brown did visit the Tallows and now they're lying low . . . '

At that moment Wesley felt overwhelmed. They had so many potential lines of enquiry, and he feared they might all lead to dead ends.

'I still think Harvey Pottinger's our best bet,' said Gerry. 'He's the one with the most to lose. He lied to us and now he's gone AWOL. This trip to the north-east is suspiciously convenient.'

Wesley found it hard to disagree. But he couldn't forget that Barry Brown had gone to Moor Barton to pursue the mystery surrounding the air crash, although nobody they'd spoken to there seemed to know anything about the missing wartime spy, Marie Leon, who may have just turned up, shot in the back and buried on the moor next to a US soldier. On the other hand, the female skeleton might turn out to be quite unconnected to the Barry Brown case.

He wondered whether Harvey Pottinger had links to Moor Barton. The team hadn't come up with any connection so far, but it was something he wanted to find out.

His phone rang and he heard a woman's voice on the other end of the line, well-spoken and authoritative, as though she was used to dealing with awkward customers.

'Is that Inspector Peterson? This is Melanie Hardcastle, Barry Brown's literary agent. I've already spoken to one of your people and they asked me to contact you if anything occurred to me regarding Barry's work.' There was a short silence, as though she was gathering some paperwork together. 'I've just had a clear-out of my spam folder and I found an email from Barry. I've no idea how it got in there, but it happens occasionally. Very annoying.'

'Yes, it is. What does this email say?'

'He said he was in Devon researching that missing spy case he'd told me about; there's always a ready market for that sort of thing. It sounds as though he'd found some promising leads.'

Wesley had been hoping Ms Hardcastle would have something new for them, and he experienced a deep feeling of disappointment. 'We already know about that. In fact we've spoken to Mr Melling, the man who commissioned him to research the case.'

He was about to thank her and end the call politely when she spoke again. 'The email goes on to say that while he was in Devon he came across another story with fantastic potential and he asked whether I thought anyone would be interested.'

'Did he give you any details?'

'I'll forward the email to you. That would be easiest.'

Five minutes later, Wesley was reading the email Barry Brown had sent to his agent. It read as though it had been composed hastily, and the contents somehow brought the author to life. He could almost sense the excitement behind the words. He called Gerry over to his desk and gave him a brief explanation before standing to one side to give the DCI a good view of the computer screen.

Hi Melanie,

I'm here in sunny Devon researching that case we discussed. That man who contacted you, George Melling, is a bit of an oddball and he's obsessed with finding out what happened to his father's cousin. From what I've found out so far, there's definitely a mystery there and a new angle on the case will make a decent book. What do you think of the idea of including some other possible wartime mysteries? A section about each, possibly? It's been a breath of fresh air to get away from celebrities for a while. As I've told you before, I think true crime will turn out to be my real passion – although of course I'll return to the autobiographies in due course because they keep the proverbial wolf from the door.

While I've been here speaking to people connected with the spy case, something totally unexpected cropped up; something that might have even greater potential for a thrilling read. What would you say to a dramatic tale of riches to rags? Thought that would whet your appetite! I won't say too much yet because I've got to do some further digging, but I think I might be on to something really interesting – and potentially very big. If my suspicions prove to be correct, I think I might have stumbled on a story with tremendous promise. Can you think of anyone who might be interested in the project?

By the way, if Harvey Pottinger gets in touch with you about his autobiography, can you use delaying tactics? As you know, I've told him I want to put off signing the contract. I've spoken to someone who wishes to remain anonymous, and if what they told me is true, Pottinger has a very a dark side to his nature and I'm reluctant to embark on a book filled with lies. If what I've been told comes out into the open, this time next year Pottinger will be hiding from the tabloids instead of swanning round patronising the proles. I know you'll tell me to think of the money and not to let scruples come into it, but I'm really not comfortable about committing myself, and if he can find another author to take on the project, good luck to him. Maybe I'm biased, but I can't stand hypocrites, as you know.

Anyway, for the moment I've got Mr Melling's mystery as well as this juicy new project to work on. I'll give you more details about that in due course, but I've a feeling I might have uncovered something pretty exciting.

I'll be in touch soon.

Cheers,

Barry

Gerry didn't speak for a while. He was taking it all in.

'It's dated a couple of days before he died,' he said eventually. 'We know he went to see Ralph Gornay around that time. And he'd been asking questions in the village. Do you think those two skeletons Neil discovered could have anything to do with Brown's murder? Has he found any records that might throw light on the matter?'

'Tell you what, Gerry, I'll ask him. Maybe he can see whether Annabel's able to gain access to any records from the time.'

'If it's connected with the SOE, wouldn't it have been top secret?'

'Yes, but if anyone can find out, Annabel can.'

'Did I hear rumours that she and Neil are engaged?'

Wesley laughed. 'That's the theory. But there's been no mention of any wedding.'

Gerry scanned the office. 'We'd better get a move on then. We need to know what Barry Brown found in Moor Barton that made him so excited. What could he have meant by "riches to rags"? We know he saw Gornay, Miss Gabriel and the lady from the vicarage, but did he talk to anyone else while he was there? And what did he find out that distracted him from the 1943 case?'

'If we knew that we might make some progress.'

'Has anything new come in on the robberies? My gut tells me there's some link with the coronation protesters, but I can't see that lot in Tradington wielding firearms, can you?'

'Not really. They say they gave those masks away to some people from up north, but they were very vague about the recipients of their generosity. Probably deliberately so.'

Gerry's phone rang, and when he'd finished the call, Wesley saw a look of smug triumph on his face. 'That was Traffic. A car registered to Harvey Pottinger was caught on camera driving towards Morbay on Sunday evening. Yolanda was right. He lied to us about not going out.'

Gerry went into his office to make a few more calls.

When he emerged, he looked as though he'd just won the lottery. 'I've spoken to Pottinger's local nick. He's arrived back in Oxford after his trip to Alnwick and is planning to come down to his Millicombe house first thing tomorrow. We'll pick him up as soon as he arrives and bring him in to be interviewed under caution. Then hopefully we might get somewhere at last.'

In spite of the unexpected discovery of the bones, Neil was pleased with the way the dig was progressing. The ex-soldiers in particular seemed to be getting a lot out of the experience, and he saw their faces come alive with genuine interest. One of them, a wiry man called Owen who'd been wounded in Afghanistan and had been suffering from post-traumatic stress disorder ever since, had even been carrying out extra research in his spare time. Neil told him to go for it. Anything he could find out might prove very useful.

Fortunately the rain had held off since the dramatic thunderstorm, so maybe now they'd be able to concentrate on what they were there for: excavating what was left of the wartime Lysander. But as soon as he'd adjusted his kneeling pad, ready to get down to some serious trowelling, he received a call from Margaret, the bone specialist. She had intriguing news.

'Neil, I've done isotope tests on those bodies you found. Want to know the results?'

'Don't keep me in suspense. What have you found out?'

'The male grew up in the States – the New England area.'

'Well we did find those US Army uniform buttons in the grave. What about the woman?'

'She's equally interesting. According to the tests, she was brought up in Brittany.'

'France?'

'That's where Brittany was last time I looked. He was American and she was French – or at least grew up there. I'll leave you to it.'

She rang off, leaving Neil to puzzle out the implications of what he'd just heard. How did an American man and a French woman come to be buried on the moor, many miles from home?

It was a mystery he wanted to solve. If he had the time.

24

Wesley received a call from Neil to say that Margaret had given him some surprising news. Tests confirmed that the male skeleton was indeed American, as they'd suspected. They'd also shown that the female had been brought up in France. Brittany to be exact. This new development was the best evidence they had so far that the woman on the moor was Marie Leon. But whether this had anything to do with Brown's murder, he couldn't be sure.

Harvey Pottinger wouldn't arrive at the station to be interviewed until the following day, and he watched a frustrated Gerry pacing to and fro, leaving his lair every now and then to see whether anything new had come to the team's attention. Like Wesley, he'd studied the image sent over by Traffic of Pottinger's brand-new Porsche SUV driving towards Morbay, the registration number clear as day on the computer screen. He'd been on the right road for Barry Brown's rented cottage in Little Rockington at approximately the time they estimated the victim must have died. Which meant Harvey Pottinger had told them a blatant lie.

According to Lenny Brice's partner, Tiffany, this wasn't the only thing he'd lied about. He'd been at the party at Brice's house, an enthusiastic recipient of the man's dubious hospitality on the night of Suzie Dix's death. Wesley was all for telling the Oxford police right away, but Gerry reckoned a few more days' delay would do no harm. He wanted to get their investigation in first before they informed Oxford that Pottinger might be involved in some very unsavoury activities. It was with some relish that the DCI announced that the smarmy celebrity's name was about to be dragged through the tabloids whether he liked it or not.

The following morning, after making sure Harvey Pottinger was back at his Millicombe holiday home, Gerry sent a patrol car over there to pick the man up. Chauffeur service, he quipped.

'I'm still waiting for Merseyside to get back to me with more info about this TR Theatre Company,' he said while they waited for their suspect to arrive.

'Strange that they're so elusive,' said Wesley. 'Surely what any theatre group wants is maximum publicity to sell tickets for performances, but this lot seem to have disappeared off the radar – apart from those business cards we found at the jeweller's in Neston and in Jay Tallow's yurt.'

'You're right, Wes. They're keeping a very low profile and that makes me suspicious.'

'Me too. Maybe Tallow will be able to throw some light on the matter – when he turns up again.'

'He's bound to appear sooner or later,' said Gerry confidently. With Harvey Pottinger's interview imminent, he was in one of his optimistic moods.

At 11.30, Wesley received a call from the reception desk. Pottinger had arrived and been taken down to the interview room. The civilian receptionist sounded quite excited about her brief brush with celebrity, and Wesley guessed she was assuming he'd come there as a witness rather than a suspect.

Pottinger had been shown into the best interview room, where they'd spoken to Barry Brown's sister, which made Wesley think that somebody else had made the same assumption as the receptionist. If Gerry had had his way, one of the grimmer rooms would have been used; the rooms that smelled of sweat and fear, with no windows and the furniture bolted to the floor.

'Mr Pottinger,' Gerry said jovially as he walked into the room. 'Good of you to come and see us.'

'No problem. Anything to help the police.' Wesley could sense nervousness behind the good-citizen act. He wondered how long he'd be able to keep it up once they presented him with what they knew.

'You've been to the north-east, I believe.'

'That's right. Just a short trip to film an episode of *Harvey's Travels*. It's a lovely part of the world. Wish I could have stayed longer.'

'Coffee?' Wesley offered, pointing to the kettle on a side table. 'We've only got instant, I'm afraid.' He calculated that the more they put the man at his ease, the more he would be off his guard when they dropped their bombshell.

'Instant's fine.'

Wesley made three mugs and set them out on the low coffee table in front of the grey sofas before taking a seat. He noticed that Gerry was watching their suspect closely for signs of guilt. But Pottinger was experienced at playing the good guy, everybody's best friend. He'd made a career of it.

Once they were settled and Gerry had switched on the discreet recording machine at the side of the room, Pottinger gave them his warmest smile. 'I promise I've told you everything I know, detectives. What happened to Barry Brown was a terrible tragedy, but I really haven't anything to add.'

'Are you sure about that?' Gerry was smiling too, but Wesley heard the threat behind his words.

'Absolutely. I only wish I could help.'

Gerry caught Wesley's eye. It was time to spring their surprise. Wesley picked up a tablet from the table and handed it to their suspect.

'I'm showing Mr Pottinger a photograph taken by a traffic camera last Sunday night at nine-fifteen on the main road leading from Morbay to Little Rockington,' he said for the benefit of the machine. 'The vehicle registration plate can be seen quite clearly. It's a Porsche SUV registered to you, isn't it, Mr Pottinger?'

He sat back and waited for a reaction. But the one he got wasn't the one he'd expected.

'For God's sake don't let Donna know about this.'

'About what?' said Gerry. 'About you killing Barry Brown to stop him exposing what you've been up to?'

'I don't know what you mean. I haven't been up to anything.' His TV persona was fading fast and there was a glint of panic in his eyes. 'I didn't kill Barry Brown.Why would I?'

'Are you sure about that?' said Gerry. 'Didn't he tell you he was planning to spend some time in Devon researching a book about a woman who went missing during the war?'

'All I know is that he wanted to postpone working on my autobiography because he was pursuing another project.

I've already been into all this. Don't you people listen?' Pottinger gave the detectives a look of wide-eyed innocence. The shock had worn off and he was regaining his composure. 'Of course I didn't kill Barry. Why would I?'

Wesley left a short silence before he spoke again. 'We've been talking to Lenny Brice.'

A look of relief appeared on Pottinger's face. 'I don't see what that has to do with me.' Wesley guessed he trusted in Brice's discretion. He hadn't reckoned with Tiffany, the invisible trophy partner in the background who said little but saw and heard everything.

'You attended a party at Brice's house on the night a girl called Suzie Dix died of a drugs overdose. You were seen with the dead girl.'

'Where on earth did you get that idea?'

'We have a witness.'

'Who?' Pottinger looked unconcerned, but the tension was clear in his voice.

'We're not at liberty to say.' Wesley suspected there'd been an unspoken pact between the guests to keep quiet about their participation, and now Pottinger was searching his memory to identify the possible traitor.

'Whoever told you this was lying. A man in my position makes enemies; people can be envious of success like mine. Tall poppy syndrome, they call it.'

'Was Barry Brown one of these envious people?'

'Of course not.'

'Were you angry that he'd let you down over your autobiography?'

'Absolutely not. The delay suited me quite well. I'm an extremely busy man.' As though to emphasise this, Pottinger looked at his watch.

'Let me put it another way,' said Wesley. 'Were you angry when Brown found out about your link with Lenny Brice and his parties? You have a certain public image to uphold. You can't afford to be associated with scandal.'

This time the colour drained from Pottinger's face. 'I . . . I don't know what you mean.'

'Let's leave that for the time being. Why were you driving to Morbay on the night Barry Brown was murdered?'

There was a lengthy silence, as though Pottinger was wondering which version of the truth would do the least damage to his reputation.

'OK. I'll come clean,' he said after a while. 'I was visiting a lady.'

'We'll need her name,' said Gerry.

'I know her as Mercedes.'

'I take it Mercedes is what we used to call a working girl?'

Pottinger answered Gerry's question with an embarrassed nod.

'Is that her real name?'

'That's a question you don't ask.'

'Address?' Gerry asked, taking his notebook from his jacket pocket.

Pottinger recited an address in Morbay. The better side of town, where white stucco villas rubbed shoulders with upmarket bars.

'I'd be grateful for your discretion.' He looked from one detective to the other with wide, pleading eyes.

'The girl who died at Lenny Brice's party was in the same line of business, I believe.'

'I wouldn't know about that.'

'As you were seen with her on the night she died, Oxford police might want to speak to you at some point.'

Pottinger bowed his head as though he'd just realised his celebrity was unlikely to protect him any longer. Then he glanced up. 'Look, ask Mercedes. She'll tell you I was with her that night. I didn't get back to Millicombe until early the following morning.'

'We know. Your return journey was caught on camera too. Are you sure you didn't know where Barry Brown was staying?'

'All he told me was that he was travelling to Devon to pursue another project.'

Gerry stood up. 'We'll leave it there for the time being. Don't go anywhere without letting us know. We might want to speak to you again.'

'Please,' Pottinger said almost in a whine. 'This could ruin me. Can't you just—'

'Thank you for your time, Mr Pottinger,' said Wesley before the man could finish his sentence. 'You're free to go.'

'For now,' Gerry added with a hint of menace.

Pottinger didn't react to the DCI's parting shot. Instead he treated them both to his man-of-the-people smile and said that he was always happy to help the police, who in his opinion did a wonderful job keeping the community safe. Once again Wesley was struck by the man's acting skills.

'What do you think?' Gerry asked as they were climbing the stairs to the CID office.

'He's definitely hiding something, although I'm not sure whether it's connected to the murder of Barry Brown. We'll get someone to interview this Mercedes, and I'm sure Oxford will be very interested in what Tiffany has to say, although I'll ask them to be discreet. If my suspicions about Lenny Brice are correct, she might be in danger if he thinks she's betrayed him.'

Gerry sighed. 'Thank God we lead dull lives, Wes.' He rubbed his hands together. 'I told you, didn't I? I had a feeling in my water this was going to be our lucky day.'

Diary of Flight Officer John Carmody

26 June 1943

The summer nights are short, so we have much less time to fly. Darkness is our friend, and this month we only have a few hours to complete our missions. We need to operate in the shadows. The Black Squadron nobody must know exists.

Tonight I picked up an agent called Albert, a Frenchman who left for England as soon as the Nazis invaded his country. We made it back safely, thank God, but Albert had grave news. Word had reached him that a number of Resistance leaders were captured near Lyon last Monday. He was clearly distressed about it, and I wondered whether he was on the verge of losing his nerve, although he assured me he was prepared to go back if he was needed. I said that if there was a danger of him being recognised, he ought to leave the job to someone else, a fresh face. But he's determined to free his homeland.

I landed back at Winkleigh at 0300 hours, desperate for sleep. There was a dance on tonight organised by the Americans at their base, and some of the chaps went to it. No doubt I'll find out how they fared tomorrow.

I met a lovely girl at the base. She told me her name

was Marie. Her father's French and she was brought up in Brittany, so she speaks the language fluently. She's due to begin her training soon. I said that if she flew with me, I could promise her a smooth journey, and she laughed. She had a lovely laugh. Ever since that night, I've been thinking of her.

25

Rob Carter could never resist looking out of the office window, especially in the summer months, when there was so much activity in the town and on the shining ribbon of river beyond the manicured greenery of the Memorial Gardens.

When he'd glanced up from his computer screen ten minutes earlier, the scene below had looked perfectly normal. Holidaymakers in summer clothes strolled through the gardens licking ice creams, and drivers in the public car park unloaded small vans as they made deliveries to local shops and restaurants. It was a typical Tradmouth summer scene. But next time he looked up, everything had changed.

Even from where Rob was sitting, he could sense the excitement, as though something unusual was going on. Then he heard a phone ring on Trish Walton's desk. And from the look on her face as she took the call, she'd just received startling news.

She jumped to her feet. 'We need to get down to the gardens. A member of the public's just reported that people are hanging jewellery on trees.'

Gerry came out of his office. 'Did I hear that right, Trish?'

'Yes, sir.'

'Well, what are we waiting for?'

Rob had never seen the office empty so fast. Officers thundered down the stairs and out into the sunshine. When they reached the gardens, Gerry and Wesley bringing up the rear, a strange scene greeted them.

People were gathering glittering objects from bushes and the lower branches of trees. Some had the glint of greed in their eyes and others seemed confused.

The assembled officers instinctively formed a human cordon around the area, and Gerry marched to the front to take command of the situation.

'Listen up, everyone. I'm Detective Chief Inspector Heffernan from Tradmouth police.' He waved a hand in the vague direction of the station. 'Can someone tell me what's going on?'

There was a lot of foot-shuffling as people looked expectantly at their neighbours, as though no one wished to draw attention to themselves by speaking out. Eventually a man broke the silence; a well-dressed, tanned individual who looked as though he'd just stepped off one of the luxurious yachts moored against the pontoons on the river.

'A group of people in masks jumped out of an old van and started hanging jewellery around the park. I assumed it was some sort of theatrical performance.' He looked round. 'They'll have been collecting up all this cheap tat from jumble sales,' he said with a dismissive smirk.

'Can you describe these people?'

'They were wearing those joke masks – the royals,' a small grey-haired woman piped up.

'Did you get the impression they were young, old, male, female? What were they wearing?'

'I think they were youngish, And they were dressed like hippies.' She sniffed. 'They might have been trying to look like the royals, but they certainly weren't dressed like them. And the one playing the King had a beer belly.'

'They looked as though they needed a good wash,' an elderly man on the edge of the group observed.

'Can everyone who has taken any of this jewellery please give it to one of my officers,' Gerry said. His mind was working fast as he watched the jewellery being collected. Some people tried to sneak away, but they were prevented by a couple of uniformed officers who'd come out to join the CID team. Citizens of a more law-abiding nature queued up to hand over their treasures.

It wasn't long before Gerry's suspicions were confirmed. To his untrained eye, the jewellery looked genuine. And as far as he could see, the items matched the list of rings, bracelets and necklaces stolen by the Royal Family gang during the raids on shops in the area.

He addressed the assembled gathering, saying that anyone who went off with any of the items would be charged with theft. This seemed to bring the waverers to their senses. Sparkly pieces were swiftly given up to officers, who placed them in plastic evidence bags, and names and addresses were taken. Statements were made by those who'd actually seen the arrival of the van and its occupants, and it was a full hour before everyone was given permission to go.

Gerry and Wesley walked back to the station with the others, and as they were crossing the small public car park, Wesley turned his head. Hanging on the hedge surrounding the Memorial Gardens, just next to the Tourist Information Centre, was what appeared to be a homemade banner; roughly painted words on a tattered off-white

202

sheet. The breeze had shifted it so that half the words were obscured. He nudged Gerry's elbow.

The DCI looked to where he was pointing, then shouted over to Rob. 'Go and take a look, will you, Rob. Your legs are younger than mine.'

They watched as the DC darted over the road, dodging traffic. When he reached the banner draped untidily on the hedge, he straightened it out so that it could be read.

**THE GLITTERING FRUITS OF
GREED AND CAPITALISM**

**YOU HAVE JUST TAKEN PART IN AN
EXPERIMENTAL PERFORMANCE BY
THE TR THEATRE COMPANY**

When Gerry looked round, he saw that Trish was standing behind him.

'What does it mean?' she asked.

'I think the Royal Family have just returned their ill-gotten gains.'

26

'It was a piece of performance art apparently. We reckon we've got most of the stolen stuff back. We just need the jewellers to identify it. There's CCTV footage of the so-called performers and their vehicle. Plenty of evidence.'

Wesley followed Gerry into his office, where the DCI brought the flickering footage up on his computer. It showed a group of four people in royal family masks, the King, the Queen, the Prince of Wales and the Princess Royal, pouring out of a Transit van, rushing into the gardens and draping sparkly items over branches and shrubs. As they decorated the greenery they danced around ecstatically, shouting something that couldn't be heard on the footage, as a small puzzled crowd stood watching. Then, as quickly as they'd arrived, they darted back into the waiting van and drove off at speed.

'Any sign of the firearm?'

Gerry shook his head. 'The good news is that one of Traffic's clever little cameras has produced a really clear picture of the van's number plate. It's registered to an address in Walton, Liverpool.'

'Where are the TR Theatre Company now?'

'They shouldn't be hard to find.'

Wesley knew that Gerry was right. After such a public stunt, surely they'd soon make arrests. It was their murder case that worried him more.

Back at his own desk, his thoughts turned to Neil's skeletons on the moor: the American man and the French woman. They'd both died far from home, but how had they ended up buried in the same unmarked grave? And could it have anything to do with Barry Brown's murder?

His musings were interrupted by a call from Ellie, who'd been sent to Morbay to track down Mercedes, the sex worker Harvey Pottinger had given as his alibi for the time of Brown's death.

'I've spoken to Mercedes,' she began. 'She says she did see Harvey Pottinger that night.' There was a pause. 'But he didn't arrive until ten-thirty. She says he spent the rest of the night with her.'

'So he would have had plenty of time to have a cosy drink with Barry Brown, adding poison to his glass, then do the washing-up to get rid of the evidence before searching the place.'

'That's right, sir. Plenty of time. But when I asked her if she'd make a formal statement, she seemed reluctant.'

'Maybe she just needs a bit of reassurance,' said Wesley. 'I'm sure you can use your powers of persuasion.'

'I just can't believe it of Harvey Pottinger. He seems so . . . lovely when you see him on the telly.'

'Never go by appearances, Ellie,' he said. 'They can be very deceptive.'

He heard Gerry calling his name. It sounded urgent, so he ended the call and rushed to the DCI's office.

Gerry's face was a picture of glee. 'We've got 'em, Wes. Their van's been caught on camera heading for Neston. I've alerted the nick there. I've never come across such incompetent robbers. Like shooting fish in a barrel.'

Wesley sat down by Gerry's cluttered desk. 'It's a protest. I think they wanted to be caught so they could make their point. I bet you they'll claim police brutality and an establishment cover-up.'

Gerry sank into his seat, deflated. 'You're probably right. Mind you, they did fire that gun at the woman in Neston.'

'But it was loaded with blanks. There was no intention to kill, just to frighten. I agree, though: they pinched cars, terrified innocent people and stole valuable items. They deserve to be brought to justice.'

A knowing grin appeared on Gerry's face. 'I'm sure your mother-in-law wouldn't agree.'

'Della has her own way of looking at things.'

'That's one way of putting it. In view of what Mercedes told us about the time Pottinger arrived at her place, let's send a patrol car to pick him up. He's got some explaining to do. According to Tiffany, he was an enthusiastic participant in whatever was going on at Lenny Brice's party. And I'm betting it wasn't the first of Lenny's little gatherings he attended. Let's face it, Wes, Brown could have ruined him, so Pottinger had every reason to want him out of the way. There's a lot of dirt underneath that squeaky-clean "everybody's best friend" act.'

'You're right, Gerry. Pottinger was expecting Brown to produce a hagiography but ... '

'A what?'

'A hagiography. An idealised account that makes the subject sound like a saint. The question is, if Pottinger was going to pay him well for this autobiography, why did Brown go off piste and start searching in the closet for nasty skeletons?'

'Maybe Barry Brown was an honest man. I'm told there are still a few of them about. And the offer from George Melling clinched it. He didn't need to write fibs about Pottinger any more.'

Their conversation was cut short by the news that the TR Theatre Company's van had been stopped on the road to Neston. Four arrests had been made and the suspects were demanding their solicitor. And they'd already notified the media that they had an important announcement to make.

27

The four robbery suspects had been brought to the station and put in separate cells. The custody sergeant, a large, calm man normally endowed with enormous patience, was looking harassed. The suspects were demanding all sorts of exotic refreshments, he complained. And they had to be vegan, from sources in Neston they'd personally approved. They'd rather starve than eat mass-produced rubbish.

In the end they began singing and chanting and the noise could be heard in the CID office on the first floor. The custody sergeant fielded vociferous complaints from a burglar and a suspected mugger who were being held in nearby cells, but all attempts to silence the group failed. In the end, he phoned up to Gerry, pleading for CID to get them interviewed and out of there as soon as possible. They were getting on everybody's nerves.

Gerry allocated Trish, Paul, Rob and Rachel to conduct the initial interviews. The charge was armed robbery, a serious offence, so bail was probably out of the question. The interviewing officers had instructions to ask whether any of the suspects had visited Barry Brown's cottage in Little Rockington wearing a mask. This was the one question they all deigned to answer with a resounding no.

None of them had ever been to Little Rockington. The pigs couldn't pin that one on them. All they'd done was protest using an innovative piece of performance art. And even though they'd *borrowed* cars, they'd always cleaned them thoroughly and returned them to safe places. They weren't criminals.

After their vehement denials, they were returned to the cells, where the chanting resumed. That was when Gerry came up with the solution. Divide and rule. They would be taken to separate stations until they could appear before the magistrate in the morning. At least that would give the custody sergeant and his other charges some peace.

The group had all made the same pre-prepared statement, parroting it like a mantra. 'We confiscated the glittering fruits of capitalism and greed to bring awareness of our cause and change the world.' That was all they said, and all they were going to say. They also sang their mantra to various tunes, none of which the officers forced to listen to their musical efforts recognised.

Once the group had been taken off to their new accommodation, Wesley looked through the messages on his desk, some from a few days previously, and found a note from the DC who'd been given the job of checking whether Craig Parker's cousin, Bella Renolds, had come back from holiday. She was still away, but a neighbour thought her return was imminent. Efforts had continued to be made to contact her mobile number, but without success.

According to Craig Parker, Bella was the keeper of the family archives, such as they were, and it was probable Brown had spoken to her before she flew off to Tenerife. Her mother had been brought up in Moor Barton, which made it easy for her to trace that side of her family. When they finally got to speak to her, it was hoped she might be able to tell them something useful. Wesley put the note to one side. There was nothing he could do until she got back, so he needed to be patient.

Ten minutes later, Gerry shot out of his office, his face so red that Wesley feared for his blood pressure. 'He's gone, Wes. Done a runner.'

'Who has?'

'Harvey Pottinger, that's who. I sent someone to tell him we'd like another word, and his missus said he's nipped over to the south of France to film an episode of *Harvey's Travels* and will be back in a day or two. She said he's a very busy man. Much in demand.'

'Wonder how long that'll last if the scandal breaks,' said Wesley.

'I got on to the production company and they confirmed the trip was scheduled after the filming in Alnwick. If it hadn't been, I would have thought he was trying to avoid us.'

'In that case, I wouldn't exactly describe that as doing a runner,' said Wesley with some amusement.

Gerry shrugged his large shoulders. 'You know me, Wes. I like to let off steam from time to time.'

'We'll just have to question him as soon as he gets back.'

'Too right we will. He lied to us about what time he arrived at Mercedes' place, and I don't like it when people lie to us. Makes me suspicious.'

'In an ideal world, we'd have more evidence against him,' said Wesley calmly. 'We've got Mercedes' statement and the fact that he was at Lenny Brice's party when the woman died, but that's hardly enough.' He was only too aware that they didn't have enough to charge him with Barry Brown's murder. But he was sure they'd make a breakthrough soon. And once they did, he might be able to turn his attention to Neil's skeletons and the mystery of Marie Leon – the reason Barry Brown had travelled to Devon in the first place.

Michael Peterson was having a great time. The students had started to regard him as one of their own, or at least a younger sibling, and he was enjoying the camaraderie of the dig and being treated like a grown-up.

That afternoon he'd been busy cleaning finds in the marquee with Harriet, but just under an hour ago she'd disappeared, telling Greg she needed something from the village shop. Michael kept turning his head, hoping to see her coming back, and Greg teased him gently.

'Missing your girlfriend?'

Michael felt the blood rush to his cheeks. 'I don't have a girlfriend,' was all he could think of to say. He saw Greg smirk and shake his head.

'Only joking.'

Harriet appeared again in time to help pack up for the day.

'Big queue at the shop?' Greg asked lightly.

'Something like that.'

After Michael had helped cover the trenches with tarpaulins, it was time to head home. As he sought Neil out for his lift to Exeter, the students were talking about a party they had lined up for the weekend. They barely seemed to notice his departure. Suddenly he felt impatient to grow up.

He could see Neil and Dave talking to the soldiers as they prepared to cover their trench, and he hung back, not wanting to interrupt. But as he waited for the conversation to finish, he felt the pressure of a hand on his shoulder. He swung round and found himself looking into the face of the man in the bucket hat. He hadn't seen him for a while, and he'd been so busy that he'd almost forgotten about him. But now the man's gaze was so intense that his heart began to pound.

'Your father's that policeman, isn't he? I saw him talking to Dr Watson the other day.'

Michael swallowed hard and nodded.

'Can you tell him I need to speak to him about that skeleton they found? The one up near the rock. And there's something else I need to tell him. Something I've only just remembered. I can't be sure, but it might be important.' Michael could hear the anxiety in his voice. 'The name's Pelham Jenks. You will remember to tell him, won't you?'

Michael nodded and the man walked away. Perhaps he'd been worrying about nothing. Perhaps Pelham Jenks had been watching him earlier because he was plucking up the courage to ask him about his dad.

'What did he want?'

Michael turned round and saw Harriet standing there.

'He asked me to tell my dad that he wants to speak to him, that's all.'

'What about?'

'That skeleton they found near the rock ... and something else he'd just remembered. He didn't say what.'

'Will you tell your dad?'

Michael shrugged. 'Suppose so. Why not?'

'Dunno. That man seems a bit of a weirdo, that's all. Might be best not to get involved.'

Michael nodded. Harriet was probably right. On the other hand, it would do no harm to mention it to his dad. He'd decide once he got home.

Diary of Edith Tallow

Sunday 27 June 1943

It's working a treat, just as Marie promised it would. Bram believes me each time I tell him I'm staying with my sister, and because he never leaves the farm, there's no danger of him discovering my lies. I'm only eighteen and I didn't realise that marrying Bram would be like a living death, and yet sometimes I feel bad about deceiving him. Hank would say it's like taking candy from a baby. I love the way Americans talk.

I've seen Hank five times now and our kisses grow more passionate with every meeting. I take my wedding ring off so he won't know I'm married, and I don't intend to tell him until I have to. Marie says I should just enjoy myself while I can. Who knows when these brave boys might be sent away to fight? Who knows whether they'll ever come back? She says it's our patriotic duty to keep up the morale of the troops – including the Yanks. If this is true, Marie should be awarded a medal.

She hasn't mentioned her hush-hush meeting recently. I asked her what was happening and she said these things take time. She sounded disappointed, because according to Marie, hush-hush equals excitement. She said that anything has to be better than milking cows at dawn and she really wants to do her bit.

Hank is the sort of man I would have searched for if I'd had any sense; not the brooding Heathcliff of my former fantasies but a tall, handsome blond man with freckles and a lovely open face. I admit that I gave in to temptation behind the huts at the base last time we met, and it was lovely; nothing like when me and Bram did it. Hank's kind and thoughtful and he treats me like a princess. He even brings me nylons and chewing gum, but I leave them with Marie at Home Farm so I can wear the nylons for the dances at the base. I daren't take them home in case Bram finds them and starts asking questions.

Old Dorcas still treats me like a servant. She frightened me the other day when Bram was out with the animals. She grabbed hold of my arm as I was passing her chair and held on to it so tightly that it hurt.

Then she hissed in my ear, 'Remember what happened to Jezebel. She was thrown from a window and dogs ate her; lapped up her blood, they did. You can't hide anything from me. I see everything. And sinners are always punished.'

There was such hatred in her eyes that I was terrified. It was as though she knew what I'd been up to, but there's no way she could have found out. Not unless she really is a witch.

I ran to the room I share with Bram, flung myself on the bed and wept bitter tears. Bram never kisses me now – or does anything else, not since our wedding night. I keep thinking of Hank. Even though I know I shouldn't, I can't help it.

I think Bram's scared of his mother. And I don't blame him. So am I.

28

Wesley decided not to mention Pottinger's imminent disgrace to Pam when he arrived home that evening. Such an indiscretion would be unprofessional, so he'd wait until the case was wrapped up – or at least until things were more certain.

As soon as he opened the front door, Sherlock rushed into the hall to greet him, his tail wagging like a windscreen wiper as usual, while Moriarty appeared at the open living room door, tail in the air, and gave the dog a disdainful look.

Sherlock was closely followed by Michael. 'Dad, someone at the dig wants to speak to you.'

'Who?' Wesley bent down to pat Sherlock's head before listening carefully to what Michael had to say.

'So you think this man Pelham Jenks was watching you?' he asked, his parental alarm bells ringing loudly.

'I was OK. Harriet and the others have been looking out for me,' Michael said proudly, and Wesley guessed his acceptance by the student group was doing wonders for his confidence.

'What exactly did he say to you?'

Michael closed his eyes, trying to recall. 'He asked me if

my dad was the policeman he'd seen talking to Neil. Then he said he needed to speak to you about the skeleton they'd found.'

'Skeleton singular? Not skeletons?'

Michael shrugged. 'Not sure. Does it matter?'

Pam had only just entered the room, and Wesley saw her frowning. 'Why are you interrogating Michael? He's not one of your suspects, you know.'

Michael looked at his mother and rolled his eyes. 'It's OK, Mum. I'm trying to think of something and you've put me off.'

Pam raised her eyebrows and retreated from the room. 'I'll leave you to it, then.'

Michael thought for a few seconds and looked up triumphantly. 'Then he said he'd just remembered something and he wants to speak to you urgently because it might be important.'

Wesley gave his son a hug. 'I've got to take Sherlock for his walk. Want to come with me?'

Michael nodded.

Wesley was thinking of Pelham Jenks as he walked to the station the next morning. Even if the man did have information about one of the long-buried skeletons, the matter could hardly be regarded as urgent. According to the experts, the remains had been out there on the moor for decades, and the police had more pressing matters to deal with. Unless Jenks had spoken to Barry Brown while he'd been up in Moor Barton. But his name hadn't come up in the investigation so far – and it was such an unusual name, he was sure it would have stuck in his memory.

He was intrigued by Jenks's claim that he'd just

remembered something important. He hadn't provided Michael with a phone number, but Wesley was sure that either Neil or the organiser of the local archaeology group would have his contact details.

As soon as he reached the CID office, he was greeted by the news that the members of the TR Theatre Company were due to be taken before the magistrate as soon as the court opened. Officers from Neston police station had interviewed the New Age group who'd been camping near Tradington – the group Jay Tallow lived with. They'd admitted that when the theatre company first arrived in the area, they'd camped with them for a couple of days. But in the end it was concluded that none of the Tradington group had actually been involved in the robberies. They'd given the theatre company their masks because they'd claimed they were needed for a special protest. However, they denied all knowledge of the visitors' real plans.

Wesley gave Neston a call and they confirmed that they'd found Tallow who'd been brought in and questioned. None of the hippies, as the officer he spoke to called them, had been held. In fact they'd been amazingly co-operative. Then, to his surprise, the officer told him that Tallow had mentioned his name and said he wanted to speak to him. He'd mentioned something about a murder, but it had all been rather vague.

Once Gerry had given his morning sermon, emphasising that getting some solid evidence that Harvey Pottinger had actually called at Barry Brown's cottage on the night of his murder was now their priority, Wesley followed him into his office and told him about Tallow's request. He also mentioned what Pelham Jenks had said to Michael.

'If I were you, Wes, I'd go and see what Tallow wants. With any luck he might have something useful to tell us.'

'Fingers crossed.'

'Then you'd better find out what this Pelham Jenks has to say for himself.' Gerry sat back and gave a heartfelt sigh. 'Until we can get more on Pottinger, we might as well try and tie up some loose ends.'

'You definitely think Pottinger's our man?'

'Don't you?'

Wesley didn't answer the question.

'Brown discovered his nasty little secrets, so he had to be silenced,' Gerry went on. 'Why else would the killer pinch his notes and laptop? Because there was something on them he didn't want anyone to see, that's why. I reckon Pottinger's mates from Lenny Brice's party closed ranks and hushed up the fact that he was there. Brice has friends in high places: MPs, senior police officers, powerful businessmen and probably a few public figures like Pottinger who'd be finished by any scandal. If the media got a sniff of what went on, it might put an end to a lot of glittering careers.'

'I realise that, but—'

'Do you think anyone's guessed that Tiffany spoke to us?' Gerry suddenly sounded worried. 'Do you think we should ask Oxford to provide her with some protection?'

'That might not be a bad idea.' Wesley cast his mind back. He was as sure as he could be that their meeting in the kitchen of Lenny Brice's house hadn't been overheard, but it would be wise to err on the side of caution.

'OK, I'll give Oxford a call while you go to Neston and have a word with Jay Tallow.'

'You're not coming?'

'Auntie Noreen wants to see me again. Says she's getting worried about the budget for this investigation. I hope she won't question our little trip to Oxford. It's not as though we treated ourselves to a luxury break at the Randolph, is it?' Gerry gave a mischievous grin.

'I'm sure you'll manage to sweet-talk your way out of it.' Wesley checked the time. If he left now, he could see Tallow before driving up to Neil's dig to find out what Pelham Jenks had to tell him. He scanned the office and saw that Rachel was sorting through paperwork. When he asked if she wanted to come with him to interview a potential witness, she leapt from her seat and followed him out of the office.

Half an hour later, they were face to face with Jay Tallow in his yurt. This time he seemed positively welcoming.

'Where's your Scouse mate?' was his first question.

'DCI Heffernan's back at Tradmouth police station,' said Rachel. 'He's a busy man, what with all these jewel robberies.'

'How much did you really know about them?' Wesley chipped in.

Tallow shook his head vigorously. 'I've been through this already with the cops from Neston.'

'Humour me.'

'OK. We knew the Liverpool lot were planning some performance art and they wanted to borrow our masks, but they never said what they were going to do. We thought they were just going to protest, like we did for the coronation. Giving them the masks isn't a crime, is it?'

Wesley and Rachel exchanged a glance.

'OK. We'll leave it at that.' The last thing Wesley wanted was to alienate the young man. If he had important information, he wanted to hear it. 'I understand you have something to tell me.'

Tallow cleared his throat. There was a strong smell of cannabis in the yurt, and Wesley suspected he'd extinguished a joint when he heard them arrive. 'Yeah. You were asking about my relatives – the ones on Dartmoor we have nothing to do with.'

'What about them?'

'I spoke to my nan – well, I call her my nan but she's really my great-gran. She's a hundred, but you'd never know it. She says if you want to know about those Tallows from Moor Barton, she's more than happy to speak to you. She said it's high time the police took an interest in them.'

'Why's that?' Rachel asked.

'Dunno. Do you want her address? It's a retirement home, and she likes to have visitors.'

Wesley wrote down the address and thanked Tallow for the information.

'Have we really got time for this?' Rachel asked as they climbed into the car.

'Even if she can't tell us anything, at least we'll be doing our good deed for the day,' Wesley replied. 'Ralph Gornay mentioned the Tallows to Barry Brown, so you never know, we might learn something.'

'The boss is convinced that Harvey Pottinger killed Brown.'

'I prefer to keep an open mind.'

'But Pottinger had an excellent motive. And he had time to call at Brown's cottage on the night of the murder. Don't forget he didn't arrive at Mercedes' place until ten thirty.'

'Linda Pugh saw someone else calling there that evening.

Someone a lot taller than Pottinger, who might have been wearing a mask.'

'She might have made a mistake. And I think we can rule out the TR Theatre Company, don't you.' Rachel looked exasperated. 'I don't know why you won't accept it, Wes. Harvey Pottinger has a nasty side to his nature, and he got rid of Brown because he was afraid he was about to tell the world about it.'

Wesley wasn't inclined to contradict her, so he stayed silent as he drove to Tallow's great-grandmother's care home in a village a mile and a half from Neston. It wasn't often that he and Rachel had a disagreement, but he couldn't forget that Brown had been looking for information about the air crash, and the Tallow family were living in Moor Barton back in 1943 when it happened.

The care home stood on the fringe of the village, housed in a substantial Victorian building that had once served as the vicarage. The village itself possessed an unremarkable church and a pub with posters in the window advertising its karaoke night. The settlement lacked the charm of a place like Little Rockington – or Moor Barton, for that matter.

The carer who answered the door examined their ID. Once she was satisfied they weren't imposters, her manner changed and she became positively welcoming. She said that Florrie, whose advanced age obviously granted her the status of the home's celebrity resident, would be delighted to speak to them because she loved detective programmes on the telly.

As she led them to Florrie's room, she seemed happy to talk, and soon they knew the ins and outs of the Tallow clan. Florrie's son and daughter-in-law had both sadly passed away a few years ago, and her grandson and his wife now lived in Spain and rarely visited. But, she added approvingly, her great-grandson, Jay, popped in every couple of days. He was a lovely boy, in spite of his appearance.

With this testimonial ringing in their ears, they reached Florrie Tallow's room. The carer knocked on the door and called out Florrie's name. After what seemed like an age, the door opened to reveal a tiny white-haired woman behind a Zimmer frame. They knew she'd reached her century, but her lively blue eyes suggested that her mind was as sharp as ever.

'Come in,' she said after the introductions had been made. 'How exciting. I hope you haven't come to arrest me.'

'Not at all,' said Rachel. 'We're just hoping you'll be able to help us.'

'I will if I can. Would you like a cup of tea?'

'Thank you,' said Wesley.

'Three teas, please, Leanne,' Florrie said to the carer, who was hovering by the door.

She addressed Wesley as soon as Leanne had hurried out into the corridor.

'Well, Inspector. You're not from round these parts, are you?'

He had grown used to comments like this over his years in Devon, and although they sometimes made him bristle slightly, his instincts told him that Florrie was simply curious about his background. He gave her a potted account of his family's travels from Trinidad to London.

'They must be very clever, your mum and dad,' she said approvingly. 'Two doctors – and you a detective inspector and your sister another doctor. But I don't suppose you're here to pass the time of day. My great-grandson said you wanted to speak to me, but he didn't say why. Jay's a good boy,' she added fondly. 'Looks after me, he does. His parents buggered off to live in Spain, so he's all I've got. But I don't feel sorry for myself. This is a nice place, and I've had my birthday card from the King. Can't ask for more, can you?'

'No, you can't,' said Wesley gently. 'Jay said you might be able to tell us something about the Tallow family. They own a smallholding in Moor Barton, I believe.'

A look of disapproval appeared on the old lady's face. 'It was my late husband's elder brother who owned the place. Bram, his name was.'

'But you lived in the village too?'

'For a while when we were first married. My Isaac left the smallholding when he fell out with his brother. Bram was ten years older than him, and they'd never got on. Isaac got a cottage on the manor estate after we left and did odd jobs for Colonel Gornay.'

'So you'd have been there when a boy called Norman went missing in the 1950s?' said Wesley.

Mrs Tallow shook her head. 'We'd left the village by then, but we did hear talk that the colonel had something to do with that lad's disappearance. But everyone knew better than to ask questions. People kept their mouths shut in those days. Not like today.'

To Wesley this sounded positively feudal. The lord of the manor had been able to get away with murder because nobody had been courageous enough to question him. Just as nobody had dared to enquire too deeply into what the distinguished guests had got up to at Lenny Brice's dubious parties. Perhaps not much had changed over the years after all.

'What was Colonel Gornay like?' he asked. He saw

223

Rachel give him a look that suggested she thought his question irrelevant and a waste of their valuable time.

'He wasn't a nice man. Had a reputation for being a bit of a tyrant. And I think his poor wife had a lot to put up with. I heard that son of his left home as soon as he could, and I'm not surprised. Never came back till the old man was dying.'

'And the smallholding – who lives there now?'

'I heard Bram died some years ago – not that we were invited to the funeral. We wouldn't have gone anyway. That man was a bad lot and I wouldn't have been able to hold my tongue if the vicar started going on about him ending up in heaven – he was bound for the other place if you ask me.' She took a deep, shuddering breath as though the memory of her late brother-in-law disturbed her.

'Last I heard, Bram's wife, Edith, was still alive. She was a lot younger than Bram – nearer my own age – and she was very pretty, as I recall. Don't know what made her tie herself to that man. My Isaac used to say he had her under his thumb.'

'Was Bram violent to his wife?' Wesley could hear the indignation behind Rachel's question.

'It wouldn't surprise me, but things like that were brushed under the carpet in those days. Isaac always used to say his brother was a bully – made his life a misery while he was growing up. And poor little Edith would never say boo to a goose. Mind you, she had her own ways of rebelling,' Florrie added with a secretive smile.

'Do you remember the plane that crashed in Moor Barton during the war?'

'Yes, but there's nothing much to tell. The pilot was taken to the Gornay Arms, but he passed away soon after.

The whole village went to the funeral to pay their respects. And I remember them coming to clear the wreckage. Some of the local kids went to watch, but they shooed them away.'

'Were you aware of any talk of a French woman going missing in Moor Barton during the war, when there were lots of American soldiers around?' Wesley was almost sure the bones belonged to the missing Marie, but he needed to explore every other possibility, and now that he was face to face with somebody who'd actually lived in Moor Barton around that time, he saw the opportunity to try and solve the mystery once and for all.

She shook her head. 'No missing women, no. Although there was talk about the crash. It was the kind of plane used to ferry spies about, you see, so people wondered if there was more to it than we were told. But later they said it had come down in the fog – a tragic accident.' Then she smiled, her watery blue eyes twinkling, 'But I remember the Yanks. They used to give out sweets to the children, and nylons to the women.' She paused. 'Why are you asking?'

Wesley gave her a brief account of Neil's discoveries, and he saw her face light up with speculation, as though she was enjoying a particularly puzzling detective programme. 'Well I never. And you think the skeletons have been there since the war?'

'The evidence points to it.'

'Fancy that sort of thing going on in Moor Barton while I was living there. And I had no idea.'

'Did a man called Barry Brown visit you? He might have been asking questions about Moor Barton.' Wesley knew this was a long shot.

To his surprise, his gamble paid off. 'That's right. Nice

young man in a leather jacket, with an earring. Said he was an author.'

'Did he say how he got your name?'

'No. But he said he'd been speaking to people about Moor Barton.'

'What did he ask you?'

'He asked the same as you: about the plane crash and whether I knew if any French women had been seen in the village afterwards. Then he wanted to know about the manor house. Asked if I knew the Gornays.' Florrie laughed. 'They didn't mix socially with the likes of me and my Isaac. Kept themselves to themselves, they did.' She leaned forward, her eyes alive with excitement. 'You don't think that was why he was killed, do you – because he'd found something out?'

It was a question Wesley couldn't answer.

29

The list of people who'd had contact with Barry Brown seemed to be growing by the moment, and Wesley had more questions to ask.

'Mrs Tallow,' he said, 'did you suggest anyone else Mr Brown should talk to?'

She shook her head. 'No, but I said that if he wanted to know about the manor, he'd have to ask Colonel Gornay's son, Ralph. He said he'd already seen him.'

'I know. It was Ralph Gornay who told us about the Tallow family. Is there anything else you can tell us?'

'I told Mr Brown to keep well away from the Tallow farm.'

'Why's that?'

She hesitated. 'My Isaac used to say it was a wicked house, but he'd never tell me why. I think things went on there; things he could never bring himself to tell me about.'

'Any idea what these things were?'

She hesitated, as though what she was about to say was deeply personal and talking about it might cause her pain. 'My son, Terry, was adopted. He passed away three years ago – a heart attack – and my biggest regret is that I never got a chance to tell him the truth about his real mother. Isaac and I weren't blessed with children, so I was glad to take him in, especially as he was family.' She paused. 'I took him in because I wanted to get him away from that farm. Especially after what he said.'

'Who are we talking about?' said Rachel, who was having trouble untangling the family relationships.

There was a long pause before Florrie continued. 'I only wish I'd been able to tell him that his Auntie Edith was really his mother.' She fell silent again, as though she was making a decision. When she eventually spoke, it was almost in a whisper. 'The truth can't hurt anyone now, can it?'

'No, it can't,' said Wesley, wondering what was coming.

'One night in 1944, Bram turned up with the baby, saying that Edith had had an affair and the little one was the result. He wanted it out of the house, he said. I knew Edith was scared of him, and I knew that if I didn't take in the poor little mite, his life would be a misery – or worse. I wouldn't have put it past Bram and his mother to do him harm.'

'Tell me what you know about Edith's affair.'

'I think it was with a soldier she'd met at some dance.' Florrie shook her head. 'You can imagine how Bram re-acted when he found out.'

'Have you any idea what happened to the soldier?'

She shrugged. 'Maybe he was just a ship that passed in the night, or maybe he never came back from the war; I don't know. Edith had another son, by Bram, some years later. His name's Ted. I haven't heard from her for years. Not since Bram died. Perhaps I should have tried harder to keep in touch.'

'Do you know if Ted still lives at the farm?' Wesley re-called the mention of the battered pickup, and Rachel's strong feeling that there'd been someone in when she and Rob had called at the smallholding.

'I don't know. Like I said, we lost touch with that side of the family.'

'What about Edith?'

'She was a bit younger than me, so if she's still alive, she'll be in her late nineties by now. I haven't heard that she's passed away, but then I doubt Ted would bother to let me know. Poor Edith,' she added. 'What a life she must have led.'

'Perhaps someone should check on her,' said Rachel, sounding genuinely concerned.

'Perhaps.' She shuddered. 'They used to say old Dorcas Tallow was a witch, you know.'

'Old Dorcas?'

'My mother-in-law – Isaac and Bram's mother. She used to make all sorts of concoctions in her little outhouse. Not that we were allowed anywhere near it. When I was little, I remember people in the village saying that a farmer had said something to offend her, so she poisoned his sheep.'

'Poisoned?' She had Wesley's full attention now.

'That's right. People were afraid of Dorcas Tallow. And some that said it wasn't only sheep she poisoned – she killed human beings too.'

Pelham Jenks lived in Whenham, a hamlet a mile and a half south of Moor Barton. When he'd retired, he'd sold his flat in Plymouth and bought a bungalow there, regarding the move as a return to his roots. He'd joined the local archaeological society because the subject had always interested him. And when the excavation of the air crash site at Moor Barton was mooted, it had seemed like a sign. He hadn't gone back to the village since his parents had moved away; he suspected he'd been avoiding the place. Until that meeting at the village hall. After that, he'd seen the dig as a chance to discover the truth about his brother at last.

He'd left a message with the boy, Michael, asking his father to get in touch with him. He hadn't yet heard anything, but he didn't intend to give up. He'd seen the people in white overalls digging up the bones, and it was high time he came clean with the police to atone for his failure all those years ago. He needed to give Norman his name back. And he needed to ensure that he had a decent burial with a proper headstone.

Then there was the other thing he wanted to mention to Michael's father; a puzzling matter that had nothing to do with Norman.

He hadn't gone to the dig that day because he had something to do. He might have made a mistake, of course. But there was only one way to find out. And that was to ask.

After their visit to Jay Tallow's great-grandmother, Rachel made a few calls. Eventually she managed to discover that there was no record of an Edith Tallow dying in the area over the past twenty years, or moving into residential care, which meant it was likely that she was still alive inside that dilapidated smallholding. Rachel wanted to check for herself, and Wesley agreed. The idea of a vulnerable elderly person living in that horrible place bothered him too. He also needed to speak to Pelham Jenks. He'd told Michael that he'd remembered something. It might be nothing, but Wesley needed to be sure.

He made a call to the lab. As Jay Tallow's DNA was on file because of his history of petty crime, he asked for a sample to be taken from the male skeleton for comparison. Could the American man buried on the moor have been Edith's lover and the biological father of Florrie's adopted son, Terry? If a match was found, it would solve one mystery and strongly suggest that Bram Tallow had killed his wife's lover. The French woman buried with him, however, remained a puzzle they were no nearer to solving.

As Rachel drove, Wesley made a mental family tree. Old Dorcas Tallow had been suspected of poisoning both people and livestock. Her son, Bram, had married the much younger Edith, who had given birth to a son by her lover in 1944. That baby, Terry, had been adopted by Edith's childless sister-in-law, Florrie. Some years later, Edith had given birth to a son by Bram called Ted, possibly the man who'd been seen driving the pickup. Florrie and her husband, Isaac, had broken off all contact with Edith and Bram Tallow at the smallholding, and later they'd moved away from Moor Barton. Terry had gone on to marry and have a family of his own, and his grandson, Jay, was now helping the police with their enquiries. Now he'd got all that straight in his mind, he felt a little more confident.

Rachel headed straight to the Tallow smallholding. It looked as derelict as she had described it, but the double doors of a tumbledown wooden garage were open and they could see a pickup parked inside the shadowy interior.

When they emerged from their car, they picked their way across a cobbled yard littered with old tyres and scrap metal.

'I think someone's at home,' Rachel whispered.

Wesley glanced up at the first floor and saw a curtain shift a little. 'Maybe we should have obtained a warrant. If they won't answer to the door ...'

'If we think an old woman's life might be in danger, we don't need a warrant.'

Wesley could see the determined look on her face. He'd seen that look before and knew she wouldn't give up until she was sure one way or the other.

There was no answer at the front door, so Rachel led the way to the back. There they saw a light on in the kitchen, a bare bulb shining weakly through the grimy window glass. She marched straight to the door and tried the handle. It yielded, and the door creaked open.

'Hello! Anyone at home,' she called out confidently.

A man appeared in the open doorway. He was six feet tall and overweight, with straggly grey hair. He wore grubby jeans and a faded checked shirt that looked too small for him.

He seemed nervous, jumpy. And the shotgun he was carrying was pointed straight at Wesley's chest.

30

Wesley took a step back and slowly, very slowly, reached into his pocket for his ID. 'Police. I'd put that down if I were you.'

The man didn't move.

'We really are police,' said Rachel reasonably. 'Now do as Detective Inspector Peterson says and put that shotgun down.'

Wesley had a sudden panicked vision of Pam receiving the news of his death; of his distraught and puzzled children; of his parents and sister being informed. He even found himself wondering whether he'd be missed by the dog. It was amazing the things that flashed through your mind when you were faced with imminent death.

The three of them stood in a frozen tableau for what seemed like minutes but was probably only seconds. Then Wesley saw the shotgun barrel lower slowly, and Rachel darted forward to take the weapon before making it safe. Once she had expertly removed the cartridges, he addressed the man, who was now standing with his head bowed.

'You live here?'

'Yeah.'

'What's your name?'

'Ted. Ted Tallow.'

'You've got a relation called Jay?'

'We don't speak to that bit of the family. Don't even know who they are.'

'Did a man called Barry Brown call here? He was an author.'

'No one calls here.'

'You sure about that?' said Rachel.

'Someone came, but I didn't answer the door. After a while he buggered off.'

'Mind if we take a look around?' she said casually, holding tight to the shotgun as she opened a kitchen cupboard.

'Yes. I do.' The man sounded as though he was ready to defend his property even though he was now unarmed. But they had the power of the law behind them.

When Rachel opened the next cupboard, Wesley saw a variety of strange-looking bottles and jars inside. Not the usual things people kept in their kitchens to rustle up a meal.

'What's in those?' he asked.

'Dunno. They've been there years. Nothing to do with me,' Tallow said, suddenly on his guard.

Wesley caught Rachel's eye. Old Dorcas Tallow, this man's grandmother, had been suspected of being a poisoner, so he wanted the contents of the jars analysed as soon as possible.

'Are you sure you didn't speak to Barry Brown? Or maybe you followed him back to the house he was renting in Little Rockington?'

'Prove it.' Ted Tallow pressed his lips together.

'I have to tell you that Barry Brown was found dead last

Monday, so this is a murder enquiry. Now can we take a look around?'

'No!' Tallow shouted as though he'd just been punched.

'Why? Are you hiding something? We can easily get a warrant, but it'd be better all round if you co-operate.'

He seemed to deflate, as though he'd suddenly realised that argument was futile. He'd threatened a couple of police officers with a firearm and admitted that a murder victim had called at his house. There was no way it was going to end there.

Rachel put on crime-scene gloves and began to search the huge kitchen dresser while Wesley kept an eye on Ted Tallow. After a few moments she pulled something out. A rubber mask. Not a royal this time, but a horror mask. Frankenstein's monster. The witness, Linda Pugh, might have been influenced by reports of the jewellery raids and been wrong about the type of mask she saw Barry Brown's visitor wearing on the night of his murder. Also, Ted Tallow was tall, which fitted the description she'd given. And yet Wesley wondered whether Brown would have invited someone wearing a Frankenstein mask into his house.

'Where did you get this?' Rachel asked, holding up the mask.

'Found it.'

'Where?'

'In Neston, the day after Halloween last year. Someone left it lying in the street and I picked it up.'

'Why?'

Tallow shrugged. 'Dunno.'

'Did you go to Little Rockington last Sunday night? Did you call at Barry Brown's cottage?'

'No. And you can't prove I did.'

'Your vehicle would have been caught on camera if you were there.'

'Like I said, prove it.' He sounded confident. Either he was telling the truth or, like many locals, he was used to taking the back lanes, where the surveillance tentacles of the traffic division hadn't yet spread.

When he was told that he was being taken to Tradmouth for questioning, he looked positively relieved, and Wesley wondered why. He took out his phone and called for a patrol car, then asked Rachel to keep an eye on Tallow while he did a spot of exploration.

As he was leaving the kitchen, Tallow bellowed after him. 'Come back! You can't go up there!'

Wesley ignored him.

First he peeped into the old-fashioned parlour next door. It was shrouded in a thick layer of dust, the sort of room once kept only for Sunday best and visitors. Clearly nobody had been in there for quite some time.

There was a narrow, steep staircase covered with a threadbare carpet of indeterminate colour. As Wesley climbed it slowly, he could still hear Tallow protesting downstairs. When he reached the landing, he experienced a growing feeling of dread. The still air smelled stale, and when he pushed open the first door, he saw a room that looked as though it was furnished for a child. A small single bed neatly made with blankets and a quilt stood against the far wall, and model aeroplanes hung from the ceiling. When he opened the wardrobe, he saw well-worn shirts and jeans hanging there, and guessed this was the room Ted had occupied since childhood.

The second door opened on to an inhospitable

bathroom with a stained bath and cracked basin. The lino on the floor was scuffed and the walls were painted a sickly green. In the third room, the curtains were drawn, and Wesley felt for the light switch. When the bulb flickered on, it took him a few moments to realise exactly what he was seeing.

The double bed was neatly made, but there was a shape beneath the blankets. As his eyes travelled towards the headboard, he saw sparse white hair spread out on the pillow. He held his breath and tiptoed softly into the room until he could see the face of the person in the bed. His hand went to his mouth in horror. The mummified corpse had clearly been there some time, lying in the bed as though she was sleeping. He was as sure as he could be that he'd found Edith Tallow.

Ted Tallow was taken away in a patrol car and the forensic team were called in. His DNA and fingerprints would be taken and they'd look for a match with any unidentified samples from Barry Brown's cottage. As he was led to the car, he protested that the old lady had died naturally; he just hadn't been able to bring himself to have her taken away. Rachel looked sceptical, as though she suspected he was concealing something even more sinister than a mummified corpse.

Harvey Pottinger was still abroad, but they now had another suspect. The substances in the kitchen cupboard had been sent off for analysis. If there'd been one poisoner in the family, there could easily be two.

Colin Bowman arrived to examine the corpse. He concluded that the elderly woman had been dead for some time, possibly even as long as a couple of years.

The thought of Ted Tallow living there alone all that time with only the mummified body of his mother for company made Wesley feel queasy. Even if he'd had nothing to do with the murder of Barry Brown, he was guilty of concealing a death and preventing a lawful burial.

When he'd called Gerry to break the news, the DCI had sounded excited. They could use the time till Harvey Pottinger turned up to get all they could out of Ted Tallow. The Tallow family's tangled relationships and a possible link with the skeletons on the moor seemed like promising leads.

But Wesley still couldn't work out how past events in the Tallow family could possibly have led to Barry Brown's death. Ted Tallow had seemed willing enough to shoot a couple of intruders, though, so maybe he'd been happy to poison Brown to guard the secret of the corpse in the upstairs bedroom.

Gerry had something else to say. 'I've had a call from someone called Pelham Jenks. He wants to speak to you urgently. He says he left a message with your Michael, but you haven't got back to him.'

'Michael passed on the message, but I've been busy.'

'That's what I told him. I asked if anyone else could help, but he wants you. What it is to be popular, eh. I asked him what it was about, but he wouldn't tell me.'

'Thanks, Gerry. I'm in Moor Barton now, so I'll nip over and see what it is he wants.'

As soon as Rachel had left with their suspect, he made his way to the dig, wondering why Jenks wanted to speak to him. He hoped it wasn't something uniform could deal with. He was too busy to waste time.

When he arrived, he was greeted by Neil, who seemed

excited about a new discovery. Fragments of the Lysander's engine that the RAF had failed to remove after the crash. Michael was working with the students, but he seemed happily preoccupied, so Wesley didn't want to distract him by saying hello.

'I've asked Annabel to look for records of the flight,' said Neil eagerly. 'She's more used to dealing with medieval documents, but she says some wartime flight logs survived. Although if it was top secret, it might not be easy.'

'I'll keep my fingers crossed then. I'm looking for Pelham Jenks. He wants to speak to me.'

Neil raised his eyebrows. 'Why's that?'

'No idea.'

'Pelham hasn't turned up today, but I've got his address somewhere.'

Wesley followed Neil to the marquee that served as finds tent, shelter and office. Neil delved into a blue ring-binder stained with soil and produced a list of his diggers' contact details. Wesley made a note of the address and took his leave.

It was only a ten-minute drive to the tiny village of Whenham, down lanes that resembled farm tracks. Pelham Jenks lived on the edge of the hamlet, in a small white bungalow with new double glazing and a glass door. The type of unremarkable dwelling in a pretty setting that many people dreamed of when retirement loomed.

Wesley rang the doorbell, and when there was no answer he walked round the side of the house and opened the wooden gate. The garden was small and neat, with well-tamed shrubs and colourful bedding plants. He kept to the path until he reached a pair of double-glazed French doors. Inside he could see a predominantly beige sitting

239

room with a three-piece suite and a large flat-screen TV. The only thing out of place was the body lying in front of the coffee table. It was too late to find out what Pelham Jenks had wanted to tell him.

Diary of Flight Officer John Carmody

3 August 1943

A few nights ago, one of our Lysanders was shot down over France and my friend Jonty bought it. The worst part of it was that the plane that shot him down was one of ours; Jonty's black camouflaged kite was mistaken for the enemy. Sometimes secrecy works against us. He was a good pilot and he had one of our most experienced agents on board, so it was a double tragedy. Our CO said it was a terrible waste. But that's war and we have to get on with it. That's what Jonty would have wanted.

There's another dance this Saturday and somebody said that Marie might be there. Another girl I met the other day said Marie had gone away to start her training for something, but she wasn't sure what. I knew that if this was SOE work, she was sure to be assigned a mission soon. So many agents have been killed or captured that new blood's always needed. I worry that Marie's inexperience will put her in danger if the enemy pulls her in for questioning. But I suppose we all have to do our bit.

It's hard to imagine Marie carrying out sabotage missions or killing someone with her bare hands, but that's what she's being trained to do. She seems so young and innocent, but I hope that will count in her favour and make her a good spy. Nobody would ever suspect a pretty young girl who enjoys dancing and having fun. At least that's what I hope and pray.

31

It took another forty minutes for the CSIs and Colin Bowman to find their way to Whenham. But before they arrived, a couple of patrol cars turned up, one carrying Gerry, and the bungalow was sealed off as a crime scene.

'Any idea what he wanted to talk to you about?' Gerry asked as they stood in the garden watching the crime-scene tent being erected by the back door.

Wesley thought for a moment. 'I have a suspicion that he might have a connection with the child Norman.'

'You suspect but you're not sure?'

'No, I'm not. But he was seen hanging round near the grave and there were signs that someone had been digging there. Maybe he either knew or suspected the child's remains were there.'

Gerry sighed. 'This is all we need, another unexplained death. Any evidence of how he died?'

'There's no sign of a struggle; no obvious gunshot or stab wounds and no apparent head injury. I couldn't see any sign of strangulation either. But there is a patch of vomit, just like at the scene of Barry Brown's murder. We'll have to wait for Colin's verdict.'

'So it could be natural causes? We might have called the circus out for nothing?' Gerry sounded hopeful.

'With everything that's been going on, I don't think we had a choice,' Wesley answered. He knew Gerry could be right. On the other hand, the fact that Jenks had asked to speak to a policeman and then died suddenly before he had the chance was suspicious in itself. Perhaps someone had wanted to silence him, which meant they needed to know where all their potential suspects had been at the relevant time.

When the CSIs arrived, they made straight for the sitting room, where Pelham Jenks lay, the centre of attention. Soon afterwards, Colin Bowman arrived with a cheerful greeting to the team, who stood aside to let him do his job.

Wesley and Gerry watched while he examined the corpse, and they saw him frown.

'Anybody found a cup or a glass?' was his first question.

Without a word, Wesley walked through to the kitchen, careful to use the CSIs' metal stepping plates. Sure enough, there were two glasses on the draining board.

'There are two glasses in the kitchen, recently washed up, I'd say.'

Gerry caught on fast. 'Just like in Barry Brown's cottage. You don't think . . . ?' He didn't bother finishing his sentence.

'I need to carry out tests before I commit myself,' said Colin. 'I can fit in the post-mortem first thing tomorrow.'

Once photographs were taken and the scene filmed, the body was removed to the waiting undertakers' van.

Gerry checked the time. 'We should get back, Wes.'

'OK, but I'd like to take a quick look round first. Jenks

wanted to speak to me and there might be something here that'll tell us why.'

'Tell you what, I'll help you look. But if we don't come across anything obvious, we'll leave it to the others.'

Wesley might have known Gerry wouldn't be able to resist the challenge.

They started in the larger of the bungalow's two bedrooms, and Wesley could hardly believe their luck. There inside the bedside cupboard was a handwritten sheet. It looked like an aide-memoire, a reminder of the facts he'd wished to convey to Wesley during the meeting he'd requested. Gerry grabbed it with gloved hands. He took his glasses from his pocket and put them on before starting to read.

'It's headed "Meeting with Inspector Peterson. Points to raise."'

Wesley raised his eyebrows. 'Very organised. Go on.'

Gerry cleared his throat. '"Point one. At the age of six, I followed my brother, Norman, even though I wasn't supposed to leave the house and he said I was a nuisance. He told me to go home, but I wanted to see where he was going. I saw my brother stealing apples from the manor orchard, then I heard shouting and a loud noise I now know to be a shot. I hid behind the orchard wall. I was terrified of being seen, but when I finally plucked up the courage to peep over the wall, I saw the man put Norman into the gardener's shed."'

Gerry looked at Wesley, who nodded. So far this fitted perfectly with Ralph Gornay's account of his father's confession.

'"Point two",' Gerry continued. '"I didn't tell my mother what had happened because she wouldn't have believed

245

me. Instead I crept out of the house the following night and went back to the manor. When I got there, I saw Colonel Gornay carrying something and I followed at a distance. He had a spade and I watched him digging by the rock they call the Sheep, but then I got frightened and ran back home. I never told anybody about it, not even when everyone was out looking for Norman. People said he'd fallen down a mine shaft or drowned in a bog, and in the end I believed that myself. I convinced myself that what I'd seen had just been a bad dream. My mother cleaned at the Manor and I knew she'd say that important people like Colonel Gornay didn't go round shooting children even if they were stealing apples. I knew I must have got it wrong."' He looked up from the sheet of paper. 'Can you believe that, Wes?'

'I think I can. If the boy was used to doing whatever grown-ups told him, he might have convinced himself that he'd imagined it all. Colonel Gornay must have been held in high esteem in the village in the 1950s. A six-year-old boy wouldn't have been believed if he came out and accused him.'

'I take your point. But you'd think he would have said something.' Gerry returned to Pelham Jenks's account. '"Point three. A few months afterwards, my parents moved to Plymouth and Norman's name was never mentioned again; it was as though my brother had never existed. I can only think that the memories were too painful and they wanted to start a new life away from Moor Barton. But looking back, they seemed to have a sudden influx of money, enough to buy a nice house, and with hindsight, I wonder now whether Colonel Gornay paid them off. Point four. Dog?"'

'Dog? What does that mean?'

'Don't ask me, Wes.' Gerry cleared his throat again and carried on.

'"When I grew up, I followed a career in local government, but I never married because I was busy caring for my parents, who had multiple health issues. Once they'd both passed away, I decided to retire, and three years ago I returned to Dartmoor, although I always avoided Moor Barton because I associated it with bad things. Even so, it was always at the back of my mind that one day I'd try to find out the truth about what happened to my big brother, and when I learned that my archaeology society were going to take part in a dig there, I knew I'd been given the chance to find the answer to the question that had festered at the back of my mind for decades. Did I really see what I thought I saw, or had I made a mistake?"'

'So he used Neil's dig as an opportunity to discover the truth once and for all,' said Wesley. 'It all makes sense now. But who would want to kill him? Not Ralph Gornay, to protect his late father's memory, because he was quite open with us about what happened. Is there any more?'

'Almost finished,' said Gerry, adjusting his reading glasses again. '"It came as an unexpected shock when I finally discovered that what I thought I'd witnessed all those years ago was true. In a way, I hoped I'd been mistaken. Then there was the matter of the dog; the suspicion that began to develop after my brother's bones were unearthed."'

'The dog again. Must be important.'

Gerry continued. '"That's why I really need to speak to somebody. Knowing that black detective is a friend of Dr Watson and father to the young man who's helping the students at the dig – the boy is a credit to his father, by the way – I thought he would be the best person with whom to share my concerns. I might be wrong, of course, but if I'm not, I fear that I might have uncovered something very sinister purely by accident. I know the detective will probably tell me I'm mistaken, but I do need advice. It isn't something I can ignore."'

Gerry grinned. 'I like the bit about your Michael being a credit to you. You'll have to tell Pam.'

Wesley smiled. 'Very nice, but what's this sinister thing he uncovered?'

'The only thing I can think of is that it concerns those other two skeletons.'

'If our suspicions are correct, they were probably buried during the war. Pelham wasn't even born then, and Norman wasn't shot until the late 1950s.' Wesley glanced at the place where Pelham Jenks's body had lain. 'And we can't ask him now, because he's dead.'

Gerry checked the time. 'There's nothing more we can do here. Let's get back to Tradmouth and speak to Ted Tallow.'

'Earlier I asked someone to get a DNA sample from the male skeleton to compare with Jay Tallow's. I have a feeling he could be Edith's wartime lover, which makes him Jay's biological great-grandfather.' He could see Gerry looking confused. 'Keep up, Gerry. Edith's brute of a husband caught them together and killed him.'

'But what about the French woman?'

'Now that is a mystery. It's starting to look as though George Melling's father was right. His father's French cousin, Marie, hitched a ride on John Carmody's Lysander after all. But how she ended up buried on the moor with an American soldier, I've no idea.'

*

248

It was coming up to 4.30 when Wesley drove back to Moor Barton to ask Michael if he wanted a lift home. The boy seemed reluctant at first, even though there was no sign of Harriet, but eventually he gathered his things and climbed into the back seat of the car. Neither Wesley nor Gerry mentioned the death of Pelham Jenks during the journey. Michael was talking eagerly about what he'd found that day and they didn't want to dampen his spirits.

After dropping his son off at home, Wesley drove on to the station. With all the new developments, there was a lot to do.

Ted Tallow was brought to the interview room. He smelled of sweat, and Wesley wished the room had better ventilation. But he knew from experience that his nostrils would soon get used to the pungent odour; after a while, he wouldn't even notice it. He'd asked Rachel to conduct the interview with him, suspecting that Tallow would need careful handling.

Ted was making do with the duty solicitor, a young woman with cropped blonde hair, a grey suit and a belligerent manner, as though she considered that her first duty was to defend the suspect from police brutality. After switching on the recording machine, Wesley gave her an unthreatening smile, which wasn't returned.

'Mr Tallow,' he began. 'You told us that Barry Brown called at your property but you didn't let him in. Is this true?'

Tallow nodded. Wesley asked him to confirm it for the tape.

'Are you sure he didn't enter your home? Because people leave DNA traces wherever they go. We can carry out tests.'

The colour drained from Tallow's face, but the solicitor

leaned over and whispered something in his ear. Then she looked Wesley in the eye. 'I understand you searched this man's house without a warrant.'

It was Rachel who answered. 'Has your client told you that he threatened two police officers with a shotgun? Besides that, we had good reason to suspect that he was involved in the murder of a man in Little Rockington. We found substances on the premises that might be connected to that death. We also found the body of a woman upstairs.'

The solicitor gave Tallow a look of distaste.

Wesley carried on. 'Did Mr Brown enter your house?'

Ted bowed his head, as though he was now resigned to telling the truth. 'The back door was open and he just walked in. Said he wanted to speak to anyone who might have been around when that plane crashed on the moor during the war. He asked if my mother was still alive. He said he'd like to speak to her. I told him she was dead.'

'But you neglected to tell him that her body was upstairs,' said Rachel.

Tallow ignored her. 'Then he asked me if she'd talked to me about the crash. I said I didn't know nothing and told him to go.'

'Did he tell you where he was staying?'

Tallow's eyes flickered from side to side, as though he was looking for a way out. 'He mentioned it, yeah. Wrote his number on the back of a card and said to get in touch if I remembered anything.'

'So you knew he was staying in Little Rockington?'

He suddenly rose to his feet. 'I don't feel well. I want to go home.' He swayed, and the solicitor put out her hand to steady him. Then his knees seemed to give way, and he sank to the floor.

'He needs medical attention,' she barked as Wesley pressed the alarm strip that would bring help running.

Twenty-five minutes later, Ted Tallow was being loaded into an ambulance.

'Think he faked all that so he wouldn't have to talk about Barry Brown's murder?' said Rachel as she stood, arms folded, at the CID office window watching the ambulance depart.

'Rachel Tracey, I never thought you could be so cynical,' said Wesley. The thought had occurred to him, but he hadn't liked to put it into words.

'I was born cynical, Wesley. You're sometimes too trusting for your own good.'

Their eyes met, and they both smiled.

'Why don't you get off home early, Rach? There's nothing more we can do at the moment. We can make an early start in the morning.'

Rachel hesitated, before hurrying to her desk to pick up her bag. Back home she'd be faced with putting young Freddie to bed then helping with whatever needed doing on the farm. No wonder she looked tired.

But before she could leave, Trish came rushing up to Wesley as though she had news of the important kind.

'Sir, a witness has come forward. He says he saw someone visiting Barry Brown's cottage at nine-thirty on Sunday night.'

The witness was a lad called Darren Williams, who'd been delivering pizzas to a holiday rental in Little Rockington on the night of the murder.

Wesley decided to pay him a visit. He could have delegated the task, but it was a sunny evening and he felt like escaping the confines of the office. Rachel insisted on going with him, and as they drove to Morbay, she confessed that she too needed a change of scene.

The young man's flat was on the ground floor of a dilapidated 1960s block in the most downmarket part of the Morbay conurbation. As they were buzzed into the building, they saw a moped parked under the concrete staircase in the communal area. When they entered the flat itself, the first thing Darren did was to apologise for the state of the place and explain that he was renting the place with three others, who weren't too fussy about housekeeping. Wesley guessed that the landlord probably wasn't aware that so many were sharing the cramped accommodation, but there was no way he'd betray the tenants' little secret. In fact he felt rather sorry for them.

There was mould around the cheap plastic windows and the floor was littered with empty pizza boxes and beer cans. Darren made a half-hearted effort to clear up as they perched on the edge of a sofa camouflaged by a filthy throw. The lad looked nervous.

'Thanks for coming forward,' Wesley began, trying to put him at his ease.

'I heard about the murder, but I've only just realised I was there that night.'

'That's OK,' said Rachel. 'Can you tell us what you saw?'

'I delivered some pizzas to a family in a holiday cottage near the village green. Two Margheritas and three meat feasts. When I started heading back to where I'd parked the moped, I saw someone at the door of one of the other cottages. It wasn't quite dark and I got a good look at him. I couldn't believe it.'

Wesley caught Rachel's eye. 'Couldn't believe what?'

'It was him off the telly. My mum loves him. Never misses one of his shows.'

'Who are we talking about?' Wesley thought he could guess, but he wanted to hear Darren saying it.

'Harvey Pottinger. I had to do a double-take. I mean, you don't expect to see someone off the telly in real life, do you?' He hesitated. 'But it couldn't have been him, could it?'

'But you thought it was?'

'If it wasn't him it was his double. I stopped for a few moments to take a good look.'

'If we send someone round to take you to Little Rockington, do you think you can identify the house for us?'

'I don't need to. I saw a picture of the murder house on my phone. It was the same place that I saw Harvey Pottinger going into at around half nine last Sunday night.'

'Are you willing to make a statement to that effect?' Rachel asked.

Darren Williams nodded.

When Wesley returned to the CID office, he met Trish at the door and told her about Darren Williams' statement.

'Harvey Pottinger,' she said, shaking her head. 'Who would have thought it. My gran loves him. She'll be devastated.'

When Gerry received the news, he was jubilant. 'I've just heard from Pottinger's production company. His film-ing finished last night and he's back in Blighty. I'll send someone over to Millicombe, and if he's home, we'll bring him in.'

The DCI seemed anxious to confront Pottinger with

their new evidence. As far as they could tell, Darren Williams was a reliable witness who had no reason to lie. But Wesley had some observations to make.

'Williams said he saw Pottinger at Brown's front door at nine-thirty. But Linda Pugh, the neighbour, said she saw someone there between nine-thirty and ten. And she thought the person she saw was wearing a mask of some kind. There was no suggestion that the person Williams saw was wearing a mask. He was absolutely sure he recognised Harvey Pottinger from the TV.'

Gerry considered this for a moment. 'Do they make Harvey Pottinger masks, I wonder?'

Wesley took out his phone, and when he'd finished his search, he shook his head. 'Well – you can't buy them online.'

'That doesn't mean they don't exist somewhere.'

'Ms Pugh also said the person she saw was tall. Harvey Pottinger is only five foot eight.'

'But don't forget it was dusk, and she was some distance away.'

Wesley had been thinking the same himself. It was easy to make mistakes when the light wasn't good.

Half an hour later, the call came in. They'd picked up Harvey Pottinger. And he wanted to make a confession.

32

Wesley called Pam to tell her there'd been a development in the case and he was going to be late again. It was 7.30 already, but she sounded remarkably sanguine about it and told him she was busy with preparations for Mark and Maritia's church fete, so could he could take Sherlock for his evening walk when he got back. Wesley had forgotten all about the summer fete, and that Pam had agreed to make notices for the stalls. As a primary school teacher, she was adept at that sort of thing, and Maritia had always believed in using everyone's talents to the full. He readily agreed to Sherlock's walk. A stroll with the dog on a pleasant summer evening would provide a welcome distraction from the case.

Rachel had ignored Wesley's earlier instruction to go home and get some rest. But when he made a solemn promise to call her later and bring her up to date with what was happening, she reluctantly left. He knew how she felt. They had a name for it these days. Fear of missing out.

When Harvey Pottinger entered the interview room, it was clear that the strain of his various filming commitments had taken its toll. Either that or the fear of being found out. His face, once smooth and tanned, had acquired a grey pallor. Any expensive moisturising regime he'd been following had been neglected over the past few days, and deepening lines were visible around his eyes and mouth. His eyes looked bloodshot, as though he hadn't slept. Wesley guessed this wasn't the image he'd wish to present to his legions of fans.

Gerry was keen to conduct the interview himself. Wesley wasn't sure whether this was due to the suspect's celebrity status or the fact that he had the best motive for Barry Brown's murder they'd come across so far.

Pottinger's solicitor, senior partner in a well-established Exeter law firm, was wearing an expensive suit. Not for Pottinger the duty solicitor – he could pay for the best available legal representation, which meant they'd have to mind their Ps and Qs and Gerry would need to resist the temptation to cut corners. Under the solicitor's sharp gaze, Wesley felt rather like a schoolboy being scrutinised by a strict headmaster.

'My client wishes to make a statement,' the solicitor began. Harvey Pottinger sat perfectly still, gazing down at the stained surface of the table as the man he'd appointed as his guard dog read from a sheet of typewritten paper.

'"I have spent the past couple of days away filming, as you well know. And I firmly deny having anything to do with the tragic death of Barry Brown. I admit now that I called at his address on the night of his death, but I assure you that Mr Brown was alive and well when I left. I know nothing about his murder."'

'Why did you lie to us, Mr Pottinger?'

'Because I didn't want to be pulled into a murder investigation. A man in my position can't afford publicity like that, and besides, I had two filming trips scheduled. Filming is an expensive business and TV companies can't afford any delay.' Pottinger gave Wesley an ingratiating smile. 'I'm sure you understand, Inspector. Besides, I didn't kill Barry and I didn't see anything suspicious, so I knew I couldn't be of any assistance to you.'

'We were told you wanted to make a confession,' said Gerry.

'That was it.' The solicitor sat back, looking smug.

But Wesley wasn't going to fall for it. 'We believe Mr Brown uncovered a scandal you were anxious to keep from the media. Perhaps anxious enough to kill him to conceal it.' He smiled politely at the lawyer, who for the first time looked perplexed. He glanced quizzically at Pottinger, who was now looking uncomfortable.

'Mr Pottinger, tell us about your meeting with Barry Brown that night.' Now the suspect was rattled, Wesley decided he might as well take advantage of the situation.

'I found out where he was staying, so I called on him to ask why he'd let me down about my autobiography. It was embarrassing, because I'd already announced it on TV and my fans had started to ask when it was due to be published. The process seemed to be going well until about six weeks ago, when Barry suddenly announced that he'd told his agent he wanted to delay signing our contract. He said he needed time to pursue another project, and it would be better if we put the autobiography on hold. As you can imagine, I was very annoyed. He was going to be paid good money, and it would take some time to find anyone as experienced.

'When I went to see him on Sunday night, I pointed out that I wasn't used to being treated like that. That was when he came out with the real reason. He said he'd found out that I was at Lenny Brice's party. I'd been seen taking drugs with a girl who'd died there.'

'Suzie Dix?'

He nodded, head bowed like a penitent. 'He said his conscience and his professional reputation wouldn't let him write a book that covered up what went on.'

'Did he ask for money to keep quiet about it?'

Pottinger shook his head. 'Nothing like that. I tried to set the record straight, of course. I told him I'd had nothing to do with Suzie's death and I'd only attended the party for a short while and left when things got a bit . . . out of control.'

'You made your excuses and left,' said Gerry, a sceptical look in his eye. 'What was Brown's reaction?'

'You don't have to answer that,' the solicitor chipped in.

But Pottinger ignored him. 'He acted all holier than thou. He said that wasn't what he'd heard and accused me of lying to protect my reputation. I told him he'd let me down badly, then I left. I admit I was angry with him, but I never touched him, I swear.'

'You didn't have a drink with him? Whisky, perhaps?'

'No. He never offered me anything. I think he was anxious to get rid of me. I felt I needed a drink after the meeting, so I went to a pub on the road to Morbay.'

'Which one?'

'The Windmill. I didn't want to be recognised, so I sat outside in the beer garden, which gave me an excuse to wear dark glasses.'

'We'll check.'

'Please do. Look, like I said, Barry was alive and well when I left him.'

'We only have your word for that. Are you sure you didn't have a drink with him?'

'My client's made his statement,' the solicitor said firmly. 'Unless you have any actual proof of his involvement in Mr Brown's death, I ask that he be released at once.'

'I'm telling the truth,' said Pottinger, suddenly humble. 'One thing I do remember about that night is that when I was leaving Barry's cottage, I saw someone hanging about.'

'Can you describe this person?'

'No. It was almost dark, and he was standing in the shadows beside one of the trees surrounding the village green. But I'd seen him get out of a vehicle, which was parked up nearby. An estate car, I think. Dark-coloured. Might have been a Volvo.'

'You say he was hanging about?'

Pottinger smiled modestly. 'I did wonder whether he'd recognised me and wanted an autograph. He certainly seemed to be looking in my direction. I'm used to that sort of thing, of course.'

'It was a man?'

'Actually, it was hard to tell. It was getting dark, and I only caught a glimpse. I just saw a figure and assumed . . .'

'Was he tall? Short? Old? Young? What was he wearing?'

'I think he was average height, dressed all in black with a hood up, even though it wasn't raining. I was in a hurry to get to my car, so I wasn't taking much notice. To be honest, Barry's mention of Lenny's party had come as a shock. And the last thing I wanted was to be obliged to be charming to a fan.'

'I have the same problem,' Gerry muttered under his breath.

'No need to be facetious,' the solicitor said haughtily. 'Are you going to let my client go?'

Gerry breathed deeply as his hand hovered over the

recording machine. 'For the time being. Providing he stays at his Millicombe address and makes himself available if we need to speak to him again.' He looked at Pottinger. 'Don't suppose you got the number of this estate car you saw?'

Pottinger shook his head. 'No, but I noticed that one of its rear lights was damaged.'

There was a look of relief on Pottinger's face as he followed his solicitor out of the room. Wesley and Gerry hung back.

'What do you think, Wes?'

'We need to talk to the residents again – see if any of them own a dark estate car with a damaged rear light, or whether any of them had a visitor that night who owns a car of that description. Pity there's no CCTV round there.'

'We only have Pottinger's word for it that Brown was alive when he left that cottage. And he could easily be making up the stranger with the estate car.' Gerry paused and looked at Wesley as though he expected him to have the answers to all the world's problems. 'Do you believe him?'

But Wesley couldn't give him the certainty he craved. 'Sorry, Gerry, I don't know. Maybe he's making up the bit about Brown taking the moral high ground. Maybe Brown attempted to blackmail him with what he'd found out.'

'We've absolutely no evidence Brown was a blackmailer.'

'That's true. Pottinger admits he was angry with him for letting him down. I reckon he still has to be at the top of our suspect list.'

'You're right, Wes. But we need evidence.'

It was time to go home at last. Gerry was looking forward to an evening in front of the telly with Alison, and Wesley knew that walking the dog would give him a chance to turn the case over in his mind.

The two men were about to leave the half-empty CID office when the phone on Wesley's desk rang. It was the front desk. Mr Pottinger had returned to the station and wanted to speak to them urgently.

The solicitor seemed subdued as they took their seats in the interview room again. Pottinger had decided to make another statement – a full one this time.

'I've just taken a call from Lenny Brice,' he began. 'Someone's been to the police and told them they saw me at his party the night a young woman died of a drugs overdose.'

Wesley caught Gerry's eye, wondering whether Tiffany had finally summoned the courage to tell the police what she knew.

'Lenny said a big scandal's about to break and there's no way he can stop it.' He took a deep, shuddering breath. 'He told me I'd better come clean about the whole thing.'

'It's not really our case,' said Gerry. 'But we can pass on your statement to Oxford.'

'I've explained to my client that he doesn't have to say anything.' The solicitor sounded disappointed that Pottinger intended to ignore his advice.

'Honesty always goes down well with juries and judges,' said Wesley.

'I don't think I've actually done anything illegal,' Pottinger said. 'The cocaine was for personal consumption, after all. I thought that if I co-operated with the police, then maybe my name could be kept out of it if no charges were brought.'

Wesley suspected that the motive for his sudden fit of openness was an attempt at damage limitation. 'Very wise.

But I'm afraid I can't guarantee that your name won't be leaked at some point if the tabloids start sniffing around.'

'I suppose that's a risk I'll have to take.'

Pottinger began his confession, his voice fading to a whisper from time to time so that Wesley had to ask him to speak up for the recording.

'I was at Lenny Brice's party on the night Suzie Dix died. I'd been with Suzie and we'd both been taking drugs and drinking heavily. She seemed to fall asleep and I couldn't wake her. Her breathing didn't seem right, but Lenny said to leave her and she'd soon come round . . . only she never did. I said that maybe we should call the emergency services, but he said not to bother.'

Wesley caught Gerry's eye. It was obvious that Pottinger was anxious to shift the blame.

'Anyway, an hour later someone felt for a pulse and found she was dead. That's when the cover-up began. Reputations and livelihoods were at stake, you see. But even if we'd told the truth at the time, it wouldn't have brought Suzie back,' he added piously.

'So Barry Brown knew the whole sorry story?' said Gerry.

'He never said how he found out. Look, I swear to God I didn't touch him. That's the truth.'

'Another question,' said Wesley. 'Have you ever met a man called Pelham Jenks?'

Pottinger frowned. 'I meet a lot of people in the course of my work, but I don't remember that name. And I think I would, don't you?'

'Have you ever been to a village on Dartmoor called Moor Barton?'

'No.'

'Were you at a village called Whenham earlier today?'

262

'You know where I was. I only got back from the south of France at lunchtime. You can check.'

'You didn't drive up to Dartmoor as soon as you got back?'

'Certainly not. You can check my phone's location.'

'You could have left it at your house,' Gerry pointed out, earning himself a dirty look from the solicitor. 'Ever had anything to do with poison? Cyanide?'

Pottinger looked genuinely puzzled. 'No. Of course not.'

'My client's made a statement and co-operated fully,' said the solicitor. 'I request that you release him. He's happy to attend the station again whenever you wish.' The man was beginning to sound as though events were spiralling out of his control. Wesley suspected this was a new experience for him.

'Very well, we'll release him for now, but we'll probably need to speak to him again,' said Gerry.

The solicitor looked as though he was about to say something, but then thought better of it. His client had already admitted to having quarrelled with Barry Brown on the night of his murder. All Pottinger's former cockiness had vanished, and he looked every inch the penitent sinner.

When Wesley arrived home, he was greeted by Sherlock, wagging his tail in anticipation of his walk. Michael followed the dog out into the hall.

'Someone said there's been another murder, Dad. Is it true?'

Wesley knew that his son's first encounter with unnatural death would come as a shock, so he told him what had happened as gently as he could. He could see that Michael was torn between horror and excitement.

'You mean someone murdered him? Why?'

'That's what I'm going to find out.' Wesley put his arm around his son's shoulder and led him into the living room, where Pam was busy cutting out triangles of colourful wallpaper. When he asked her what she was doing, she replied that she was making bunting for the fete. 'Maritia says it's all hands to the pump,' she said with a roll of her eyes. Wesley understood. His sister was a hard woman to say no to. In some ways he felt he'd lived in his brilliant sibling's shadow during his formative years.

'Let's take Sherlock for his walk,' he said to Michael, deciding that the boy needed a distraction. He would share his news with Pam later.

That night he found himself lying awake in bed as he went over all the possibilities in his mind. Next to him, Pam slept deeply. He'd always been envious of her ability to switch off from whatever had happened during the day.

Gerry seemed convinced that Harvey Pottinger was their man, but Wesley wasn't so sure. He certainly had a motive for silencing Barry Brown. But Wesley couldn't see poison as Pottinger's weapon of choice, especially if it turned out that Pelham Jenks had been poisoned with the same substance.

The following morning, he got out of bed at six-thirty, creeping around the bedroom to avoid disturbing Pam, who was making the most of the school holidays by getting up later than normal. She opened her eyes, checked the time and grunted before rolling over and going back to sleep.

Once downstairs, he drank two cups of strong coffee to wake himself up and set off for work before the rest of the family had emerged from their rooms. As he walked down the hill, the sun came out, but just as he was enjoying the view over the town rooftops and the glistening river, his phone rang. It was the station to say that the DNA results had come through. Jay Tallow was related to the unknown American buried on the moor. A familial match that suggested the soldier was his great-grandfather.

There was something else too. The buttons found in the grave had been positively identified as belonging to an American military uniform from World War II, so enquiries were being made to find out whether any US soldiers posted nearby had gone AWOL during the war. It might have been assumed that he'd deserted, so there was sure to be a record of it somewhere. But how he'd ended up in the same grave as the French woman still remained a mystery.

33

When he arrived at the station, Wesley made straight for Gerry's office to discuss the DNA results.

They now had a clearer picture of what had happened. Edith had become pregnant by her American lover and the baby had been taken in by her childless sister-in-law, Florrie. They agreed that it was likely that the American had been shot by Edith's husband; the age-old story of the jealous husband killing his wife's lover. In France, such a crime of passion would traditionally have earned lenient treatment. But in this case it seemed that the lover hadn't been the only one to die. The French woman had been shot in the back, suggesting that she'd been running away, which raised a question: if she was Marie Leon, as they strongly suspected, who had shot *her*? Perhaps there had been enemy agents at large on Dartmoor that fateful night, although this was a possibility nobody had mentioned. Wesley was determined to find out the truth if at all possible.

Gerry pointed out that, intriguing as the mystery was, the deaths had occurred over eighty years ago, so there was no chance of bringing anyone to justice now. Edith had lived with her secret until her death and Wesley couldn't help wondering how the murder of her lover and having to give up her firstborn child had affected her life. But at that moment there were more urgent matters to attend to.

Pelham Jenks's post-mortem was scheduled for 9.30, so they walked to the mortuary along the embankment. It promised to be a fine day again, with a warm, gentle breeze, and the yachts were out in force on the river. Gerry cast longing glances at the water, and Wesley knew he was yearning to be out on the *Rosie May* in such perfect sailing weather.

But it was not to be. Instead they found themselves in Colin's mortuary, where two covered bodies lay on steel tables.

'I'll start with the old lady,' said Colin through the microphone.

When the sheet was removed, it revealed a tiny, desiccated body that reminded Wesley of an Egyptian mummy. Colin worked gently and efficiently before delivering his verdict.

'I can't see anything suspicious about this one. I think she probably died of simple old age. But I'll send samples to toxicology just in case.'

The body of Pelham Jenks proved more challenging. Jenks lay pale and thin on the table, receiving the attention Wesley suspected he'd never had in life. He'd spent his entire existence nursing the secret of what he'd witnessed as a child. He'd cared for his parents; never married; never had children of his own. As Wesley watched Colin cut into his flesh, he couldn't help feeling sad for the man.

Colin kept up a commentary as he worked, and once he'd finished, he gave his verdict.

'There are definite similarities to that other body you

brought me – the chap from Little Rockington – and tests showed that was cyanide poisoning. I can detect a smell of bitter almonds in the stomach contents too, so if I were a betting man, I'd lay odds that the tox results, when they come back, will say the same.'

'Thanks, Colin,' said Gerry, looking at his watch.

'Have you gentlemen got time for a cup of tea? There are some rather decent new biscuits you might like to try.'

Wesley could see Gerry wavering, torn between pleasure and duty. Eventually the latter won. 'Sorry, Colin, we've got a lot on. Let us have those tox results as soon as you get them, won't you?'

'Have I ever let you down, Gerry? At least you can release the old woman's body for burial. I haven't found anything to contradict the version of events you've been given.'

'And all that time her son was living in the same house as her corpse.'

Colin shook his head sadly. 'Some people can't let go, I suppose.'

Wesley hadn't thought of it like that before. He'd assumed Ted Tallow hadn't reported the death because he wanted to avoid contact with the authorities. But he and Edith must have been close. Perhaps Colin was right and he just couldn't bear to be alone.

As they left the mortuary, Gerry took a call. When he'd finished talking, he turned to Wesley.

'Ted Tallow's recovered from his funny turn. He's been checked over by the doctor and is now enjoying the custody sergeant's lavish hospitality in one of our well-appointed luxury cells. Let's have a word, eh. We can let him know he can bury his mum at last.'

Wesley nodded. He was sure Ted knew more than he'd

admitted. He'd told them that Barry Brown had called at the Tallow farm, and they needed to know more about the encounter.

Half an hour later, the two detectives were sitting opposite Tallow and the duty solicitor in the interview room. Wesley didn't want a repetition of the suspect's collapse the previous day, so he asked him if he felt up to talking. To his relief, Tallow said he was feeling much better, and Wesley went on to tell him that he had the go-ahead to arrange his mother's funeral.

'You know you should have done it as soon as she passed away,' said Gerry.

Tallow bowed his head, avoiding looking the detectives in the eye. 'I didn't want anyone in the house poking around ... and she looked so peaceful. I just shut the bedroom door and—'

'OK. Let's talk about Barry Brown,' said Wesley. In his opinion there were more urgent matters than failing to report a death, and they were wasting valuable time. 'Can you tell us what you discussed?'

'I told you before. He'd heard about a mystery in Moor Barton. Something to do with the plane that came down in the war and some woman who might have been on it. I told him that plane crash was a very long time ago so it couldn't have anything to do with me.'

'Did he say who'd told him about this mystery?'

'A man had asked him to write a book about some relation who went missing during the war.'

'Did he mention Harvey Pottinger?'

'Who?' Wesley hadn't noticed a TV in his house, so maybe he was one of the few people in the country who didn't know who Pottinger was.

'He's a well-known TV personality.'

'Don't know nothing about that. And I don't think he mentioned the name.'

'Did Mr Brown say anything else?'

Tallow shook his head.

'Those potions found in your kitchen. When did you last use them?'

'I've never used them. They belonged to my grandma, Dorcas. They said she was a witch.'

'Did your mother, Edith, ever use them?'

'She never touched them. Said they were the work of the Devil.'

The door opened and Ellie walked in with a note for Gerry. He paused the recording while he read it. Then he started the machine again and looked Ted Tallow in the eye.

'We've sent the bottles in your kitchen cupboard for analysis. Any idea what we'll find in them?'

Tallow shook his head vigorously. 'I've never touched them. I was never allowed to. Everyone in the village used to come to old Dorcas for cures. She made the stuff in one of the outhouses but no one was ever allowed in there. Everyone was scared of her, but they still came when there was something up with them or their livestock.'

'Cyanide was used to kill Barry Brown and we suspect it was used to poison a second victim too. If we find that any of those bottles contain cyanide . . . '

Tallow's eyes widened with fear. 'Old Dorcas made her own potions. I don't know what was in them.'

'Ever heard of a man called Pelham Jenks?'

A flicker of recognition appeared in his eyes. 'There was a family called Jenks in the village once. They had a kid who was a bit older than me. He disappeared back in the

1950s and they moved away. But that was a long time ago. I never really knew them.'

'The boy who went missing was called Norman Jenks. Did you ever play with him?'

'No. We kept ourselves to ourselves. My mum liked it that way.'

'Norman was found buried up near the crash site, not far from the body of an American soldier and an unknown woman. They'd both been shot.' Wesley paused. 'Tests have proved that the soldier was the biological great-grandfather of Jay Tallow. I think Jay's a relative of yours. Your half great uncle to be exact.'

'We never had anything to do with that bit of the family. My father wouldn't let us.'

Wesley knew he was about to drop a bombshell. He looked at Gerry, who gave him a small nod. Best to get it over with.

'Would it surprise you to learn that your mother, Edith, was Jay's great-grandmother? During the war, a decade before you were born, your mother gave birth to a baby; a boy who was your half-brother.'

The puzzled look on Ted's face told Wesley this was something he hadn't been aware of. The family secret that had never been revealed. Until now.

'The baby's father was the soldier we found buried on the moor. He was shot. Did your father own a revolver?'

All of a sudden Ted Tallow's eyes filled with tears. 'I got something to show you,' he said after a few moments, his voice shaking.

Wesley glanced at Gerry. 'What is it?'

'I can't show you while I'm stuck in here.'

'OK,' said Gerry. 'We'll release you on bail and take you home. Then you can show us. That suit you?'

'You're letting my client go?' The solicitor sounded surprised.

'Pending further enquiries,' said Gerry with a business-like smile. 'But he's not out of the woods yet.'

While the formalities were being carried out in the custody suite, Wesley and Gerry retired to the CID office. When they walked through the door, Rachel looked up eagerly.

'Well? Have you charged Tallow?'

Wesley shook his head. 'The fingerprint report has come back, and his prints aren't on those bottles.'

'He could have wiped them.'

'I don't think so. There are other prints on them that aren't on record. We need a motive to tie him in with Brown's murder. And as for Pelham Jenks, I can't see why he'd want to kill him, can you?'

'Unless Jenks and Brown found out about the corpse he'd been hiding.'

'Is that a reason for murder?' Wesley knew people had killed for less. But he still wasn't convinced.

Gerry had been listening to the conversation, and now he chipped in. 'Can you really see Ted Tallow driving to Little Rockington, having a drink with Barry Brown, poisoning him, then calmly driving back home to his dead mum? It just doesn't fit with what we know about him. Also, his pickup wasn't caught on any of Traffic's handy little cameras, and it's quite a distinctive vehicle. Of course, he might have killed Brown to stop him revealing to the world that his dad shot his mum's lover. Family honour?'

'But that happened long before he was born. And would Tallow actually kill to hide something like that when nothing could hurt his mother any more?'

'I agree, Wes. Harvey Pottinger, on the other hand, had an awful lot to lose. Reputation in tatters and career ruined, to say the least.'

Gerry's phone rang. It was the custody sergeant to say that the paperwork had been completed and Tallow was free to go. It was time to find out what he'd wanted to show them at the smallholding. As soon as they reached the door, however, he received another call, this time from the chief super. He was wanted immediately in her office on the top floor. A look of bitter disappointment passed across his face.

Wesley glanced at Rachel, who jumped to her feet. He would never have admitted it, but he was glad to have someone else take on the responsibility of driving down the Dartmoor lanes.

'So Tallow wants to show us something?' Rachel said as they walked down the stairs to reception.

'That's what he said. I get the impression it could be important.'

'I asked my parents and my in-laws about the Tallows, but they didn't know anything about them. Hadn't even heard the name,' Rachel said. 'They're aware of most of the farming families in the area, but the Tallows are a bit of a mystery.'

'They've always kept themselves to themselves. Which is why Ted found it so easy to conceal Edith's death. Hopefully he's about to let us in on some family secrets.'

'Including murder?'

'I suspect so.'

'It sounds like a classic crime of passion to me,' said Rachel. 'Woman has affair with handsome American soldier. Husband finds out and shoots him, then makes her give the baby up to a childless relative.' She shook her head and came to a halt on the half-landing. The last thing they wanted was for Ted Tallow to overhear their conversation. 'I bet the husband gave Edith a tough time after her fling. I'm surprised she didn't leave him.'

'He'd killed her lover, so she was probably terrified of him – and his mother, Dorcas the witch. And later on, she had Ted to care for.'

'What about the female skeleton?'

'With any luck, Ted's about to throw some light on how she came to be there.'

They passed the journey in amicable silence, with Ted Tallow in the back seat. When they arrived at their destination, Tallow climbed out of the car and opened his front door. Wesley thought he looked exhausted after his short period of incarceration.

'You'd better come in,' he said, leading them into the parlour. 'Wait there. I'll get it.'

They heard scrabbling and banging above their heads, as though furniture was being shifted and floorboards lifted. Wesley realised that the room above was the bedroom where until recently Edith had lain in the sleep of death. Eventually Ted returned holding an old shoebox. He handed it to Wesley, who peered inside and saw a woman's shoe; it looked like the partner of the half-rotted one found in the double grave. Beside the shoe was a pair of oval identification tags on a chain. They were embossed with a name – Hank Oppenheimer – together with a service number and other information, probably medical. They now had a name for their skeleton on the moor. At the bottom of the box was an old notebook with foxed pages. Wesley took it out and passed it to Rachel.

She looked at Tallow. 'Have you read it?'

His face turned red. 'I don't read too well. Never got the hang of it. Mother hid it under a loose floorboard. She told me it was there just before she passed away.'

'Thanks for showing it to us,' Wesley said gently. If he'd promised his dying mother that he'd stay silent, sharing the notebook with them was a major thing. 'Did the shoe belong to your mother?'

Tallow shook his head and took something from his pocket. Wesley's heart quickened when he saw that it was a revolver, and it was pointing in his direction. For a few long seconds he held his breath.

'You need to hand that over,' he said after he'd recovered from the initial shock. 'Please, Ted.'

They stood there frozen for what seemed like an age. Then, unexpectedly, Ted began to cry. Tears streamed down his face as he gulped back the grief.

'Mother was all I had.'

'I understand,' said Wesley.

'I couldn't let her go, could I? While she was still here, I didn't feel alone. Keeping her here wasn't wrong, was it? What harm did it do?'

Rachel caught Wesley's eye. 'You're not alone, Ted. You've got relatives. We've spoken to some of them. We can ask them to contact you. You should give the gun to Inspector Peterson.'

Wesley hadn't expected him to hand over the weapon so meekly. When he took it, he checked to see whether it was loaded, and found that it was. But the chamber only held three bullets. The other three were missing. Maybe they'd been the ones that had killed the skeletons down at the mortuary.

'Where did the gun come from?'

'Mother found it in my dad's things after he died. I think it was my grandad's gun from the first war. She didn't tell me about it until she knew she hadn't much time left.' The tears started again.

'Do you mind if we take the book away with us?' said Wesley. 'It might contain something important. We'll let you have it back once we've finished with it.'

Ted shrugged his shoulders. Wesley had rarely felt so sorry for a suspect in a murder inquiry. He'd spent his life caring for his mother, who'd endured an abusive marriage. He'd even tried to keep her with him after her death. He knew they should get back to the station with the gun and the notebook, but he was reluctant to leave the man on his own. Besides, he had more questions to ask.

'You're sure you can't remember anything else Barry Brown said when he came here?'

Ted shook his head. Then he suddenly raised his hand as though he'd remembered something. 'He dropped something when he left. Don't think he meant to. I ran after him to give it back, but he'd driven away by then. I don't know if it's important.'

'Have you still got it?'

Ted went to the huge dusty dresser on the far side of the room and opened one of the drawers, then another. Eventually he found what he was looking for.

Wesley recognised the name printed on the business card at once. '"Bella Renolds, Beauty Consultant",' he read, and Rachel raised her eyebrows.

Bella Renolds, Craig Parker's cousin and the keeper of the family archives, was, frustratingly, still away on holiday, but speaking to her had now taken on a new urgency. And the presence of her business card confirmed that Brown had met with her before she'd gone away. But what had she told him? He turned the card over and saw some scribbled words on the back. *Moor Barton. Riches to rags?*

Riches to rags. Those words were familiar. Wesley remembered they'd featured in the email Barry Brown had sent to his agent. He wondered whether something Bella had told him had made him follow another trail. One potentially more interesting than an SOE agent who'd gone missing in 1943. But what did the words mean? Surely they couldn't refer to Marie Leon?

He stepped outside and called the number on Bella's card, not really expecting a reply. But it turned out to be his lucky day. The phone was answered by a breathless Bella, who said she'd only arrived home from the airport an hour ago and was busy unpacking. She'd be free to see them in an hour.

Wesley needed to head to Tradmouth as soon as possible, but he was reluctant to leave Ted Tallow on his own. He suspected that he was on the verge of becoming emotionally involved. Tallow was elderly, lonely and had been through the trauma of losing his beloved mother; once when she actually died and again when the police removed her body. He returned to the parlour and took Rachel to one side to whisper the latest news. He was about to ask Ted if he'd be OK if they left him, but Rachel spoke first.

'We'll need to talk to you again, Ted,' she said, her voice sympathetic.

'Will I get into trouble for having that gun? I never took it out of the floorboards till now, I swear.'

'We'll be in touch,' said Rachel firmly. She knew they could pull him in again any time they wanted, so she was unwilling to make any promises. 'And we'll return the notebook as soon as we've finished with it,' she added more softly. 'Promise.'

As they were driving away with the shoebox full of evidence, Wesley called Gerry. He'd want to know about this latest development.

Moor Barton had a village shop, just opposite the Gornay Arms. Pam had given Michael money to buy something to go with his lunch because she hadn't had time to visit the supermarket. Chocolate or crisps; both things on the naughty list as far as nutritionists were concerned but temptations every busy mother yielded to from time to time.

Neil had given them an hour's break for lunch, so Michael decided it would do no harm to walk to the village. He looked round for Harriet, but there was no sign of her.

'Greg, have you seen Harriet?' he asked.

Greg straightened up from where he had been uncovering a piece of metal. 'I saw her slipping off about five minutes ago. I think she might have been making for the village. Why?'

Michael felt the blood rushing to his cheeks. 'No reason,' he said. 'I fancy buying something from the village shop. Coming with me?'

Greg shook his head.

Michael started walking, hoping to catch up with Harriet. But when he arrived in the village, there was no sign of her, and to his disappointment, the little shop, which sold everything from brushes to milk and doubled as a post office, had closed for lunch; an old-fashioned arrangement he hadn't bargained for. He was about to stroll back to the dig when he heard voices, one of them familiar.

He walked on a little further, and as he rounded a bend, he saw Harriet some distance away with a man he recognised because he'd seen him talking to Neil. But before he could catch up with her, she started to hurry off with the man by her side. He decided to follow, half in the hope that Harriet would know when the shop was due to open and half out of curiosity. To his surprise, the pair vanished down a path next to the churchyard, the man's dog trotting obediently at his heels.

He knew that was the way to the manor, and he wondered whether Harriet had somehow persuaded the owner to give her privileged access. He didn't want to be left out, so he carried on, and when he reached the house, he saw that the front door was open. But there was no sign of Harriet.

Then he heard a voice. 'What are you doing here?'

34

On the way back to Tradmouth, Wesley and Rachel decided to pull into a lay-by to have a quick look through the notebook they'd been given. It wasn't easy reading. The first section outlined how Edith Tallow had been subject to bullying and threats by her controlling husband. The modern term for it would be domestic abuse, but they didn't suppose that had been a concept back then.

Just over halfway in, the tone of Edith's entries changed. She'd decided to help the war effort by working as a land girl on a local farm, and had started sneaking off for nights out with friends she'd made there, including a girl called Marie, who'd been raised in France. At a dance, Edith had met an American soldier stationed nearby, and they'd begun meeting in secret. The budding relationship had transformed her life, and she'd looked forward to their rendezvous with the eagerness of a teenager experiencing first love. Wesley was holding the book so they could both read, and he heard Rachel gasp and tut from time to time as the narrative went on. However, they had to abandon the story before the end; if they didn't set off again, they'd be late for their appointment with Bella Renolds.

Bella's house stood on a new estate on the fringe of the

town. Even further away from the river than Wesley's own address. Unless you were fit enough to tackle the mile-and-a-half walk up the steep hill, you'd probably drive into the town centre; or take the bus if you couldn't face the often fruitless search for a parking space.

She had sounded open and friendly when Wesley had called her, telling him that she'd been very surprised to find messages from the police on her phone and that he could pop in any time. She'd sounded positively keen to help, and he felt this boded well.

He had never had cause to visit Tradmouth's newest estate before, possibly because the residents of the four-bedroom detached houses with open-plan kitchens and en suite bathrooms had so far proved to live ordered and law-abiding lives.

'Nice,' Rachel said as she parked outside Bella's address.

As soon as they got out of the car, the front door opened as though Bella had been on the lookout for their arrival. She was a chatty woman in her fifties with dyed blonde hair, a recently acquired tan and a figure that suggested a love of the good things in life.

'Come in, come in,' she said as she ushered them into a cream-coloured living room. 'Do sit down. I must say, I'm terribly curious. I don't think I've broken any laws recently,' she said with a giggle. 'There was terrible signal at the resort where I was staying, and when I was on my way home I found I'd had a few missed calls. My neighbour's just told me that officers have been round asking when I'd be back. They didn't tell her what it was about, so I'm sure she thinks I'm some kind of criminal mastermind,' she added with another giggle. 'Anyway, I'm here now. Would you like tea or coffee?'

'Tea, please,' said Wesley. Rachel said she'd have the same.

Once the drinks were in front of them, Bella sat down, her face a picture of innocent curiosity. Wesley suspected she'd had few encounters with the police in real life, though the little pile of crime novels on the coffee table suggested she was a fan of mysteries.

'We wanted to speak to you about a visit you received from a man called Barry Brown.'

Her eyes lit up with recognition. 'That's right. He's a writer. He wanted my help with his research,' she said proudly. 'He'd been given my name by my cousin.'

'Craig Parker?'

'Yes. Craig's a blacksmith. Does very well. I've got a few of his things in my garden.'

'We've spoken to him. He told us you're into family history. Do you know a village on Dartmoor called Moor Barton?'

'Yes. My mum was brought up there.'

'Did Mr Brown mention an air crash during the war?'

'He did. He told me that a man called George Melling had asked him to discover what happened to a French cousin of his father's who went missing in 1943. George's father was ground crew at an airbase near Millicombe, and our grandad worked with him.'

She took a breath before she carried on. She was the talkative sort; always good in a witness.

'Anyway,' she continued, 'apparently George was ab-solutely convinced that this woman's disappearance had something to do with the crash. He said his dad actually saw her board the plane, and that my grandad was with him. When Barry told me that she was a spy who went on

282

secret missions to France, I told him that George's dad had probably been mistaken and she most likely went off on another mission and got killed or captured. Everything was a huge secret at that time.' She looked disappointed that the solution to the mystery seemed so obvious. 'He said he wanted to write about her disappearance, but I said I couldn't help him. As far as I'm aware, there are no family stories about Grandad seeing her fly off or anything like that.'

'The skeleton of a woman has been found buried near the village of Moor Barton,' Wesley said. 'Tests show that she was brought up in France, which fits with what George Melling told us. We still have to compare George's DNA with the remains, but we think she was his relative; the one Barry Brown was trying to trace.'

'Well that's the mystery solved then. Barry will be pleased. Do you know how she came to be buried there?'

'That's what we're trying to find out.' He paused, guessing that his next statement would upset Bella. But there was no gentle way of breaking the news.

'I'm sorry to have to tell you that Barry Brown was murdered just over a week ago. Last Sunday. The day after you went away.'

There was no mistaking the shock on her face. 'That's awful. What happened?'

'He was found in the house he was renting in Little Rockington. He'd been poisoned.'

She shook her head in disbelief. 'Who on earth would want to do that? He seemed so nice. He told me he'd ghost-written lots of books for celebrities. Maybe he'd found out that one of them had a dark secret.' She looked as though she hoped she'd been able to solve their case for them.

Wesley smiled. 'We're following a number of leads, but we're particularly interested in Moor Barton. You said that was where your mother was brought up.'

'That's right. She lived there until she was a teenager. Barry asked if he could speak to her, but I had to tell him she passed away last year.'

'I'm sorry. What was her maiden name?'

'Cregan.'

Wesley looked at Rachel. Miss Gabriel had mentioned a family called Cregan who'd lived in Moor Barton for generations.

'Mum's parents moved to Tradmouth in the 1970s, after she'd left home. She said a little village on Dartmoor had been great to grow up in, but it had been really boring when she was a teenager. She was an only child and the last of the Cregans to live in Moor Barton,' she added.

'Did you mention this to Barry Brown?'

'Oh yes. Even though she wasn't born until 1948, Mum used to talk about the wartime air crash. I think it was probably a big thing at the time; sort of village folklore. Barry asked me if I knew anyone in Moor Barton he could speak to about it.'

'Did you give him any names?'

'I remember Mum mentioning someone called Miss Gabriel; I think she was the postmistress.'

'We've spoken to her,' said Rachel.

'Mum loved a bit of gossip, and she told me Miss Gabriel got involved with a man but her parents didn't approve. That's all I know about it, I'm afraid.'

Wesley saw Rachel glance in his direction. He hadn't met Miss Gabriel himself, but from what Rachel had reported about her, she hadn't seemed the type to fall for bad boys.

But people did all sorts in their teenage years they later came to regret.

'Did your mum ever mention the Tallows?'

'Oh yes. People in small communities have long memories, and I remember her saying something about the father being a brute who made his poor wife's life a misery. There were rumours that his mother was a witch, but I don't know how true that was. People make things up because they like a bit of drama, don't they.'

'What else did you tell him?'

'We spoke for ages and he made a lot of notes. He'd started off asking about my grandparents, but I could tell he was more interested in the history of the village. I told him about the Gornay family, who lived in the manor house. Mind you, I've heard the village has changed beyond recognition. I believe all the old families, like the Southens, have gone and their places have been sold to newcomers. Shame really, but times change, don't they.'

There was a long pause, and Wesley's instincts told him that she had more to say.

'My mum knew Ralph Gornay when she was young, and she said he was a cocky little so-and-so.' Bella leaned forward. 'Do you know, Mum and I went to London twelve years ago, for a birthday treat, and we actually saw him there. He wasn't so cocky then.'

'Mr Gornay told us he used to live in London. He returned to Moor Barton when his father fell ill.'

'Mum said old Colonel Gornay was a right Tartar. They were all terrified of him. He was a sort of bogeyman to the village kids.'

Wesley wasn't inclined to mention the shooting of young Norman Jenks. He did ask Bella whether her mother had ever mentioned Norman's brother, Pelham, but the answer was no.

Then she came out with something completely unexpected. 'It was terrible seeing Ralph Gornay like that,' she said suddenly. 'Mum was so shocked.'

Wesley was puzzled. 'Like what?'

'Drunk and living on the streets, poor man. Mum recognised him at once. I tried to stop her approaching him, because I thought it couldn't possibly be the Ralph Gornay she'd known, not looking like that. But she still went up and spoke to him, and it turned out it really was Ralph Gornay from the manor.'

She shook her head in disbelief. 'Mum said you could have knocked her down with a feather. He looked so ... dishevelled. And he had this horrible gash on his forehead. Really nasty. Mum said he should get it seen to. He told us he was hoping to stay in a hostel that night, and Mum gave him twenty quid. She told me she'd never particularly liked Ralph when she was young, but I could tell she felt sorry for him. How are the mighty fallen, she said. Just shows you, you never can tell.'

'So let me get this clear: you saw Ralph Gornay in London twelve years ago, and he was homeless?'

She nodded. 'That's right. Mum said it was incredible when she thought of everything he'd had at one time: that lovely manor house, posh school ... Mind you, from what she told me, having the colonel as a father was probably enough to drive anyone to drink.'

'We've spoken to Ralph recently and he's definitely put all that behind him,' said Rachel. 'He went home to the manor when his father became ill and moved back in there.'

'I already knew that. Mum read in the local paper that he'd opened the church fete in the village. She was relieved that he'd got over his bad patch and pulled himself round.'

'Did you mention this to Barry Brown?' Wesley asked.

'Yes. He seemed really interested. Quite excited actually. He said it would make a fantastic story. Riches to rags than back to riches again.'

Wesley's heart suddenly began to beat a little faster. Those were the words that had been written on the back of Bella's business card; the one Brown had dropped at Ted Tallow's place. And they'd also featured in Brown's email to his agent.

Bella raised her hand as though she'd suddenly re-membered something. 'There are some old photographs belonging to my mother in the loft. I haven't had a chance to sort through them yet, but I can see if I can find any from her Moor Barton days. Would that be any use to you?'

'It might be. Thanks.' Wesley wasn't sure if this was true, but he nursed a hope that pictures from the past might provide some sort of clue.

Suddenly impatient to get on, he stood up and thanked Bella for her time, handing her a card with his contact details. He had a feeling he could be on to something important.

'You will come back again?' she said cheerfully.

He smiled. 'Possibly.'

'What are you thinking?' Rachel asked as she drove fast down a single-track lane.

'Ralph Gornay never mentioned that he'd been in bother.'

'Maybe it was something he'd rather forget.'

Wesley's phone rang. It was the lab to say that they'd

analysed the contents of the bottles found at Ted Tallow's place. Three of them had contained cyanide.

Ted Tallow wasn't used to company, and the police questioning had left him exhausted. He'd concealed his mother's death and he'd been told that was a crime. Only it hadn't felt that way at the time.

There was a knock on the door and he froze. He didn't have many visitors – apart from the police and that writer who'd died – and he was torn between curiosity and a desire to be on his own. In the end, he shuffled to the door in his slippers, thinking that the police must have come back. He hoped they weren't there to arrest him. He hadn't liked being in the cell. He needed freedom. Open spaces. Dartmoor. He'd always liked walking at the site of the plane crash but it hadn't been the same since the archaeologists took over his private space. When they'd first arrived, he'd stood and watched them tearing up the earth, wondering what they'd find. But he'd hurried away before anybody could see him and ask questions.

There were things he hadn't told anybody. He'd kept quiet when his mother's spirit left her wizened body. Then there was the other thing, although he couldn't be absolutely sure he'd got it right. He'd mentioned it to his mother, and she'd told him to keep quiet. It was none of their business, and silence, she'd said, was the only way.

He hoped it was the black detective who'd come back; at least he'd seemed kind, and kindness was something Ted hadn't experienced very often in his lifetime. His father had communicated by shouting and doling out regular beatings, and his mother had been too cowed with fear to show him much affection.

When he opened the door, though, he saw a visitor he hadn't been expecting, and the surprise rendered him speechless for a few moments.

'I need to speak to you, Ted.'

He stood aside and the visitor walked in.

'Have you been talking to the police?'

He nodded, suddenly feeling uneasy.

'When I last came here, you said your mother was too ill to receive visitors.'

Ted's heart was beating fast. He could hear the blood pumping in his ears.

'I heard they took her body away. You should have told me she was dead.'

He bowed his head, feeling like a naughty child. What he'd done was wrong, and he didn't need to be told that. He took a deep breath. There was a question he had to ask. He just needed to summon the courage.

'When you came here before, did you take anything from one of the bottles in the cupboard?'

The visitor smiled. 'Your memory's not what it was, is it, Ted? I hope you didn't tell the police I did. They'd just think you were stupid. Couldn't even read the labels on those bottles, could you? Old Edith had to read everything for you.'

'The police took the bottles away to be tested.'

'That's a shame,' said the visitor, taking a step towards him.

'I never told them nothing. I swear.'

When the visitor took another pace closer, Ted closed his eyes.

Diary of Edith Tallow

Thursday 15 July 1943

We hear little of the war here on Dartmoor. We dig for victory and see lots of soldiers and airmen around, our own and the Yanks, but the actual fighting seems a long way away. Bram's mother refuses to get a wireless, saying such contraptions are the work of Satan. Everyone else has a wireless to keep up with what's happening and listen to music and funny shows, but we live in silence.

I only get to hear the news when I go to Home Farm. Marie tells me she's leaving, but she can't say where she's going. She seems really excited about it and maybe a bit nervous. She says our boys are fighting in Italy and that our Yanks – we think of them as ours now – might be sent there. She's been into the church to say a prayer for her brother because she thinks he might be there already. She doesn't know for certain, of course. They're not allowed to tell anyone their whereabouts when they write home. Marie told me she said a prayer for herself as well. I'll really miss her when she goes, but we all have to do our bit.

I've been meeting Hank in secret, and if Bram ever found out, I don't know what he'd do. I'm sure his mother's guessed there's something different about me and I know I've got to be careful. Perhaps she is a witch after all.

Marie says I should leave Bram, but where would I go? My sister's got four kids and she doesn't want another mouth to feed. Besides, we've never been close; she didn't even come to my wedding. I could go to Isaac and Florrie maybe? Bram and Isaac have never got on, but they say blood is thicker than water, so I can't be sure they'd take my side once they find out what I've been up to. They don't have kids, though; Florrie said they've been trying but they've had no luck.

Something has happened – or rather hasn't happened. And I'm feeling sick in the mornings. I told Marie and she says I might be in the family way. She asked me if I'd told Bram yet, but how can I tell him when I know it won't be his – not when he's put off you know what because his mother's lying next door and the walls are so thin? Bram says Dorcas doesn't sleep much and she might be listening, so we haven't done it since our wedding night when we stayed in that guest house in Morbay. If I am in the family way it must be Hank's, and I don't know what to do. Marie says I should brazen it out and tell Bram it's his, but I'm not a liar.

I've decided to tell Hank. Once he knows I'm having his baby, I'm sure he'll want to take me away from all this when the war's over. I'd love him to take me to America. He says he's got a ranch; that's like a big farm. I can't wait to see it.

35

'Put your foot down,' said Wesley.

'Why?' Rachel sounded amused. It wasn't like Wesley to be so dramatic.

'Because I'm worried.'

'What about?'

'Ted Tallow, if you must know. I think someone took the poison from that cupboard and Ted must know who's had access to it.'

'Wouldn't he have told us?'

'Maybe he didn't realise it had been taken. '

'Maybe Edith gave it to someone. Or his grandmother, the witch, did.' Rachel sounded sceptical about this talk of witchcraft.

'She died years ago, and according to Colin Bowman, Edith's been dead a couple of years, so neither of them could have poisoned Brown and Jenks. I think someone probably helped themselves to the contents of those bottles more recently. Unless the poison was taken while Edith was alive and stored in case it was needed. In which case, it must have been someone she trusted.'

'Ralph Gornay?'

'I can't see him visiting the Tallows, can you?'

'I suppose not.'

Wesley was busy thinking things through. 'Two people were poisoned with the same substance,' he said after a lengthy pause. 'And they trusted their killer enough to have a drink with him or her. And after what Bella told us ... Let's check Ted's OK,' he said. 'Then we'll have another word with Ralph Gornay. He never mentioned Brown asking him about his riches-to-rags story, so there might be other things he's neglected to tell us.'

Even though Rachel was driving as fast as the country roads allowed, the journey seemed to take an age. When they eventually drew up outside the Tallow place, they saw Ted's pickup parked by the tumbledown wooden garage to the side of the building, but there was no other sign of life. Wesley had a bad feeling when he saw the front door was slightly ajar. He rushed towards it with Rachel close behind, hesitating for a heartbeat before pushing it open.

His worst fears were realised when he saw Ted Tallow lying face-down on the floor, apparently lifeless. Blood was seeping from a wound to his head, and Wesley fell to his knees to check that he was still alive.

'Call an ambulance,' he shouted to Rachel, who already had her phone to her ear. She made the call before helping Wesley put Ted into the recovery position.

Wesley looked round and spotted a heavy iron doorstop lying on the floor nearby, stained with blood and hair. He felt helpless as he willed Ted to regain consciousness. His parents had been keen for him to follow in their footsteps and become a doctor, and he'd never regretted disappointing them ... until that moment, when he wished he could do something useful for the unconscious man.

Then he started thinking like a detective. If it was Barry

Brown's killer who'd attacked Ted, they'd changed their MO. Or perhaps they had known that Ted would be unwilling to share a friendly drink, so violence had been the only option.

It was an anxious quarter of an hour before they heard a deafening roar, like the beating of dragon's wings. Rachel ran outside and shouted to Wesley that the air ambulance had arrived; a far more practical alternative on the moor, where emergency vehicles might be impeded by impassable lanes and slow-moving tractors. It came as a relief that responsibility for the unconscious man was about to be taken on by those more capable.

'Will he make it?' Wesley asked the doctor. The medic was non-committal, which didn't make him feel any better.

His phone made a noise. It was a text from Neil. *Know where Mike is?*

No. Thought he'd be with you. He told himself that his son was probably with the students; they'd lost track of time and they'd return to the dig soon, but Neil's text still made him feel slightly uneasy. However, there was nothing he could do about it just at that moment, because Rachel was striding back to the car, and he had to hurry to catch up with her.

'Where to now? Ralph Gornay?' she asked once she'd called the crime-scene team. The medics had probably destroyed evidence in the course of their life-saving efforts, but there was always a chance that Ted's attacker had left some clues behind.

'There's someone else I want to see first.' When Wesley told her where he wanted to go, she looked surprised.

'Are you sure about that?

They said nothing for the rest of the short journey, and

when they pulled up outside the Gornay Arms, Wesley got out first.

'You met Miss Gabriel. What did you think of her?'

'I thought she was just a nice old lady; the village spinster.'

'According to Bella Renolds' mother, she had a colourful past.'

'So do lots of people, Wesley.'

'Can you show me where she lives.'

Rachel led the way to Miss Gabriel's cottage. Wesley banged on the front door, while Rachel hovered behind him looking worried.

'Let me do that,' she said. 'She's met me.'

Wesley stood back, and when he looked up at the cottage, he saw an upstairs net curtain move a fraction.

'She's in,' he said.

'She might be having a nap – or getting changed.'

'Either that or she doesn't want to speak to us.'

'I can't believe that. She's just a straightforward old village lady. I've come across dozens of them in my time.'

'Any who used to have an undesirable boyfriend?'

'Which of us hasn't?' Rachel said with a grin.

'They say poison's a woman's weapon.'

'To be honest, Wes, I can't see Miss Gabriel in the role of Lucrezia Borgia. Come on. We're wasting time. We'll try later. We need to see Ralph Gornay.'

Wesley's phone pinged, and when he checked it he saw that Bella Renolds had kept her word and sent through a photograph. It showed a group of children aged from around eight to their early teens; the youngsters of Moor Barton circa 1965. Some of the boys were wearing cricket whites. Presumably Bella's mother was among the girls, but he didn't know which she was. Then he saw that she'd sent another image: the back of the photograph showing the names of the children neatly printed in order.

He studied the photos for several minutes before handing the phone to Rachel.

'That arrogant-looking boy in the front row wearing an immaculate white jumper and trousers and pristine cricket shoes. According to the names on the back, that's Ralph Gornay. But see the boy in the scruffy polo shirt? The name printed on the back is Keith Southen.' He reached over and enlarged the image.

Rachel peered at the screen, and after a few moments she let out a gasp. 'I see what you mean.'

As they drove to the manor house, they noticed people in the street hanging round and talking. The landing of the air ambulance not far away had probably brought them out to speculate about what had happened. Wesley needed to speak to Ralph Gornay as soon as possible, and on the way he called Gerry to bring him up to date with the latest developments. Gerry said that he'd ask a patrol car to take him out there as soon as he could get away, but he wasn't sure how long he'd be. He claimed he wanted to be in on the action, but Wesley guessed he was as eager to escape the clutches of bureaucracy as he was to join in the investigation.

Rachel knocked on the door of the manor house, and when there was no reply, they walked round to the outhouses at the back. There they found a row of empty stables, relics of the time when the owner of the manor kept a number of horses for transport and hunting. Adjoining them was a coach house with large wooden double doors.

One of the doors was open a fraction and Wesley peeped inside. Then he turned to Rachel.

'Harvey Pottinger said he saw someone get out of a dark-coloured estate car on the night of Barry Brown's murder. Was that ever followed up?'

'Yes, but none of the residents knew anything about it. We haven't got round to asking Traffic whether anything like that was caught on camera.'

'Maybe there's no need. There's an old dark blue Volvo estate in there.' He nodded towards the coach house. Rachel raised her eyebrows. 'Pottinger said the car had a broken rear light. Take a look.'

He stood aside so Rachel could see inside the dim garage. Sure enough, the passenger-side rear light was damaged. Without another word, they made for the back of the house, searching for an entrance.

As they walked around the building, Rachel glanced through the windows. Suddenly she stopped and reached out to touch Wesley's arm. Sensing something wasn't right, he came to a halt and saw that she'd bobbed down to avoid being seen. Automatically he did the same.

'What's the matter?'

'He's in there. Someone's with him, but I didn't see who it was.' She hesitated. 'I think I heard your Michael's voice. But I could be wrong.'

Wesley felt his heart thumping in his chest as he straightened up slowly and peered through the glass. But the room beyond was empty and he began to relax a little.

'There's no one there, Rach.'

They carried on walking until they reached the back door. It was unlocked, and when Wesley opened it, he found himself in a large old-fashioned kitchen with stone flags on the floor, wooden dressers and a large scrubbed-pine table. The Labrador lying in a shabby dog basket raised his head to look at the newcomers, then resumed his nap. Fine guard dog he was. Wesley came to a halt and listened.

'I can definitely hear voices,' Rachel whispered behind him.

She was right. Muffled conversation was coming from some distant room. He crept towards the sound on tiptoe, and Rachel followed him out into the corridor. When they reached the end, the voices grew louder.

'Look, I didn't mean anything. Honestly. I just thought . . . ' It *was* Michael's voice, and he sounded frightened. Wesley was unable to stop himself from turning the door handle.

'What's going on?' he asked as he burst into the room, his eyes fixed on his son. He'd come to ask some searching questions. The last thing he wanted was to involve Michael. 'Michael, what are you doing here?'

The boy was facing Ralph Gornay, who was standing beside the girl from the dig, Harriet. As soon as he heard Wesley's voice, Gornay swung round.

'This boy was intruding on my property.' He sounded calm and reasonable, but Wesley thought he could hear a hint of threat behind the words.

'I saw Harriet come in and I wanted to ask her something, that's all.' Michael sounded puzzled as Rachel moved forward to usher him out.

'Michael, Harriet, I suggest you go back to the dig,' said Wesley calmly. 'I had a text from Neil. He's wondering where you are.'

But Harriet didn't move, and Michael stood there waiting for her to take the lead.

'I value my privacy,' said Gornay. 'I resent it when people pry into things that don't concern them.'

'Like Barry Brown did?'

Gornay didn't answer.

'You said you resent people prying. What exactly do you mean? You were quite open about your father shooting little Norman. What's changed?' Wesley tried to sound genuinely puzzled. He wanted Gornay to talk. And with any luck, to betray himself.

But Michael chose that moment to step away from Rachel's protective arm. 'I only followed Harriet here because I thought she'd know what time the shop opened,' he said, sounding anxious.

Harriet swung round to face him. 'I didn't want you to follow me. Where I go is none of your business.'

Michael looked devastated, as though she'd just delivered a physical blow. Someone he'd admired, his first crush, had just turned on him.

Suddenly, to Wesley's surprise, Gornay strode over to an umbrella stand in the corner of the room and took out something long and thin. At first he took it for a walking cane. Then he realised it was a shotgun.

'Don't do anything stupid, Gornay. Let the kids go,' he said, making a great effort to keep calm.

He glanced round and saw that Rachel was no longer in the doorway. Hopefully she was calling for backup. He focused his attention on Michael, who was standing absolutely still, frozen with fear. Harriet was edging closer to him, and Wesley hoped that she'd relent and lead him to safety.

Gornay raised the shotgun. 'I've nothing more to say to you. Get out of my house. You're trespassing.'

This was an entirely different Ralph Gornay from the affable man Wesley had encountered a few days before. And Gornay's reaction served to confirm the suspicions that had been bubbling in his mind since he'd seen Bella Renolds' photograph.

He was about to try and defuse the situation when Harriet let out a scream as a face appeared at the window. Wesley recognised Neil at once and knew that his friend had no idea what he'd wandered into.

Gornay was momentarily distracted. He fumbled with the weapon, then Wesley heard a loud bang followed by another scream.

Next time he looked at the window, there was nobody there.

36

Ralph Gornay's shock was unmistakable. He stood quite still, looking at the window that his gunshot had shattered, paralysed with the horror of what he'd done. If he was the killer, as Wesley suspected, poison had so far been his weapon of choice and he'd never had to face his victim as death approached. Apart from Ted Tallow, of course: that time violence had been his only alternative. Even then he'd hit him from behind so he wouldn't have to look him in the eye.

Wesley darted forward to seize the weapon, but Gornay recovered quickly, grabbing Michael's arm and dragging him towards the front door. 'Leave my son alone!' Wesley shouted, but with the gun pointed at him, he could only watch helplessly as Michael looked over his shoulder to shoot him a pleading glance.

Once they'd gone, he rushed to the window. Through the shattered pane he saw Rachel kneeling anxiously beside Neil, who was lying still on the ground.

His friend was down and he felt a sudden wave of panic. Not only that, but his son was in grave danger.

'I've called for backup and the air ambulance,' Rachel shouted to him.

Wesley knew the sensible thing to do was to leave the pursuit of Ralph Gornay to the armed response unit. Soon the whole circus would arrive, possibly with a trained negotiator. He tried to convince himself that once they got there, everything would be OK. But he couldn't just wait around. If there was a chance he could rescue his son, he needed to take it.

He rushed outside. He hadn't heard a car engine start so he guessed they were still nearby. As he headed for the outhouses he saw that the big double doors to the coach house were shut. When he stopped in the yard and looked round, he heard a voice coming from inside the building: Ralph Gornay swearing. He assumed Harriet and Michael were in there too, terrified and held at gunpoint.

He crept towards the doors and squinted through the gap. In the gloom, he could make out the shape of the car and a figure standing over the open bonnet. It seemed Gornay was having mechanical trouble. The shotgun was propped up next to the headlight, just within the man's reach. He couldn't see Michael, but he knew he needed to stay calm. Professional.

He reckoned he had the advantage of surprise, but he hadn't bargained for the noise the old wooden door made as it scraped against the ground. The sound made Gornay swing round, grabbing the gun in one fluid movement and pointing it in Wesley's direction. His only option now was to keep the man talking until the ARU arrived.

'Where are Michael and Harriet? Are they all right?'

To Wesley's amazement, the front passenger door opened and Harriet emerged from the vehicle.

'What's the matter, Dad? Why can't you get it going?'

Wesley wondered if he'd misheard her.

'You called him Dad,' he said, his eyes searching for Michael. Then he saw a figure in the back seat. His son was looking out of the window with pleading eyes, on the verge of tears. His hand was on the door handle, but Wesley guessed the child locks had been activated. He was trapped.

'Didn't I say? This is my dad.'

Wesley remembered Ralph mentioning a daughter and he cursed himself for not having put two and two together. On the other hand, how could he have known? Michael had never mentioned that Harriet had family nearby, let alone that her father owned the manor house.

Harriet took the shotgun from her father's hands and pointed it in his direction as Ralph continued to tinker with the engine. Michael was still looking out of the car window, and Wesley fought the urge to rush over and reassure him. He needed to give Gornay and Harriet his full attention.

'Did you use Michael to find out how my investigation was progressing?' He addressed the question to Harriet, who was looking a little nervous as she tried to hold the shotgun steady.

'It wasn't difficult. He never shut up about it. Seemed proud of having a detective for a dad.'

She spat out the words, but for a split second Wesley found her verdict quite gratifying. Like most kids of his age, Michael usually appeared to regard his parents as an embarrassment.

'I'd hoped for more inside information,' she continued. 'But it seems you don't go into many details at home.'

Wesley was relieved. He'd been racking his brains for things he might have given away; confidential matters he might have shared with Pam and Neil in Michael's hearing. But it seemed he hadn't let anything slip.

'Your father killed Barry Brown.' He watched her face for a reaction.

'Prove it,' she said defiantly.

'And he's just shot Dr Watson.'

Ralph straightened up, his hands stained with oil. 'I didn't mean to shoot him. I fired by accident. Will he be OK?'

It was a question Wesley had been asking himself. 'You're not usually so concerned about your victims.'

He saw father and daughter exchange a look.

'Why did you do it, Ralph? Though Ralph's not your real name, is it?'

But before Gornay could respond, Wesley heard approaching sirens. It was time the matter was brought to a close.

Harriet tightened her grip on the shotgun. And Wesley knew that a nervous person with a firearm was more dangerous than someone who was calm and controlled.

'It's over, Harriet,' he said gently, speaking to her as he would to a terrified animal. 'Hand the gun over, otherwise the officers outside will shoot you. They'll have no choice if they feel my life is in danger.'

For a while, nothing happened. The three of them stood quite still, a tableau of fear and indecision. Then Ralph spoke.

'It's over, darling. Give him the gun.'

Wesley had been holding his breath, and he exhaled with relief as Harriet handed the weapon over. He removed the remaining cartridge, then threw the gun to the ground and kicked it away. He didn't want armed officers mistaking him for the threat and shooting before he had a chance to identify himself.

'That gun used to be my father's,' Ralph said unexpect-edly. 'It was the one that killed that kid, Norman. He gave it to me just before he made his deathbed confession.'

Wesley felt confused. He'd begun to suspect the man was an imposter. But now he wondered whether he was the real Ralph Gornay after all.

His heart leapt with relief when two armed officers burst in, shouting for everyone to hit the ground. Wesley did as he was told, and one of the officers was about to cuff him when he shouted out that he was DI Peterson, Tradmouth CID, and that his ID was in his pocket. The officer fished it out and examined it, then hauled him to his feet with a mumbled 'Sorry, sir. Had to make sure.'

Wesley pointed at Harriet and Ralph. 'Cuff them, please. I need them taken to Tradmouth for questioning.'

He dashed to the car, almost tripping over in his anxiety to release his son. He pulled the door open and took the tearful, terrified Michael in his arms. The child lock had prevented the boy from escaping, but he knew this had been a good thing. If he'd managed to get out of the car, he would have put himself in danger.

As Gornay and Harriet were being dealt with, Wesley asked one of the officers the question that had been on his mind since he left the house. 'Have you heard how the casualty is; the man who was taken off in the air ambulance?'

The answer was a shake of the head.

The prisoners were on their way to Tradmouth, and now that Michael was safe, Wesley's main concern was Neil. He knew he'd been taken to hospital in Exeter, but there were no details of his condition at this stage. He rang Annabel, because he thought she needed to know. She sounded close to tears, quite unlike the confident Annabel he knew, and said she'd go to the hospital at once. She'd been conducting research for Neil's dig, contacting the Imperial War Museum to ask if there were any records about SOE operations in Devon. But at that moment, history wasn't her chief concern.

He'd been putting off calling Pam until he knew more about Neil's condition, but now he had no choice. He rang her and told her what had happened. She sounded stunned at first. Then her shock turned to anger as she ordered him to bring Michael home at once.

Wesley was grateful when Rachel offered to drive them both back to Tradmouth. He sat in the back with a silent Michael clutching his hand. For once, the boy didn't object to the parental show of affection.

During the journey, he called Gerry to bring him up to date with events in Moor Barton. Gerry asked him whether he felt up to conducting the interview with Ralph Gornay and his daughter. Wesley said he did. He wanted to be in at the finish.

37

When Wesley arrived home with Michael, Pam rushed to the door with Sherlock at her heels, barking as though he knew something was amiss. The dog wagged his tail and jumped up at his master while Pam stood there looking furious.

'What the hell's been happening? Is Michael OK? And what about Neil?'

'Michael's fine. Aren't you?' he said before guiding the boy forward into Pam's waiting arms.

Michael didn't answer, but Wesley guessed that once the shock had worn off, the story of his adventures would be told around school, possibly embellished with heroic details. Providing, that was, Neil pulled through.

'Neil's having surgery,' he said. 'I've spoken to Annabel. I'll ring the hospital later for an update.'

'How on earth did he come to be shot?' Pam shook her head in disbelief as Michael extracted himself from his mother's embrace and disappeared upstairs with the dog.

'He was in the wrong place at the wrong time, that's all. We've made a couple of arrests, so I've got to get back to the station to conduct the interviews.'

Pam's eyes filled with tears as she clenched her fist

and thumped her husband's chest. 'You put Michael in danger – and Neil,' she sobbed. 'What if he dies? And it could have been you.'

He took hold of both her hands before hugging her. He knew her fury was born of worry, and if he told her that an hour ago he'd been looking down the barrel of a shotgun, she'd probably order him to hand in his notice at once. She'd often confessed she had nightmares about him facing mortal danger at work, but he'd assured her that in CID his contribution relied more on brainwork than chasing armed villains. The events of the last few hours had proved that to be false, but he'd keep that from her if he possibly could.

'Look after Michael,' he said. 'I'll call you as soon as I know anything about Neil.'

Rachel was waiting for him in the car she'd parked at the end of the drive. 'Everything all right?' she asked as he got into the passenger seat.

'Pam's upset. Can't really blame her.'

She asked him how he was feeling.

'A bit shaken. And worried about Neil.'

'He'll be OK. He's indestructible.'

'That's what we feel about everyone we're close to. Until events prove otherwise.' He took a deep breath. He wasn't looking forward to facing Gornay and his daughter again, but he needed to know the full story. He needed to know why Neil had ended up in an operating theatre, possibly fighting for his life.

When they reached the CID office, Gerry hurried out to greet them. 'How's Neil?' was his first question. Wesley had to tell him there was no news yet.

'I feel I've missed all the excitement. What happened?'

Wesley followed the DCI into his office and took a seat before going through everything that had occurred that day. The attack on Ted Tallow; Bella Renolds' claim that she and her late mother had seen Ralph Gornay in London. Bella had mentioned that he'd had a deep wound on his forehead, the kind of wound that would certainly have left a scar. The Ralph Gornay Wesley had spoken to had no such scar.

Then he mentioned the photograph taken in the 1960s that Bella had sent him. That photograph had shown two boys who looked remarkably alike; one the son of the manor, confidently dominating the front row; the other lurking at the back.

'So you think the man at the manor house is an imposter?' Gerry sounded puzzled. 'Surely people in the village would be able to tell.'

'Most of the families who lived there when the boys were young are long gone. That picture looked as though it was taken at a village cricket match, but normally the Gornays didn't mix much with the locals. Maybe nobody got that close to the real Ralph. Luckily Bella's late mum had a very good memory for faces, and she recognised him right away when she saw him in London. Have the two suspects been taken to the interview suite?'

'Gornay's in room two and the girl's in number three. Gornay called his solicitor as soon as he got here.' Gerry hesitated. 'You look as though you could use a drink.'

'I'll get a tea from the machine later.'

'I reckon you need something stronger. But that'll have to wait.'

The two men walked down the stairs to the interview rooms. Trish Walton and Paul Johnson were going to speak to Harriet, but Wesley and Gerry had chosen to interview the man claiming to be Ralph Gornay themselves.

When they entered the interview room, Gornay was waiting for them in his shirtsleeves. He seemed to have lost the lord-of-the-manor confidence he'd shown previously.

'Mr Gornay,' Gerry began after the recording equipment had been activated. 'Is that your real name?'

'What makes you think it isn't?' There was a note of defiance in the man's voice.

'Because the real Ralph Gornay had a scar on his forehead. Someone who knew him as a child saw him in London a number of years ago. He was homeless, living on the streets. He was drinking heavily and had lost everything.'

'I've made no secret of the fact that I used to live in London. Is that all you've got?'

'No.' Wesley found the picture Bella had shown him. 'That is you, isn't it?' He pointed to the boy on the back row. Keith Southen, according to the names Bella's mother had printed on the back.

'That's me in the cricket gear on the front row,' he said warily.

'But you admit there is a strong resemblance between the two of you. You and Keith Southen could be twins.'

Gornay didn't answer. Wesley glanced at Gerry. What he was about to say was pure guesswork, but he wanted to see the suspect's reaction.

'I think your real name is Keith Southen and you and Ralph Gornay were half-brothers. I think your father, Colonel Gornay, got a village woman pregnant and you were the result.'

The man didn't say anything.

'When Ralph reached his late teens, he argued with his father and left to start a new life away from Dartmoor. I'm guessing from our witness's account of seeing him in London that things didn't work out too well for him and he fell on hard times. You'd left Moor Barton too and moved to London for work, as many people do.'

Wesley leaned forward and looked the suspect in the eye.

'Did you come across Ralph Gornay while you were in London and see the state he was in? Is that what gave you the idea? He was in a bad way. One of the anonymous homeless. You thought nobody was going to miss him, so you decided to assume his identity and return to Moor Barton to take his place. You probably told yourself that you were Colonel Gornay's son as much as he was, so it was your birthright. You heard somehow that the colonel was near to death and you calculated that if you came back after so many years, nobody would realise the deception, including your father, who hadn't seen Ralph – or you, for that matter – for decades. You admitted that the colonel was confused near the end and that his eyesight was bad. You and Ralph were very alike, so you were sure you could get away with it. Am I right?'

The suspect had bowed his head so that it wasn't possible to see his expression. 'No comment.'

'Harriet is your daughter. Where's her mother?'

He didn't answer the question directly. 'We separated when Harriet was little, but she never really got on with her mother and she blamed her for the divorce. She had an affair, you see. Recently my daughter and I have become very close. That's one of the reasons she chose to study in Exeter,' he said fondly. 'To be near me.'

'I understand. But I'd like you to tell me who you stayed

311

in touch with in Moor Barton. Someone must have kept you up to date with all the news while you were living in London or you wouldn't have known about the colonel's health.'

'No comment.'

Wesley persisted. 'It must have been someone who'd known you before you went to London. And let's face it, there aren't many people left in the village who remember that time.' He paused. 'I think we can rule out the Tallows. The Southen family and the Cregans are no longer there, but what about Miss Gabriel? I expect she's always had her finger on the Moor Barton pulse.' He left a few seconds of silence. 'I noticed that when Barry Brown asked you who was worth talking to in Moor Barton, you left out the most obvious person. You told him to talk to the vicar and the Tallows, but you didn't mention Miss Gabriel. Is she the person you kept in touch with?'

'No comment.'

The solicitor requested a break in the interview, and Wesley was relieved when Gerry agreed. He needed to phone the hospital again. And he wanted to speak to Pam and check on Michael.

The news from the hospital was good. Dr Watson was out of theatre and it turned out his condition wasn't as bad as Wesley had feared The shotgun wounds were superficial, but when he'd fallen he'd broken his leg in two places, and he'd had pins inserted into the bone. Wesley rang Annabel, who was sitting by the patient's bedside playing the devoted fiancée. Somehow he still couldn't see them as a couple, but it seemed he'd got it wrong. Fine detective he was, he thought with a smile; he felt smiles were permitted now that he knew Neil was on the mend.

He called Pam, who told him that one of Michael's school friends had called round and they were playing computer games upstairs; normal service had been resumed. He said something about children being resilient, and Pam agreed. 'Sorry for before, but I'd been frantic with worry. You understand that, don't you?'

'Of course. But it's over now and Neil's going to be OK. I don't know what time I'll be back tonight.'

'So what's new?' she said before ending the call.

There was someone else he needed to check on, and that was Ted Tallow. He rang Morbay hospital for an update and was told that Ted had regained consciousness and was up to speaking to the police. Wesley felt like punching the air. Ted's testimony might help ensure the poisoner's conviction, and he asked Rob to go to the hospital right away to take a statement. Rob looked pleased with himself as he left the CID office, as though he knew he was the one who would put the final piece of the jigsaw in place.

Gerry agreed that they should wait to resume the interview with Gornay – or Keith Southen, if Wesley's suspicions were correct – until Rob reported back. Once they knew the identity of Ted's deadly visitor, there would be no more doubt.

The wait for Rob's call seemed to take an age, but Wesley used the time productively by asking Trish and Paul what they'd learned from Harriet. The answer was nothing. She wasn't talking, answering 'no comment' to every question they'd put to her.

Wesley feared Gerry would wear a groove in the office carpet tiles if he carried on pacing up and down for much longer. Then his phone rang, and when he heard Rob's voice, he rushed over to the DCI and activated his speaker.

'You'll never guess, sir,' said Rob, sounding unusually excited. And when he told them the name of Ted Tallow's visitor, Wesley smiled to himself. With any luck, everything was about to fall into place.

Diary of Flight Officer John Carmody

22 September 1943

I meant to write in this journal every day, but I've had to leave it for a while because our drops are getting more frequent as operations over in France are stepped up a gear. More people are needed for sabotage missions and the Resistance grows in strength. At least that's what we've been told. We can only pray it's true.

Another night, another mission. Tonight it's a pickup. A man called Lucien. He's to be taken to Bolt Head, where someone's waiting to debrief him. That's fine by me; after I've delivered my precious cargo, it'll just be a short hop over Dartmoor back to my base. We all put on a brave face, but the old butterflies in my stomach always start fluttering their wings whenever I make my descent into a torchlit French field. But I take a deep breath and carry on. It's the only way.

What terrific luck. I delivered Lucien safely into the capable hands of Bolt Head, and who should be waiting there, looking lost and very pretty, but Marie. She seemed nervous, so I gave her a cigarette and we got talking. She told me she'd just returned from a mission. She said it was nothing like what she'd been doing before she started training for the SOE. I asked her what that was, and she said she'd been working as a land girl on Dartmoor.

'What?' I said. 'Milking cows and ploughing fields?'

She laughed. 'It turned out to be valuable experience. I've been staying on a farm over in France, so it helped me blend in. Hopefully no one ever suspected I was sending back intelligence from the Resistance.'

'It must be exciting,' I said.

'I suppose it is, but I do miss the other girls.' She looked sad when she said it, and I told her I understood. What she's doing must be lonely. And frightening.

She said she'd already completed several missions, and I said it was a pity she hadn't flown with me. She asked if I was flirting with her. When I said I was, she smiled. She has a lovely smile.

She'd been promised a lift back to the base at Winkleigh, but the car hadn't turned up, so I asked her if she wanted a ride in my old black kite. She said that would be super.

She noticed I was carrying this journal and she asked to see it. I said there were some top-secret things in it but I might show her one day once we knew each other better. She asked when that would be, and I told her there was a dance next week and asked if she'd like to go with me. I can't wait to spend some time in her company. That's if she doesn't get sent away on another mission.

Then a car drew up and someone shouted her name. It was her lift, so I supposed I'd be flying back without a passenger after all. But then she put her finger to her lips and laughed.

'If we keep quiet, he'll think he's missed me. I'd much rather come with you.'

38

Wesley remembered learning from Rachel that the Southens had been the Gornays' tenant farmers, but they'd left Moor Barton many years ago and their farmhouse had been sold to a lawyer from Exeter. Nobody had been able to trace them, so it had seemed like a dead end.

Speaking to someone who knew the family was now a priority, and Rachel made a few calls to farming contacts of her husband and parents – farmer to farmer. As she made the final call, Wesley watched the expression on her face change to one of triumph as she looked over at him and gave him the thumbs-up sign.

She'd spoken to a woman called Jenny Pirie, née Southen, who now lived up in Scotland. And she'd just provided the final piece of the jigsaw.

Rachel Tracey knocked on the door of the little cottage opposite the Gornay Arms, but there was no answer. She turned to Rob, who'd offered to go with her as soon as he'd returned from Ted Tallow's bedside, eager to wrap the case up once and for all.

When there was still no reply, she knocked again. But there was no sign of life

She turned to Rob. 'Let's try the back.'

'Are you sure about this?'

'Jenny Pirie told me that her brother, Keith, had been adopted. She also told me the name of his birth mother.'

Rob didn't question her further. When they reached the little back yard, they found the kitchen door unlocked. Rachel went in first, calling Miss Gabriel's name. The heavy stillness inside the neat little cottage gave her the feeling that something was wrong. She went from room to room. Everything was pristine, as though it had been tidied and dusted recently; almost as though the occupant was expecting visitors.

When she reached the bedroom, she realised that the visitors Miss Gabriel had been expecting were the police. She lay there on the bed, lifeless and at peace; a small bottle stood on the bedside table beside an empty glass that bore traces of red wine. A last drink before oblivion.

'Suicide?' Rob whispered.

Rachel put on her crime-scene gloves and picked up a trio of old photographs lying by the dead woman's left hand. The first was of a very young woman nervously cradling a baby. A second picture showed a boy aged around ten, the boy they now knew from Bella Renolds' photo as Keith Southen. The third showed a man she recognised immediately as the Ralph Gornay who'd been living in the manor house. The Ralph Gornay who'd threatened Michael Peterson and shot Neil Watson. The Ralph Gornay whose real name was Keith Southen. Miss Gabriel's son.

She took out her phone and called Wesley. He'd want to know that Ted Tallow's last visitor was dead.

*

When Wesley and Gerry broke the news of Miss Gabriel's death to Ralph Gornay, alias Keith Southen, the man cried. Real tears rolled down his cheeks and Wesley passed him a tissue from the box on the table.

'Miss Gabriel was your mother,' said Gerry with surprising gentleness.

Southen nodded and blew his nose.

'Let me tell you what I think happened,' said Wesley. 'I'm sure you'll correct me if I get it wrong.'

The suspect sniffed and looked away.

Wesley continued. 'Your father, Colonel Gornay, had a fling with a young woman from the village. Jane Gabriel.'

Gornay looked up, his eyes suddenly blazing with anger. 'A fling? She was sixteen. He raped her.'

Wesley sat stunned for a few moments. 'I'm sorry,' were the only words he could think of to say. He was relieved when the suspect began to speak.

'My mother found she was pregnant. The colonel arranged for her to go away to have the baby, and for his tenant farmers, the Southens, to take me in. They already had a daughter, but my adoptive mother couldn't have any more children and she seemed happy with the situation. I'm not sure whether there was any financial arrangement, but the Southens welcomed me into their household and my real mother knew I was in good hands. Of course in those days nobody acknowledged the truth. Everything was brushed under the carpet.'

'Just to get things clear, your real name is Keith Southen?' said Wesley.

The suspect took a deep breath. 'That's the name the Southens gave me.'

'I presume they knew you were the colonel's son,' said

Gerry. 'They probably felt obliged to the lord of the manor. It was an arrangement that suited everyone.'

The suspect didn't answer.

'Our sergeant has spoken to your adoptive sister, Jenny, up in Scotland. She filled us in on a few things.'

Southen looked away.

'The Southens brought you up and did their best, but you never really felt you belonged with them,' Wesley continued, and the look on Southen's face told him he'd got it right. 'Is that why you went off to London as soon as you were old enough? You met the real Ralph there, didn't you? Your half-brother. He also got out of Moor Barton as soon as he could.'

'Seeking the bright lights,' added Gerry. 'Just like you.'

Southen nodded; he looked as though he was beginning to relax a little. 'There was nothing in Moor Barton for me. Like you said, Ralph got out as soon as possible, and so did I.'

'When did you find out that Colonel Gornay was your father?' Wesley asked. He wanted to get his facts straight.

'My adoptive parents told me just before I left for London.'

'What was your relationship with your biological father?'

'I didn't have one.' There was a long silence before Southen spoke again. 'I'd heard rumours that he'd once shot a boy from the village. A lad called Norman. I didn't know whether it was true, but it wouldn't have surprised me. When I was young, everyone was frightened of him, so I tended to avoid him. It was only when I came back from London that my birth mother told me what had really happened – that she'd become pregnant when the colonel forced himself on her. I didn't owe the Gornays anything,'

321

he added bitterly, before looking away. He obviously found the facts distressing, and Wesley could understand why.

'What about Ralph? Did you have much to do with him while you were growing up?'

'No, he was sent away to school and he didn't mix with the village kids.'

'And Miss Gabriel? When did you find out she was your mother?'

'At the same time I was told about the colonel – just before I left for London. It came as a hell of a shock. Maybe that's why I felt I had to get away.'

'But when you returned to Moor Barton, you became close to your birth mother?'

'I was reconciled to the idea by then and I went to see her. I knew she was the one person I could trust to keep my secret.'

'Let's get back to Ralph. What happened?'

'He might have been my half-brother, but when we were kids, he was arrogant. He was the lord of the manor's son and we were the peasants. Of course he had no idea about our relationship back then, and when he left Moor Barton, I didn't know where he'd gone or what had happened to him. And I didn't particularly care.'

'Did you keep in touch with your adoptive family?'

'Only to send Christmas cards. I was living a new life in London and I was doing OK. I worked for an estate agency and I got married to a woman twelve years younger than me. We had a daughter, Harriet, and lived in the suburbs. For many years I never gave Ralph Gornay a second thought.'

'What changed?'

'Ten years ago, my adoptive parents both passed away

within weeks of each other. I didn't go back for the funerals. I'd put that life behind me.'

'They treated you badly?'

Southen shook his head. 'No. But I'd been hurt by what they'd told me about my real mother. I was angry that they'd kept the truth from me for all those years.'

This seemed harsh to Wesley, but he said nothing.

'My sister wrote to me to let me know they'd gone. She told me the farm had been sold to someone from Exeter and she was moving up to Scotland with her husband later that month. She also said the old colonel was very ill. He had dementia and wasn't expected to live for long. By sheer coincidence, just after I received her letter, I was in the centre of London and I came across Ralph Gornay.'

'Came across him?'

'Yes, after all those years, our paths crossed again. I was working near Soho and was walking down St Martin's Lane one day after a meeting, and there was Ralph; he was in a bad way and asking strangers for money. At first I thought it couldn't be him. Then I summoned the courage to speak to him and he told me who he was. I could hardly believe it. The Ralph Gornay who'd had it all at one time, reduced to sleeping rough and begging on the streets. How are the mighty fallen, eh.'

'You hadn't seen him before then?'

'London's a big place.'

'Did he recognise you?'

'Yes, after a while it dawned on him who I was. I took him to a café and bought him a hot meal. He told me he hadn't spoken to our father since he left home. He said he was having problems and nobody could help him.'

'Did he know you were brothers?'

Keith shook his head. 'No. And I wasn't going to tell him. I thought he had enough to deal with. He started telling me his life story: how he'd gone travelling as soon as he left Moor Barton, and once he'd blown all his money he was too proud to contact his father. He ended up in London working backstage in theatres at first, then he graduated to working in hotel kitchens and even opened a restaurant of his own, but that failed after a few years. He started drinking and his life spiralled out of control. I told him the colonel was ill, although I don't think the news sank in.'

Wesley glanced at the recording machine. He knew the suspect needed to tell the story at his own pace.

Southen cleared his throat before continuing. 'Things weren't going well for me at the time. My marriage had just broken up. Harriet stayed with her mother, but the break-up hit her very badly.' He hesitated. 'Soon after I met Ralph, I was made redundant. I was divorced and living alone. My bitch of a wife was keeping my daughter away from me, so there was nothing to keep me in London – apart from the hope that I'd be allowed to see Harriet from time to time. Then my ex-wife announced that she was moving out of London and buying somewhere in the West Country because she'd got a new boyfriend who lived in Morbay. I had no job, so I thought I might as well move back to Devon to be near my daughter. To tell the truth, I was worried about her. Harriet's always been very . . . intense, and I thought she needed me. Her mother's never been good at handling her, you see.

'Then I had an idea. Ralph and I had always looked very alike, and the chances of him returning to Moor Barton seemed to be nil, so I reckoned that if I went back and took his place, I could inherit the manor when the old colonel died. Most of the people who lived in the village now were newcomers, and those that weren't hadn't seen me or Ralph for decades. The colonel had dementia and the Southens were gone, so I was sure I'd get away with it. It seemed like a victimless crime. When I told my ex-wife I was moving back to Devon, she agreed to let Harriet keep in contact. She was only eight at the time.' He smiled fondly. 'I told my ex I was going to inherit a manor house, but she wasn't impressed. She was living with her new partner by then, but Harriet couldn't stand him. He's long gone, I believe. Harriet told me she drove him away. She can be ... difficult.'

'What happened to the real Ralph?' said Wesley, leaning forward.

'I'd been living in the manor house for about four years and I'd got to know my real mum. Everyone seemed to accept me as Ralph.' Southen gave a bitter laugh. 'The vicar even asked me to open the village fete, would you believe.'

'We heard. I understand it made the local papers.'

Keith nodded. 'Yes. I wasn't too happy about that, but I thought I'd got away with it.' He paused. 'Then everything began to go wrong.'

'What happened?' Wesley prompted

'Ralph arrived at the front door one day out of the blue, saying he'd turned his life around. He'd found himself in a Salvation Army hostel when he'd hit rock bottom and they'd helped him get back on his feet. He'd come back to see if his father was still alive. Started throwing his weight around like the Gornays always used to. Even ordered me to get Castor, my dog, out of the room. He seemed surprised to see me at first, then it became obvious that he assumed I was acting as some sort of caretaker. But I knew the game was up.'

'So you poisoned him.'

Southen shook his head. 'Not me.'

'Let me guess,' said Gerry. 'It was Miss Gabriel. She was your mum, and mums will do anything for their children. I expect she knew old Edith from the Tallow place, and she'd have known about the stock of poisons that Dorcas Tallow kept in her cupboard. If she paid Edith a friendly visit, she could easily have helped herself to some poison while she was there.'

From the man's reaction, Wesley knew Gerry had guessed correctly.

'My mother said my position would never be safe unless we got rid of Ralph,' Southen said quietly. 'She came to the manor while he was there and put the poison in his tea; he'd given up the booze, you see.' He paused. 'My mother's dead now, so whatever I say can't harm her. But she killed Ralph. She did it for me.'

'What did you do with his body?'

'He's buried in the walled garden at the manor. I can show you where.' Keith seemed resigned to the inevitable.

'What about Barry Brown? Why did he have to die?

'He said he'd heard I was living rough at one time and that it would make a fantastic story. Overcoming adversity and turning your life around and all that. He asked if there was anyone in London he could talk to who'd known me on my "journey". He seemed so enthusiastic about it. Said he usually wrote about celebrities, but my story – or rather Ralph's – was far more interesting. "Inspiring" was how he put it. When I told my mother, she said that if he went ahead, it would put me at risk.'

'So he had to die?'

Keith didn't answer.

'What about Pelham Jenks?'

'He saw me at the dig and told me that he used to live in the village when he was very young.'

'You thought he suspected something?'

Keith nodded.

'Your ex-wife – what's her name?' Wesley had an idea, and he wanted to know if he was right. 'There'll be records, so we can easily find out,' he added.

Southen's answer explained something that had been puzzling Wesley. An untidy loose end. At the beginning of the investigation, they'd been misled by the testimony of one particular witness. But sometimes witnesses lied if they needed to protect someone they loved.

'Interview terminated at four thirty-five,' said Gerry, stopping the machine.

'Where's Harriet? Can I see her? Is she all right?'

'All in good time,' said Gerry, catching Wesley's eye as they hurried out, leaving the suspect with his solicitor.

39

Their two suspects, father and daughter, were being held in the cells, and Gerry had assured the chief super they'd soon have enough evidence to charge them both.

But there was somebody else they needed to speak to first. After that, they hoped the final piece of the jigsaw would fall into place.

Wesley drove to Little Rockington. The sun was shining and tourists were ambling about, recording the picture-postcard scene with their phones. The village green looked at its best, but tattered blue and white crime-scene tape still fluttered in the gentle breeze outside one of the cottages; a reminder of murder.

Wesley marched straight to the cottage opposite the crime scene and the door was answered by Kylie Mountjoy, dressed in her cleaner's tabard and holding a yellow duster in her hand.

'Hello, Kylie. Is Mrs Pugh at home?'

'Yes.'

'Don't bother to announce us, love,' said Gerry, barging ahead into the living room, where Linda Pugh was sitting on the sofa reading a glossy magazine.

'Ms Pugh – or should I say Mrs Southen?'

The woman turned pale and stared at Gerry, lost for words. After a few moments, she gathered her thoughts. 'What do you want?'

'We've come to tell you that your ex-husband and your daughter have been arrested on suspicion of murder.'

She didn't look as surprised as Wesley expected.

'You lied to us, didn't you? I think it was your daughter you saw visiting Barry Brown's cottage on the night he died.'

When she didn't deny it, he carried on. 'You told us you saw a tall man wearing a mask, but that wasn't true. Did you get the mask idea from the reports of the jewellery raids? The royal family masks they wore?'

Linda Pugh opened her mouth to speak, but no sound came out. Then she nodded.

'You saw your daughter, Harriet, going into that house. You misled us about the tall man in the mask to protect her, didn't you?' said Wesley.

The answer was another nod. 'I couldn't allow her to become a suspect, could I?' Linda continued. 'It would have interfered with her studies and turned her against me even more if she found out I'd ... betrayed her. She obviously had nothing to do with what happened to that man, but I still needed to protect her.'

Wesley understood. Mothers could have blind spots where their children were concerned. He glanced at the photographs on the mantelpiece. The smiling, innocent little girl. The young Harriet.

'Did you know your ex-husband was calling himself Ralph Gornay?'

'He told me it was a condition of a relative's will. He said he had to change his name if he wanted to inherit that manor house.'

'And you believed him?'

'Yes. I've heard about things like that before.'

'Would it surprise you to learn that he had no right to that house? He took the place of the rightful heir.'

The disbelief on the woman's face was unmistakable.

'Barry Brown, the writer who was staying opposite, stumbled on what was going on when he started asking questions up in Moor Barton,' Wesley continued. 'He found out that the real Ralph Gornay had been homeless and at rock bottom and he felt it would make a great story. The wealthy man who lost everything, then turned his life around. Riches to rags then back to riches. Harriet and her father were afraid his deception was about to be found out. That's why Harriet killed Mr Brown.'

Linda shook her head in disbelief. 'You're wrong. My daughter's not a murderer. She can't be. OK, I did see her calling there, but she told me it was something to do with her university course. She asked me not to say anything to the police because she didn't want to get involved.'

'You didn't have to lie about seeing someone else.'

'Harriet said it would make sure they didn't bother her.'

'You believed her?'

'Yes, of course. She's my daughter.' The uncertainty in her eyes told Wesley this wasn't altogether true.

'Tell us about Harriet.'

Linda hesitated. 'She's always been . . . ' she searched for the right word, 'focused.'

'Obsessive?'

She didn't answer. 'Since the split, she's been fixated with her father. He can do no wrong in her eyes. She worships him. She was always a lot closer to him than she was to me, and she blamed me for the divorce. She was really bitter about it and she resented any relationships I had after her father and I split up; made sure they never lasted.' Wesley could see her eyes glazing with unshed tears. 'After the divorce, she wanted to live with her father but it had been agreed that she'd stay with me, which turned out to be a mistake because those years became a nightmare. As soon as she was eighteen she went to him and, I know this is a terrible thing to say, I was relieved. She was going to move out of her student accommodation next year and live with him in that manor house he'd inherited. She told me she didn't need me any more, which broke my heart. She even said she'd become close to her grandmother, Keith's mother, which I thought was strange. He'd told me both his parents were dead so I don't know whether she was making it up to hurt me.' She took a deep breath. 'Harriet was always a ... difficult child. She was very clever, but she had a lot of problems. But you never stop loving your children, do you?'

Wesley nodded. 'Did you know Keith lied about inheriting the house?'

She shook her head vigorously. 'I honestly had no idea. It happened after we'd broken up and I didn't ask questions because I had my own life to live.' She paused and dabbed her eyes with a tissue. 'Harriet was enthralled by the idea of her father being lord of the manor. It made her even more obsessed with him. In her eyes he was some kind of saint.'

'She'd do anything for him, that's quite clear,' said Wesley with a hint of bitterness. Harriet had pretended to be Michael's friend, the big-sister figure looking out for him. She'd admitted that she'd cultivated the friendship to discover how the police investigation was progressing, and he hoped the experience wouldn't dent Michael's youthful faith in human nature. Although discovering that not everybody is as harmless as they seem might not be a bad lesson for an adolescent boy.

Wesley saw tears trickling down Linda's cheeks. 'We'll send someone round to take another statement from you.' He didn't mention the possibility of charges; perverting the course of justice perhaps. He felt Linda Pugh had received enough shocks for one day.

When they returned to the station, Gerry decided to have a go at speaking to Harriet. Now that they had some facts to confront her with, he hoped they'd have more luck than Trish and Paul.

Her face was impassive as they entered the interview room. Wesley found it difficult to see the petite girl with the auburn plaits in the role of murderer. But her apparent harmlessness was probably why Barry Brown and Pelham Jenks were so ready to admit her to their homes. Who would suspect a friendly young student, bearing a bottle, calling for a chat about the dig – or in Barry Brown's case, wanting to talk about the air crash?

'Harriet, we'd like to ask you a few questions,' he began, giving her an unthreatening smile. He found it hard to appear calm and friendly, given what she'd put Michael through.

'OK.'

'I'd better tell you that we've spoken to your father and your mother and we know the whole story. I also have to tell you that your grandmother, Jane Gabriel, is dead. We think she ended her own life.'

For the first time, Harriet showed some emotion. Her eyes filled with hot tears as she looked at them defiantly. 'You're lying.'

332

'It's the truth, love,' said Gerry. 'She was sorry for everything she's done. She left us a note.'

Wesley waited for the girl to compose herself before carrying on. 'Your mother told us she saw you visiting Barry Brown's cottage on the night of his death.'

She nodded. 'Dad said that man had been round asking questions. Prying into our lives. He might have ruined everything for us, so I dealt with it.'

'You took his laptop and his phone.'

'I didn't know what was on them. I couldn't take the risk. I took all his notes too.' She sounded almost proud.

'Where did you get the poison?'

'From my Grandma Jane. I told her about Brown and she said I needed to protect Dad, just like she'd always done. She told me what to do.' She looked Wesley in the eye defiantly. 'My dad deserves the manor. That house is his birthright, but his biological father treated him like one of the peasantry – beneath contempt. My bitch of a mum did too. I've always been on Dad's side. Me and Grandma Jane were the only ones who had his back.'

'What about Pelham Jenks?'

'My grandma told me he lived in the village when he was a kid and his mother used to clean for Colonel Gornay. Jenks spoke to my dad when the dig started, and when he saw Castor, Dad's dog, he asked if he'd got over his allergy. He remembered his mum mentioning that Colonel Gornay's son was terribly allergic to dogs and cats. Couldn't have them anywhere near him or he became quite ill. His face used to swell up.'

Wesley nodded. He now understood the reference to the dog in Pelham Jenks's notes. 'I believe people can grow out of allergies,' he said.

But Harriet wasn't listening. 'When Grandma found out what Pelham had said, she told me we couldn't take the risk. And once you've killed, the second time's easy.'

The cool way she said the words sent a chill through Wesley's soul.

'I did whatever was necessary to protect my dad and our rightful inheritance.'

Wesley looked into her eyes. They were hard and cold, with no human emotion behind them. He was about to ask her whether doing what was necessary included killing Michael. But he said nothing. Maybe he couldn't bear to hear the answer.

The next few days were spent gathering evidence. Miss Gabriel's fingerprints were matched to those found on the poison bottles in Ted Tallow's kitchen cupboard. Once they'd finished with the bottles, the CSIs offered to get them disposed of safely. Ted was quick to agree, relieved that someone was willing to take the responsibility out of his hands.

Forensic evidence was found in Dorcas's makeshift laboratory that she'd used laurel leaves to create cyanide, still lethal decades after the alleged witch's death.

Ted said that his mother had received many visits from Miss Gabriel over the years, so she'd had plenty of opportunity to help herself to the contents of the bottles, although he'd never wanted to touch them himself. They'd belonged to his grandmother and she was a witch. There were some things you didn't interfere with.

Miss Gabriel's prints were also found on the cast-iron doorstop used in Ted's attempted murder, and they now knew that she'd also poisoned the real Ralph Gornay, whose body had been found buried exactly where Keith Southen said it was.

There was no evidence that Southen had actually committed any of the murders himself, although he'd helped his mother bury Ralph's body. It had been Harriet who'd disposed of Barry Brown when she suspected he was about to stumble on her father's secret. And she'd also killed Pelham Jenks because he'd known about the real Ralph's allergy to dogs so had been surprised to see her father in the company of Castor the Labrador.

Castor and Pollux, the heavenly twins. According to Greek mythology, Castor had been the mortal son of the King of Sparta and Pollux had been conceived when Zeus, in the form of a swan, raped Leda. Keith and Ralph had been called the twins at one time and Wesley wondered whether the dog's name might have provided a clue.

Miss Gabriel had attempted to kill Ted Tallow in case he put two and two together and realised that she was one of the few people who'd had access to Dorcas's poisons. Fortunately she'd been too weak to finish the job, and when she realised that the truth was about to come out, she'd taken her own life, the prospect of prison being intolerable.

Ted was recovering well and would soon be released from hospital. Rachel had contacted Kylie Mountjoy to ask her whether he could hire a team of cleaners from her agency to clear out his house. Kylie suggested that she herself could call in from time to time to help him keep the place straight.

Rachel had also let Jay Tallow know about Ted's situation. As Jay and his friends hadn't taken part in the TR Theatre Company's 'performances', their only role being innocently supplying the masks, Gerry reckoned there were no charges to answer. And when Jay promised to call in on his Great Uncle Ted, Wesley felt optimistic. Family feuds were all very well, but Edith's violent husband, the man who'd killed his wife's lover and an innocent French woman, was long gone. And Edith herself was lying in the mortuary in Tradmouth awaiting burial. In Rachel's opinion, it was time for reconciliation. A new beginning for the Tallows.

The DNA taken from the female skeleton on the moor confirmed that she was indeed related to George Melling. Marie Leon had been found, but there was one loose end left, and that was how she had ended up buried on the moor. They'd been too busy with the case to take a look at the small notebook with the foxed pages found beneath the floorboards in Edith Tallow's bedroom. But now that the case was cleared up, apart from the paperwork, and Harriet and her father were in custody awaiting trial, Wesley yielded to temptation and dug the diary out of the evidence store in the hope that it would throw some light on the mystery.

He couldn't forget that Barry Brown had come to Devon in the first place because George Melling had wanted to know what had happened to his father's cousin. In a way, the mystery of Marie Leon had led indirectly to Brown's death.

But as soon as he settled down at his desk to start reading, he heard Gerry's voice behind him. 'What are you up to, Wes?'

'It's that diary we found under Edith's floorboards. I'm just looking through it to see whether there's anything relevant to the case.' It wasn't exactly a lie, but he knew it was stretching the truth a bit.

Gerry patted him on the back and ambled back to his office, hands thrust in his pockets.

Edith's handwriting was neat and easy to read, and Wesley was soon absorbed in the narrative unfolding on the pages.

Her husband, Bram, had been all charm at first, but after their marriage, when Edith moved into Tallow Farm with her new husband and his mother, Dorcas the witch, everything changed. Her mother-in-law was a malign influence on the household; controlling her son and treating her new daughter-in-law as a servant. Wesley was surprised that Edith put up with the situation for so long, but he told himself that things were different in those days. Writing a secret diary might have been the only available act of rebellion in that particular household. Edith had poured her resentment out onto the pages along with her innermost secrets, and Wesley found it heartbreaking. Then she managed to persuade Bram that she should do her bit for the war effort and help out as a land girl on the Southens' farm nearby. He could tell she relished her taste of freedom and the new friends she'd made. These friends, especially a vivacious French girl called Marie, had given her a new way of seeing the world; a world no longer confined to the four walls of the Tallows' smallholding.

It was when he came to an entry in September 1943 that he realised that the puzzle of how the bodies came to be buried on the moor was finally about to be solved.

Diary of Edith Tallow

Wednesday 22 September 1943

My heart is broken. Hank's being sent away this week and I don't know what I'm going to do. I've told him the truth about Bram and that I'm in the family way. I swore to him that the baby is his and not my husband's. He said he was pleased about the baby and he's promised to come back for me as soon as the war's over and take me to the States. In the meantime, he has to do his duty and fight. He says I should leave Bram and move into the Southens' farm with the other land girls, although it wouldn't be the same now Marie isn't there any more. I don't know what Farmer Southen will think of having a pregnant woman sleeping in his outhouse, but Hank said he'll make it all right. Hank's the type of man who can do anything.

He says he's going come into the house and tell Bram the truth. I told him not to. I said I'd rather sneak out to meet him because I need to do this my own way. I hope he won't do anything rash.

I need to make sure the chickens are locked up for the night. It's misty out there and the witch says you soon won't be able

338

to see your hand in front of your face. I wouldn't be surprised if she conjures the mist herself.

Hank says he'll come tonight, and I'll be waiting for him.

Thursday 23 September 1943

My hands are shaking and it seems like a nightmare. Maybe it was. Maybe when I go downstairs I'll find out it never happened. I can hardly write this, but maybe putting it into words will help to make sense of the horror.

Last night there was a terrible crash. It sounded like thunder and Bram said the Germans must have dropped a bomb on Moor Barton, although I couldn't see why they'd want to – unless it was aimed at the American base. I thought of Hank, praying he was safe, and felt a fluttering in my tummy like a tiny butterfly.

Dorcas sat on her rocking chair in the corner, muttering something that sounded like a spell, and Bram said we should take shelter under the table in case more bombs were dropped. But there were no more bangs and I told him that any bomber would be a long way away by now.

Then there was a hammering on the door and I ran to open it, even though Bram ordered me not to. I was shocked to see Hank standing on the doorstep. He'd kept his promise. Even through the thick mist, he'd found his way to me.

'A plane's come down outside the village,' he said. 'Some of the boys from the base are going over to see if there are any survivors. Don't know if it's ours or theirs. It's painted all in black.'

I reached for my coat. If I was quick, I could snatch the little suitcase I'd kept ready and the crash would provide perfect cover for my escape. But Hank was already inside the house, facing Bram like cowboys in a film squaring up to each other.

'My name's Hank Oppenheimer,' he said.

I knew what he was going to say next, and I grabbed his arm. This wasn't the time or place. Not with Bram's mother watching. But I could tell he'd made up his mind, and there was no stopping him.

'Me and Edith have been seeing each other. She's having my baby. It's best to tell it straight, honey.' He looked at me, but I was too terrified to say anything. 'I'm taking her back to the States once this war's over. Sorry and all that, but the lady's made her choice.'

He looked at me and smiled and I knew he'd done the right thing. A clean break. I saw a golden future. Then, with a sudden explosion, that future was shattered.

Dorcas had risen from her rocking chair and the smoking gun in her hand was pointing straight at Hank. I'll never forget the startled look on his face as he put his hand to his shoulder, and when he drew it away, I could see blood. He was wounded, and I let out a scream. But before I could go to him, a figure staggered through the open front door. I recognised her at once. It was my friend Marie. For a second I thought she'd come to my rescue.

Then I saw that her clothes were tattered and filthy and her stockings were torn as though she'd crawled across the moor on her hands and knees. Her eyes were wild with shock. I'd never seen her like that before and I knew something terrible must have happened. She was saying something I couldn't make out. I think it might have been in French.

I heard another deafening bang, like an explosion, and I saw Hank fall to the floor. Then I saw the life leave his staring eyes. I wanted to take him in my arms, but before I could move, I heard Marie scream and saw her spin round, ready to run away.

Then I heard another explosion, then another, and I saw her collapse to the ground. She'd witnessed Hank's murder, so she couldn't be allowed to live. And I feared that the same fate awaited me.

40

Before returning the diary to the evidence store, Wesley made a copy of the relevant pages. He'd promised Pam that he'd be home at a reasonable time, and he could just as easily read through it at his leisure. He let Gerry know that he was heading home. With everything that had happened to Neil and Michael, Pam needed his support.

'You get off, Wes. We've charged the suspects and collected all the statements.' The DCI gave a heavy sigh, and as he sat back in his chair, it creaked ominously under his weight. 'I've told everyone to go home. We'll be busy tomorrow preparing the files for the CPS.' He looked up. 'What's the latest on Neil?'

'He's being discharged tomorrow, and Annabel's moving into his flat to look after him.' He'd never thought of her as the devoted nursing type, but sometimes you could misjudge people. 'What's happening to Keith Southen's dog?'

'One of the uniforms has taken him home for the time being. If Southen gets sent down, he'll have to find a new home.' The DCI smiled. 'Nice dogs, Labradors.'

Wesley arrived home at six, and Pam greeted him in the hall, looking worried. 'Michael's in his room,' she said. 'He

342

won't come out. Said he wants his dinner on a tray. I told him we don't do room service. This isn't the Ritz.'

Wesley had been afraid that the shock of Harriet's betrayal would dent the boy's confidence. And now he had to break the news that she was a killer. It was something he wasn't looking forward to.

'I'll go up later and have a word,' he said, kissing his wife's forehead. 'You OK?'

'I've spoken to Annabel. She says Neil's desperate to get back to the dig. Proves he's on the mend.'

'At least that's good news.'

'There's more good news. I had a call from your sister.'

'What did she say?'

'That your parents are coming the week after next.'

'Perfect. Our case should be wrapped up by then.'

'And she had more news.' Pam paused. 'She's expecting again. Dominic's going to have a little brother or sister.'

This revelation made Wesley smile. He knew Maritia and Mark had been trying for a second baby for a while and that they would be rejoicing at the news.

But he couldn't help contrasting his sister's joy with the emotion Edith must have felt when she found herself pregnant by her American soldier lover. Then there was Miss Gabriel, who'd been assaulted by Colonel Gornay and had to give up the resulting child; a child whose secret she'd later committed murder to protect.

'That's fantastic news. They must be thrilled,' he said as he followed her into the kitchen, glancing up at the staircase. In days gone by, Amelia would always come bounding down to greet him, but like Michael, she was at the stage where she considered herself too old. Enthusiastic greetings were now left to the dog.

Michael did appear for dinner, but he picked at his food. Wesley assured him that Uncle Neil was on the mend, hoping this would cheer him up, but the boy said nothing. When he returned to his room, Wesley followed.

'What's happened to Harriet?' Michael asked.

Wesley wondered how much to tell him. He would have liked to shield him from the horror. But in the end, he knew he had to be honest, so he broke the news as gently as he could. Michael looked as though he could hardly bring himself to acknowledge the truth. It was a bitter lesson to learn so early in life. When he said he wanted to be alone, Wesley crept out of his room

Once out on the landing, his phone rang and he saw Annabel's name on the caller display. When he answered, she started speaking straight away. Someone had once said that Annabel was like the head girl of some excusive boarding school; well-spoken and confident. How she had come to be attracted to Neil, Pam had never been quite sure.

'I've been looking in the National Archives and the archives of the Imperial War Museum, and I think I might have solved the mystery of the French woman buried on the moor for you.'

'I think I've already solved it.'

'Really?' She sounded disappointed.

'But I'd be grateful for any information you've got.'

'OK. I came across a journal donated by the granddaughter of a pilot called Paddy Smith who flew Lysanders from Devon airbases during the war. She found it when she was clearing out his attic after he'd passed away. The journal was written by someone called John Carmody, who apparently gave it to Paddy for safe keeping before his plane crashed on Dartmoor. He talks a lot about a girl he fancies called Marie. Then there's the very last entry, which explains how she came to be on his plane. You ready?'

'Sure,' said Wesley, impatient to solve the mystery once and for all.

'OK. The entry is dated 22 September 1943, and was written at 2245 hours. Carmody writes: "My luck's held. The driver didn't come back to look for Marie and in ten minutes we'll be up in the Lysander together. Just shows that dreams can come true. I'll finish this for now and give it to my friend Paddy to look after. He hasn't got a drop tonight so he can let me have it back tomorrow. Someone said there's a danger of mist over Dartmoor, but I told Marie not to worry. If we can beat the enemy, we can beat the weather."'

'So she sneaked aboard the Lysander because she fancied John.'

'Romantic, isn't it?'

Wesley was about to say that it wasn't romantic when you considered what happened to John and Marie. But he didn't. Now that they had Edith's diary and John Carmody's account of what had happened, they knew the whole truth. Marie had dodged her driver and accepted John's offer. It was a decision that had cost her her life.

He was pleased that they'd now managed to give names to all three of the bodies found on the moor. Norman Jenks, Hank Oppenheimer and Marie Leon. He knew that efforts would be made to trace their relatives, and that Neil would contact the local vicar so they could be given decent burials.

He chatted with Annabel for a while longer about Neil and the arrangements she was making for his convalescence. She sounded exasperated when she spoke about how anxious he was to get back to the dig. But Wesley suspected that if anyone could force him to take it easy, it was Annabel. She wasn't a woman who would stand any nonsense.

He felt he should call Melling to bring him up to date. The mystery of his father's French cousin's disappearance had been solved once and for all. Melling's father had been right all along when he said she did board that ill-fated flight.

Melling sounded stunned at first. Then he announced that he intended to commission another author to write the story. It was one that needed to be told. He would dedicate the book to Marie and John Carmody. *The bravest of the brave.*

Pam was watching a detective series on the TV when Wesley returned to the living room. It reminded him too much of work, so he began to read the copy he'd made of Edith's diary.

And by the end of the evening, he knew the rest of Edith's story.

Diary of Edith Tallow

I haven't even looked at this diary for ten years. It's been hidden from sight beneath the loose floorboard in the bedroom, lying there like an unexploded bomb since that last entry; the one I wrote after that terrible night.

I realise now that I was in shock and that's why I felt I had no choice. I had to do as I was told or else I would have ended up dead like Hank and poor Marie. I still can't believe she's dead. She was so full of vitality and courage, and to this day I don't know how she came to be here. People in the village said the pilot of the crashed plane had been alone, but seeing the state Marie was in made me wonder whether she'd been on board as well. If it was something to do with secret missions, I don't suppose we'll ever know. The pilot survived a while and they took him to the Gornay Arms. I heard that the only word he said before he died was 'Marie' – or at least that's what someone thought it sounded like.

The bodies of Hank and Marie lay in the parlour until the following night, when Dorcas gave me something to drink that made me sleep. When I woke up, they had gone I asked

Bram where he'd buried them, but he wouldn't tell me. I wish I knew, because I'd like to lay flowers on the grave.

Since that night I've lived as a prisoner. Dorcas herself delivered my son. I was hardly allowed to see him before Bram took him off somewhere. I don't know where he went. I only hope they took him to Isaac and Florrie, because I knew they wanted children so badly and they weren't blessed. I wish I knew what had happened to him. Does he look like Hank? Is he happy? So many questions.

Dorcas passed away last year, but this house is still my prison. It's as though she's still here, watching me, calling me a Jezebel who must be punished. Even in death she gets her own way, and my whole life is an endless punishment. I never went back to the Southens' farm after that night, because Bram wouldn't let me. He said if I'd never gone there I wouldn't have met Hank. And I'd never have become a whore.

We keep ourselves to ourselves now. As soon as his mother died, Bram became a husband to me again, and I have another baby now— a boy called Ted. I know Bram will keep him here, just as he keeps me. He still has the gun his mother used to kill Hank and Marie, the gun his father brought back from the first war. Perhaps one day I'll be free. Although since Hank died, I've stopped caring. I don't have the strength any more.

I won't write in this diary again. I'll hide it where Bram won't find it and live what's left of my life – for Ted's sake.

41

The next morning Wesley walked to the station knowing he had another day of tying up loose ends ahead of him. It was a glorious day; a bright blue cloudless sky hung over the shining river and the good weather had lured the tourists out of their hotels, B&Bs and holiday cottages to stroll through the Memorial Gardens and along the embankment. He decided to take a detour through the gardens, where the shrubs had been stripped of the glittering decorations the Royal Family had festooned on them during their 'performance'. The loot was to be returned to its rightful owners, and the culprits, still protesting that the whole thing had been an artistic prank, were in custody awaiting trial. They might have been granted bail were it not for the shot accidentally fired in Neston and the fear they'd created among the innocent jewellers of the south-west.

That case was wrapped up, as were the murders of Barry Brown, Ralph Gornay and Pelham Jenks. Ted Tallow was back home and Jay had become a regular visitor. Gerry said all was well that ended well, but Wesley couldn't forget the people who'd died – and Harriet, the young student who was facing a life sentence for murder.

When he arrived in the office, the atmosphere seemed lighter as the formalities were completed. There was chatter about Trish and Paul's wedding. Gerry threatened to sing in the choir and perform his own rendition of 'A policeman's lot is not a happy one' during the signing of the register. Wesley joined in with the laughter.

At midday, Gerry received a phone call and summoned Wesley into his office before switching on the loudspeaker. The caller was a DCI Smith from Oxford, and he had news. The police had been questioning Harvey Pottinger and various other people about drugs offences, and Pottinger's production company had put out a statement saying that Mr Pottinger had stepped down from his media commitments due to an ongoing health issue and was currently being treated in a private clinic, although it assured his many fans that his life wasn't in any danger.

'Sounds like he jumped before he was pushed,' said Gerry with a roll of his eyes.

'At least we've got Lenny Brice on a charge of supplying drugs and perverting the course of justice,' said Smith. 'We've been wanting to get something on him for a while, but he's as slippery as an eel in a greased wetsuit.'

Wesley had to smile. That sounded like one of Gerry's sayings; it seemed the DCI had found a soulmate.

Wesley had assumed that after his traumatic experience, Michael would want nothing more to do with the Moor Barton dig. But it turned out his son was made of sterner stuff. Within a couple of weeks, Neil had convinced his doctors that he was fit to resume his duties, albeit from a fold-up chair set up in the finds tent, and Michael insisted that if Uncle Neil felt up to going back, so did he.

Wesley had arranged to drive the boy up there on his first day back, and when he arrived in Moor Barton, he found Neil presiding like a monarch on his throne, receiving offerings in the form of finds trays, which he examined before giving his verdict on the contents. According to Neil, Harriet's absence hadn't been mentioned by her fellow students. Perhaps they'd wanted to forget what she'd done. And Wesley couldn't blame them.

As both Harriet and her father were awaiting trial, Wesley wondered what would happen to the manor house. He supposed that, as Colonel Gornay's natural son, Keith might have a legal right to it. But after all the deception, together with the murderous activities of his birth mother and his daughter, it was unclear what would happen once he'd served his sentence. All Wesley's instincts cried out that he shouldn't benefit from his lies – but the law often wasn't the same as justice.

He was about to return to Tradmouth when Neil called him back.

'I've got something to show you. The soldiers in the trench we've just expanded found something interesting last night.' He pointed to a finds tray on one of the trestle tables and Wesley brought it over to him. 'There, look.'

Wesley picked up a delicate chain, tarnished after decades in the ground but probably silver. The clasp was broken, and attached to the chain was a crucifix. When he turned it over, he saw something engraved on the reverse. As he brushed off the dirt, Neil handed him a magnifying glass.

It was difficult to read, but after a while he was able to make out the letters. *Marie*, it said. *Première communion.*

He glanced up at Neil. 'It belongs to the woman buried

on the moor; must have been given to her at her first communion.' He looked back down at the necklace. 'I think it should be buried with her.'

Neil nodded. 'I'm sure that can be arranged.'

A couple more weeks passed and Wesley started to feel that all was right with the world. He'd even managed to put his mother-in-law's return from her latest retreat out of his mind. She'd called round and announced her intention to open a retreat of her own using therapeutic goats, and had ordered him to ask Rachel whether she could supply the animals from her farm. Wesley hadn't bothered to mention it to Rachel. Hopefully Della would forget about it soon enough.

The remains of Hank Oppenheimer, the US soldier, had been returned to the States to lie with the rest of his family, but the bodies of Marie Leon, Edith Tallow, Norman Jenks and his brother Pelham had been buried with great ceremony in the churchyard at Moor Barton. The whole village had turned out to honour them, and Marie's coffin had been draped in the French flag. George Melling led the mourners, and Wesley saw the glint of tears in his eyes. Gerry had been there too, and both men had found the event moving.

But now the sorrow of the funeral had lifted and his own parents, paragons of common sense compared to Pam's mother, were staying at his sister's. It was good to see them again and hear all about their day at Buckingham Palace, where his father had received his knighthood from the King – the real one this time.

And when the day of Trish and Paul's wedding arrived, Gerry's prayers were answered and there were no reports of any criminal activity, almost as though the villains of Tradmouth had decided to launch a go-slow as a wedding present. Everyone from CID was at St Margaret's church in the middle of the town. The bells rang, Gerry resisted the urge to serenade the congregation, and as the happy couple emerged into the outside world, their colleagues formed a guard of honour, making an arch with old-fashioned police truncheons somebody had found in a station storeroom.

As Wesley and Pam were both guests at the wedding, his parents were looking after Amelia for the day while Michael was at the dig. They came to watch the newly-weds coming out of the church, Dr Cecilia Peterson – now Lady Peterson – holding her granddaughter's hand proudly as they enjoyed the spectacle.

It was a joyful occasion. And there was far too little joy in the world.

Author's Note

I've always been a great fan of *Time Team*, and ever since I saw an episode about the excavation of a World War II aircraft, I've been longing to feature a similar dig in a Wesley Peterson novel. However, I'd always assumed that most RAF activity during the war took place in the east of England – after all, Lincolnshire is famously known as 'Bomber County', and the Battle of Britain was fought mainly over the south-eastern counties. When I began consulting Google, searching for Devon wartime airfields. I anticipated that south-western bases might have provided training and airborne backup for the D-Day landings (which were rehearsed in the county) but little else. I thought Devon was probably a bit of a backwater as far as airborne heroics were concerned. How wrong I turned out to be!

More than forty planes crashed on Dartmoor during World War II, although only a few were the result of enemy action. It seems that bad weather, especially fog (as in this book), was responsible for many of these tragedies, resulting in the horrific loss of many brave airmen from both the RAF and the USAAF.

In the course of my research, I also came across a

remarkable story of courageous spies and secret missions into enemy territory.

I'd walked around Bolt Head near Salcombe, but little did I know that aircraft taking Special Operations Executive agents over to Europe during the war's darkest years had actually been stationed there. Bolt Head and Winkleigh in north Devon were bases for the secretive Black Squadron (the pilots were known as the 'cloak-and-dagger boys').

Thanks to their ability to land and take off from short airstrips, Westland Lysanders were used for the missions. They were painted black for camouflage and flew on moonless nights so they could sneak into enemy territory undetected. They were adapted with the addition of long-range fuel tanks beneath the fuselage and a ladder fixed to the side to allow the secret agents to enter and exit the aircraft quickly.

During the war, many resourceful men and women who were fluent in foreign languages (like my fictional Marie) were recruited to land in occupied Europe and blend in with the locals, working with resistance groups to send back intelligence or sabotage enemy infrastructure.

Many of these brave men and women of the SOE lost their lives, and because of the secrecy of the operations, occasionally camouflaged Lysanders were mistaken for enemy aircraft and shot down by their own side. After learning about their activities, I was humbled by the courage of both agents and pilots. As a writer, you need to imagine yourself in the place of your characters – and I concluded early on that I wouldn't have possessed a fraction of their bravery.

To turn from heroism to more sinister matters. Old beliefs and superstitions lingered for a very long time in isolated country areas. Rumours often spread that women like Dorcas Tallow, who provided folk remedies for their community, used their herbal knowledge for evil as well as good. Marks giving protection against witches are often found in old buildings in Devon and beyond, some dating to as late as the early twentieth century. Such superstitions take a long time to die out – if they ever really do.

I hope you've enjoyed reading Wesley Peterson's twenty-ninth investigation. I'd like to thank my husband, Roger, for his patience and support (and for providing all those cups of tea and coffee when I shut myself away in my writing office at the bottom of the garden). A big thank you too to my sons: Tom for his technical support and Olly for his historical and archaeological advice. Huge thanks also to my agent, Euan Thorneycroft, and to my excellent editor, Hannah Wann (without whom Wesley's cases might flounder in confusion).

Finally, a very special thank you to all the bookshops and libraries who've supported me over the years. And, of course, my readers. You make it all worthwhile.